Devil Wind

Also by Deborah Shlian and Linda Reid
Dead Air

Also by Deborah Shlian
FICTION
Rabbit in the Moon
Nursery (Re-released as Double Illusion)
Wednesday's Child

Also by Linda Reid
FICTION
Where Angels Fear to Tread (aka Yolanda Pascal)

DEVIL WIND

A Novel

Deborah Shlian
&
Linda Reid

Oceanview Publishing
LONGBOAT KEY, FLORIDA

Los Angeles Is Burning
Words and Music by Brett Gurewitz and
Greg Graffin © 2004 EMI BLACKWOOD MUSIC INC., SICK MUSE SONGS and POLYPTERUS MUSIC All Rights for SICK MUSE SONGS. Controlled and Administered by EMI BLACKWOOD MUSIC INC. All Rights Reserved. International Copyright Secured. Used by Permission.
Reprinted by permission of Hal Leonard Corporation

Devil Wind
Words and Music by Bob Welch © 1979 GLENWOOD MUSIC CORP. and CIGAR MUSIC. All Rights Controlled and Administered by GLENWOOD MUSIC CORP. All Rights Reserved. International Copyright Secured. Used by Permission.
Reprinted by permission of Hal Leonard Corporation

ISBN: 978-1-933515-89-2

Published in the United States of America by Oceanview Publishing, Longboat Key, Florida
www.oceanviewpub.com

2 4 6 8 10 9 7 5 3 1

PRINTED IN THE UNITED STATES OF AMERICA

To our husbands,
Joel Shlian and Anastasios Chassiakos,
with love and thanks

Acknowledgments

Many thanks to the following people without whom we couldn't have written *Devil Wind*.

Professor Anastasios Chassiakos for his engineering expertise that ensured the resonator resonated.

Detective Steve Teplitsky for his valued consultations on California police procedures—and his gentle reminder that detectives ride in "plain wraps" and not "patrol cars."

Experienced pilot, Bob Woodhams for explaining how the Santa Anas would affect Prescott's Gulfstream on its way to L.A.

Dr. Warren Strauss for his cardiology reviews.

Dr. Joel Shlian for serving as a contributing medical editor—and the inspiration for Dr. Wyndham.

Avid thriller readers Steve Manton, Sharon Hanley, Joan Cochran, and E. G. Stassinopoulos for their generosity in reviewing and critiquing multiple drafts of our manuscript.

Bob and Pat Gussin, Susan Greger, Frank Troncale, Maryglenn McCombs, and Susan Hayes from Oceanview for their help in bringing the second of the Sammy Greene thriller series to life.

George Foster for another gorgeous cover.

Finally, thanks go to our spouses for their unfailing love and support.

Deborah Shlian and Linda Reid

Well hello little girl, welcome to this big town
I've been patiently waiting, let me show you around
Did you bring lots of money, do you have nerves of steel
And are you ready to gamble, put your heart on the wheel
Oh oh, the devil wind
Big town claims another win
Is this how it all begins
How the innocents have changed...
After the devil wind stops blowin´
Wake up and find your heart´s been broken

—"Devil Wind" lyrics by Bob Welch

When the hills of Los Angeles are burning
Palm trees are candles in the murder wind
So many lives are on the breeze
Even the stars are ill at ease
And Los Angeles is burning

—"Los Angeles Is Burning," Bad Religion, 2002

Devil Wind

Prologue

Operation Desert Storm
Northeast Saudi Arabia
50 kilometers from the Iraqi border
February 16, 1991

The young man's screams resonated through the mobile army surgical unit, drowning out the piercing wails of the brutal winter sandstorm. The desert winds rocked the trailer in rhythm with the corporal's cries.

"Can't medivac him out til morning," whispered an aide to the senior medic. Both knew it was too risky for the flight from Germany to land before the winds died down. "Should I get the chaplain?"

"Bishop," the medic responded. "Get Bishop."

The trailer door blew open, flapping against the aluminum siding. A tall, muscled man with grizzled hair strode in, "I'm here," his only greeting as he rushed to the young man's side. Despite the storm, his uniform was pressed and immaculate. Dr. Franklin Bishop was an officer's officer.

He laid a gentle hand on the soldier's writhing abdomen, noting the absence of legs below both knees. Lifting the sheet, the doctor saw that the amputations had not been surgical. The burned skin on the corporal's thighs was black, the fever of infection would no doubt kill him by morning. "Ten mg of morphine stat," Bishop ordered. The opiate would make his last hours more comfortable.

As the pain medicine gradually dulled the young man's agony, his screams became words. Whispered words that only Bishop, leaning his head close to the soldier's lips, could hear.

"Many children. Dead. Innocents. Stop the resonator. Stop the murder." The soldier's next words dissolved into gibberish as he fell into a deep sleep.

Bishop stood erect, shaking his head. Resonator? Murder?

The soldier's body shook and shivered, his breathing grew more labored. Bishop clasped his hand and gave it a firm squeeze. In the morning, he would call Miller. See what the Company man could spill. For now, Colonel Bishop's duty was to stand by this brave young man's bedside so that he would not die alone.

The trailer was eerily quiet except for the howling winds. Cocking an ear, Bishop was certain he heard the winds echo the soldier's words: *resonator . . . murder. . .*

CHAPTER ONE

Each winter, hot dry winds sweep from the deserts across the L.A. basin, and for a few days, blow away the hazy smog, exposing the glittery beauty of the City of Angels. Newcomers delight in the unexpected clarity, the ability to see snow-capped Santa Monica Mountains and azure Pacific Ocean emerge against a lavender sky. But those who stay a while soon learn why some call these Santa Anas *devil's breath*, others, *murder winds*, and not just because they can whip parched chaparral into explosive fuel feeding deadly wildfires. No, it's something about the winds' effect on the inhabitants of the city's hills and canyons, making senses sharper, on edge. As Raymond Chandler once wrote, while these winds blast, *anything can happen*. Anything.

Neil Prescott's Gulfstream G650 shuddered and rolled, slammed by gusty Santa Anas thundering over the Sierras. The gray-haired congressman considered the luxury plane a fitting thirtieth anniversary gift from his oil heiress wife. Enjoying the wild ride, he took a dramatic swig of his martini before leaning over to clap his distressed guest on the shoulder.

"Didn't know you could get so pale under that Saudi suntan." Prescott's ample midriff shook as he chuckled.

Fahim al-Harbi, stroked the neatly trimmed salt-and-pepper mustache and beard that covered much of his olive complexion, then, jaw still clenched, calmly put down his Glenlivet and rocks and brushed the arm of his Armani suit. "I should prefer my death to be in the company of the female gender," he said in cultured Oxford English.

"Aren't you people supposed to get seventy-two virgins in heaven?" Prescott watched the last drops of his martini splash onto his shirt with the Gulfstream yawing and bucking in the turbulence. "I'd sign up for that," he added, remembering to remove his wedding ring and slip it into his jacket pocket.

"Good news. Captain says we'll land in L.A. twenty minutes early." Prescott's second guest, no stranger to most of the "players" on Capitol Hill, stumbled down the aisle from the cockpit when the jet jolted yet again. Slim and ferret-faced, Albert Miller was ID'd by true insiders as a senior CIA operative. Had his sense of irony inspired him to wear that gray flannel suit? Gazing out the window, he muttered, "Five seasons."

"Beg your pardon?" Fahim asked.

"Miller's referring to the California seasons: earthquakes, floods, mudslides, riots, and fires," Prescott explained. "Santa Ana winds, with a little help from the firebugs, set the mountains aflame each year. Burns all the slopes. Then, as soon as you get spring rain, the mudslides." The politician swooped his free hand downward to demonstrate the lava-like flow.

"Bite your tongue, Neil," Miller snapped, settling down next to them and opening his Macbook. "I have a bungalow in Laguna Hills."

"For now." Prescott turned to Fahim, "Hope you're up for a great party in Bel Air tonight, pal. There'll be a little thank-you gift for making all the, um, arrangements."

Fahim's brown eyes narrowed. "I shall still expect full payment when the 'items' are delivered next week." He leaned forward, gripping his leather armrests, "And tell your Madam Kaye, no Arab girls this time."

"Santa Ana winds are bringing record high temperatures and stoking blazes in the San Gabriels and Simi Valley," interrupted Miller who was scanning CNN from his 2-bit LAN connection. "Fire officials expect a severe fire season ahead due to lush growth left behind by last year's El Niño."

Prescott anticipated Fahim's question. "El Niño's a weather pattern that turns the climate upside-down. A lot of rain, then a lot of drought. Accident waiting to happen." He shook his head. "Like Y2K."

"Your country seems to be hysterical about the end of the millennium," Fahim observed.

"You heard the Deputy Secretary in D.C. this morning. Y2K is the electronic equivalent of El Niño. Our control of computer systems, aviation, weapons, power supply—everything could go up in smoke."

Prescott turned his gaze to Miller's laptop. The computer screen now displayed a picture of the charismatic president stumping for his charm-challenged VP to win the Democratic nomination in next year's race. He nodded at the monitor where the crowd was chanting the president's name. "They still adore him. Look at them. A bunch of fat and happy sheep." He sneered. "Time we restored some dignity to the office, dammit. We can't let these bastards have another four years in the White House." Prescott slammed his fist on the cedar table just as the jet lurched upward.

"You honestly think you can persuade the American people to vote for change?" Fahim asked after a moment of strained silence.

Miller glanced up from his computer. "Our researchers have been studying fear since the Cold War. An effective tool that unites people against a common enemy." The expression in Miller's blue eyes grew cold. "Let the sheep enjoy this holiday season for a few more days. With your help, before the sun rises on the new millennium, this entire country will wake up certain there's an enemy out there intent on ending America as we know it. Believe me," he declared, "first, they'll be terrified, and then they'll be begging for change."

•   •   •

The madam picked up the call on her personal line after the first ring. ID displayed *private caller*. Though he didn't give his name, she recognized Miller's gravel voice.

"You're back in L.A." The demure tone belied her irritation at the fact.

"Blew in on these damn winds," he said. "Listen, Kaye, I need a short order for a party tonight in Bel Air. Blonde. No implants." He didn't bother to say hot, sexy, or beautiful. Those adjectives were implied. "Someone who's comfortable with—the exotic."

"Who's the client?" the madam demanded, her suspicions aroused by his hesitation.

"Our Saudi friend."

"*Govno!*" she cursed silently in her native Russian. The Arab had roughed up one of her girls a year ago. She'd told Miller then that he was on her blacklist.

"You there?" he asked when she hadn't answered.

"I'm not comfortable with this."

"Twelve thousand for a couple of hours. How uncomfortable can you be?"

More dead air on the line as the madam considered Miller's proposal. Twelve thousand was four times the usual fees. Hard to hang up on that. And, it might be an opportunity to kill two birds with one stone. Sylvie had gotten too cocky lately. Making foolish noises about leaving the fold. Going out on her own. By sending Sylvie to the party tonight, they'd have a chance to search the girl's flat for the client list she'd stolen. *That was another stupid mistake, Ms Sylvie: underestimating Madam Kaye.*

"All right," she said. "It's a deal."

The winds gusted soft and warm, a siren song caressing the nubile bodies dancing and drinking by moonlight on the poolside patio of the sheltered Bel Air estate with the movers and shakers of Tinseltown. An exclusive gala of a music mogul who'd just signed a multimillion-dollar record deal—only the beautiful and wealthy were welcome. The deafening beat of the producer's latest artist's rap album made conversation impossible. But, truth was, the partygoers were there to be seen, not heard. This event was 10 percent business, 90 percent show.

Two young blondes, sporting identical hairstyles and dressed in identical tight cocktail dresses, sat at a table in a darkened corner cradling flutes of champagne, surveying the scene like hunters stalking their prey. Sylvie adjusted her décolletage to expose more cleavage. "It's well past eleven. Kaye said he'd be here by ten."

"You don't think playing both sides is a little dangerous?" her "twin" wondered, wishing Sylvie hadn't confided her duplicity.

"Come on, Ana, L.A.'s a rough town and we've got a rough gig," Sylvie replied. They both knew she meant the life of a high-priced call girl. Or "escort" or "working girl" or "whore," it was all the same. Underneath the city that glittered, there was plenty of grime. Sylvie had long ago accepted that reality. Ana still hadn't made her peace with it.

"Why are we doing this?" Ana persisted. It was something she'd been thinking about more and more.

Sylvie tilted her head and leveled her blue eyes that glistened from the hit of coke she'd taken before leaving the apartment. "You're kidding, right?"

"No. You're smart, you're beautiful. I thought you wanted to be an actress."

Sylvie ran her tongue over her full, sensuous lips. "I *am* an actress. People like you and me, we're survivors. We do what we have to do. Besides, there's always Plan B. Payless shoes, remember—"

Ana looked away, catching a glimpse of several newcomers just stepping onto the patio and nudged Sylvie with her elbow.

"Shit, that's him," Sylvie said, blindly grabbing the designer string purse behind her chair. "At this hour, I'll be all night. Find your own way home, okay." It wasn't a question.

Ana observed her roommate as she shimmied on her Manolo Blahniks toward a swarthy man whose salt-and pepper-hair, though stylishly coiffed, betrayed at least a couple of decades beyond hers.

Sylvie flashed a luminous pink metallic smile and whispered some-thing in his ear. When he nodded, she took his manicured hand and led him toward one of the guesthouses where Ana had no doubt they would share a line of high-grade coke—and much more.

Damn. It had been a mistake to come with Sylvie tonight. Still, Madam Kaye could be quite convincing. She'd insisted they both attend, and, so, here they were. Ana scoured the crowd until she spotted a stocky man she'd seen many times on TV standing by the bar—popular Orange County, California Congressman Neil Pres-cott, reputed to be one of the madam's occasional and less avaricious clients. Perhaps Kaye was right. The night wouldn't be a total loss. The congressman would be good for a pair of wheels, and maybe a couple of thou for next month's rent.

Straightening her dress, Ana rose and reached behind her to grab her own purse hanging from the chair. Slowly, she approached the congressman with practiced modesty, and an unwelcome twinge of regret. This scene was getting old, and, in her mid-twenties, so was she. "Hi," she shouted over the music, "mind if I join you?"

The politician gave her long blonde hair and well-toned body an appreciative once over, then pointed to the gyrating crowd with a broad smile. "Too noisy. Let's get out of here. I have a place."

It was almost midnight when the silver Mercedes drove past the two muscled bouncers manning the gates of the Bel Air estate. The music had been cranked up even louder, the beat reverberating in the abyssal canyon. The party would no doubt go on all night. Ana felt a slight shiver as the wind began picking up strength around them. Was that scent a hint of smoke? Unleashed, the Santa Anas could whip the night into a fiery frenzy. By morning, the streets would be strewn with the victims—dead branches of once beautiful palms, rotting in the gutters that are the shadowy underbelly of Eden.

CHAPTER TWO

Breathless, Sammy Greene sprinted into the radio studio, slid into her seat, and pulled on her headphones at one minute before midnight. She flashed a broad, slightly guilty smile at her producer on the other side of the glass. "Am I late?"

Jim Lodge punched the button for the network feed harder than really necessary. As the sounds of the national news for the top of the hour came in over the loudspeaker, he turned to the window between them with a wry expression. "Bad hair day?"

"*Gut gesuked.*" Sammy ran her fingers through her disheveled red mop and tossed off her grandmother's Yiddish equivalent of *I'll say*, adding, "I've lived through hurricanes and I've never seen hot winds like this."

"Santa Anas," the producer said.

Sammy reached into her satchel and pulled out notes for her upcoming show. "Aren't winds supposed to be cold? Wind *chill.*"

Jim shook his long gray locks and took a sip from a large mug of steaming coffee. He lowered his voice to a hush. "Devil wind."

"Huh?" Sammy repositioned her mic and leaned over to turn on the small TV monitor she had set up next to her board. She liked to run it muted on the national news networks or C-SPAN to keep up with breaking events while she was on the air.

"They fly from the desert, from Death Valley, and soar over the mountains, bringing the flames of Hell to the denizens of Paradise." He waved a torn sleeve at the window and the sea of lights beyond.

"How Dante-esque." Sammy's colleague, his full beard, ponytail, and ragged togs identifying him in her mind as the last surviving hippie, could get a little creepy at times. "And I thought I'd only have to worry about earthquakes."

Frowning, Sammy surveyed the gloomy studio, buried within a ratty wood-and-stucco building in the bowels of Canyon City, a wannabe middle-class community just south of Beverly Hills. When she'd begun her broadcasting career, she'd never imagined ending up two years later on the night shift in a tiny shack like this.

She glanced over at the adjacent monitor, now tuned to CNN. High-tech graphics whizzing across the screen cost thousands of dollars—more than a year's wages at the Washington TV network where she used to work. Despite the low pay and long hours, she'd gladly have stayed there if she could. She'd loved being near the action, especially with an election coming up next year.

Sammy felt no regrets leaving Ellsford University after graduating on the five-year plan in '97. Her campus radio experience landed her the dream internship in D.C. at the television network and a gig six months later as one of the youngest associate producers for investigative reporter Barry Kane and his show, *Up Front D.C.* Sammy'd never had illusions about landing in front of the camera. Her frizzy red hair and strong Brooklyn accent didn't fit the popular Barbie Doll image. She was happy as a journalist pounding a beat, thrilled to be trolling for stories from K Street to the hallowed halls of Congress, catching the scent of corruption hovering over the Capitol.

Maybe she shouldn't have pushed so hard on the Senator Treadwell story. After all, he was a fishing buddy of the network's CEO. Still, she never figured she'd get sacked for doing her job. Even the parade to the door through the studio by a security guard escort hadn't dampened her certainty that another news organization would appreciate her skills in the tenacious pursuit of truth.

Only after months of mailing out résumés and calling on colleagues once counted as friends, did the message sink in. She was persona non grata in Washington. And New York. And Boston. And—

"Los Angeles," advised her colleague, Vito, one of the few D.C. news pros still willing to lunch with her. "It's the city of second chances. People don't care about your past there."

Ironic. Vito couldn't have known that some of her past—make that, some*one* from her past—was in that very city. That was why she'd resisted his offer to contact an old buddy at a tiny, low-budget, low-wattage Pacifica radio station on the Very Left Coast. She'd waited weeks, until every feeler she'd put out had been rejected and her bank account nearly drained, before swallowing her pride and asking Vito to make the call.

Her career in tatters, Sammy had ended up back where she started. In front of a talk-radio mic. Lighting Chanukah candles in ninety-five degree Los Angeles heat. She walked over to the almost empty coffeepot. "Thanks, Jim," she muttered, pouring the last few drops into a clean cup. Returning to her seat at the board, she began to arrange her notes for Hour One.

She'd scoured the morning papers, bypassing election news and holiday features until she found what she was looking for near the back page of the L.A. *Times*—a story about a homeless protest en-campment, a tent city growing this past month outside the Canyon City Hall, just a few miles from the station. Sammy had come so close to being out on the street herself. She felt passionate about helping the thousands in her new city who could not afford shelter. With Christmas just over a day away, it was time for action. Sammy would try to rally her listeners to offer their aid. She glanced at the clock. Almost five after twelve. "Jim, we ready?"

The producer nodded and began a five-finger countdown to her cue.

A Miles Davis fusion riff filtered through Sammy's headphones as she flipped open her mic and in a practiced sultry voice an-nounced, "Sammy Greene on the L.A. scene. Turn up the radio, turn down the lights, and cuddle up in bed. That is, if you *have* a bed, lights, a radio, a home, a roof. Because many Angelenos don't."

She shuffled her papers near the mic as a sound effect. "According to the L.A. University Center for Public Research, at least two hundred thousand individuals are homeless in L.A. County. On any given night, half have nowhere to sleep. Women and children make up more than a third of this group; over eighty percent of homeless families are headed by women. Folks, this is a national tragedy. How can we sleep at night when so many men, women, and children in Los Angeles are crying out for help?"

Her cries for help went unanswered, drowned by the incessant beat of the deafening music from the patio outside the Bel Air mansion. The naked blonde in the guesthouse bedroom knew she was going to die. If only she hadn't taken the wrong purse.

Fahim had gone to the bathroom, leaving Sylvie sprawled on the crumpled sheets, groggy from the Ecstasy and wine they shared. As soon as the door closed, she'd tiptoed out of bed and lifted the Handspring personal digital assistant he'd laid on the night table. Sex was only one part of her job. Kaye expected Sylvie to bring back any client secrets she could find. That's why the madam had insisted she seek out the Saudi tonight.

Sylvie thought she'd done her part well—scanned the last few e-mails as quickly as she could, then grabbed the phone from her purse, texted the critical information as a short message, and keyed in the phone number to Ana's cell. Hit "Send," and the traces would disappear, to be retrieved safely in the morning from her roommate. Sylvie would be back on the bed, pretending to sleep. It wasn't until the text message boomeranged to the phone in her hand that she realized she had Ana's cell—and purse.

The minute it took to resend the message to her own number and slip the phone back into the purse was one minute too long. Fahim had grabbed her from behind and shoved her against the wall before she could replace the PDA.

Sylvie didn't stand a chance as, towering over her tiny frame, Fahim pounded the life out of her, the loud beat of the party's music masking the fatal blows and her final screams.

•   •   •

"Anybody in there?"

Fahim wiped the sweat from his brow with his shirtsleeve before opening the front door of the guest cottage a crack.

A uniformed officer was pointing at the Bentley parked behind him. "You here alone?"

Fahim swallowed and nodded.

"Better get this beauty and yourself outta here. We're evacuating everybody. Fire's at Mulholland."

"Fire?" Fahim shook his head to clear it. "Yes, of course. I'll, er, get my things."

The officer waved as he left with a last admiring glance at the car Fahim had rented on arrival. "Don't wait too long. Be a shame if she burns up."

As soon as Fahim shut the door, he pulled his cell from his pants pocket and, dreading each step back toward the bedroom, dialed a number he'd preferred not to call.

"You're sure the girl's dead?" It was same cold tone Miller had used on the plane that afternoon.

"Yes, it was an acc—"

"Name and address," Miller interrupted, obviously not interested in the circumstances.

Fahim balanced his cell in the crook of his neck as he looked into the silk purse and read off the license: "Anastasia Pappajohn. An address in Santa Monica."

"Okay, listen carefully." Miller gave him a road map to get rid of the body. "When that's done, take off. Get a room somewhere where the cops can't find you. Just in case."

"But, I thought—"

"Isn't that the problem, Fahim? Not thinking." Miller didn't wait for a response. "I'll keep you out of this and clean up your mess, but you owe me, pal. Big time."

CHAPTER THREE

Prescott turned his Mercedes east onto Sunset Boulevard. "I keep a place in Beverly Hills since I do lots of business in the city. That way I don't have to fight traffic back to the O.C."

Ana nodded and sat back in the comfortable leather seat of the Mercedes, closing her eyes. She didn't know how much longer she could keep up this game. She'd be twenty-seven next month. Over the hill in this market of young and younger. She'd been clean for over a year, but the bills for Teddy's leg braces alone cost her more than she netted from weeks of work. Kaye saw to it that her girls got just enough take-home to keep coming back for more.

Her fingers brushed the simple gold cross she always wore around her neck. A gift from her father when she was his innocent child. Those days were long gone. Ironic that *putana* was one of the names her father had called her when he'd booted her out into the cold Boston winter ten years before for shacking up with a gang-banger fresh out of juvie. She'd certainly lived up to his expectations.

She'd run away with her boyfriend, all the way to the West Coast. The first few months on the road had almost been fun. At seventeen, sleeping in alleys, begging for handouts and food, and sharing good dope was an adventure. If they got cold or hungry, there was always a homeless shelter to spend the night. For the first time since her mother's death, Ana had felt alive. And her father could rot in hell.

Until her boyfriend moved on and never came back.

Teddy was born in the hallway of L.A. County General Hospi-

tal seven months later, amidst the screams and cries of dozens of suffering people waiting for the few crumbs of help the overburdened
facility could offer. She'd always blamed herself for his cerebral palsy.
There had been no prenatal care on the streets. Ana had also never
forgiven her father. If he hadn't turned her away—

Well, she and Teddy were on their own, and she wasn't going
to go back to daddy on bended knee. She'd been waiting tables at a
hip café, struggling to make the rent and pay for her son's care when
Washington pulled the plug on public assistance programs. With no
other options, she finally surrendered Teddy to her social worker and
foster care. That day her heart had been irreparably broken.

Drugs made a lot of the pain disappear—for a while. Another
waitress, Sylvie, always seemed to have an unlimited stash of meth
and coke to share. And somehow, plenty of dollars. Best of all, a
Santa Monica apartment with an extra bed.

Only one move-in condition. "You have to meet Kaye."

Six years later, Ana still knew Kaye only by her first name,
though Henry Higgins could not have done a better job transform-
ing the dark-haired waitress into a glamorous blonde. Then, like the
serpent of Eden, the sophisticated middle-aged madam had slowly
introduced Ana to a lifestyle she could merely dream of—glittering
parties, beautiful clothes, champagne and caviar, top executives and
movie stars—all to be hers if she agreed to barter her body for a taste
of paradise.

In the end, a Faustian bargain. Very soon, she was hooked on
crack and dependent on the money she made as an "escort" to maintain her supply. The sex was sometimes kinky, sometimes even violent, but never, ever satisfying. And, in the mornings, when she
would finally fall into a fitful sleep, she'd see Teddy's face crying for
her in her dreams.

Teddy was the reason Ana had entered rehab last year. Without
drugs, she might be able to save enough to quit the life and bring
him home.

Home. Could she return? she mused now. Perhaps this time the
old man wouldn't throw her out. He'd actually responded somewhat

politely to the e-mail she'd sent last spring. Said he was thinking about retiring from his university job and moving in with Aunt Eleni in Somerville. Maybe he'd softened up enough to accept a prodigal daughter's visit. And a grandson he'd never known about.

The purse vibrating on her lap made Ana open her eyes. Fishing inside to shut off her phone, she realized that something wasn't right. Instead of the single key she carried, her fingers found a large loop of keys. Opening the purse, she realized the problem. The keys, the wallet, the cell phone all belonged to Sylvie. Damn! The girls had bargained for identical silk bags in a little shop on Melrose last week. "Two for one," Sylvie had chuckled, when she'd brought the price low enough. That was Sylvie. Always bargaining. In her haste to meet her mark, Sylvie must have grabbed the wrong bag. Yep, that was Ana's own number calling with a text message—Sylvie must have figured out the mix-up, too.

"So how much is this going to cost me?"

Ana turned her attention back to business. "The usual. Three thousand."

That number seemed exorbitant to her, even after all these years. Still, the gurgling sound she heard in response was unexpected. Kaye's girls were the crème de la crème. Surely the price couldn't be a surprise to the congressman. What *was* a surprise was the Mercedes beginning to weave on the fairly empty boulevard. Ana turned to see Prescott clutch his chest, his features contorted. *He must be having a heart attack!*

Ana seized the wheel and straightened the sedan's frightening yaw. Sliding into Prescott's lap in the driver's seat, she intended to pull to the side of the road and call 911 from his car phone, but the street sign up ahead changed her plans. She jerked the wheel to the right and turned south onto Beverly Glen Boulevard. In less than a couple of minutes, she could make it to the ER at L.A. University Medical Center.

A few miles north, the dark, late model Bentley navigated up the serpentine Roscomare Road, buffeted by the strong winds that were bringing in ever-thickening smoke from the Bel Air hills above. Visibility diminished as black flecks of soot filled the air, settling on the windshield like a swarm of strange insects. Fahim heard the sounds of sirens following him up the canyon well before he saw the flashing red lights in his rearview mirror. Praying that they heralded the fire brigade and not pursuing police, he pulled over toward the far edge of the road and turned off his headlights.

Lucky Prescott had insisted he park next to the guesthouse. Now that his all-nighter had evolved into a journey of a different sort, the estate's private drive had become an escape route allowing him to bypass the mob crowding the valet stand at the front gates.

The sedan shook as the fire engines skimmed by. Once the last truck had passed, Fahim maneuvered the Bentley a few hundred yards north until he could make out a gravel shoulder on the right.

Stopping his car again, he waited, listening for passing traffic, but only hearing distant echoes of retreating sirens and whistling winds. Shrouded by thickening smoke, he stepped from the car and opened the trunk. Eyes and nose watering, he lifted the bruised and battered body of the young blonde and dumped it in the brush next to the gravel. Judging by the dense fumes and growing heat, the fire couldn't be too far away. He assumed the flames moving down the canyon would reach her body and consume it.

Gagging and coughing, Fahim raced back to close the trunk. In it, to his dismay, he spied the woman's silk purse. Cursing, he threw it next to her feet and hopped back into the driver's seat, gasping in filtered breaths of air through the Bentley's vents as he fled the burning cloud of sparks.

CHAPTER FOUR

Dr. Reed Wyndham dabbed a little jelly on the ultrasound probe and slowly glided it around the teenager's tattooed chest. "So tell me again how you got shot."

"I was on this guy's roof. I didn't do nuthin'." The boy threw a defiant look at the LAPD officer standing guard in the corner of the examination room.

"And why were you on the roof?" Reed asked as he studied the black-and-white moving picture of the patient's beating heart on the monitor by his side.

"I was taking the TV."

Reed pushed the probe a little more to the left. "*His* TV?"

"Yeh, but he didn't need it."

The ER resident who'd paged Reed down for a cardiac consult snickered. The cop just shook his head.

"I see." After spending four years at Boston Medical, the last as chief resident in internal medicine, not much surprised the thirty-year-old doctor. He pointed to the monitor, and said to the ER physician, "No pericardial effusion."

"What's that mean?" the young man interjected.

"That means you were lucky this time, kid. The bullet missed your heart. Next time—" He stopped what he sensed would be a futile lecture, shut down the machine, and peeled off his latex gloves.

"He's all yours," Reed said to both the ER resident and the cop, knowing that once the kid was patched up, he'd be shipped to juvie for a few years of criminal training. Nothing more he could do, Reed appeased himself with a sigh. He was a cardiology fellow, not a psychiatrist.

Finished with his consult, Reed ambled over to the corner of the ER where a half dozen of the staff compared notes by the coffeepot. At one a.m., he didn't think he could get back to sleep. Besides, odds were he'd just get paged again the minute he hit the pillow. He poured himself a cup of the lukewarm brew and grabbed a piece of leftover cruller.

"—and when I asked the guy to pull down his pants so I could see his rash, he hands me his cell phone with a picture of his penis!"

"And the rash?" another resident asked, laughing.

"Picture perfect chancre."

"Full moons and Santa Anas." Lou, the desk clerk, invoked it as if it were a curse. "Betcha the loons are out tonight." He turned up the volume of the radio boombox he'd balanced precariously on a pile of charts.

"Go ahead Brenda from Venice. You're on," the announcer encouraged.

Reed froze. That seductive voice couldn't totally mask the Brooklyn accent. Sammy!

"The homeless are dangerous. They're aliens."

"Now wait. Some may be undocumented immigrants, but—"

"No, they're aliens. Real aliens. From space. This happens when Mercury's in retrograde. They're here watching us, trying to—"

Lowering the volume, Lou caught Reed's astonished expression and chuckled, "See? Told you."

"No, no." He shook his head. "I know her."

"The loon?"

"No, the DJ. She's uh," he hesitated, "an old friend. From back East."

"Yeah, she's new. Only been on a couple of months. Better than the deadhead they used to have on after midnight. Jim something. She's pretty good. Knows how to stir things up."

Reed didn't think he said the words out loud. "That's for sure."

•   •   •

"I work for a living. If you ask me, the police should pick 'em all up and lock 'em in the hoosegow. That's where they belong." The caller clearly wasn't the compassionate type.

"Even the children?" Sammy rolled her eyes and made a face at Jim. This was the third *meshugganah* nutcase in a row.

"Shouldn't have children unless they can afford them's what I think," the caller continued. "Don't want *my* taxes supporting somebody else's kids."

"You're dating yourself," Sammy said. "'Greed is good' went out with the eighties. We're approaching a new millennium. And we've got a chance to make it the best ever." She hung up the line and added, "Right after these capitalist messages."

As the series of commercials began playing in her headphones, Sammy clicked off her air mic and turned on the intercom. "Hey, Jim, I thought you were supposed to be my screener."

"It's the winds, baby. Brings out all the crazies."

"Swell."

"Speaking of winds, Merry Christmas," the producer pointed to the TV monitor beside Sammy, its orange glow casting an eerie light in the dark studio. "Looks like the hills are alive—"

The screen displayed a fiery inferno shot from a news helicopter hovering overhead. Horrified, Sammy watched the CNN reporter gesturing at the hillside behind her, the wind whipping long tendrils of hair around her beautiful face. Without sound, Sammy squinted to read the moving crawl under the pictures of the blaze. *Where?*

The caption on the crawl read Beverly Glen. How far that was from Canyon City, she had no idea. She'd only been in L.A. a few months. The myriad names of the hundreds of neighborhoods here that passed for a city still confused her. Hancock Park, Baldwin Park, Baldwin Hills, Beverly Hills. It would take years to become familiar with the hundreds of small towns that together made up this very sizeable metropolis.

Sammy suppressed a shudder as the camera panned the scene.

Fanned by the winter winds, the blaze seemed to be spreading un-controlled down a forested hill. Like dry kindling in a fireplace, a house nestled among the trees burst into a firestorm of sparks and was soon immolated under the intrusive lens of the helicopter cameras.

I hope they had time to get out.

Unlike Brian. She swallowed a sob at the memory of losing her old friend more than four years ago. The pain was no longer there every day, but when it returned, it was as potent as ever. The fire inside her college's rickety radio station had trapped her talk-show engineer, burning him alive. His warm smile and loving soul would be scorched into her heart forever.

"Ten seconds," Jim's voice interrupted. "You okay?"

Nodding, she switched on her mic and began on cue, "We're back, let's talk to Bill from Bel Air. You're not anywhere near the fires, are you?"

"Hi. Actually, yeah. The smoke's pretty bad, so we're getting out. But, that's not why I called. We can't get through to 911, and I need to tell somebody about the burned body we almost ran over on Roscomare Road."

Ana tried deep breathing to quell the adrenaline surge that had fueled her maniacal drive to the hospital. Pulling up to the emergency room entrance, she jumped out of the Mercedes and ran into the lobby screaming, "He's having a heart attack." Then she watched, terrified, as a tall blonde doctor whose nametag read "Michelle Hunt, M.D." and two nurses raced to the car and pulled the barely conscious congressman onto a gurney.

"He clutched his chest and just blacked out," she explained, her voice trembling. Prescott's color was no longer his ruddy hue, but a cadaverous ashen. "Is he dead?"

Intent on their tasks, no one bothered to answer. The gurney rolled into the triage area with Ana in tow. "BP one sixty over one ten, pulse one thirty," a nurse called out. The doctor nodded, tossing her stethoscope back around her neck. "Heart sounds are faint," she reported to a large-breasted nurse behind the triage desk, "rule out MI."

When the doctor pushed Prescott through another set of doors, one of the nurses thrust a hand in Ana's face. "Sorry, you can't go back. Have a seat in the waiting area. We'll call you as soon as your husband's stable."

Ana stood motionless for a long minute, dazed, and deaf to the world.

"Your car, miss?" the desk clerk repeated. "If it's out here, you'll have to park around the side." He handed her a four by eight card. "Put this on the dashboard."

Ana accepted the parking permit and walked out without a word.

The radiology tech bounded into the nurses' station and headed for the boombox. "Turn on the news. Fire!"

Lou rolled his eyes. "Hope it's not nearby, or we'll be bombed tonight."

Paused in his charting, the ortho resident reluctantly aimed the remote at the TV mounted on the far wall, switching it from the sports update to cable news. The screen showed video of a blazing hillside while the crawl scrolled locations of mandatory evacuations that encompassed some of L.A.'s richest neighborhoods. *Very* close to the hospital.

"Bombs away," Lou announced just as the buxom triage nurse strode in barking orders.

"Nobody leave the area, We've got three on the way. One GSW, one burn victim, and one spaced-out starlet. ETA for all three is ten minutes." She pointed to the desk clerk, "Keep the paparazzi out of here, all right?"

Lou saluted with four fingers. "Aye-aye, cap'n."

Frowning, the nurse spun to face Reed. "Dr. Wyndham, would you please come with me?"

Reed put down his coffee. "Sure. What you got?"

"Rule out MI."

Reed followed her, registering surprise. As a cardiac fellow, he was usually called to see a patient *after* the ER resident had finished an examination, ordered appropriate tests, and made the diagnosis of myocardial infarction.

"Who's the resident on the case?" Reed asked as he caught up to the triage nurse.

"Dr. Bishop wants you to take over this one. He's on his way in, but he lives in the Palisades, and the fires are backing up traffic."

Reed understood. If his chief was getting out of bed in the middle of the night, it must be for someone important. With the hospital surrounded by mansions of Hollywood players, he'd seen his share of celebrities and was used to the occasional change in protocol. "VIP?" Reed ventured and picked up his pace.

The triage nurse whispered, "Heard his wife drove him here in a fancy Mercedes."

Reed rushed past the nurse and sped to the cardiac unit at the end of the hall. If this was a full-blown heart attack, every second was critical. The moment he pushed through the electronic doors he sensed trouble. It was written all over Michelle Hunt, the ER resident's face. The distinguished-looking gentleman had already been wired to a bevy of beeping monitors, nasal oxygen, and an IV.

"Fifty-eight-year-old white male had a sudden onset of severe chest pain while driving. Apparent brief LOC," Michelle reported, using the medical acronym for loss of consciousness. "Just gave him his second nitro and his ASA," she added, stepping aside. "Heart rate's down to one twenty. BP's holding at one ten over seventy-five. Pulse ox is up to ninety-two."

A quick glance at the S-T elevations on the EKG confirmed a heart attack. Reed didn't need to wait for the serum troponin or CPK-MB levels or any other labs to know that this patient probably had complete blockage of at least one of his coronary arteries.

"Thrombolytics on standby," Reed ordered. "Is Eisenberg in house?" he whispered to a nurse at his side. "I'd like to do an angio and I want some backup if he crashes."

"Wrapping up in the OR," she responded. "Shall I page him?"

Reed nodded. The cardiothoracic surgeon would never turn down a chance to crack a chest if a problem cropped up during the cardiologist's procedure.

Giving Michelle's shoulder a reassuring pat, Reed stepped up to the bed and glanced at the patient's name on his wristband. "Mr. Prescott, I'm Dr. Wyndham, the cardiology fellow here. Dr. Bishop asked me to take good care of you."

Prescott, groggy from the morphine he'd received in his IV, barely nodded.

Another nurse handed Reed a hospital chart. "Congressman Prescott was here for knee replacement last June," she summarized. "Dr. Bishop did a full pre-op cardiac evaluation. Normal EKG. No meds. No allergies. Recovery from surgery was unremarkable. His wife didn't know about any health problems."

The nurse leaned into Reed's ear again. "They were just a couple of blocks away. She took over the wheel and drove him right in. Probably saved his life."

Lucky his wife was with him, Reed thought. So Prescott was a congressman. No wonder he rated special treatment. Reed hadn't been in town long enough to recognize the man, but if he was Dr. Bishop's patient, that was all that mattered. After spending years climbing up the medical career ladder, Reed had grown along with his professional experience. He knew a good word from the chief was the key to the next rung after his fellowship—an academic appointment at a university hospital, perhaps even out here, in the land of eternal sunshine. He hated to think where a misstep might lead.

"Sir, it looks as though you've got some blockage in your heart. If we can do a procedure to open it up right now, we can make you feel much better. Okay?"

Prescott produced a weak nod.

"Good." Reed turned to the nurses, "Take him next door and prep him for emergency cath. I'm going to speak to his wife and give Dr. Bishop a heads-up."

Reed already had his back to Prescott, so he didn't see the congressman's attempt to shake his head or hear his whispered "no."

Ana found the Mercedes still idling at the ER entrance. She opened the door and sat down in the driver's seat. Still shaking, she turned off the engine and leaned back, easing her head against the soft headrest. How had she gotten in this mess?

Kaye. She'd know what to do. Ana zipped open the purse she'd left on the passenger seat and withdrew Sylvie's phone. Maybe her guardian angel *was* on duty tonight. Sylvie was one of the few girls who had Kaye's private line. After years on the payroll, she'd earned the madam's trust. Ana scrolled down the phone's contact list and pushed CALL.

"How'd you get this number?" Kaye demanded.

Ana began to describe the mix-up in purses, but, hearing sirens approaching, quickly relayed the news about Prescott and their journey to LAU Med.

Kaye responded with a volley of Slavic curses. "Grab a cab and get out of there. And keep your mouth shut! The man's running for reelection. I can't afford a scandal!"

"Ambulance pulling in!" a nurse announced from the ER doorway just as one approached, its siren blaring, missing the Mercedes's front fender by mere inches.

Ana hung up and ducked down inside the car to avoid being seen by the crowd of doctors, paramedics, and nurses gathering in the ambulance bay. This would be a good time to make her escape. Opening the passenger door, she slipped out just as an EMT jumped from the arriving ambulance and began unloading his patient. Behind the medical vehicle, a phalanx of black SUVs appeared, disgorging a stream of photographers and flashing lights.

Ana heard a piercing scream. And then another. Turning, she could see a disheveled-looking brunette struggle against the leather restraints on her wrists and ankles. A third scream was followed by raucous laughter. *Courtney Phillips?* Ana barely recognized her. She and the singer/actress had spent several weeks at Promise House together last year. Obviously, rehab had failed. Ana knew her old friend would be in for a rough night—like so many *she'd* had before quitting drugs.

"God damn fuckers," the brunette ranted.

The ER's lone security guard held out his arms, a human fence against the horde of paparazzi.

"Courtney Phillips, Hollywood's very own teen idol. The girl *my* little girl looks up to," the EMT said with disgust as a young doctor strode up to take charge.

"Hey you fuckers, get this shit off of me!" Jerky neck movements and wild laughter accompanied Courtney's epithets.

The doctor shook his head. "I heard she'd found God and sworn off the hard stuff."

A TV cameraman pushing past the guard began filming the raving actress. Laughing, he raced back to his truck with the ER's security guard on foot pursuit. Unnerved by the camera's lights, Ana instinctively stepped farther back into the shadows as a few more rapacious photographers saw their chance to move in.

"Let's get her inside so she doesn't wake up the rest of the city," the young doctor said. "I want a CBC, chem seven, cath UA, and stat drug screen." He leaned over the gurney to check Courtney's pupils, took a whiff of her breath, and added, "ETOH too," a blood alcohol. He swung around and almost bumped into the Mercedes. "And whose damn car is this?"

Another pair of sirens was followed by screeching tires. Two black-and-whites drove up behind the SUVs, with uniformed officers jumping out to join the fray. Ana swallowed another gasp. Police. How would she ever be able to sneak away?

She sidled over to a sheltered spot in the bushes near the front of the second ambulance. The driver had just opened the doors to unload the patient as another young doctor joined them. Ana caught a glimpse of a woman's blonde hair and a face obscured by the tape holding an endotracheal tube in place. The smell of burning flesh made her gag.

"This one's bad," the EMT reported, shaking his head. "Found her in Benedict Canyon. Second- and third-degree burns over most of her body. Dried blood on her scalp. Looks like her jaw's fractured too."

"We'll need the police here." The doctor nodded at the officers who'd managed to herd the paparazzi behind a line of yellow tape. "Any ID?"

The gloved tech reached into the ambulance and grabbed a charred silk purse. Gingerly, he pulled out a singed driver's license from the inside.

Ana stood immobilized in horror. The unburned parts of the woman's purse were unnervingly familiar.

"Name's Anastasia Pappajohn. Address in Santa Monica. Born nineteen seventy-three."

In the chaos of the scene, no one heard Ana's cry, no one saw her stumble backward, dazed. Her heart beat wildly as she tried to make sense of what was happening. Sylvie, injured and burned! Dear God, what the hell happened tonight? Sylvie always lived on the edge, taking risks. Didn't Ana warn her it was dangerous to play both sides?

Sick with grief, Ana didn't know what to do next. All she knew was she had to get out of there. And fast.

Reed stepped into the hallway and nearly collided with Michelle, whose right ear was now wrapped in gauze.

"What happened to you?"

"Courtney Phillips took a bite when I tried to draw a drug screen. The girl's gone over the edge."

"Lou thinks it's the crazy winds."

"Nothing against Lou, but I'm betting this one's due to meth." Michelle spoke with the cynicism typical of an overworked resident in a busy ER. "The politico going to cath?"

"Yup. We're on our way now. He'll probably need a stent." Reed held up a clipboard with a consent form.

"You interventional cardiologists get all the fun stuff," Michelle said, heading off toward the treatment area.

"Just call me the 'balloon man,'" Reed laughed and waved. "That's why they pay us the big bucks." Or will someday. But for now, his fellow's salary barely covered rent and food in this very expensive city. Pride had made him reject family money to pay for medical school—Wyndham endowments never came without unwanted strings. Instead, long nights working in labs and ERs along with student loans had seen him through the years of training. Now that he could see the light at the end of the tunnel, it felt good to know he'd done it all on his own.

Reed walked over to Lou who was on his way back into the treatment area, "Did you happen to see where Prescott's wife went?" he asked. "I'd like her to sign off on the procedure too. He's fairly sedated."

"Pretty young blonde?" Lou raised his eyebrows salaciously. "She should be in there." He pointed toward the waiting room around the corner before turning back to the raft of ringing phones.

"Thanks," Reed hurried off in the direction the clerk had indicated. A quick scan of the crowded room revealed no one with the description "pretty young blonde." Every seat was filled with old and young patients-to-be, coughing, sneezing, moaning, sleeping—none of them pretty in their pain. Reed hurried back to the lobby and peered out at the ambulance bay, leaping back as the doors opened to admit a team of doctors and nurses wheeling in a dirt-caked blonde. The smell of singed flesh identified her as a burn victim. The paperwork that flew off her gurney identified her as Anastasia Pappajohn.

Reed picked up the scattered papers and handed them back to the nurse, sighing as he watched them take her away. The few spots of skin that weren't burned looked to belong to a young woman. Too bad her survival chances were grim.

As soon as Ana had hung up, Kaye snapped her cell phone shut. "*Bliad!* Slut! Stupid, stupid girl!" Beauty was no guarantee of brains. And brains were no guarantee of street smarts. At forty-seven, Kaye's own youthful beauty may have been a few years past its bloom, but her razor-sharp intelligence and Moscow-bred savvy were still at their peak. No way would she let a multimillion-dollar escort business go to hell because of a foolish girl's screw-up. Time to call in a few markers.

Reopening her cell, Kaye scrolled down her contact list. She'd have preferred that the ambulance take Prescott to St. Johns Hospital in Santa Monica, where the priests and nuns knew how to keep secrets. She found Franklin Bishop and speed dialed his number, hoping the doctor's reputation for discretion would guarantee that no boats were rocked.

Kaye stood by the bathroom window for a few minutes after hanging up with Bishop. The long silver rays of moonlight glistening in the water far below her hillside home were shattered by the churning of swaying sailboats, yachts, and motorboats docked in the marina. Even her new cabin cruiser seemed to be straining in its slip. Leashes had to stay tight, or the consequences could be fatal.

Kaye latched the window and, examining herself in the mirror, brushed a hand to smooth her shoulder-length sable hair. She eased open the guest bathroom door and tiptoed down the long hallway, across the polished marble toward the master bedroom. As she slid under the sheets beside her sleeping mate, she slipped her cell phone in its usual nest under her pillow. Closing her eyes, she could hear the Santa Anas whistling under the eaves of the mansion. *Winds of hell.* No matter where she'd lived, they would always come and find her.

Inside the cath lab, beneath sterile blue drapes, the sedated congressman lay naked on the table, only his shaved and prepped left groin exposed to the room's chill. One of the critical-care nurses had hooked up the cardiac monitor while the other had started an IV in his right arm.

Unable to find Prescott's wife for official consent, Reed had consulted with Bishop, still stalled in fire-created traffic. "He was conscious enough to scribble his signature on the form, but—"

"I've just spoken with Julia—his wife. Go ahead with the procedure. I'll be there as fast as I can."

They both knew that "minutes mean muscle." The sooner a patient like Prescott had his blocked artery opened, the lower the risk of damage to his heart from lack of oxygen, and the greater his chances for survival.

Now, masked and dressed in clean scrubs, Reed held up a small tapered plastic tube in his gloved hand. "Okay, Mr. Prescott, you may feel some pressure in your groin. I've numbed the area so you shouldn't have pain. You'll be sedated, but conscious enough to tell us if you're uncomfortable." He nodded to one of the nurses who administered the IV propofol and watched as within seconds, Prescott's eyelids fluttered closed. "I'll make a small incision, then put a thin wire through this sheath into your femoral artery."

Reed took a deep breath, said a silent prayer, then deftly placed the rigid sheath through the puncture site and slowly threaded the wire toward the congressman's heart. A fluoroscope moving above Prescott's chest documented the guide wire's journey. While Reed and the team could observe the procedure in real time, the fluoroscope had an X-ray subsystem recording on videotape for instant replay as needed. No doubt, Bishop would be reviewing and analyzing his performance. By his second month of fellowship, Reed had mastered the skills so that he reveled in the challenge of a procedure demanding such precision. All his years of training culminated here. Like an athlete running a championship race, Reed's focus had narrowed to succeeding in his task with a winning performance, his goal, perfect technique, his patient, temporarily forgotten. As long as things didn't go wrong.

Carefully, Reed inserted a flexible tube through the sheath over the wire. "A little more pressure," he warned the congressman, threading the pigtail catheter across the aortic valve to the left ventricle. Satisfied it had reached its destination, he motioned for a syringe filled with contrast. "You might notice a warm, flushed sensation or slight nausea when I inject this dye. Don't worry, that's normal."

Reed's eyes were focused on the fluoroscopy monitor. The injected dye illuminated the left ventricle allowing Reed to determine the level of damage in the pumping chamber.

"Ejection fraction's sixty percent. Normal," he said, pulling the catheter back out and exchanging it for a left coronary catheter.

"Keep an eye on the rhythm," Reed told the resident, as he adjusted the table, moving it back and forth to view the coronary arteries from several different angles.

Within moments of the second injection, the contrast media defined the route, fanning out into the coronaries like a road map.

"Widow maker," Reed pointed to the middle of the left anterior descending artery that was over 90 percent occluded. Blockage of this critical blood vessel could lead to permanent heart damage and even death. Reed's skills at reopening the vessel with an expandable balloon and putting in a stent would give the heart muscle a second lease at life. Reed injected a little more dye to visualize the right coronary artery, which, fortunately, was open. He withdrew the catheter and turned to the resident.

"Okay, let Eisenberg know we're going for an angioplasty and a stent. Have him stand by just in case."

"Thirty-five minutes," reported the critical care nurse, indicating how much time had passed since the patient entered the hospital. Assuming Prescott had gotten to LAU within twenty minutes of his heart attack, Reed calculated nearly fifty-five minutes had gone by. The time between a patient's arrival at the hospital to the time a stent was placed—what doctors called door-to-balloon time—should be no more than ninety minutes. He felt a rush of adrenaline as he realized he had less than thirty-five minutes to beat the clock.

"Mr. Prescott, we found a serious blockage in one of your arteries. That's why you had the chest pain."

Prescott's eyes fluttered open. His monitor registered an increase in blood pressure and heart rate.

"We'll fix it, don't worry," Reed said. "If this works, we can avoid surgery."

Prescott's smile was feeble. His heart rate and blood pressure remained elevated.

Reed nodded to the team. "Ready?"

A nurse handed him a flexible catheter with a tiny deflated balloon surrounded by a wire mesh stent on the end. He threaded the tip of the catheter through the opening in Prescott's groin, following its progress on the fluoroscope until it reached the blocked artery.

"Now I'm going to inflate the balloon. In a few minutes you should be feeling much better."

The congressman's face went slack. "Uhhhh."

"He's crashing!" the resident shouted.

Reed's gaze flew to the monitor. The tracing showed ventricular fibrillation. The heart chambers were no longer contracting. Instead, individual muscle fibers were twitching erratically, turning the heart into a flaccid, useless bag.

One of the nurses grabbed the defibrillator and charged the paddles.

"Do it!" Reed ordered. "Clear!"

Everyone moved from the table as the nurse delivered a four hundred-joule jolt to the now unconscious patient.

Shit. Still in V fib.

"Should we call Eisenberg?" the resident suggested.

"One milligram epinephrine IV, then shock him again," Reed snapped.

The second nurse injected a bolus of epinephrine into the IV line.

"Clear!" Again the group stepped away from the table as the paddles discharged, sending a second burst of electricity through the patient.

Reed held his breath as he watched the chaotic rhythm on the monitor slowly respond—first one regular beat, then two, then three, each perfectly formed and evenly spaced.

Slowly, the congressman opened his eyes.

Reed let out a sigh. "Welcome back," he mumbled, willing himself to appear calm even though his own heart beat wildly. Fearing another complication, Reed quickly inflated the balloon inside the artery, compressing the occlusive plaque against the wall. The fully expanded balloon also extended the surrounding stent, pushing it into place in the vessel. Within the widened passageway, blood could now flow freely to the starved muscles of the heart. Almost immediately, Prescott's color improved. His vital signs now stable, the congressman slipped into a restful sleep.

Reed deflated the balloon and removed it along with the catheter. His own heart rate had slowed to normal, and the butterflies in his stomach were gone.

The resident shook his head in awe. "Great save."

A voice cracked on the intercom. "Dr. Wyndham. I'm calling for Dr. Eisenberg. Do you need him?"

Reed looked at the wall clock. Twenty-five minutes had passed. In total, eighty minutes from door-to-balloon time. Reed allowed himself a grin. It *was* a great save. He'd opened the artery and saved a life.

"No, no," he said, pulling off his latex gloves. "We're okay now."

Kaye almost didn't hear the muffled ring of her cell phone over the sounds of the roaring winds rattling their balcony doors. By the time she pulled it out from under her pillow, the caller had hung up. ID read *Private Caller*. Again.

Kaye tiptoed into the study as the phone rang a second time. It could only be Miller. No one else had the nerve to call her private line in the middle of the night.

"An unfortunate accident at the party tonight," Miller began.

That bloated pig, Prescott, no doubt. Kaye waited to hear news about the porcine congressman.

Instead: "One of your girls is dead."

Dead?

"We may have had some leakage. I'm sending my men to sweep her apartment."

Now Kaye was on high alert. "For what?"

"The girl was a snitch."

Kaye felt her heart jump. It had been a gamble sending Sylvie to spy on that Arab. Despite wavering loyalty, Sylvie had always been the best foxhound on her team. For years Sylvie's pillow talk reports had kept the madam and most of her girls out of jail. Clients were much less inclined to disclose Kaye's business once they realized she possessed secrets about their business. And every now and then, a few of those tidbits fed to a "friend" at the LAPD kept the vice squad from knocking at her door. To the cops, Kaye was more valuable gathering dirt on the street. Dirt that could bring down a white-collar target.

"My girls are straight shooters," she said. "Someone has an active imagination." Her phone read 2:14. Yevgeny should've found the client list Sylvie had stolen by now. Annoying enough having to convince Ana to join Sylvie at the party so Yevgeny could search the girls' flat. It would be more than inconvenient to have Miller's people run into her undocumented Russian hatchet man there.

"Fahim caught her spying."

"I don't believe it," Kaye feigned indignation, though her emotions were a mixture of anger and ice. *Damn that Sylvie.* After ten years, the girl had gotten too overconfident, too aggressive. Kaye wouldn't be sorry to see Sylvie out of the way—once Yevgeny found the copy of that list.

"So sad, such a young girl." Miller's concern was unconvincing. "Apparently too much cocaine and went off half-cocked running down the road. Poor Fahim tried to stop her, but she was too fast. She must have stumbled, knocked herself out. And then the fire. Such a tragedy."

Kaye wasn't swallowing the story. She was outraged that that Arab john had murdered one of her girls. She'd catered to the tastes of sadistic clients many times, but there *were* limits. "Where is 'poor' Fahim?" she asked, the edge now clear in her voice.

"We'll take care of Fahim," Miller said, "and Anastasia's body, of course."

Anastasia? Kaye frowned. She'd told *Sylvie* to go with Fahim.

Ana had hooked up with that cock-driven congressman, Prescott. Hadn't she?

"Anastasia Pappajohn. She *is* one of your escorts?" The question had the barest hint of menace.

"One of my personal assistants, yes," Kaye said smoothly. *Who had spoken to her on the phone less than an hour ago. About Prescott, not Fahim. Wait. What had that stupid girl said? Something about losing her purse?*

"Well, then, Kaye, my deepest condolences." Abruptly, Miller clicked off.

Kaye stood staring at her cell, her mind racing. *Anastasia's body.* So Miller believed *Ana* was dead. Kaye allowed herself a small smile as the truth dawned on her. Considering Sylvie's unforgivable betrayal, perhaps it was a stroke of luck that Sylvie was the real victim. Yevgeny would soon return the stolen information to Kaye's safekeeping, and Sylvie would no longer be a threat.

Kaye's smile vanished with a new fear. Might Sylvie have bought herself a backup plan? Spilled the info on Kaye's clients and their Achilles' heels to Ana? If so, there would still be loose ends, running loose.

Kaye speed dialed the next number without looking. "*Dobroye 'ootro*, Yevgeny."

CHAPTER FIVE

L.A. is a city that thrives on scandals, so, by the two a.m. break, news of the fires had been relegated to the crawls running under the video footage of Courtney Phillips's tumultuous journey to the ER for what was diplomatically labeled "exhaustion." Eager to learn more about the burn victim discovered earlier, Sammy had asked Jim to follow up with the police.

As she waited, she gazed at the TV monitor in frustration. The shaky, grainy videos of the screaming starlet playing on the screen hinted at a more substantive cause for her trip. Or, more accurately, "substance-tive."

Jim hung up the phone and flicked on his intercom. "They found the fire victim. Young woman. Breathing. Took her to LAU Med." He added in a patronizing tone, "Los Angeles University Medical Center."

So she was alive. That was lucky. It'd be nice to give the listeners some good news. Frowning, Sammy checked her clock. Five more minutes until her third hour. She glanced again at the TV screen now displaying a chaotic scene at the LAU Med ER. Drug-addled actors, keystone cops, and frenzied paparazzi. Welcome to L.A. "Can you *please* call the hospital? See how she's doing?"

"Sorry," Jim hit *Enter* on his keyboard. "Just sent you the number. I gotta go to the can." Still clutching his coffee, the producer grunted as he rose and shuffled out of the studio.

Shaking her head, Sammy opened the e-mail on her computer, which typically displayed callers' names and topics. If she had any, that is. Despite the excitement in the Santa Monica Mountains and at the Westwood hospital, the phone lines were mockingly unlit. She pressed the button of an open line and dialed the digits for the medical center.

"I can't tell you anything," the triage nurse responded after several transfers. "You'll have to talk to a doctor. Please hold." Again.

Two minutes left. Sammy drummed her fingers on her board, impatient. Finally, after multiple rings, someone in the doctors' lounge answered. "Hello?"

Sammy dived in, "I'm looking for information on the young woman just brought in from the fire zone."

There was a pause on the other end of the line. Then, "Hello, Sammy."

A voice from the past. Reed. An unwelcome giggle rose in her throat. "Hey, what are you doing here? I mean, I *know* you're a doctor, but I thought you were still in Boston."

"Just started a cardiology fellowship out here in July. Glad to hear you on the radio again," Reed said.

"Yeah, me, too. We, uh, gotta catch up, you know." One minute on the clock. "Listen, you wouldn't happen to know what happened to that fire victim?"

"Actually, I saw her, but she's not my patient. They're working on her now. Kind of touch and go."

"Thirty seconds," intoned Jim, back on the other side of the glass.

"I hope she makes it. Any ID?"

"You can't put it on the air. They'll need to contact family first," Reed explained.

"I understand," Sammy said, her tone implying the opposite, "but you can tell *me*. I promise to keep it under wraps until you give the okay."

"Good try. But she's not my patient—and I can't afford trouble with the HIPAA police."

The clock showed ten seconds to go. No time to argue about the new, stringent privacy law that had hospitals running scared of violations. Sammy jotted down Reed's cell number and promised to connect again. In fact, that connection would probably be very soon. It was just a fifteen-minute drive to Westwood from the studio. She could go after tonight's show. With Reed as an entrée, she might wrangle information on the burn victim *and* Courtney Phillips.

Jim's finger pointed and Sammy rushed to click on her mic. "Welcome back, night owls. Sammy Greene on the L.A. Scene. The City of Angels is under fire. But this time, *don't* head for the hills—"

"You okay?" Lou dumped another stack of charts in the doctor's in-box and eyed Reed with concern.

Reed forced a smile. "Just talking to an old friend." He replaced the receiver on the cradle. "What do the Buddhists say about fate being like two rivers flowing together downstream?"

Lou shrugged, heading for the door. "Dunno. I'm Catholic."

Reed smiled and picked up his microphone to finish the dictation on Prescott's case. He hadn't seen Sammy in over two years, since that last difficult weekend when she'd come up to see him in Boston. They'd both agreed it was time to move on. For good. And now, here she was. Next to him. Downstream.

They *had* had a couple of great years together. Life since Sammy had become much more predictable, boring even. Reed had to admit that he missed the sense of excitement and adventure he'd felt being around her, though more than once her need to get at the truth had gotten her into major trouble.

He thought back to how he'd rushed into the Nitshi Institute that day years ago to save her life, with that portly campus cop waving his pistol right behind. Pappa—? Reed sat up, startled. *That's* where he'd seen that name before. Of course. Pappajohn. The burn victim whose papers he'd gathered had the same last name as the Ellsford University chief of campus police.

Now that was a scary coincidence. Pappajohn didn't seem to be a common name. Could this poor young woman be a relative?

Reed hoped not. Chances of her making it were zero to none. And, after their partnership to rescue Sammy and catch her kidnappers, Reed had developed a soft spot for that grumpy old cop.

Well, no matter. The police here would do their job and track down the girl's next of kin. Reed had enough on his plate with Prescott, and Dr. Bishop would be arriving any minute.

He clicked on the dictating machine, and, visualizing Sammy also at her mic, began, "inserted a 22-gauge catheter in the left femoral vein, period."

"You gonna keep going?" The nurse's question sounded more like a suggestion.

Flushed and sweating, Michelle's forearms ached with the effort of closed chest massage. Despite the infusion of drugs and three jolts of electricity from the defibrillator, the chaotic, undulating blips on the EKG monitor had refused to respond. If only Reed were by her side.

"Time?" she asked one of the bystanders.

"Twenty-two minutes."

Michelle's eyes welled with tears as she looked down at the young burn patient—Anastasia—and then at the half dozen nurses and techs crowded around the gurney. Their expressions reflected her own sense of sadness and defeat. Even Reed—heck even Dr. Bishop—couldn't fight the fatal prognosis of third-degree burns over 80 percent of Anastasia's body. From the moment she'd been wheeled into the ER, everyone knew she was facing a death sentence. Still, the used syringes, drug vials, and crumpled packaging on the floor confirmed how hard they'd all battled to beat the odds. Michelle fought back her tears. It was now her job to let Anastasia go.

"Okay. Let's call the code," she said, reaching past the tangle of wires and IV tubing to shut off the cardiac monitor. Within seconds, the oscilloscope went black. She looked at the watch she'd pinned to her scrubs and, noting the time, said softly, "Two fifteen."

•   •   •

The driver of the Bentley switched the audio system from AM to CD. The fading sounds and growing static of Christmas carols and L.A. news stations were replaced by the soothing melodies of Rabeh Sager. When he'd called Miller earlier, he'd assured him that the whore was dead. Since hearing reports of a burn victim rescued in Benedict Canyon, he'd been frantic, flipping from station to station, listening closely for further news that the victim might somehow have survived and fingered him.

For two hours Fahim had driven south on Pacific Coast Highway, too nervous to stop at his penthouse hotel in Marina Del Rey. It would be better to hide out much closer to the Mexican border, just in case. Now he saw a sign for Oceanside up ahead, took the turn-off and pulled into the lot of a seaside Hampton Inn. Not quite up to his luxurious standards, but it would do for the next few hours. He needed time to think.

After registering as Mr. Smith and accepting the key from a somnolent front desk receptionist, Fahim drove the Bentley a few blocks away and parked it in an inconspicuous spot obscured by palm trees. He hiked back to the motel and rode the elevator up to the third floor. Inside his modest room, he undressed and walked naked into the bathroom, stopping abruptly in front of the mirror.

His dark eyes studied his reflection, carefully taking stock. His handsome face, framed by his neatly trimmed mustache and beard, was free of bruises. The nails on his strong hands still had their manicures intact, but a line of scratches with dried blood like scarlet ribbons were clearly visible across his muscled chest.

He tried to calm his growing fears. Even if the rescued victim had been the whore, and, somehow, by some miracle, she *had* survived, what could she say? She'd never seen him before tonight, didn't know his real name, where he lived, or what he did. Besides, in the midst of the revelry of the party, no one would remember seeing them together. Thank Allah all his e-mails were in code. She could learn nothing for her trouble. And she deserved what she got.

Now Fahim stepped into the shower, turning the water on full blast, letting the spray stream over his body to cleanse it. At forty-eight, he was old enough to have mastered self-discipline, to put mission before pleasure. But, freed from the bounds of his homeland and his brothers, he could not resist the temptations so forbidden halfway round the world. He knew he should shun the unholy and impure, but it was an irresistible addiction.

Wrapping himself in a bath towel, Fahim raided the motel's minibar and gulped down the contents of several tiny bottles inside. Only when the alcohol had washed over his brain could he begin to forget. He lay down on the lumpy mattress and, praying that not even Allah's eyes had seen him take a life, fell into a fitful sleep.

Guided by moonlight, Ana plowed through the thorny bushes of neighborhood yards, avoiding sidewalks and streets. A few more blocks and she would reach the towering high-rises that lined Wilshire Boulevard as it wended toward Beverly Hills. The luxury buildings had opulent lobbies manned by doormen who could discreetly call her a taxi. She'd been a "guest" at one of their towers last year at the invitation of a retired film director.

Scurrying from house to house, her nose, mouth, and lungs stinging from the smoky air, she turned into the rear alley behind two of the Wilshire luxury behemoths. Brushing twigs from her dress and smoothing her windblown hair, Ana trailed a maintenance worker into one tower through a back door. After a detour to the thirty-seventh floor on a balky freight elevator, she returned to the ground floor and entered the marble lobby. Marshalling all her skills to portray a nonchalant wealthy sophisticate, she strode over to the elderly doorman and requested a cab.

Charmed by Ana's enthusiastic nattering about a "recent Mediterranean cruise," the doorman didn't seem to mind that the only tip offered was a warm kiss before she stepped into a taxi. As soon as he shut the cab door, Ana rested her head back and breathed a sigh of relief, eager for the safe haven of her apartment. There was nothing she could do for Sylvie tonight. For herself, a warm bath, clean clothes, and a few winks would tide her through until she could reach Kaye in the morning.

The driver was a big, burly, middle-aged man with a bushy mustache who reminded her of her father, though his accent had traces of Hispanic roots rather than Greek. Without twisting around to acknowledge her, he fiddled briefly with the meter, then put the cab in gear. "You're not going anywhere near the fire?" The question was clearly rhetorical.

"No, uh, Ocean Park." Ana gave her address.

"Good, I can take Santa Monica to Twenty-third. Too much traffic on Wilshire." He stepped on the gas and turned up his radio. Ana recognized the station, a small, liberal outlet known for its radical perspective. She smiled. No way would daddy have ever tuned in to KPCF.

As the taxi drove through Brentwood toward Santa Monica, Ana listened to the female host engage her callers in a spirited discussion about the homeless.

"So you think they should all be herded up and shipped back home?" the host challenged in a strong Brooklyn accent. "Well, roll out the welcome mat, bubba, because most of them are from *your* town, *your* neighborhood, *your* street. People with mental and physical health problems that needed a helping hand and all they got from you *and* our government was a door slammed in their face."

"Maybe if they'd learn English they could get a job instead of expecting me to pay for their health care—"

"Do *you* know English? Did you understand a word I just said?" the host interrupted the caller. "Most of the homeless are *not* undocumented immigrants. They're people like you and me, who—"

"Illegal aliens," the driver interjected, drowning out the radio, "are killing my business!" He leaned over to straighten the American flag waving from his dashboard. "I'm a citizen. Since eighty-five. Working my butt off not so some *cholo* can come take my job." Glancing back at Ana, he raised a fist in pride. "America for Americans, right?"

I know that look, Ana thought. It went along with the "Reagan for President" bumper stickers on her father's Dodge pickup. The world according to Gus Pappajohn.

Closing her eyes, she could see him standing at the door, ranting that life's consequences came from wrong choices, not bad luck. Didn't he understand how easy it was to lose control of your own fate?

"You said Sixteenth, right?"

Ana opened her eyes, surprised to feel dampness on her face. "Yes, Ashland should be up ahead."

"*Mierda!*" The cab driver slammed on his brakes and gave a one finger salute to the lone pedestrian scurrying across the street, dodging eddies of dirt and paper being blown about like bits of tumbleweed.

"I can get out here." Ana opened the back door, grabbed the twenty she'd secreted inside her shoe, and handed it to the driver for the $17.65 fare. Her apartment was just around the corner. "Keep the change," she added as she slid out of the cab into the hot, dry winds.

The cab sped off, tires screeching, no doubt a show of the driver's displeasure at a mere two dollar tip. Ana felt little sympathy. The twenty would've gone a lot farther if he hadn't amped up his meter. *This town. Everybody's got an angle.* Weary, she hurried down the block toward her building's side entrance. All she wanted was to get home and shut out the world.

By 3:05 a.m., Sammy had signed off, passing the baton for the next three hours to her soporific producer. Jim didn't bother to return her conciliatory "goodbye." Not even a wave as he leaned into the mic, welcoming his audience with a dull monotone that guaranteed them quick sedation and a good night's sleep.

No wonder all I get is crazies, Sammy thought. It wasn't easy waking up listeners used to Graveyard Jim to her passionate, activist brand of radio. She headed for the station exit, vowing to try for an earlier shift as soon as she could.

Pressing against the door, it took all her strength to open it.

The moment she stepped outside, the dry winds slammed into her with such force that she half expected a tornado to lift her up and carry her small frame across the deserted parking lot.

Jeez, Toto, we're not in Kansas anymore. She dived through the gale to her Toyota Tercel, fumbled to unlock it, and, with the door slamming behind her, slipped inside. Safe in the tiny cocoon, she examined herself in the rearview mirror, aghast at the damage to her frizzy red mane. *Bad hair day for sure.* Last year, tired of resembling a freckled pixie, she'd let the natural curls grow out, so that now, when she took the time to tame them, they fell softly on her shoulders.

As she anchored down the errant strands, Sammy wondered what Reed would think of her new look. They'd finally called it quits two years ago, but she had to admit she'd always have feelings for the young medical student she'd met at Ellsford. Not only because Reed had literally saved her life, but because he'd helped her come to grips with the pain of losing her mother to suicide and her father to a pot of gold. Sammy laughed at the image. Somewhere over the rainbow—in L.A.

And now Reed was in L.A. too. Pulling out of the lot onto Venice Boulevard, Sammy felt a surge of excitement she was reluctant to acknowledge. Reed had helped to soothe Sammy's pain, but, in the end, he couldn't break through the armor she'd built around her heart. Love, for Sammy, had always led to loss. And Reed, exasperated, had finally given up trying to overcome her fears. Seeking an intimacy she couldn't offer, he—they—had decided to move on. *His* loss.

At the intersection, a honk from the car behind jolted her alert. The light had already turned green. Driving north on Robertson, Sammy could see high-intensity beams from hovering helicopters bathing the distant Santa Monica Mountains. Eager for an update on the fires, she punched in KPFK on her radio to catch the latest news. The progressive NPR station was very unlikely to be wasting time with Cocaine Courtney.

The newsman on the scene reported that gale-force winds had transformed hillside canyons from Hollywood to the Getty into giant blowtorches. At least a half dozen multimillion-dollar homes had been lost. Shelters were being set up all across the foothills for those displaced by the evacuation. Traffic tie-ups along Sunset and Pacific Coast Highway had resulted in a couple of incidents of violence as people raced to escape the flames. "It could be days before firefighters get a handle on the situation," he reported.

The fury of the Santa Anas was turning L.A. into a tinderbox, Sammy realized. As she traveled along Pico, the usual clusters of ragged men and women she'd often see huddled in the dark doorways of closed storefronts had been driven away by the winds. Instead, scraps of litter danced above deserted pavements like confetti, but with no living souls standing by to enjoy the parade. Where were *these* poor homeless victims sleeping tonight?

Less than a mile away was the Avenue of the Stars, a wide tree-lined boulevard of luxury shopping and opulent high-rise hotels where heads of state and Hollywood stars paid thousands a night for a suite. Except for the swaying and flickering Christmas lights strung along its median, the avenue was deserted too. Century City residents were no doubt celebrating their wealth inside the glass, chrome, and steel towers that kept them safe from the winds—and the homeless.

Passing the grand Fox Plaza skyscraper, Sammy recognized the address of her father's new corporate offices. When she'd talked with his second ex a few months ago, Susan had mentioned something about her father moving to Century City as his business grew. Now that Sammy was in L.A., she made a mental note to pay Susan a personal call. That summer between freshman and sophomore year, Sammy had come here to reach out to her father, but it was her stepmother who'd made the visit bearable. Sammy's father? Well, people could be unavailable even if they lived in the same city *or* the same house.

Wiping a tear from her eyes, Sammy muttered, "Damn winds!" and pushed the dashboard button switching the ventilation to recirculate.

After swinging west on Santa Monica Boulevard, she arrived

in Westwood within minutes. A right on Sepulveda brought her to the gates of L.A. University. The Schwarzenegger Hospital and its emergency room, a small part of the enormous LAU Medical Center, were located just inside the south gate off Montana. Sammy parked the Tercel in the hospital parking lot beside two media vans and walked around to the emergency entrance. At least a dozen teenaged Courtney Phillips fans, some looking as stoned as their idol, were standing vigil behind yellow police tape, waving and mugging for the local reporters filming updates on Courtney's condition in the ER driveway.

Sammy pushed past the group and strode toward the entrance.

The uniformed guard held up a hand to block her. "You can't come in unless you're a patient."

Experience had taught Sammy to try honey before vinegar. Flashing a warm smile, she reached into her purse and pulled out a paper bag holding her uneaten dinner sandwich and banana. Looking at the sea of press and groupies, she shook her head sympathetically. "Tough job, I don't know how you do it. I'm Dr. Reed Wyndham's fiancée. He said he was hungry."

"Heart doc, right?" the guard asked, squinting.

Sammy nodded. "It's been a long night."

"I'll say. Go ahead on in." He winked, "And, hey, next time, I'll take a ham on rye."

Sammy waved and returned his smile. "You got it," she promised as she stepped inside the ER's double doors.

Sylvie's apartment was in one of the older buildings on Ashland Street, surrounded by tiny aging boxes—single-family bungalows with grills on the windows—that sold for over a million dollars. Despite its vintage, this former working-class neighborhood's proximity to the beach and good schools now attracted upwardly mobile young professionals who gladly paid hefty monthly rents for a westside address.

Ana scurried through her building's unlit courtyard and up the side stairs to the third floor. Even before she reached 3B, she sensed something amiss. The door to her apartment, which she was sure they'd locked, was slightly ajar. Beyond, only darkness. Ana paused, waiting, listening for any sounds, but all she could hear were the violent winds rustling through the leaves and branches of the nearby trees.

Tentatively, her body pressed against the wall, she nudged the door open with her foot and waited. Nothing happened. She carefully inched her head closer to peek inside, ready to jump back at a moment's notice. Again, nothing. Finally, after scanning the hallway one more time, she tiptoed over to the doorframe and reached in to flick on the light switch.

Her jaw dropped as she viewed the scene. The entire living room had been trashed. Papers were tossed everywhere, bookcases upended, and CDs scattered all over the floor. Even the cushions on the sofa bed where she slept had been slashed. Neither kitchen nor bathroom had escaped the devastation. *My God, what were they looking for?*

It'd been over a year since Sylvie had stopped dealing. She and Ana had been doing so well with clients, it was no longer worth the risk. The coke Sylvie used herself appeared untouched, still in the sugar bowl next to the tea cozy. They must have been after money. Ana checked inside the box of tampons under the bathroom sink. The four hundred dollars she'd hidden there had disappeared. Damn.

Sylvie's jewelry. Most of it was paste, but Sylvie did have a few genuine pieces she'd gotten from some of her favorite clients as gifts. Ana raced into Sylvie's bedroom, to find it similarly ravaged. Everything, from the bed linens to the clothes in the closet had been tossed onto the carpet. Sylvie's jewelry box, hidden inside a now open Payless shoe box was missing. Money *and* jewelry. Shit.

Ana caught the reflection in the mirror and gasped. Sylvie's computer was smashed into tiny pieces on her desk. Ana spun around and stared at the damage, shocked by the violence of the destruction. This was not the work of a common burglar. Whoever had done this must have felt incredible rage.

A wave of dizziness overwhelmed her. She knew she couldn't stay in the apartment another minute. Forcing herself to calm down and breathe more slowly, she quickly dressed in a clean T-shirt and jeans, and exchanged her designer heels for clean socks and tennis shoes. Money. She needed money. Ana remembered that Sylvie had kept a few dollars of "just-in-case" funds in a special location somewhere in her closet. But where?

Sylvie's words came back to her. Payless, remember? Of course. The Payless box. Sylvie'd always kept that in the middle of the closet as a joke. Grabbing a sturdy kitchen knife, Ana pushed the box aside to pry up the wooden slats. Slowly, they creaked loose to reveal a small hole where a wad of twenty dollar bills lay wrapped around a thick disk. Ana pocketed the money and frowned as she examined the disk. It was thicker than a typical 3 1/2 inch floppy and had only the label Jazz etched into the plastic. Sylvie had dated a musician recently, so maybe the disk contained her boyfriend's music. But then why not keep it with her CDs near the stereo? This had to be Sylvie's Plan B.

The faint sound of a siren far in the distance jarred Ana into action. The police might be on their way to the apartment. They had her ID and address inside the charred purse on Sylvie's gurney. Ana opened Sylvie's pristine purse and fished out her roommate's cell phone and her thin wallet with its license and money. No point in leaving something else for visitors to steal.

She threw Sylvie's purse on the closet floor, stuffed the wallet, the money, and the disk in one pocket, the phone in another, then ran back to the kitchen to replace the large knife with a smaller one that slid into the waistband of her jeans. The answering machine by the kitchen counter was blinking. Estimating the sirens to still be a few blocks away, Ana pushed the play button. The first two calls were hang ups, followed by a message from Kaye: "Ana, where are you? Call me as soon as you get in. We have to talk."

Ana erased the voice mail. She was in no mood to talk to anyone just yet. Not Kaye and certainly not the police. It would be daylight in a few hours. She had to get away while she could. Right now she needed to find a safe place to hide and to rest.

As the sirens grew louder, Ana rushed out the door and down the back stairs to the alley behind the building. Through the yards of the houses she passed, she could see the flashing red lights of police cars speeding toward her address. By the time the black-and-whites had arrived at the apartment, Ana was at least ten blocks away, at the neighborhood play area and park. Filled with mothers, nannies, and young children during the day, the playground was deserted after dark, except for a few of Ana's old homeless friends who sought shelter among the trees. Tonight she would join them.

Only hours before, she and Sylvie had been mingling with the glitterati. And now, as her luck would have it, the glitter had burned away to ashes.

Reed was writing orders for Prescott's admission to the CCU, enjoying the silence of the doctors' lounge, when the door squeaked open. He smiled broadly as Michelle shuffled in and parked her five foot nine frame down in a chair beside him. She was one visitor he welcomed. In fact, he'd been struck by her California-blonde beauty at the hospital orientation months ago, but had only found time to ask her out weeks later. Between his schedule as a cardiac fellow and hers as a new resident, most of their dates were casual encounters over coffee in the hospital cafeteria or under the sheets in the doctors' call room.

Their conversations were brief, stolen time away from patients and responsibilities. Still, he'd learned enough to know they shared much in common. Michelle's father was a successful Santa Barbara stockbroker, her privileged background mirroring his as the son of a rich New England banker. Though the physical attraction was genuine, he knew something was missing. Michelle hadn't made his heart do somersaults the way Sammy Greene had that night they'd met.

But he was older now, and somersaults were a little harder to handle. He had come to the conclusion that relationship success for him was more likely with the familiar rather than the unpredictable. After the pain of his affair with Sammy, Reed was less inclined to seek challenges again.

Now Michelle's exaggerated sigh made him ask, "Bad night?"

"First the crazy cannibal." She pointed to the fresh bandage on her right ear where she'd been bitten. "Then the burn victim."

Reed knew she'd had no rest for the past twenty hours. Thirty-six hour shifts were routine for first years. But her wide hazel eyes reflected sadness more than fatigue.

"Didn't make it?"

Michelle just shook her head.

Reed patted her arm. "With the extent of her burns, the odds were against her."

"I know." Michelle pulled the rubber band from her ponytail and let her long blonde tresses fall loosely around her face. "But that doesn't make it easier." She choked on the last word and looked away.

"No," he whispered, "no, it doesn't." He reached an arm over to her, pulling her close. "The best we can is all we can do." He brushed a few strands of hair from her face and leaned over to meet her lips with his.

"Where? I've been looking all over this *ferdemta* place." From the other side of the door, the New York accent was unmistakable. The Yiddish curse nailed it.

"In here? Thanks." The door opened, admitting the voice that had once belonged to a mischievous pixie. It now belonged to a mature young woman whose red hair fell softly across strong shoulders, and whose bright green eyes quickly focused on his. Her left hand held a rather bruised banana.

"Hey, Reed," she said, without batting a long lash, "Hungry?"

Blushing, Reed disentangled himself and eased a few inches away from a frowning Michelle. "Sammy? What are you doing here?"

"Didn't mean to interrupt your work," Sammy said, "I just thought you might like to share breakfast, seeing as we were both doing graveyard."

"Night shift is what she means," Reed explained to Michelle.

"Yup, radio talk." Smiling, Sammy extended her right hand. "Sammy Greene on the L.A. Scene. KPCF. And you are?"

"Michelle Hunt." Though Michelle shook Sammy's hand, her tone was decidedly cold. "I take it you and Reed are friends."

"Well, uh," Reed stammered.

The lounge door opened again and the uniformed guard stuck his head in the room. "There you are, Dr. Reed. Dr. Bishop asked me to find you. He's in the heart suite with the big cheese." The guard nodded at Sammy. "Your fiancée can wait here."

Reed struggled to compose himself as he hurried to the ER's cardio-vascular suite. Amazing how after all these years, Sammy could just appear and throw him off kilter. The hurt look on Michelle's face was sure to set their nascent relationship back to the word go. Or stop.

Entering the suite, Reed was surprised to find his chief already at Prescott's side, examining the congressman. Bishop was a lean man with razor-cut gray hair and military bearing fostered by his years at Walter Reed Army Medical Center and as an Army MASH unit commander in the deserts of Saudi Arabia. According to the hospital buzz, after Bishop made colonel during the Gulf War, he'd been on his way to a couple of stars and an influential billet at the Pentagon. But in ninety-three, he'd inexplicably decided to retire into the private sector and academia. LAU Med was quick to snap up one of the nation's leading cardiovascular experts. For Reed it was a chance to train with the best.

Normally dressed in sharp, tailored suits, tonight Bishop wore an open-necked polo shirt and khakis, evidence that he'd rushed to get to the hospital for his VIP patient. Seeing Reed, Bishop pulled the stethoscope from his ears and cracked a trace of a smile.

"Nicely done, Reed." Not given to effusive praise, Bishop added that he'd already reviewed the videos of the procedure in the cath lab and had been impressed with both the technique and the result. "Dr. Wyndham here saved Neil's life, Julia," he told the attractive fifty-something brunette hovering anxiously just behind them.

Hiding confusion, Reed smiled at the dignified woman who reached over and clasped her husband's hand. *Hadn't Lou said Prescott's wife was very young and blonde?*

"Thank you, Dr. Wyndham, from the bottom of my heart."

Prescott's intense stare telegraphed an unspoken message.

Nodding at the congressman, Reed understood what was expected of him. Something he'd learned as an adolescent dealing with his father's same penchant for attractive young mistresses. Smile, and keep up pretenses at all cost. "You're very welcome, Mrs. Prescott. Don't worry. We'll take good care of your husband."

Prescott visibly relaxed, and, closing his eyes, rested back on his pillow. Though Reed smiled politely, he had a strong urge to take a long, cleansing bath.

Left alone in the break room, Sammy and Michelle studied each other like opponents before a tennis match, wondering whether one possessed a killer serve or a trick drop-shot. To Sammy, it was no contest. Her heart-shaped freckled face gave her a perpetual elfin look that her copper colored hair and green eyes only amplified. Michelle, on the other hand, was a goddess. California-style.

Sammy would have liked to dismiss the tall, lanky blonde as mere eye candy, but Michelle clearly had brains too. After all she was a doctor, like Reed. *Toughen up, kid, You're the one who broke up with Reed. Can't play the jealous girlfriend now.*

Exhaling, Sammy broke the strained silence. "No. I'm *not* his fiancée. Never was, in fact. We *are* just old friends."

"I didn't ask."

"But you wanted to."

Michelle returned a faint smile. "Reed doesn't like bananas."

"Neither do I," Sammy admitted, tossing the fruit squarely into an open wastebasket by the door. "What happened to your ear?"

"One of my patients was a little, uh—?"

"Crazy Courtney?" Sammy probed.

"I really can't say." The quiver in the set of Michelle's jaw said it all.

"Detox, psych ward, or both?"

"Really." Avoiding Sammy's gaze, Michelle picked up several charts. "So you can gossip on your talk show? You media people are so nosy."

Sammy countered, "I *am* authorized as press—"

"No one's supposed to know about Prescott! How'd you find out?"

Sammy stopped in mid-sentence. *Prescott? Congressman Prescott? Head of the House Armed Services Committee? So Courtney wasn't the big cheese.* "I'm an investigative reporter," she said. *Or at least I used to be.*

Shaking her head, Michelle strode by Sammy, her charts tucked under one arm. "Well, you're not finding out anything from me," she said at the door.

Sammy kept her expression blank, hoping to hide the fact that she could read the patient names on the files, though their significance only struck her after Michelle had disappeared down the hall. One, *Courtney Phillips*, was no surprise. But the other—

Sammy could never forget the name of the man who'd saved her life back at Ellsford University. *Pappajohn.* Campus police chief Gus Pappajohn. How often had he told her she reminded him of his daughter, Ana, who'd run off years before to L.A.? *Anastasia Pappajohn.* Could Michelle's patient be *that* Ana?

An abandoned lanyard with a doctor's ID lying on top of a pile of charts at the back of the lounge gave Sammy an idea. She quickly slipped it around her neck and, fingers crossed, checked the photo. Ajit Subramanian, MD, had black hair, dark skin, a full mustache, and no freckles. With no other option, Sammy flipped the card over and hoped for the best.

Stepping into an empty hallway, she took a deep breath and adopted a confident stride toward the ER nurse's station, her goal to locate the rooms assigned to Courtney Phillips and Anastasia Pappajohn.

The whiteboard listing emergency patients was mounted for maximum visibility from all corners of the central area. Sammy leaned casually against the counter beside an anemic desktop Christ-mas tree and watched the clerk erase Courtney Phillips's name. Turn-ing, he said, "And may she rest in peace."

"Courtney died?"

The clerk laughed. His ID badge read "Lou Costanza" and with his pudgy boyish face, wire frames, and thinning hair, he could eas-ily have been a doppelganger for his namesake on *Seinfeld*. Sammy decided not to make the obvious comment.

"Not this time. I meant she needs to rest. And the rest of us need some peace," Lou said, chuckling. "Psych ward." He spun his index finger next to his temple in the familiar gesture.

Nodding politely, Sammy scanned the board for the name "Pap-pajohn." It wasn't there.

"Who you looking for?"

"Pappajohn. Anastasia."

Lou sobered up quickly. "They've already taken her to Arnold Schwarzenegger."

"Beg your pardon?"

"You know," he said, lowering his voice, "in the Arnold Schwarzenegger Hospital next door. The morgue."

Morgue? Oh, my God. I hope it isn't Pappajohn's daught—

"Such a shame, young woman like that. 'Bout your age."

Just like the ex-cop's Ana. Oh, my God.

A pair of nondescript automatic doors several labyrinthine hallways past the nurses' station connected LAU Med's ER to the newly in-augurated Arnold Schwarzenegger Hospital. Maintaining her adopted air of confidence and avoiding eye contact, Sammy dodged and weaved past patients and staff until she reached the adjacent hospital tower. Assuming the morgue would be located somewhere in the basement, she entered an open elevator car and punched the buttons for all three B levels.

While one and two lit up, Sammy noticed the B3 button had a lock beside it that failed to activate. When the doors slid back to re-veal a darkened radiology center on B1, she decided to wait for B2.

This time the elevator opened on a dimly lit hallway. A sign pointing straight ahead read DECEDENT AFFAIRS. *That has to be it.* Sammy stepped out before the doors slammed shut.

Her footsteps echoed loudly down the deserted corridor. More than once she stopped to stare nervously back into the shadows, but saw nothing there. She was totally alone. After passing several closed and unlit offices, Sammy reached a set of large metal double doors under a small tarnished bronze sign that read MORGUE. Taking a deep breath, she pressed the automatic opener.

The morgue resembled a large bank vault rather than the dissecting room she expected from watching TV crime shows. Fortunately no bodies lay on the half dozen metal tables. Sammy guessed the dead were all resting inside the drawers stacked like large lockers on both sides of the sterile space. Though several of these compartments had nametags, none were marked PAPPAJOHN. Dreading the idea of checking them all, Sammy glanced around the room until she spotted one unlabeled drawer, slightly ajar. Edging closer, she tried to suppress the tension filling her chest as she slowly drew it open.

A naked body lay inside a translucent bag, like a developing butterfly in a protective cocoon. Reluctantly, Sammy pulled down the zipper. No stranger to death; the memory of her mother lying in her cold coffin still haunted her more than two decades later.

Gazing at this corpse, she couldn't contain the wave of revulsion that passed through her. Afraid she might scream, Sammy covered her mouth with her hands. It was too horrible. She could only guess that the victim was female by the few long strands of blonde hair surrounding a blackened face, its features melted like a candle.

About to turn away, Sammy noticed a charred handbag at the bottom of the drawer. On impulse, she reached down for it. Inside she found a pair of diamond earrings, a single key, a singed driver's license, some condoms, a warped cell phone, and a few twenty dollar bills.

Sammy flipped the license over to check the photo and the name. The young woman pictured there was—had been—beautiful, with brown eyes and soft blonde hair, framed by the faintest row of dark roots. That Costanza guy was right. They *were* close to the same age. Only twenty-six. Sammy's eyes welled up. Poor Gus. The name on the license was the only part of his daughter that had survived the fire: *Anastasia Pappajohn.*

The vibration grew stronger and stronger, the shaking more and more violent. Alarm bells rang insistently, intrusively, louder and louder.

Fahim shot up in his bed, bathed in sweat. Earthquake?

Disoriented and half-awake, he turned on the night table lamp and looked around. The room itself was still. Only his mobile phone jangling on the pillow. Relieved, he reached for it and flipped it open.

"Yes?"

"You're one lucky bastard."

Fahim recognized Miller's voice and his anxiety returned.

"Your little inconvenience. She died at the hospital before re-gaining consciousness."

"I told you—"

"You told me she was already dead. Lucky for you she never woke up. But there *is* a problem."

"Oh?" Fahim fought to keep his voice steady.

"You were right. About her spying."

"And that is a problem? Why? You just said she was dead."

"She wasn't dead when she text messaged information from your PDA to her roommate's phone. Let's see, the rommate's a Sylvie ...uh, Pauzé."

Fahim swallowed a string of curse words. He hadn't been quick enough. "But I do not even know this Sylvie!"

"Fortunately, we plugged the dam before it leaked out of black ops. I don't expect Ms. Sylvie to give us much trouble once we track her down. But, thanks to you, I've had to allocate precious resources to that task. That doesn't make me happy."

Miller's menacing tone raised the caution flag higher.

"So my friend, you're going to help me implement a Christmas Day surprise. Sort of a trial run for your ultimate target."

"I don't understand."

"I'll explain everything when we meet at the Montagne Olympus. If you leave in half an hour, you'll be there by seven."

Fahim checked the square red digits on the bedside clock. 5:30 a.m. He'd slept just a few hours. The new über-luxury hotel in Newport Beach was over an hour to the north. "Do I have a choice?"

"Not if you want customs to wave you through on your next trip home."

Fahim knew the threat was real. One word from Mr. CIA Special Ops and his cover as a wealthy Saudi businessman and friend of America would be blown. *Fuck you*, Fahim thought in English, but said through gritted teeth, "All right. At seven."

"Drive safely," Miller said. "All these winds and fires. You don't know who'll get burned. And who'll survive."

Not bothering to say goodbye, Fahim clicked off and threw his phone onto the bed. This time he cursed out loud.

"Don't touch that! It's evidence."

Startled, Sammy dropped the license on the floor of the morgue. "Jeez, Reed, you scared me!"

"Good. You have no business here. But when has that ever stopped you?"

"How'd you find me?"

"One of our more alert nurses saw you get in the tower elevator going down. I figured you'd be looking for the burn patient." Reed's tone reflected his exasperation. "What is it with you? Always breaking rules."

Sammy pointed to the license on the floor. "It's . . . she's Gus Pappajohn's daughter, Reed. Ana Pappajohn."

"Gus? You're sure?"

Sammy nodded, her eyes puddled. "His kid ran away from home years ago and came to L.A. She and I were almost the same age."

Sammy's quivering lip seemed to soften Reed's irritation. He leaned over, picked up the license, and placed it gently on the tray. "I'm sorry, but—"

"I've got to call her father."

"That's for the police to do."

Sammy was genuinely shocked. "That is so cold, Reed. I'm his friend. I thought you were too." She'd already pulled out her cell phone and was scrolling down a very long list of contacts.

Reed reached out a hand to stop her before she dialed. "They haven't done the post—the autopsy, yet."

"Wasn't it the fires that killed her?"

"Probably, but . . ." Reed seemed to hesitate.

"But what?"

"But nothing," Reed finally responded. "It's standard operating procedure in a case like this. We have to wait for the medical examiner to determine the official cause of death."

Sammy rolled her eyes and drew her phone from Reed's reach. "That could take days. I'm making the call now. He's her father and," Sammy nodded at the body resting in the open drawer, "she needs him."

Detective Montel De'andray forced a polite thank you to Michelle and her team for their detailed reports on the unfortunate burn victim. He watched them file out of the lounge, irritated that his paperwork had just doubled. Could this crazy night get any worse? The victim bought herself an autopsy now that the doc had mentioned head trauma and a displaced jaw along with the burn. If the girl was knocked out *before* the fire, it could be homicide.

Sergeant Emilio Ortego walked in and pulled up a chair next to his partner. Colleagues at the West L.A. precinct called the thirty-something duo "Mutt and Jeff." At six foot two, the slender African-American De'andray dwarfed the muscular Chicano ex-Marine by half a foot.

"Headquarters checked the name Anastasia Pappajohn." Ortego looked at his notepad, "She's got a sheet."

De'andray nodded. "No surprise."

"One arrest for misdemeanor drug possession in ninety-six, got off with a slap on the wrist. Felony arrest in ninety-eight, mandatory rehab." Ortego looked up from his notes. "Bet *this'll* surprise you, Dee. Dad's ex-Boston PD."

De'andray shrugged. Hadn't Ortego read about the Orange County case where they'd just busted the son of the assistant chief? "Where's Daddy now?"

"Last we have, he's a rent-a-cop for some college in Vermont. But get this," Oretego said, "Anastasia did her rehab at Promise House."

Now De'andray was suprised. "Daddy didn't pay for that on a cop's salary." Promise House was a rehabilitation facility only the rich could afford.

"No shit. Apparently Dad refused to come out for arraignment, trial, anything."

De'andray rubbed his temples. "A Sugar Daddy then?"

"Yeah. Dealing or hooking?" Ortego wondered aloud.

"Neither'll get you a suite at Promise. Can't make that kind of money on the street."

"Bel Air don't use the street, Dee. One phone call gets you high-class *chucha*, amigo."

De'andray chuckled. "Not on a cop's salary." He stood up slowly. "Okay, amigo, looks like we're stuck with a full-on investigation. You alert the coroner, and I'll give her pappy a call."

"*Efharisto.*" Sammy whispered the Greek word for thank you before hanging up her phone. "That was just awful," she said to Reed.

"It never gets easier."

Sammy shook her head. "I don't know how you do it."

"We do what we have to do," Reed said. "The police hadn't called?"

"No. Maybe they tried his old number in Vermont. He's been living in his sister's house near Boston since he retired six months ago. She moved back to Greece and got married." Sammy's voice was heavy with regret. "I kept Eleni's number on my contacts list. She took care of me after that horrible trip to New York. For years, I'd call whenever I needed a mom. In place of Grandma Rose's Yiddish, I'd get a dose of Aunt Eleni's Greek wisdom."

Reed gave Sammy's shoulder a comforting squeeze. "You did the wise thing, calling."

"I hope so." She blinked to push back tears. "Gus didn't say much. It was," Sammy thought for a minute, "almost like he'd been expecting bad news." She told Reed how, according to Pappajohn, Ana had run away almost a decade ago, blaming him for spending too much time at work when her mother was dying of cancer. "I don't know if she ever forgave him."

"Fathers and daughters."

Sammy was glad Reed didn't say more. She knew he was aware of her estrangement from her own father. She certainly didn't want to talk about that now. "Pappajohn plans to catch the noon non-stop from Boston. I think I'll meet him at the airport."

"You want me to come?" Reed leaned down and closed the drawer.

"Thanks, but you don't need to. Besides," Sammy added with a soft smile, "you've been up all night."

"Yeah, and I can't get out of here til after the Y2K disaster drill tomorrow." Reed checked his watch. "Today."

"This town and Y2K." Sammy shook her head. "Then you'd better get a few hours of beauty rest."

Reed made a vain attempt to straighten his rumpled white lab coat and ran his long fingers through his thick sandy blond hair. "I must look terrible."

Sammy's admiring glance didn't need a voice, but she said it anyway. "Actually, you look pretty good."

"You, too. I, uh, like the hair." Reed took her arm and gently turned her toward the doors. Obviously uncomfortable, he added, "We'd better go before we're caught in here."

"Just say it was my fault. As usual," Sammy offered, half joking as they left the morgue and headed down the hall. After several uncomfortable moments of silence from Reed, she ventured, "Speaking of my fault, I'm sorry I, uh, rained on your parade earlier. With Michelle."

At the elevator, Reed finally spoke. "There's no parade. But I did figure *I* wasn't on your contact list any more."

Sammy stared at her feet, wishing the elevator would hurry. "I still have your number in Boston."

The elevator doors opened, and Reed extended a hand to wave her into the car. His tone was only lukewarm as he said, "Welcome to L.A".

CHAPTER SIX

Ana woke just before the first gasp of daylight, smoke burning her nostrils. Blearily, she looked around to get her bearings. She was in a Santa Monica park, blocks from her apartment. The two homeless women in the nearby bushes she'd found last night in the darkness were still asleep, sharing a thin blanket, curled against each other on the cold ground like stray cats. This was no dream.

Slowly, she stood, rubbed a twinge in her back and stretched, trying not to wake the women. Neither looked familiar. There was no point in involving these poor souls in her troubles. And she was, she thought with regret, in deep trouble.

At least Teddy was safe. Her son's foster mother had taken him up north to Hayward to visit a sister for Christmas and they wouldn't return until Wednesday. Ana hoped Teddy liked the Nintendo Game Boy she'd bought him. She desperately wished she could spend the holidays by his side.

She brushed dirt and grass from her T-shirt and jeans and made a futile effort to smooth her hair. She longed for a shower and a bite to eat. Neither would be an option until she figured out what to do. Sylvie was in bad shape. Ana had no doubt someone had tried to kill her friend. The same person who ransacked the apartment? And smashed Sylvie's computer?

Why? What were they looking for?

Ana picked up the disk she'd laid on the ground so as not to damage it while she slept, and tuned it over and over in her hand. She stared at the *Jazz* label. Sylvie's boyfriend was a really lame musician. His tunes couldn't be worth much. But, if the disk had no value, why would Sylvie take such trouble to hide it? It had to be Sylvie's Plan B.

Better find out what was on it, Ana finally decided. She'd need access to a computer. The Public Library on Sixth Street had free PCs, but opened at nine. Without a watch Ana had to guess the time. From the way the sun's rays were starting to burn through the haze, she figured it was no later than seven a.m. She took out Sylvie's phone and saw that the battery was dead. Damn, Sylvie was so forgetful. Now she'd have to find a charger. Going back to the apartment was out of the question.

Ana's stomach growled, a reminder that her last meal had been midday yesterday. She selected a twenty from the roll of bills stuffed in her pocket and tucked it under the blanket where the women slept. At least they'd have something to eat for the next few days.

Tiptoeing off in the direction of Lincoln Boulevard, she headed for a twenty-four-hour diner on the corner of Lincoln and Broadway. She could wash up, grab a cup of coffee and some breakfast, and use the pay phone to call Kaye. The madam had always taken care of her girls.

On the eighth floor CCU of the Schwartzenegger Tower, Julia Graves Prescott stood by her husband's bedside until he was fast asleep. She refused to acknowledge the part of her that wished his sleep would be permanent. She'd done her duty for thirty years, and would do so for thirty more if the fates so decreed.

Still, Julia was grateful that Franklin Bishop had been here tonight. Memories of her high school sweetheart had always remained fond ones, despite the years and their divergent paths from Houston. The Graves family fortune that had paved Neil's path to the Capitol, had sent the man she once loved to the Killing Fields. Frank's survival was a miracle; her marriage to Neil, her penance.

Who would have thought they'd find themselves together again here in Southern California? The fates, indeed.

Sammy hesitated before declining Reed's offer to follow her home after his shift. A polite gesture or something more? Sammy wasn't sure. She only knew that seeing Reed again had roused feelings she'd assumed long dead. The few years and hard-earned smile lines had made him even more handsome. Perhaps just being alone in this new, impersonal city at the holidays was behind the stirring in her heart. Better to keep some distance between herself and Reed until she could sort things out.

Rays of pink began painting streaks in the brown night sky. The sun would soon be visible, and Sammy was eager to get home, take a bath, and catch a few winks before facing Pappajohn at LAX. Morning rush-hour traffic was just getting into full swing by the time she'd driven from Westwood to Palms. Weary, she parked her car and trudged up the stairs to the second floor. Then as she did every day since moving into this matchbox of an apartment, Sammy stepped inside her door and cursed the lack of heavy brick construction and thick insulation used in buildings in the Northeast. Through the thin plasterboard walls, she could hear her next door neighbor taking his crack-of-dawn shower and singing his out-of-tune version of "Cabaret" that woke her each morning after too few hours sleep.

Too tired for a bath, she took a quick shower with the building's remaining hot water, gobbled a cup of yogurt from her fridge, and, wearing only a long T-shirt, hopped into bed. She set her alarm for noon. The airport was no more than half an hour away on surface streets. The old blinds didn't keep much sunlight from the room, so she grabbed a second pillow and covered her face.

Though her eyes were shut, she clearly saw the unwelcome image of Ana lying in the hospital morgue, her pale features horribly burned. A picture so at odds with the one in Pappajohn's wallet years ago. How terrible those last moments must have been, running to escape the flames whipped up all around her by the winds. The smoke getting thicker, choking her breath, the ashes singeing her tender skin and burning and blinding her eyes. Stumbling on twigs and roots, falling, her head cracked by a branch or a stone. Unconscious as the fire washed over her, leaving charred footsteps behind. Or injured, but awake, feeling every second of the the hellish blaze.

Sammy sat up, agitated by memories of the fire that had killed her engineer at the college radio station years before. The doctors had assured her that Brian had been anesthetized by the smoke as he'd burned alive. It was the only straw she could grasp to make her old friend's death bearable. That in the end, he hadn't suffered. But Ana?

Sammy frowned, replaying the scene with Reed in the hospital morgue.

Wasn't it the fires that killed her?

"*Probably, but—*

But—Sammy knew Reed. Something about his hesitation made her wonder now if he'd been hiding something.

Sammy lay back down. *But what?* If not the fires, what else could have killed Ana? *Or*, she shuddered, *who?*

We have to wait for the medical examiner to determine the official cause of death.

Okay, she'd wait. Acknowledging her exhaustion, Sammy considered that she might be going off the deep end this time, looking for murder where there was just a terrible, tragic accident. Moments later, when she fell into a deep sleep, she dreamed of Reed and Ana and Gus Pappajohn. Of old friends, past lives, fathers and of daughters. And loss.

For the president of Greene Progress, LLC, there was no question that L.A. had given him a second chance. Born on the wrong side of the Hudson River, son of a paperhanger, scion of what the well-to-do disdainfully called the "road-and-tunnel crowd," he'd spent years trying to make a go of it in New York City, without success.

Yes, he'd made plenty of mistakes. Got married the first time too young. Even worse, had a kid right away. Twenty-three years old and living in a duplex in Brooklyn, with a hysterical wife and Bubbe Rose, the mother-in-law from Hell. Between his wife's drama and her mother's harping, there was no room to breathe. "Monster Mama" wouldn't stop nagging him to "get a real job," calling him a loser, trying to crush his big dreams. Which was why he finally had to get away from the voices of defeat. Before they defeated *him*.

With two women to micromanage her upbringing, his daughter would be fine. Girls needed mothers anyway. Or grandmothers who never stopped being mothers. No sense in compounding a mistake by sticking around. If he was going to start fresh, he needed to put distance between himself and his past and travel light.

Whoever said "Tip the world over on its side and everything loose will land in Los Angeles" was a very smart man.

Now, twenty-one years after leaving New York in his rearview mirror, Jeffrey Greene stood at the window of his corner office, on the thirty-sixth floor of Fox Plaza with a view to the sea, admiring the city he'd conquered. The "loser" from Brooklyn had become king of a multimillion-dollar real estate empire, on a first name basis with Hollywood megastars, business tycoons, and powerful politicians.

Marrying Susan had been a good move. She'd helped him get his real estate license and capitalized the first fixer-uppers he'd flipped in the early eighties. But, when the market started to heat up, and the time was ripe to strike it big, she got cold feet. Leveraging, buying everything he could find with only 10 percent down, and racking up dozens of 18 and 19 percent mortgages—*that* was the ticket. Susan never got it. People like him, people who weren't born with silver spoons in their mouths, *had* to take risks. No risk, no reward, he'd tell her. It didn't take long before she started to say "no reward" back to him more and more.

Her loss. Because now he'd found the key to the big leagues. He was playing pro, and he needed a pro by his side. Susan couldn't cut the mustard, so he'd had to cut the cord. For the briefest moment, Jeffrey wondered how his ex-wife was doing. Last time they spoke—almost a year ago—she was selling the Encino ranch and moving to a condo down the coast in Costa Mesa. Which, of course, she paid for in cash. So typically Susan.

Thank goodness Trina had come into his life at the perfect time. Not only beautiful, smart, and gutsy as all get out, she was a pro, a partner who didn't fear taking chances and who seemed to know everyone who was anyone from San Francisco to San Diego. Everyone, in turn, was captivated by her exotic beauty, blending the grace of a Monaco princess with the sexy earthiness of Sophia Loren in her prime.

It was Trina who helped Jeffrey start a real estate partnership, bringing in investors like Danny Tice from CompCity.com, Barry Rogers from Panoramic Studios, even a few Saudis with money to burn. It was her political connections that greased the bureaucratic wheels to make the big deals happen. The old cliché: "it's not what you know, but who you know" sure had it right. Thanks to receptive politicians like Congressman Neil Prescott, Jeffrey Greene was a very rich man today.

Jeffrey turned his back to the view and sat down behind his antique mahogany desk. Trina insisted he make the high bid at Sotheby's last winter. "You work so hard, *cheri*. You deserve it," she'd said. Well, she was right, dammit. He lived to work. Even with the fires raging in the city, he'd slipped out of bed at five a.m., ran an hour on his home treadmill, then fought the still backed-up traffic from Orange County to Century City to arrive at the office well before the secretarial staff. He needed some privacy to make his call this morning.

Jeffrey unlocked the desk drawer and removed a file labeled PLAYA BELLA PARTNERSHIP #2. This was his deal of deals. For years he'd set his sights on the last remaining undeveloped tract of land in Southern California where the Marine Corps was closing its El Avestruz air station. A dream property with hundreds of open acres right next to the ocean-misted hills overlooking Newport Beach, one of Orange County's most popular coastal resorts. Tipped off by Trina, who never actually told him her source, he'd snapped up an adjacent old hotel built on land leased from the Marines, giving him an inside track to buying the rest when the base finally shut down.

Prescott, head of the House Armed Services Committee, had introduced him to the Department of Defense official who could work out a sale. When talks stalled over price and water supply, Prescott's legislative aide had smoothly interceded, resolving the matter with one call to a deputy assistant secretary at the Pentagon. Jeffrey had finally bought the land for twenty million, obtaining an unusual guarantee from the Marines that gave him a generous water allowance outside the standard allocation process—a bonus that he knew had rankled municipal officials like that prosecutor in Irvine.

Trina was sure the prosecutor was the reason the county commissioners balked at his renovating the historic landmark. Lucky for Jeffrey the jerk ran his Mercedes into an eighteen-wheeler last year. Dead on impact. Six months later, Jeffrey had sold the just completed five-star hotel for two hundred million. Playa Bella Partnership #1 had made a tenfold profit in less than three years. Not bad for a poor slob from Brooklyn.

Now he craved an even bigger prize: the two Navy golf courses sold to the city of Mission Alto. He lifted the brochure featuring a four-color rendition of the proposed high-end condominiums and luxury inn by the links in the rolling hills, a project he'd described in an internal memo as *World Series, final game, out of the park, grand slam, home run.*

Courting local officials and potential partners, he'd assured them that his close relationship with Prescott would help cut through any red tape in dealing with the Department of the Navy. And that was no lie. He and Trina had been one of the platinum fund-raisers for the congressman. You scratch my back—

Up to now, Prescott had come through. When Mission Alto solicited bids last year to develop the world-class resort, Prescott had made a few phone calls to the city council and Greene Progress LLC flew to the top of the list. But now there was a serious glitch in the deal. Jeffrey needed Prescott to assist the city in a water dispute before they'd give final bid approval. Just one final step. Last week when he'd asked him to drop a line to the Seaside city manager, Prescott had balked.

"I can't," he'd said. "With all this Clinton crap, the media is looking for dirt on every candidate. It's too close to the election for me to do anything that might appear inappropriate."

Jeffrey would have liked to laugh in the hypocrite's face, or, better yet, spit in it. All the money he'd raised for that bastard and his cronies. The congressman hadn't worried about "inappropriate" when Jeffrey had let Prescott's staff use his Century City office to make fund-raising calls. But Jeffrey was savvy enough to play it cool and try his backup option. Trina had assured him *she* could sweet-talk Prescott into reconsidering his position.

He looked again at the beautiful brochure and then at the date on his calendar. December 24th. Prescott's Savings and Loan buddies were shutting down operations the week between Christmas and New Year's to do their Y2K computer retrofits. That meant the deal he'd lined up had to be funded by five p.m. today.

Jeffrey shook his head. Y2K. What a crock. Didn't those fools know the doom and gloom predictions were all manufactured hype? As far as he was concerned, it was just a ploy by IT nerds. He'd read somewhere that the U.S. had spent close to one hundred billion dollars preparing for the so-called coming disaster. *I should've gotten a piece of that,* he thought, as he started to dial a number on his multi-line desk phone. Right now the only disaster to worry about was Prescott not coming through on this dream project.

Feeling his blood pressure rise with each digit he pressed, he keyed in the congressman's private number.

"Fresh cup? That one's got to be cold by now."

Ana glanced up at the weary looking waitress holding a coffeepot, wondering if the remark was a subtle message that she'd overstayed her welcome. She'd been sitting in the booth at the back of the diner for almost two hours, downing cups of caffeine, waiting for a decent time to call Kaye.

"No thanks. Three's my limit."

The waitress removed Ana's breakfast plate and slapped down a check. "I'm off duty in ten minutes. With these fires, I'll be lucky to make it to the Valley and feed my kid before I come back for the night shift. Christmas Eve too. Can you believe it?"

Ana conveyed her understanding of the woman's plight with a sympathetic look. She'd been in her shoes, waiting tables, trying to stretch tip money between rent and food for Teddy. She handed over enough for the check plus several dollars extra and started to get up. "Keep the change. I'm just going to use the phone."

The waitress pocketed the tip, "Sure, honey."

Ana hurried over to the pay phone next to the rest rooms and made a collect call to Kaye's number. The diner was beginning to fill up with the morning crowd, so she tried to keep her voice low. "It's me," she whispered when she heard Kaye accept the charges.

"Where the hell are you?" Kaye demanded.

"I can't really talk," Ana said, afraid of who might be listening. "Not on the phone. Can I meet you, uh, at—?"

Ana didn't expect Kaye to suggest her place, a well-kept secret. As far as Ana knew, none of Kaye's girls had a clue where the madam lived. Rumors abounded, of course, and stretched from Brentwood to Beverly Hills, from Santa Barbara to La Jolla. But, as Sylvie had explained, Kaye had to be discreet. For herself as well as for her famous clients, few of whom had ever actually met her in person. Kaye conducted her million-dollar business on the phone or the Internet. The only two times Ana had seen the madam had been at their apartment.

"I'm booked with meetings until three," Kaye responded, adding curtly. "I'll come to you."

No surprise. "Then how about Third Street?" Ana improvised. Several blocks of the Santa Monica street close to the ocean had been turned into a pedestrian open-air mall. They could lose themselves among the crowds and talk privately.

"All right," Kaye said through a clutter of static. "I can meet you at the pier, by the carousel, at four."

The Santa Monica pier with its amusement park, shops, and restaurants was also a popular attraction. Ana agreed, disconnecting. The graffiti-etched pay phone burped, and Ana heard the clanking of a quarter in the return slot. She reached in and picked up the coin, smiling at the small good omen. She briefly considered calling her father in Vermont, but twenty-five cents wouldn't be enough for long distance. And if the operator did reach her father, would he accept her collect call?

On impulse, she dropped the quarter into the slot and dialed her cell, the phone Sylvie had accidentally grabbed. It rang repeatedly without an answer, defaulting to voice mail. Ana heard her own voice asking callers to leave a message. She hung up, eyes welling with tears.

"God damn it!" Jeffrey Greene slammed down the receiver. Prescott was hiding in the fucking hospital, hanging him out to dry! What the hell was he going to do? Jeffrey glanced at the speed dial list on his phone. He'd have to ask Trina to work her magic once again.

Trina picked up after a half dozen rings. Though her greeting was warm, Jeffrey caught the faintest edge in her tone.

"*Es nada*," she said when he called her on it. "Too many headaches here, but for you, *carino*, always time. What do you need?"

He filled her in on the news he'd just learned: Prescott had had a heart attack and was in the hospital. "Julia refused to let him take my call," Jeffrey said. "You think you could sweet-talk Neil out of the CCU and back into our deal? I'd hate to think his bout of indigestion is going to take down our multimillion-dollar arrangement. And us with it."

There was a pause on the other end of the line before Trina responded. "None of us would want to see that happen. Don't worry, I'll handle it."

Kaye pressed the button on her cell phone. Did you get it?" she asked in Russian.

"*Nyet.*" Yevgeny was clearly anxious as he responded in their language. "I found nothing and now police are all round the building."

Kaye sat up in her Porsche Boxter, her expression showing more than a hint of alarm. "Police? Why?"

"One of the doctors thought the girl was beaten. A cop said the body's gone to the county morgue."

"*Govno*." Miller was supposed to handle things so there'd be no investigation. Now she'd need to create some excuse to call her LAPD "friend" and see what was going on. Until she found the client list Sylvie stole, it would be better for people to believe Ana had died in the fire.

"Get over to the morgue right away. If Sylvie's "treasure" is there, take it!" Kaye snapped the phone shut.

If the list wasn't with Sylvie's body, Ana would probably have it. Well, that would be convenient. Kaye wasn't about to take any chances. Like a Mafia don whose turf had been invaded, she decided to send her enforcer Yevgeny to the pier that afternoon. He could handle Ana easily, get Sylvie's information and kill, literally, two birds with one stone.

At half past seven, Fahim and Miller were the only guests having breakfast on the oceanside patio. *Just as well*, Fahim thought. Forced to rush to the meeting, he'd had to wear the wrinkled suit from last night. Miller, on the other hand, appeared crisp in pressed tan slacks and a blue blazer over an open-collared cotton dress shirt.

"I can never get enough of this view," Miller said as he sipped champagne and gazed at the blue Pacific whose waves crashed rhythmically against the shoreline less than twenty yards from their table. This morning a cool ocean breeze kept the smoke and dust of the Santa Anas at bay. "An American Eden, don't you think?"

Fahim had to agree. Open only six months, the Montagne Olympus already rivaled the finest five-star luxury hotels from London to Dubai. But he wasn't here to admire the view or make small talk. For half an hour, he'd been anxiously waiting to hear about Miller's change of plans.

What had he gotten himself into? After years of small-time arms dealing, Fahim thought he'd finally found in Miller the right partner to impress his contacts in the royal family. One suitcase nuke delivered to the prince's man al-Salid by the New Year, and his Vegas debts would disappear. That's all he'd wanted in the beginning.

And then he'd seen in Miller an irresistible opportunity. Intensity reflected in the man's cold blue eyes no different from that of the fanatics within his own country who talked of annihilating infidels. Miller's "us-versus-them" oligarchic worldview was as obsessive and misguided as that of any jihadist.

Less motivated by politics than practicality, Fahim had hoped to play both sides and stay neutral. Feeding Miller manufactured news of impending terrorist threats had placed the Saudi on the unofficial CIA payroll. "Consultant" certainly sounded better than "arms dealer." It also paid a whole lot better. And allowed him to indulge his yen for hot women and cool deals.

But now it seemed he was being drawn further and further into some high-level secret plot that Miller promised would ensure the election of a president who favored a much more aggressive approach against the enemies of America and her Saudi brothers. Despite the cool breeze, Fahim felt sweat drip from his collar. With a sweep of his linen napkin, he wiped an errant piece of omelet from his lips. "So you have a surprise?" he asked, feigning nonchalance.

"That I do." Miller grabbed his Macbook from the empty seat beside him and opened it on the table where they could both watch the screen. With a few keystrokes, he summoned a photo of an abandoned fifteen-story building standing squarely in the middle of a dirt parcel filled with overgrown weeds and trash. "Voila, Eden 1.0."

Fahim raised an eyebrow.

"That ramshackle tenement was the Palacio Real Hotel—the vacation spot for Hollywood's biggest stars of the nineteen thirties."

Up went the other eyebrow.

"Needed a little face-lift, wouldn't you say?" Miller sipped his champagne. "A real estate partnership bought the place planning to do major surgery. Unfortunately, the Orange County commissioners declared it a historic landmark and Jeffrey Greene, the principal investor, was left holding the bag. All they'd let him do was a seismic retrofit, but, hell, you'd need Atlas himself to keep that Tinkertoy up in an earthquake. As it turns out, Neil Prescott had some of his own money in the deal and you know Neil," Miller said. "He hates to lose anything."

Fahim nodded, though he wondered where this story was going

"Watch this." Miller pressed a few more keys and in seconds, the QuickTime program played a video with a more distant perspective of the dilapidated hotel. Construction equipment surrounded the building's concrete and steel frame, and bulldozers ringed the ground floor. A large crane hovered menacingly to one side. "Greene Progress has almost completed the seismic retrofit and is ready to begin renovating the inside of the old rattletrap," Miller narrated. "Their engineers were putting in an active seismic control system in the mechanical rooms under the roof."

Fahim stifled a yawn.

"In a minute, the construction team will start blasting a hollow for a new underground parking garage." Miller pointed to the edge of the screen just as several booms shattered the silence. "Keep your eyes on the hotel."

As both men watched the monitor, the hotel began to weave slightly back and forth in reaction to the explosion's ground shock wave. Instead of stabilizing quickly, the weaving became increasingly exaggerated and irregular, until the building's concrete started to crack and crumble. Within seconds, the vibrations had become so strong that the men could see the structure's steel beams bend and fissure. The entire building seemed to lose its balance, collapsing in on itself, disappearing in a mammoth cloud of dust.

"Oops," Miller said to an awed Fahim. "Everyone thought it was an unfortunate accident, including Jeffrey Greene." Miller's voice dropped to a gruff whisper. "Except that obsessive prosecutor Taylor. Didn't shed any tears at his untimely death." He swept his hand toward the hotel, "With this wonderful coastal landmark destroyed, the county commissioner practically begged Greene to build the Montagne Olympus on the site."

Fahim was impressed. "You will tell me how this *accident* happened?"

"Remote active seismic control."

"Sorry. I studied economics at university, not engineering."

"Here, let me show you. Active seismic-control systems are found in many of the newest tall buildings and skyscrapers." Miller reached over and grabbed the crystal saltshaker from the center of their table. "Normally, in an earthquake, buildings sway in rhythmic sync with the ground forces generated—what's known as resonance. In severe quakes, the swaying gets so strong, that—" He tilted the saltshaker roughly from side to side, until it fell over.

"Yes. That is clear. We lost many buildings in Tabuk," Fahim said, referring to the 1997 quake in northwest Saudi Arabia.

"To prevent this, many structures like L.A. City Hall are now installing base isolation systems just under their foundations. It's like putting a pillow between the building and the ground to dampen the earthquake waves."

Miller folded his napkin into a small square and inserted it under the saltshaker. He slipped one hand palm up under the napkin and wagged it to simulate an earthquake. Cushioned by the napkin, the saltshaker wiggled on his palm, but didn't tip over. "For extra protection you can combine base isolation with an active seismic-control system—computer sensors that dynamically monitor a building's sway and instruct rooftop weights to counter the motion. You not only cushion the forces of a quake, but you can actually resist them." Miller wagged his hand again, and, as the saltshaker started to tilt, he thrust out his other hand to push its tip in the opposite direction. "The building stays up."

"The hand of Allah, to keep us, safe, eh?" Fahim said. "That's what they needed there." He pointed to the frozen image of the destroyed hotel's dust cloud displayed on Miller's monitor.

"Actually, Greene Progress *was* installing a seismic-control system in the old hotel."

Fahim frowned. "But it was not yet ready—"

"That's what's on the public record. Normally, this hand of God can keep a building up. But, let's say a remote wireless signal worms into the control system's computer and changes the programming. Instead of instructing the weights to counter the quake forces, now they magnify them." Miller lifted the saltshaker with one hand again. "The building will start resonating, swaying in sync in rhythm *with* the ground forces more and more." He extended a long finger and pushed the top of the saleshaker with increasing pressure until it fell off his supporting hand onto the table with a thump, spilling salt on the pristine tablecloth. "Boom. It'll come down."

"And you have this—hand of God?" ventured Fahim.

"*We* call it a resonator," Miller said quietly.

"This resonator?"

Miller nodded as he sprinkled a pinch of the salt over his left shoulder. "And, tomorrow, on Christmas Day, you'll have it, too."

"ID please."

"Huh?"

The librarian slid Benjamin Franklin half-lenses along her narrow nose and peered at Ana as if she'd just arrived from Mars. "To use the Santa Monica Library Internet," she explained, exasperation evident in her tone. "We need proof that you live in the city."

"Oh, sure." Ana pulled Sylvie's license from her jeans pocket and waited anxiously as the older woman studied the information. Fortunately, the resemblance between Ana and Sylvie was so close—especially after Ana had dyed her hair blonde—that no one was likely to question her identity. It was something the two of them often joked about.

Still, Ana held her breath until the librarian handed back the license and indicated the computer room across from the stacks. "You can use it for one hour if no one's waiting."

At just past ten a.m., six of the eight PCs were already occupied. A few people glanced up when Ana entered. They quickly resumed their own work once she'd settled down at a free computer farthest from prying eyes.

She pulled the thick Jazz disk from her pocket. There were several slots on the computer. One by one, Ana tried them all without success. None fit. Now what? Ana stared at the desktop icons for a moment, then double clicked on Internet Explorer to enter the World Wide Web. She located CNN's homepage and searched the text for details of the California fires. Scanning the story, she drew in a sharp breath when she saw that a victim found on Roscomare Road had been taken to LAU Medical. Roscomare wasn't that far from the party!

Could they have been writing about Sylvie? But why would she leave the mansion without her car? Ana reread the article, searching for more details. There was no name reported, no other facts. If Sylvie *was* the victim, there had to be a good reason why she'd been alone and gotten caught by the flames. Trying to escape the people who'd destroyed her apartment? Ana prayed her roommate would recover quickly in the hospital. And then resolve in the future not to take so many risks.

Behind her a teenager dressed all in black hovered, tapping his foot. Ana craned her neck to see him point to his watch, mouthing "five minutes." She nodded and turned back to the keyboard, typing in the log-on to open e-mail. Her inbox was empty.

Feeling very alone, Ana made a quick decision. *Dear Baba,* she typed to her father, *Don't worry, I'm okay. I've been clean for a year. I have more news. I'll try to get in touch as soon as I can. Merry Christmas.* She sat staring at the screen, ignoring the youth's toe tapping, considering how to sign off. It had been years since she'd offered endearments to her father, longer still since he'd offered them in return. Impulsively, she typed, *Love, Ana,* then quickly logged off.

Ana gathered her things with calculated slowness and finally eased her chair back so she could stand up and stretch. She favored the angry teen with a sneer as she sauntered past him out of the computer room and into the stacks. In one corner she found a well-worn chair and soon settled into its comforting arms to take stock.

Ana was certain that Kaye would take care of things. The madam was known to have LAPD connections. She could call off the cops. Then Ana could go home, and get things ready for Sylvie once she was discharged from the hospital. She'd help nurse her friend back to health. *Nurse*, Ana thought ruefully. That was what she'd wanted to be when she volunteered as a teenage candy striper in Boston. Before she ran. Before Teddy.

Ana closed her eyes and tried to conjure up Teddy's smile.

The librarian shook her gently. "Sorry, miss."

Ana opened her eyes, realizing she'd been sleeping.

"It's almost three. We're closing early because of the fires and Christmas Eve. You can't stay here. You have to go."

Donning a white coat pilfered from a clean laundry stack delivered to the county hospital next door, Yevgeny took advantage of the lax security in the understaffed, overworked Los Angeles County morgue and followed two technicians returning from a late lunch into the back entrance, down the stairs to the basement. He waited until they'd disappeared into one of the labs off the narrow corridor, then hurried to a room marked PROPERTY.

He jiggled his penknife to open the locked door. Stepping inside, he flipped on the overhead light, illuminating a small dusty room with rows of wire trays on shelves labeled with the names of victims. After a few minutes, he located a tray for Pappajohn, A. and lifted it out from the top row. Inside a large manila envelope were a charred silk purse, a driver's license, one key, and a few dollars. Nothing that could conceivably hold Kaye's client list. Yevgeny looked through the purse again and then searched the tray. Didn't the girl have a cell phone? There was none in sight. Damn!

Cursing, Yevgeny returned the belongings to the envelope, and placed it and the tray back on the shelf. Turning off the lights, he peeked out the door to see an empty hallway and slipped out, aiming for the back exit, mission unaccomplished. Kaye was not going to be happy.

Trina Greene waited for Julia to step into the elevator going down before emerging from the shadows at the far end of the hallway and heading for the Coronary Care Unit. Though she and Jeffrey had socialized with both Prescotts for years, Julia always managed to remain somewhat aloof. Perhaps as a second-generation debutante from a rich Texas family, she considered the Greenes and their real estate fortune nouveau riche.

Or maybe Julia was wary just because Trina's Euro-glamorous allure never failed to turn a male eye and she knew her husband was not above temptation. Prescott *had* come on to Trina—more than once—but she'd rebuffed him. Not that she hadn't enjoyed a dalliance or two herself now and again. She simply imagined the congressman's stodgy conservatism would make him a less than imaginative lover. For Trina, Neil Prescott was a stepping-stone to building Greene Progress into a billion dollar corporation. Why complicate their relationship with sex?

Trina pressed the button for admission to the Coronary Care Unit and walked briskly past the nurses' station to bed three, ignoring their protests. Prescott was easy to spot in the glass-enclosed cubicle across from the entry. As Trina walked up, he was resting with his eyes closed, opening them at the clicking sound of her high heels. "How did you—?"

"Jeffrey tried to call this morning. Julia wouldn't put him through."

"I just had a heart attack. She's trying to protect me."

"If I didn't know better, I'd swear you were trying to avoid us."

"I already explained to Jeffrey last week. I can't do anything that the press could use against me. Have you seen what they're doing to our so-called president?"

"Don't worry, love, no incriminating evidence here. Jeffrey just needs a quiet word from you to the folks at Seaside, and the Playa Bella Partnership deal goes through. Easy. Let me remind you, without that deal, our campaign contributions might come up a little... short. And I might have to start charging you for damage control."

She said nothing more, but the grimace on Prescott's red face and the few extra beats erupting on his cardiac monitor indicated that she'd made her point. "We both share secrets," he whispered.

"True, though right now I honestly think you have more to lose than me." Trina put a manicured hand on Prescott's arm. "Don't you agree?" Without waiting for a reply, she leaned over and pressed her lips to his cheek, "I'll tell Jeffrey he'll be hearing from you within the hour," she said, then turned to go. "Oh, and Neil," she added, looking back at him, "remember, the electorate may be fickle, but I'm true to my word. If Greene Progress goes down, *you* go down."

Fahim sat back in his chair, considering Miller's "surprise." If this resonator truly worked, it would be a far more spectacular weapon than any dirty bomb. How much might the young prince be willing to pay for such a weapon? Billions?

Years of gambling in Vegas and Monte Carlo had taught Fahim to estimate odds. If Miller stayed true to his track record, this resonator could be a winner for Fahim *and* for *al-Arabiyya*. It wasn't as if Miller was backing down on the original plan. He still promised that the miniaturized nuclear weapon—the suitcase nuke—would be in Fahim's hands on Wednesday. Plenty of time to deliver it to al-Salid and his men so it could be secreted in place by New Year's Eve to disperse its deadly radiation.

No. No downside. Either way, even without the resonator, Fahim would still be twenty million dollars richer. Enough to clean his tab and give him spending money for a New Year's celebration in Las Vegas.

A sudden blast of wind blew the salt shaker over again and Fahim smiled. The hand of the devil. A good sign. As long as Fahim played his cards well, his web of deceit might not backfire after all.

The Klaxon reverberated throughout Schwarzenegger Hospital at exactly 11:37 a.m. The paging system echoed the alert: "Dr. Firestone, Dr. Firestone, please come to Room C294, Dr. Firestone."

On every floor of the tall tower, nurses and medical assistants hurried from room to room, trying to calm patients aroused by the sirens and the sounds of hospital personnel racing through the halls. "It's only a drill. Everything's going to be fine."

Riders on the high-speed elevators screamed as the cars shuddered and stopped their ascent, then dropped smoothly to the ground floor. Frightened visitors flew out as the doors opened, moments before the elevator lights and power shut off.

Crashing computers, darkening monitors, silent TVs, all fell victim to the damaging blaze reportedly out of control in the ultra-modern high-tech, high-security Incident Command Control Center in the subbasement.

The fluorescent lighting that brightened the labyrinthine hallways of the hospital faded to black, wing by wing, like a series of falling dominoes, replaced by recessed lights that signaled the launch of generator power. Fire doors, hermetically sealed when closed, clanged shut as negative pressure ventilation systems began operating in each section.

"Dr. Firestone, Dr. Firestone—" The incessant pages were drowned out by shouts from staff ordering those able to ambulate to move to the lighted atria near the fire stairs at each corner of the building.

Assigned to clear out the cardiac Step Down ward, Michelle helped move patients in wheelchairs through the panicked crowds to the "fortress," an auditorium-sized steel well in the center of the tower containing generator wiring and a fire-resistant freight elevator. Flushed from her own efforts, she wondered how Reed was faring, knowing he had a much harder challenge in the CCU with the acutely ill cardiac patients. Thank God this drill wasn't real!

Like burrowing ants, five members of Hassan al-Salid's terrorist cell used the cover of the disaster drill to practice infiltrating the hospital.

Two clean-shaven Arabs dressed as orderlies, complete with fake identification provided through Miller, helped Michelle move patients to the secure core of the tower. Another two men, formerly with the Irish Republican Army, had taken their places with the facilities staff, making their way through the electrical and plumbing conduits implementing rarely used shut-down protocols.

The fifth man, al-Salid himself, entered the high-security Incident Command Control Center, ICCC, on level B3, by scanning his microchipped Emergency Operations Officer badge through the Omnilock. He nodded curtly to his colleagues, all diligently monitoring the "emergency." Hospital Security Chief Richard Eccles waved, revealing the perspiration stains on his too-tight uniform shirt.

Miller was right. Hospital security here was a small-time operation. Smart to use former IRA, rather than al-Salid's Arab compatriots to infiltrate the ICCC. The Belfast men, both fair-haired and freckled, easily passed as Americans. The fact that al-Salid had inherited his German mother's green eyes and light skin and acquired a flawless German accent while living as a teen with her, made his own false identity—an engineering graduate student of Turkish descent from Hamburg—all the more acceptable to Eccles when he'd applied for the job.

Al-Salid slipped into an empty seat at a workstation in the far end of the room, smiling as he passed the tall, stiff, gray-haired man in the pressed white coat whose gaze remained fixed on the data reports and visuals popping up on three screens. Dr. Franklin Bishop was ex-military. Despite Miller's reassurances, it was best to remain on guard.

Al-Salid typed a log-in for Hans Sanger, his manufactured German-American persona, on his own keyboard, and watched several fifteen-inch flat-panels facing him come to life, each recording images of hospital staff guiding patients to the safety of the core with its independent, filtered ventilation system. The core, he knew, on December 31 would baptize them with focused radiation from one carefully targeted dispersal device. A *dirty bomb*.

"Dr. Firestone, Dr. Firestone—"

Reed apologized as he reached out a strong arm to guide Prescott into a wheelchair. "We'll get you moved to the Step Down unit as soon as this drill is over." He attached Prescott's nasal cannula to a portable oxygen tank and transferred the IV to the wheelchair's IV pole. "Is your wife here?"

"She went home to get some sleep," Prescott said. "Where's your boss?"

"Dr. Bishop's the medical director of our disaster response programs. Probably monitoring us right now from Mission Control."

Prescott's vital signs jumped, causing his monitor to eek out a beep. "Mission Control?"

"Level B3, in the basement. Dr. Bishop took me there when we first launched the Y2K response training. Looks like NASA Houston. High tech-equipment, computers, monitors, power center. Runs the entire hospital," Reed explained. "Hospital security's got a whole emergency operations center down there. We're lucky to have Dr. Bishop's army experience on board. Heard he commanded a MASH field unit in Desert Storm."

Prescott didn't respond right away. In fact, Reed thought the congressman seemed more than a little agitated. No surprise, with all this commotion, and what he'd been through the last twelve hours. And maybe before with that blonde.

Reed laid a comforting hand on Prescott's shoulder. "Please don't worry. You're perfectly safe. With all the high-tech gear, Dr. Bishop said he can see and hear everything." He pointed to a tiny camera mounted on the ceiling overhead. "Security wants to make sure everyone's trained and ready in case something goes wrong on Y2K." Reed began wheeling Prescott out of the cardiac unit. "Boy Scout motto: Be Prepared."

Running late, Sammy cursed the midday traffic, which had slowed to a crawl. It seemed as if the entire city was out on the freeway heading for the airport. Rush hour usually started after four. *Wasn't anyone in L.A. working today?* Swinging off the freeway onto Century Boulevard toward LAX and Terminal Two, she entered the parking garage, her frustration unrelieved. Not a single free parking space on the lower floors. Amazing how many people traveled on Christmas Eve.

Sammy carefully steered up the last ramp onto the uncovered roof where spaces were surprisingly plentiful. It was only when she drove into the sunlight that she understood why most had avoided this area. Not only was it unseasonably warm from the Santa Anas—ninety degrees in December—but the winds buffeted her Tercel like a Hot Wheels toy. Turning into a free slot, Sammy shut off the engine and struggled to push open her car door. Outside, she guessed that the fires still blazed, judging from the sky, browned by haze. From her high vantage point, she could see menacing puffs of black smoke clouds drift up between distant mountains to the north.

Racing toward the elevators, Sammy had a fleeting worry that the winds might whisk her off the edge of the building and blow her clear over the runways into the cold Pacific Ocean. Fortunately, the elevator doors opened quickly. Inside, she relished the respite, though not the annoying synthetic holiday music that accompanied her down to the ground floor.

Only as the elevator reached its destination did she recognize the tinny instrumental as "Let it Snow." When the doors opened to the blasting furnace of smoky heat, she laughed at the irony. Christmas in Los Angeles, an oxymoron if there ever was one. For a moment, she missed the soothing comfort of a blanket of freshly fallen Vermont snow. And Grandma Rose's Chanukah latkes.

Pappajohn's flight was due in less than fifteen minutes. Sammy grabbed her purse from the X-ray conveyor belt and made a beeline for the arrival area. *Poor Gus.* How difficult this journey must be for him. He hadn't often mentioned his daughter, but when he did, his references to Ana had always seemed a mixture of anger and regret.

First-class passengers had disembarked by the time Sammy reached the gate. *Flight must've come in early*, she guessed, scanning the waiting area for her old friend. About to check at the counter, she spotted him, shuffling slowly up the ramp with a small carry-on slung over his shoulder. Sammy hadn't seen Gus Pappajohn since graduation from Ellsford University three and a half years ago. Still, this man was a shock. He appeared as if he'd aged a decade, the salt-and-pepper hair turned the color of slate, his mustache almost white.

And though he'd kept his ample paunch—probably from his penchant for Greek sweets—it was now accompanied by stooped shoulders.

"*Ya'sou*," Sammy greeted him softly as their eyes met. His twinkle had vanished, she noted, though he managed a weary smile.

"*Shalom*," Pappajohn returned, sticking out his hand for a shake.

Sammy drew him into a hug instead. "I'm so sorry."

Pappajohn pulled away, nodding.

"How did Eleni take the news?"

"I didn't want to spoil her holiday, he said, his voice cracking. "Besides, what could she do here? She'll know soon enough." Changing the subject, he pointed to his carry-on bag. "I brought you some *kourambiedes*, though after that rough flight, they're probably all broken up in pieces."

"Yeah, the Santa Anas have really kicked up. The weatherman's predicting more "devil wind" for the next few days."

Sammy reached to take his bag, but Pappajohn shook his head, and continued his trek to the exit. "I'm fine."

"My car's across the street." Sammy guided him. "This airport's a maze."

"You seem to know your way around. How long have you been out here?"

"Two months tomorrow. I'm a quick study," Sammy said as they stepped out into the heat and smog and headed for the garage elevator. "You'll never guess who else is here."

Pappajohn nodded again. "Are you living with him?"

Sammy's expression reflected surprise. "Uh, no. We broke up a couple of years ago."

Seeing Pappajohn's puzzled features, she added, "Reed. Reed Wyndham. My old boyfriend. He's at LAU Med doing a fellowship. We're, uh, just friends now. Who did you—?"

The elevator arrived.

"I meant your father," Pappajohn said, following her inside. "You told me he was out here."

Sammy focused on the lighted numbers moving from two to six.

The elevator doors opened and she waved a hand to urge Pappajohn out onto the roof. "Yeah, guess I did," she finally answered. "No, I've got my own place. But, I'll give him a call. It's, uh, on my list."

Sammy unlocked the passenger side of the Tercel and squinted at Pappajohn. The haze and the winds were obviously irritating his eyes too. Sammy noted they were a trace watery.

Pappajohn opened his door, but didn't get in before adding, "You should. Now while you still can—" The rest of his sentence was lost in the wind as he coughed and slid into his seat.

An hour later, Sammy had located the North Mission Road address in Boyle Heights and angled into a visitor's space behind the L.A. County morgue. Two men in blue jumpsuits were unloading a body bag from a coroner's van.

Sammy gasped, stealing a glance at Pappajohn whose sullen expression hadn't altered since they'd left the airport. He'd insisted they drive straight downtown despite Sammy's suggestion that he rest after his long flight. He had to see his daughter, he'd repeated. After Sammy had reluctantly agreed, Pappajohn had sat, grim and silent, staring out the car's side window for the rest of the trip.

Now Sammy worried that the sight of the body bag would cause Pappajohn's stoic pose to crumble. But he maintained his composure and stepped out of the car even before Sammy had turned off the ignition. He was already inside talking to one of the clerks when she entered the foyer of the three-story brick building adjoining the massive L.A. County Southern Medical Center.

"Oh yes, here it is." The middle-aged black woman ran a manicured finger down a list of names on her clipboard. "Anastasia Pappajohn. Admitted nine-o-six a.m. this morning." Looking up at Pappajohn, her expression registered confusion. "That's odd," she said, "usually takes two or three days to complete the autopsy, but I guess with everybody called in for overtime, you know, 'cause of the fires and all, there's already a disposition—I mean a—"

"I'm a cop, I get the jargon," Pappajohn said flatly. "So you're saying, I don't need to identify my daughter?"

"Well, it seems that's been confirmed and the case is closed."

"Can I see her at least?" Pappajohn asked, his voice so soft that Sammy could barely hear, though the stoop of his shoulders proclaimed his grief.

The clerk must have recognized it too because she dropped her matter-of-fact tone, her expression now empathetic. "Of course. I'll need to get one of the staff. Please," she said, pointing to the two red leather couches in the middle of the room, "have a seat."

Five minutes later, an older bespectacled man in a crisp white coat approached Pappajohn and shook his hand. "I'm Dr. Gharani, assistant chief medical examiner. Let me first say how sorry we are for your loss."

Lips drawn tight, Pappajohn merely nodded,

"Reception said you wanted to see your daughter."

"Yes."

Gharani removed his glasses and rubbed the deep furrow between his weary looking eyes. "Okay," he said with obvious reluctance, "but, please understand, I'm a father, too. Your daughter— she's been through a terrible, terrible fire. If you wanted to forego—"

"No, I need to do this." Pappajohn was firm.

"All right, then." Gharani slipped his wire frames back on and led Pappajohn toward the elevator to the basement. Sammy introduced herself as a family friend, and, with a nod from Pappajohn, followed them into the car.

Ana paced back and forth near the merry-go-round, the sense of urgency growing in her gut. Nearly ten minutes late. Where the hell was Kaye? Anxious to share her fears and hopefully get help, Ana had hiked from the library to Colorado Avenue, arriving at Pacific Park just before the four p.m. meeting time.

Located on the Santa Monica Pier, this amusement park's roller coaster, Ferris wheel, midway games, oceanfront specialty food outlets, and seaside shopping attracted hordes of tourists and locals alike. Now it seemed as though all of L.A. sought relief from the fires. Though flecks of soot still floated down from the blazing hills to the east, at least here, over the ocean, the salty sea breeze made it easier to breathe.

A chilly marine layer of clouds had moved in over the pier in the last half hour. The moisture would help the firefighters, but the approaching sunset with its drop in temperature made Ana shiver. She'd hurried over to a vendor selling hot drinks and paid for a tall decaf—she'd had enough caffeine for one day. Back at her post, she circled the carousel once again. No sign of Kaye. Just the happy faces of children waving to mothers and fathers from astride fancifully painted horses and chariots. Her heart leapt at the sight of one little boy with the same tousled brown hair that framed her own Teddy's round face. Oh God, she missed him, how she wanted him in her arms again.

A tap on the shoulder made her spin around.

"Ana?" The man towering over her had bulging biceps and a thick Russian accent.

Who—? How did—? Ana was instantly suspicious. "Where's Kaye?"

"In the car. Come."

Ana frowned and took an uncertain step backward, leaving a few feet between her and the man. Her alarm bells had gone off full tilt. Shaking her head, she said, "I'll meet her here. That's what we agreed."

His intense stare made Ana's whole body tighten. The Russian grabbed her arm, "Come now!"

Looking around at the crowd, Ana made a split-second decision. With her free hand, she threw her hot coffee in the man's face. Pain registered in his expression, and the moment he released his grip on her arm, she scrambled past him, and sprinted out onto the pier. With a loud roar, only seconds behind her, the Russian appeared between Ana and the ramp that led off the pier to Ocean Avenue.

Desperate to escape, yet not wanting to call attention to herself, Ana threaded her way through the oncoming throng of pedestrians in the opposite direction. As she hurried, she stumbled and fell, then picked herself up, narrowly missing a woman and her baby. She staggered to her feet, breathless. The man was still on her tail, closing the gap between them. She could see an earpiece glued to his left ear. Talking to someone on his cell phone?

Spying a photographer posing a wedding party in formal attire, Ana slipped behind the group, then ducked into the busy arcade. The sound inside was deafening as teenagers challenged each other at video games that pinged and buzzed. Surveying the huge area for somewhere to hide, Ana located a space between two unoccupied video displays. Her heart thumped wildly, her palms were wet with fear. She wanted to scream for help, but she knew that would only bring the police and right now she didn't know who she could trust. Instead, she crouched down, peeking out every few seconds to see if she'd been followed.

She froze when she spotted the Russian scanning the room. *Please don't look this way.* Less than ten feet to her right, a sign pointed to the Hall of Mirrors. The moment he turned in the other direction, Ana rose and made a mad dash for its entrance, racing past the befuddled checker. Inside, the mirrored halls were dimly lit and the passages narrow, heightening the illusory experience and making it difficult for Ana to see exactly where to go.

She chose one path and bumped up against a young couple laughing at their deformed reflections, first tall and skinny, then short and wide. Apologizing, Ana rushed past them, her pulse racing. Like a lost lab rat, she traveled the bewildering maze of mirrors, frantically seeking an exit until she heard her name.

"Ana, Kaye knows you have it. She's waiting."

Have it? What was he talking about? Ana stopped to listen, focusing to determine the origin of the disembodied voice. Somewhere in back. But how close? She searched for the man's reflection. Down an empty path, she ran hard into a hidden mirror blocking her path. Looking up, she could see his distorted image behind her and swallowed a scream. She spun around and shot out her hand, now clutching the knife she'd hidden in her pants. He was gone. Where?

Panicked, she stumbled to her right until finally she heard young voices and saw a ray of light up ahead. Hoping it was a way out, she slipped the knife into her side pocket and quickly elbowed past a troop of giggling Brownies to the emergency exit, bursting back out onto the pier just beside the Ferris wheel. She closed the exit to block the overhead spotlight and threw a large empty metal trash can on its side in front of the door, so that anyone rushing out would likely trip.

At five p.m., the late December sun had already sunk over the horizon. Artificial lights strung up all along the Ferris wheel sparkled green and gold and amber against the moonlit sky. Refusing to look back, Ana joined a line moving to get on the ride.

"Ticket?" a young man wearing a Pacific Park T-shirt demanded when she reached the front. Only one empty bucket remained to be filled.

"Sorry, I lost mine." Ana handed him a twenty with a wink.

Without missing a beat, the ticket taker pocketed the bill and waved her in. Ana crouched low, the knife back in her hands, and held her breath until the ticket taker pushed a lever on the side of the ride and swept her bucket high up into the air.

At the same moment, Ana heard what she guessed was a Russian expletive as the sound of someone falling hard on the wooden pier below made everyone else turn in its direction. Knowing she had just seconds to hide, Ana slid down all the way in the bucket. Trembling, she peeked through the cage. Flat on his face, the Russian tried to stand, refusing all offers of help from several good Samaritans who'd rushed over. Although she hovered far above him, Ana could not miss his frustrated expression when, after getting up, he scanned the crowd for several minutes, spoke into his earpiece, and finally walked away in the direction of the parking lot. What she did miss was Kaye hidden among a group watching a sidewalk artist, a cell to her ear, her elegant features contorted with rage as Yevgeny gave her the news that he'd lost Ana.

The mingled smells of disinfectant, sweat, and something sweet permeated the air. *This was death.* Sammy shivered as she followed Dr. Gharani and Pappajohn down the morgue's basement hallway. She noticed the cracked cement walls, missing ceiling tiles, and chipped plaster and thought of how the lobby had been so pristine, like the entrance to a funeral home. Here, in the mortician's workshop, no one tried to hide the imperfections.

"From the ninety-four Northridge quake," Gharani explained with a shrug when he saw Sammy eyeing the damage.

Several white-coated staff, all looking harried, hurried past, ducking into doors that Sammy guessed led to autopsy rooms or forensic labs. A few of the coroner's crew nodded greetings to Gharani, but none stopped to chat.

"Busy day," he explained to fill the silence. He stopped just outside a steel door and turned to Pappajohn. "You're sure about this?"

"I'm sure," Pappajohn responded, his expression grim.

Pappajohn followed Gharani inside the chamber.

For a moment, Sammy hesitated, unsure if she could face another viewing of poor Anastasia, but Pappajohn's shuffling gait convinced her he'd do better with her by his side.

The viewing room was a long, narrow space painted entirely in white. On the table in the middle lay a body covered by a white sheet, the overhead fluorescent lights bathing it in a rectangle of iridescence. Gharani moved to one side of the table while Sammy and Pappajohn stood on the other. Slowly he pulled back the sheet, exposing the head.

Sammy shut her eyes. But when she heard Pappajohn's rapid expulsion of breath and felt the trembling hand that grabbed hers, she opened them again.

"*The-eh mou*, what happened?" Pappajohn cried. "I don't even recognize her."

Gharani quickly recovered the body and came around the table. Sammy stepped aside as he draped a comforting arm around Pappajohn's shoulder. "From what we can gather, she was running away from a fire in Bel Air. The smoke got pretty bad so it's likely she got disoriented, fell, and was knocked unconscious. Unfortunately, by the time the EMTs found her, she'd been badly burned. There was nothing they could do. I'm sure she was out long before the flames and didn't suffer at all."

As if a dam had burst, Pappajohn began to sob. Sammy could barely make out his words, repeated over and over, a gasping prayer, *"Theos horesteeneh."* God forgive her.

Like a caged rat trapped on a spinning wheel, Ana stayed crouched in the Ferris wheel's bucket for what seemed to her an eternity. Her fingers unconsciously crept to her cross, repeating the prayer she'd learned years before in Sunday school. *The Lord is my Shepherd—*

Her twenty dollars had apparently bought her a quarter hour's worth of rides. Enough time, she fervently hoped, for that goon to give up. Occasionally, her bucket would stop at the top, affording Ana a panoramic view of the pier when she dared to peek over the edge. After ten minutes or so, the Russian had disappeared, hopefully gone for good.

The earnest face of the ticket taker leaning into her bucket made Ana jump. "Want to go again?"

Ana eased herself up and looked around. The coast was clear. She patted the young man on the hand and shook her head. "Not in this lifetime." Hopping out, she sped off toward the crowded parking lot, where ducking behind a car would be easy if the man turned up again.

Scanning the rows of parked cars, Ana spotted a Porsche nestled between two sedans. The vanity license plate USPEH made her look twice. Hadn't Sylvie told her that was Kaye's motto? *Success* in Russian? Ana stepped back and surveyed the lot. If this was Kaye's car, was she here too? Then why hadn't she met as planned?

The implication hit Ana like a slap in the face. Kaye must have sent that man after her to—to what? Kill her? Was he the one who'd trashed the apartment? And destroyed the computer? Imagining the rage with which he'd smashed it made Ana's panic rise. Heart pounding, she crept away as fast as she could, hiding in the next row of cars behind a large SUV. Minutes later she saw the Russian sprint into the lot and unlock the passenger side of the Porsche. By the light of its open door, the car's mirror reflected an agitated Kaye.

As soon as her well-muscled lackey slammed the door shut, the sports car revved out of the parking space, and, tires squealing, sped off. Ana leaned against the SUV, shocked and feeling very much alone. There was no safe house to which she could return. What had happened? She'd been so sure that Kaye would be her savior. *My God, did Kaye really want her dead?* Why? The only person who knew all the players in this drama was Sylvie, who was in no condition to help.

Fear tightened across Ana's chest like a vise. She was a sitting duck now with no one to turn to and nowhere to go.

On duty for over twelve hours, the detective was dreaming of a Double-Double at In-n-Out Burger before hitting the sack. He'd already filed the report on the dead girl, and all that stood between him and his cheeseburger was the call he'd expected this morning. For which he was still waiting. Frustrated, he tried his contact's number for the second time that afternoon. Once again, the line rang through to voice mail. This time though, the message he left was far from polite.

The sun had set over Santa Monica while Ana leaned against the creaking wood railings at the end of the pier, wondering what to do. Beneath the pilings below her, a group of teenagers huddled against the wind's chill. Their boom box blasted an old Everclear rock song Ana knew to be Sylvie's favorite: "Father of Mine." According to Sylvie, the lead singer, Art Alexakis, had never gotten over his father's leaving him when Art was just ten.

"Neither did I," Sylvie had admitted one night when she'd returned home stoned. Her father's last words had been whispered in her sleeping ears, "*Au revoir, ma petite.*"

She'd gone on to tell Ana how Art had attempted suicide as a teen somewhere near the very spot where Ana now stood, filling his pockets with weights, then getting high on marijuana and jumping off the pier. "He claimed the vision and voice of his dead brother, Donald, made him survive," Sylvie had explained, choking back a sob. "We cling to what we can."

In her head, Ana could still hear Sylvie singing that sad song as she'd staggered off to her room.

Dejected, Ana shuffled along the wooden planks. Below her, through the cracks, she could see the churning Pacific waters washing over the sand. The sound of the ocean seemed to call to her, inviting her to find a home in its depths. This is how Art must have felt standing here all alone many years ago. Desperate to go home.

A little boy with his parents stepped out of a taxi that had turned into the lot to drop them off. Teddy. How Ana missed him. Though she gazed longingly at the ocean, she couldn't forget her promise to her son.

I'll be back for you, my love. As soon as I can.

The DJ came on the radio with breaking news. "Update on our own Courtney Phillips. Word is she's AWOL. That's right, slipped out of Schwarzenegger Hospital sometime this evening. Where she's gone is anybody's guess. Her manager refused to comment, ri-i-ight," the DJ chuckled. "I'll bet she headed straight back to Promise House one more time. Promises, promises. So how 'bout we toast her well-worn road to recovery with some "Lithium" from Nirvana."

Promise House. Of course. Ana *had* made a friend at the rehab facility, a friend who'd helped her get clean and save her life. Courtney Phillips. The public didn't know the real Courtney, a sweet kid who'd made it too big too soon, with too many people making demands—her mother, her agents, her fans. Everyone wanting their piece of her, thinking it was so easy to live your life with hordes of paparazzi always following you. No surprise she'd sought solace at the end of a line of coke.

If Courtney had snuck out of the hospital, Ana doubted she'd go to the rehab facility. That would be the first place the press would think to look. There *was* one other possibility. On impulse, Ana leaped for the empty taxi ready to drive off, and, tugging open the door, slid into the backseat. Her brain struggled to remember Courtney's address from her visit to the mansion last summer.

"Malibu," she told the driver. "Malibu, Sea View Dri—no, Sea *Vista* Drive."

Hours after the disaster drill, Prescott was still seething. Reed's revelation that everything in the CCU might be monitored had unnerved him. What if someone from hospital security had overheard his discussion with Trina? Could they claim undue influence on behalf of Greene Progress? Bishop himself had a well-earned reputation for an over-developed sense of morality. Recently the *L.A. Times* had made a big deal, calling him a hero, for refusing millions in research funds from an international pharmaceutical company, citing conflict of interest.

If Bishop disclosed an under-the-table real estate deal, that revelation would be the nail in the coffin for Prescott's political career. No doubt Julia would leave him the moment he was out of office—something Prescott couldn't afford. What he'd squirreled away could never keep him living the lifestyle to which he'd become accustomed.

Prescott lay back in his bed, thinking. Bishop had left the army rather abruptly a few years back. Unusual for lifers. If something had happened, if there was any buried dirt, Prescott knew the one person to uncover it.

Reaching over, he pulled the phone to his side, lifted the receiver, and tapped in the private numbers. Miller time.

The trip to the foyer had allowed Pappajohn to recover his composure. Overwhelmed by the sight of his daughter's fatal injuries, he sat on one of the leather couches, holding his head in his hands.

Wearing a look of concern, a lab-coated aide sidled over and handed the coroner a manila envelope.

Gharani motioned to Sammy to approach them out of earshot of the grieving father. "These are some personal effects Mr. Pappajohn might want to have."

"Thank you," Sammy whispered, accepting the package labeled PAPPAJOHN, A.

Gharani checked his watch. "It's after five. Christmas Eve and we've still got several cases backed up. Tomorrow we'll only be dealing with emergencies because of the holiday. We probably won't have the paperwork done until Monday. You can make arrangements to have her—uh—picked up anytime after noon," he said, starting as the sounds of Sinatra's "My Way" erupted from his pocket. Without another word, he reached into his white coat for the phone, spun around, and walked off to answer the call.

"I'll, uh, talk to him." Sammy stuttered as she watched Gharani disappear into the elevator. Puzzled, Sammy headed back toward Pappajohn, wondering if it had been her imagination or was Gharani more than a little on edge.

"Everything's taken care of," the caller told Miller. "The phone's in the incinerator and the autopsy report's been filed. Cause of death, third degree burns. Accidental. Case closed."

"No problems with the cops?"

"Too busy with fallout from the fires—looting, fistfights on the freeway. You can't believe the chaos. These Santa Anas have really brought out the worst in people. One dead hooker is one less headache for the LAPD."

"Good work, doc. And that little matter of those missing drugs?"

"Yes?" the voice trembled.

"Case closed." Miller said, clicking off before adding, "for now." If his man at the morgue thought these fires had created chaos, wait until he saw what Christmas and New Year's would bring.

Lit only by its headlights, the taxi wended slowly through the Malibu hills. Hugging the ocean, the dry offshore winds carrying fresh ash from the hills to the west formed a thick blanket, impeding visibility. Acres of blackened trees stood as testaments to the power of fires that had raged through the area last year. Lack of reforestation's only saving grace was a slightly lower risk of this canyon breaking out in flames again now.

Still, downed signs and power lines on the narrow road made the steep ascent treacherous—enough for the driver to ask if Ana would like to go back. In response, she leaned over the front seat and handed him an extra twenty.

As the cab climbed the slope, fewer and fewer cars passed by. Fearing she might have been followed, Ana kept peeking out the rear window. Near the top of the hill, the taxi rolled to a stop at a pair of cast-iron gates nested within a two-meter-tall brick wall. There was no sign of life outside the car.

The driver turned to face Ana. "This the address?"

Ana nodded and fished out another forty dollars from the pocket of her jeans.

"You want me to wait?" the driver asked as she stepped out into the darkness.

"No, I'm fine," she replied with a confidence she didn't possess.

A moment later, watching the taxi do a five-point turn on the narrow lane and disappear back down the dusty hill, she wondered if she shouldn't be running after it. Hazy moonlight through burned tree branches cast threatening shadows—arms reaching out to grab her. She shivered as another strong gust of wind blew across the deserted crevasse.

How unusual this city was. From crowded skyscrapers to desolate wilderness in less than half an hour. That's why Courtney said she loved this place. It was far from the action and the paparazzi that surrounded her Hollywood Hills home. Somehow, Ana figured, Courtney would come here to get well *and* escape after her hospital stay. She rang the doorbell and waited for a response from the intercom.

The house was invisible from the gate, through which she could only see a winding stone path leading into the darkness. No answer. After a few minutes, she tried again. Still nothing. Maybe she'd been wrong to think Courtney would come to this haven after all.

Ana walked up and down a few feet in each direction from the gate, eyeing the wall as she dodged several three-foot-tall hexagonal signs planted in her path. The signs, common around the richer neighborhoods in L.A., warned that a security company with armed response protected the estate. She saw no real foothold to scale the bricks, and the height of the barrier was far above arm's reach.

The distant crunching and grinding sound of a car's tires rolling on the lane, very, very slowly made her pause to listen. A driver too drunk or someone after her? Her throat tightened.

As the faint wisps of headlights turned the corner of the road below, Ana dived into an irrigation gully in front of the brick wall away from the gate. She lay flat, holding her breath, waiting until the car drove by.

Only it stopped, idling at the gate. She heard a window lowered, saw the beam from a flashlight scan the area, barely missing her cowering body in the grass. For an eternity, the cone of light searched, then, to Ana's relief, was extinguished. She listened as the window rolled up, and the car continued slowly toward the end of the lane.

Finally, daring to peek, she saw that instead of the white security van she'd expected, the vehicle creeping up the road was blacker than the darkness of the night. Ana shuddered. She knew that road was a dead end and that in a matter of minutes, the car would return. Even if she ran, it would catch up with her eventually. And?

Sounds of tires sliding on the ground, then turning.

Now she had no choice. She had to get over that wall. The thought came to her out of the blue. It was her only chance. One by one, she tugged a pair of the security company's metal signs out of the ground. Pushing with all of her might, she stuck the metal posts back in the dirt next to each other, abutting the wall. As the turning sound stopped and the rolling sound began in the distance again, Ana placed one foot on the flat edge atop each of the signs and stepped up, balancing her body with both hands on the rough surface of the brick wall. Yes! The height of the signs had given her enough lift so her fingers could reach the ledge.

Without pausing to look behind her and ignoring the throbbing in her arms, Ana pulled herself up, her feet clambering in the small ridges of the brick as she climbed. The black car's headlights inched into her peripheral vision. She figured two more seconds before she'd be exposed. With a burst of energy driven by terror, Ana gave one last pull and swung her torso over the top of the wall, landing roughly, but safely, on the manicured lawn on the other side.

She scurried along the base of the wall as far from the gate as she could, hiding among a bed of rosebushes a few feet north. Still panting, her eyes and throat burning from the particles of ash in the air, she watched a pair of hands struggle to open the gate. Fortunately, it didn't yield and the reach of the flashlight's beam through the gate wasn't strong enough to expose Ana's crouched and shaking form. She heard a loud guttural sound of frustration, then saw the light extinguished. A moment later, the car squealed, its tires grinding through the gravel as it headed off down the road.

Not until her heart stopped racing, did she allow herself a victorious grin. This was probably the first time in history anyone had used a security company's protective gear to break into a house.

"Just for tonight," Pappajohn had insisted when he'd entered Sammy's apartment earlier that evening. They'd come straight from the morgue. She'd suggested they stop for a bite to eat, but he'd told her he wasn't hungry. He'd tried to tell her he didn't want to impose, that he needed to be alone, but she'd refused to listen.

"You're exhausted. I'm working all night. You'll have the place to yourself. There's not much food in the fridge, but feel free. If you want to leave in the morning, you can check into a hotel. No problem," she'd said. "In the meantime, *mi casa es su casa.*" Waving a hand at the living/dining/kitchen half of her small one-bedroom home, she'd added, "All I can afford in this town, but at least it's furnished."

Reluctantly he'd agreed, dropping his carry-on next to a well-worn living room couch.

True to her word, after showing him around her tiny place, Sammy had disappeared into her bedroom to prepare for her show. Pappajohn had laid his stiff and weary body down on the lumpy couch for what he'd thought would be a short catnap.

Now, hours later, he woke with a start, his body drenched in sweat. The image that had soothed him in slumber, his daughter and wife, Ana and Effie, smiling at a St. Sophia Church picnic had dissolved into a nightmare. Flames leaping from the barbecue pit had enveloped Ana and were burning her alive, her screams of "Daddy, Daddy," a knife to his heart. Desperate, he searched left and right for his wife. Nothing.

Water, I have to get water.

No matter how hard he tried, he couldn't move his limbs. Ana's pleas grew stronger and, still, he remained frozen, his daughter agonizingly beyond his reach, until her screams faded and her body collapsed onto the charred grass.

No, onto a cold slab in a downtown morgue.

Clawing his way out of sleep, Pappajohn opened his eyes, trying to remember where he was. The morgue? He sat up stiffly, peering through the darkness at the strange room. Oh, yeah, Sammy's. Right. She must have thrown a blanket over him. Relief at waking from his nightmare lasted just seconds, as the reason for his being here in Los Angeles punched him in the gut like a champion boxer's strike. Ana was dead.

Pappajohn kicked off the hot covers and lay back on the couch for a long while, straining for sounds he recognized. Traffic noise mixed with sirens and helicopters. So different from the bucolic Ellsford University campus in Vermont, or even suburban Somerville outside Boston where he'd moved in with his sister Eleni. The rattling of the sliding doors to Sammy's balcony indicated that those smoky winds had picked up again. The fire department would have a bad night trying to control the flames.

Too edgy to sleep, Pappajohn got up and wandered into the adjacent hallway leading to Sammy's bedroom. A faint shaft of illumination spilled out from the partly opened bathroom door.

"Sammy?" He glanced at his watch: one a.m. She'd obviously been gone for hours. Hadn't she said her radio show ran from midnight to three?

He went inside to use the toilet, relieved himself, then washing his hands, stood in front of the mirror, staring at his reflection. The old man who returned the gaze had *ena pothi ston tapho*, one foot in the grave.

"What happened to you?" Jim asked when Sammy rushed into the studio at three minutes to midnight, "I know this is radio, but *I* still have to look at you."

Sammy crinkled her nose at her producer. Where Brian, the engineer at her college station, had been a loveable teddy bear with whom she'd enjoyed good-natured sparring, Jim was a cynical Ichabod Crane look-alike with three-day-old salt-and-pepper scruff, whose barbs she no longer found amusing. Especially tonight. "You're not exactly a vision of loveliness yourself."

"Hey, it isn't the face that gets the ladies, it's my charm," he said in his trademark monotone before zooming in for another bite of his *grande* burrito.

Sammy deposited the slew of papers she'd brought on the desk section of her console and leaned over to turn on the TV monitor next to her mic. "Bet your phone never stops ringing."

Jim swallowed and shook his head. "I don't give out my number," he chuckled, "Don't take it personally. I calls it like I sees it, men or women. So, who ran over you with a truck?"

Sammy plopped down in her chair. The news would be over in a couple of minutes. How to summarize twenty-four hours of tragedy? "The victim we got the call about last night?"

Jim nodded as he chewed.

"She didn't make it."

Jim washed the bite down with a swig of coffee. "That's too bad."

"I knew her."

The producer looked surprised.

"No. Not really knew her. Knew of her. She was the daughter of a friend. I had to tell him."

"Life sucks," Jim said, his attempt at consolation.

Sammy slipped on her headphones, and watched Jim's finger for her cue. "Yeah, it does." His finger dropped, and her theme music filled the studio, to be faded away as she turned on her mic.

"Sammy Greene on the L.A. Scene. Everybody breathin' easy tonight? Well, me neither. The L.A. fire chief just reported fires moving west through the mountains toward Malibu. Apparently, there are scattered power failures in the area. Hope that doesn't keep any of you from tuning in. Because it isn't just the fires and the smoke, people. It's knowing that there are over ten thousand on the street tonight. On Christmas Eve. Half of them in Red Cross shelters. We're all praying that your homes will be saved by the firefighting heroes on the front line.

"The other half have been kicked out of home after home, and the only place they have to go is a tent city. That's right, folks, five thousand men, women, and children, at last count, are living under tarps on a parking lot next to Canyon City Hall at the dawning of the twenty-first century. That's a crime and *we*, you heard me, *we* are the criminals!"

Sammy took a quick sip of cold coffee before continuing. "How much did you give the man standing at the on-ramp this morning? Nothing? Didn't have change after buying that barrel of java at the 7-Eleven? Maybe you could've read the *National Enquirer* in the checkout line and given three bucks to the woman in the parking lot instead. How much more about Courtney Phillips do you really need to know? She's got a drug problem, but *she* can afford to get help. The homeless can't afford to eat!"

All ten phone lines were blinking insistently, Sammy noted with pleasure. She was looking forward to some heated exchanges with her listeners once she'd finished her rant. Even Jim, with receivers in both ears, had a hand free to give her a thumbs-up.

"Canyon effing City is spending over fifty million dollars to renovate a bell tower on its City Hall! A bell tower! A *shonda*! Look, I wasn't here in ninety-four, but aren't there cheaper ways to make structures earthquake safe? Why not just take the tower down and use the leftover money to help starving children? In our own city!

"Because we don't want them in our city, isn't that right? Not if our city's Beverly Hills anyway. Apparently, Congressman Prescott was one of the movers and shakers behind this year's new 'Not In My Backyard' law in the old 90210 zip code. Didn't want any homeless wandering around his expensive rental properties to clash with the landscaping. That's right. The same Beverly Hills PR firm that did that 'Safe Streets for Beverly Hills' campaign just ran a two-million-dollar fund-raiser for Orange County's senior representative and didn't let in a single grocery cart. Hey, Neil Prescott, you're all heart. Speaking of heart, I guess God's not too happy with our congressman right now. He was admitted to Schwarzenegger last night with a heart attack."

Sammy clicked off the mic to clear her throat, then clicked back on. "Maybe He's trying to tell you something, Congressman. You're a big shot in D.C. As soon as you're back on your feet, show some heart and get some funding out to California to help poor people in need. Earn you some points with the big guy, eh?

"We'll be right back to take your phone calls after we pay our dues. Fifteen after."

Trina Greene switched off the radio show in disgust. "That daughter of yours is going to ruin everything. You have to do something."

"What do you want me to do?" Jeffrey asked. "She's an adult now. I haven't seen her in years. Besides," he said, desperate to calm his wife's legendary temper, "no one listens to that rinky-dink station."

"Trust me. It's an election year. Someone is listening. And if word gets out that Prescott's involved in any kind of scandal your daughter stirred up, he'll pull your deal."

"All right. I'll have a talk with her, have her come to the office next week."

Trina gave him a pointed look. "Now, Jeffrey. Call that cabrona right now!"

•   •   •

From the bathroom, Pappajohn wandered into Sammy's bedroom. Hazy moonlight smothered by smoke and ash filtered through the window, bathing the tiny space in undulating speckled shadows. Los Angeles's version of a snowy Christmas Eve.

As his eyes adjusted, Pappajohn explored the small bedroom, thinking how much it reflected Sammy's personality—a kind of passionate chaos. Books on politics and several daily newspapers were thrown on the hastily made bed. The utilitarian wooden desk was cluttered with scribbled notes, a small radio, and a computer. Posters of Martin Luther King and Bobby Kennedy were taped to the wall. Pappajohn smiled in spite of himself. The girl hadn't changed. In the footsteps of martyred heroes, fighting impossible battles. Though he didn't agree with the way she'd rush headlong into the fray, he had to admire her spunk.

Wondering at what windmills she was tilting, Pappajohn walked over to the desk and flipped on the radio. As expected, it was tuned to Sammy's show. He pulled out the chair, which squeaked loudly as he sat. Leaning back as far as he dared, he closed his eyes and listened to her scolding voice.

"We have a duty to help. I don't know about you, Mark, but I intend to be in Canyon City tomorrow serving turkey, ham, and spuds for Christmas dinner to the homeless."

"And you think that's going to make any difference?" the caller challenged. "The tents'll still be there the day after. A drop in the ocean."

"Enough drops and you create an ocean. Make a commitment. Come out tomorrow at noon and help us feed starving families. All of you. KPCF is donating food for five hundred. Come join us. Bring some toys for the children. Clothing, shoes, blankets, anything. Be a drop, and drop by.

"Twenty-eight after."

"God damn it, I *said* I don't want to go on air. I just want to talk to Sammy. Is that so difficult to understand?"

The rising timbre of Jeffrey's voice failed to move Jim. As a longtime producer in talk radio, graveyard shifts were his specialty. He was used to handling crackpots. "If you tell me what you'd like to discuss, I can see if it fits in with tonight's topics and—"

"Where do they get these idiots?"

"Hey, that wasn't nice. If you insist on being rude, I'll just hang up now."

"All right. Fine. Sorry. Can't you just leave her a message with my number?"

"I guess."

Jeffrey gave the producer his name and cell number. "Just tell Sammy her father called and he'd like to see her at the Century City office of Greene Progress first thing this morning. Six a.m. sharp. It's important."

Jeffrey hung up, leaving a bemused Jim shaking his head. Well, well. What do you know? Jeffrey Greene of Greene Progress, Sammy's father? Now *that* was a story. Jim wondered if Sammy's bloodhound instincts could ever be aimed at her father. Jeffrey Greene and Neil Prescott seemed to be in bed together more than Cocaine Courtney and her manager. Jim looked at the paper with Jeffrey's number and, smiling, switched on his intercom line.

"Hey, Sammy. You've got mail."

While Sammy took a break at the half hour for the news and commercials, Pappajohn sat back in his chair thinking about her show. A drop in the ocean. Tens of thousands of young girls caught up in the underbelly of this city, living desperate lives with no one to turn to. That was the ocean. But there was one drop in that ocean he could've helped. Ana. Why had he been so hard-hearted when she'd turned to him, refusing to appreciate her feelings, to forgive her youthful impulsiveness? If only Effie had been there to help him understand that his daughter was more important than a principle. And now it was too late.

His hand brushed against a manila envelope on the desk. He picked it up and saw that it was stamped with an L.A. county coroner's logo, and labeled PERSONAL EFFECTS: PAPPAJOHN, A. He sat up and opened the packet, tilting it so that its contents slid out onto the desk. This was all that was left of a daughter he'd so carelessly discarded. A charred silk purse. A single key. A pair of fake diamond earrings. A tube of melted lipstick. And Ana's license.

Pappajohn gazed at the streaked photo. Even though she'd obviously dyed her dark hair blonde, she was still a beauty. Like her mother. The ebony eyes staring back at him so reminded him of Effie. Now he'd lost them both. Stifling a sob, he kissed the photo and whispered softly, "S'agapo."

For a long time he stared at the few items strewn across the desk, then grabbed the envelope and shook it to make certain he hadn't missed anything. Empty. *Where was her cross?* he wondered. She'd never taken it off, not even for a day, since her baptism. She'd run from her family, but had she also turned away from God?

The pain of his loss grew into a real discomfort deep in his gut—an internal fire alarm he'd battled for years. Searching his pocket for the Rolaids he usually carried in packs, he realized he'd forgotten them in the rush to make the plane. He rose with a loud grunt and wandered back into the bathroom to check Sammy's medicine cabinet. Except for toothpaste, toothbrush, antiperspirant, and a tiny bottle of makeup that appeared to be a sample, the shelves were bare. No antacids. *No surprise,* he thought wryly. Sammy was the type to give rather than get heartburn.

Pappajohn walked down the hallway into the tiny alcove that served as a kitchen and opened the refrigerator. Sammy was not kidding when she'd said there was "not much" food. Only a carton of skim milk expiring the next day, two wrinkled tomatoes, and a few bagels hard as rocks sat on the otherwise empty shelves. Kid was no homemaker. He reached for the carton, smelled the contents to make sure the milk was still fresh, then poured himself a glass.

Settling back down on the lumpy living room couch, he picked up the remote on the adjacent coffee table and aimed it at the small TV on the newspaper-littered stand across the room. Channel after channel had infomercials. Whatever happened to the days when stations ran classic old movies in the middle of the night? Bogart, Cagney, *It's a Wonderful Life*, Something to take his mind off of—

He stopped surfing on a local news station displaying a graphic map of the Los Angeles fires with at least ten iconic flames scattered throughout the city's hills and canyons. The weatherman spoke soberly about the unrelenting winds that hadn't given firefighters a break since the first ember ignited the Bel Air brush twenty-four hours earlier, then shifted gears to flirt with the skimpily dressed, olive-skinned female anchor.

Pappajohn took a gulp of milk to quiet his stomach pain while the woman gushed about some actress, Courtney something, who'd left the hospital against medical advice. The male anchor reported the official story of exhaustion, then winked at the camera, disclosing the "buzz" suggesting too much partying. Sniff, sniff.

Pappajohn threw the remote on the carpet. Fires and young girls on drugs. Everything came back to Ana. He thought back to how as an idealistic young cop he'd volunteered for the toughest assignments in Boston's South End. He'd been what they called a "street dog"—out there pounding the pavements—getting rid of pimps and pushers, addicts and johns, cleaning up the neighborhoods so kids like Ana could have a future. For all the awards and commendations he'd received, what good had any of it done for his daughter?

Scolding himself for his weakness, he blinked the tears from his eyes, and reached over to pick up the remote just as the screen displayed a video of Courtney's transport and admission to the LAU Medical Emergency Room. By the time Pappajohn had returned to watching the TV, the camera's brief glimpses of Ana in the ER parking lot had passed.

"How'd he find out I was in L.A.?" Sammy groaned when Jim delivered the message from her father. She let her purse and papers drop on the counter as she sat in a chair beside Jim.

The producer looked at her with cool amusement. "I take it you and your father are not on speaking terms."

"Hardly. I haven't seen or heard from the *schlepper* in six years. Never seemed to have time for a kid in his life."

"Most moguls only make time for their ambitions," Jim said as he pushed some buttons on his console. The three a.m. news feed bored through the speaker in his studio.

"Mogul? You know my father?"

"Everyone around here knows your father, so to speak." Jim was unable to hide a smirk. "Jeffrey Greene is California's answer to Donald Trump. With better hair," he chuckled.

Sammy digested his information. "I had heard he'd moved into fancy new offices in Century City."

"Speaking of which, he wants to see you there this morning. Six a.m. sharp, I quote. Says it's important."

"You're kidding. Nothing for years and suddenly it's a command performance?" Sammy shook her head. "Well, I'm not going. We've got the Christmas food drive today." She stood. "Next week, if I find time. Or maybe next year."

"Suit yourself." Jim shrugged. He put on his headphones and turned his back to her, reaching for his mic. "By the way, word is your father and Congressman Prescott are pretty tight."

Sammy's brow lines converged again. "You don't say."

"Could just be a rumor. Then again, in this town, where there's a rumor, there's a fire." Jim clicked on his mic and welcomed his listener or two with his sonorous voice. Frowning, Sammy gathered her purse and papers and tiptoed to the door. She missed Jim's reflection in the glass eyeing her as she eased out, including the satisfied smile inching across his face.

•   •   •

Pappajohn wasn't the only insomniac glued to the flickering screen of a TV. Troubled by the fiasco at the Santa Monica pier, Kaye had forsaken the comfort of her bed and was now seated at her kitchen counter, nursing a vodka on very few rocks. Other than to refill her glass, she'd remained on her stool, clicking from channel to channel, hoping not to hear disturbing news about Prescott or Sylvie.

Thankfully, nothing. The names of fire victims were likely

being withheld until families could be notified. That would give Yevgeny a few extra hours to find Ana before her name was plastered on the TV. Before Miller learned the truth.

Kaye drained her drink and poured another. Now that they'd shown their hand, the girl would never give herself up. It would take serious detective work to track her down in this enormous city. Assuming she hadn't already hightailed it for the border.

The news program running had shifted to weather and descriptions of the hot, windy Christmas Eve.

"It's been smoky enough flying above the city tonight," the TV meteorologist joked. "Santa's not gonna want to shimmy down any chimneys. He'd better be careful his reindeer don't get road burns. And tomorrow's picture's no better. Wind gusts up to sixty miles an hour are expected across the canyons—"

Unsmiling, Kaye took another swig of her drink. After the requisite insipid back-and-forth chitchat, the gray-haired anchor turned to update the pre-dawn audience on Courtney Phillips's status. As if anyone gives a damn. *No discipline, that one. Not like my girls.*

The screen replayed the chaos of Courtney's arrival at LAU Medical the night before. The camera zoomed in to reveal the disheveled, combative star. About to turn off the TV, Kaye noticed a flash fill a tiny corner of the scene, the camera's light momentarily exposing a familiar looking woman.

Govno! She knew that face. Ana must have been hiding behind the ambulance while the paparazzi stalked Courtney. Kaye was filled with rage. How much more trouble could that girl cause? What if Miller saw this footage and realized that Ana was still alive? And assumed that Kaye had double-crossed him? That was something Kaye could not afford.

She grabbed her cell and dialed Yevgeny. Waiting for his pick up, she vowed to find Ana and make sure the girl disappeared for good.

Jeffrey Greene and Neil Prescott.

Sammy wondered about Jim's stake in all this. He sure seemed to have an ax to grind. Still, the lure of a juicy story was ultimately too tempting to rebuff—even if it meant going to see her father when she didn't feel emotionally prepared for the confrontation.

Biding her time in the dark and deserted sales office, Sammy surfed the web, typing in the names Neil Prescott and Jeffrey Greene on the search engine. *Interesting*, she thought, as she digested the stories she found. In some ways, Prescott's history paralleled her father's. Both men were born in homes where money was scarce— Prescott in a working class neighborhood in Houston, Jeffrey in an even poorer area of Brooklyn. Neither were great students, but both had married well—Prescott on the first try with the heiress to a Texas fortune, Jeffrey after abandoning Sammy's mom and then Susan.

Prescott had parlayed a medaled army stint from his tour of duty in Germany during the Vietnam War into a long, winning career as a California congressman. Jeffrey had built a successful empire by buying up choice California real estate. Sammy noted that most of his mogul multimillions had been made in the past five years—*after* his marriage to Trina. Several online features recounted the couple's philanthropic endeavors as well as galas her public relations firm hosted for local politicians such as the congressman. Interestingly, although there were lots of pictures of her father beaming at local officials, shaking hands with Hollywood movie stars, even one in a hard hat at a ground breaking ceremony for a project in Laguna Hills, Sammy couldn't locate any of Trina. She'd like to have studied the woman who seemed to have literally transformed her father's life.

Just before logging off, Sammy found an account on *The Orange County News* website of a recent lavish ten-thousand-dollar-a-plate dinner for Prescott held at the Greene's Orange County mansion. According to the article, the couple had raised more than two million for the congressman's reelection. *What do you know?* Sammy had just outed Prescott on air, decrying his failure to allow homeless in the Beverly Hills neighborhood where he owned property. And who would she guess had helped finance the *shmuck?* Her own father!

If their biographies were to be believed, Neil Prescott and Jeffrey Greene were both pillars of the community, without the slightest blemish in their public relations-polished images. Sammy knew that what she'd read online was obviously the whitewashed version. In fact, besides the dirt she'd already broadcast on her show about Prescott, she was sure she remembered hearing something smelly about him from her Washington days. But what? She'd need to do some real digging—after the Christmas food drive and once she'd helped Pappajohn bury his daughter.

Sammy glanced at her watch. 5:30 a.m. She should blow off her father's command, drive home, and check on Pappajohn. That would be the more compassionate choice. And, she sighed, the easier one.

At four a.m., the corridors of the Schwarzenegger Hospital had slipped into the eerie twilight zone suffused with the soft lights and muted voices that typify the night shift. The sound-absorbing plush carpeting of the VIP ward masked Miller's footsteps as he walked past closed doors that muffled an occasional cough or moan.

Slipping into the men's room off the empty corridor, Miller pulled out his cell and speed dialed a contact, initiating a prearranged call to the nurses' station. Several minutes later, he opened the bathroom door a crack to see the one nurse staffing the floor head off in the direction opposite his destination. Quickly, he crossed the corridor and entered suite 501.

Annoyed at having to risk being seen, Miller shook Prescott awake.

"Wha—? You—?"

"Yeah, it's me. Listen, I only have a few minutes. We're almost in the homestretch. I need to know you're a hundred percent on board."

Prescott sat up, eyes wide. "Of course I am. This was as much my plan as yours."

Miller gave him a pointed look. "When the game is over, neither of us will be taking credit. Understand?"

"Of course."

"So what do you think Bishop heard?"

"Not sure," Prescott admitted sleepily. "The cardiology fellow said there's some spy center in the basement recording everything. I've got a real estate deal I need to keep private—among other things."

"I'm sure you do," Miller said. "But, if he's referring to the Incident Command Control Center on B3, don't worry. We've got that covered. My man will make sure none of your conversations ever happened."

"That may keep me clear in superior court, but I'm concerned about home court. If Bishop gets suspicious and starts asking Julia questions, I could face some tough cross-examination."

"After all these years, she still controls the purse strings? Stop worrying about Bishop. If that happens, we'll just remind him that curiosity killed the cat." Miller's expression left no doubt about the sincerity of his threat. "You get some rest now, and make sure you're discharged before Friday. Operation Y2K goes off at midnight sharp."

At the door, Miller looked both ways to be sure the coast was clear before hurrying off to the elevators down the corridor. He didn't see the nurse at her station—she was still on a well-engineered wild-goose chase at the other end of the ward. And he didn't notice Reed, on his way to check on Prescott, standing behind the open door of the adjacent empty suite.

Back in his high-rise office, oblivious to the pink streaks of the rising sun painting the gray sky outside his panoramic window, Miller was crouched over his monitor and keyboard, worming his way into the confidential files of the secretary of the army.

It took only a few minutes to find the file he sought. Uploading it, he scanned page after page. Franklin Bishop, MD, FACP, Col. USA, Ret. Age 61. Divorced, no kids. Born in a working-class suburb of Houston, Texas. Attended River Oaks Prep on a football scholarship. Eschewed Texas A & M for West Point. Medical School at Baylor. Internal Medicine residency at Walter Reed, Cardiology Fellowship at Baylor under DeBakey. Spent 29 years in uniform, starting with two tours in Nam. Stationed at Brooke, Stuttgart, Madigan, Tripler, and many years at Walter Reed. Exemplary performance reviews from all his superiors. Made Colonel two years early. Buzz about his being up for flag rank. Billeted as assistant chief medical officer in Desert Storm.

Then came the bump in the road. In the last days of the Gulf War, Bishop was wrapping up a tour of duty in Saudi Arabia when he began drinking heavily and behaving erratically. Enough to have him sent to Germany for a psych evaluation. According to the medical record, while going through the DTs there, Bishop insisted he'd lost a burn patient because of a test weapon used to target civilians, claimed his demand for an army investigation had been denied, that no one believed him. The psychiatrist who diagnosed alcoholic delusions secondary to PTSD suggested immediate discharge.

Miller shook his head, remembering his concern in nineteen ninety-one. If the resonator was going to be a trump card in the next theater, he couldn't afford the other side hearing about those early trials. His team had had to bury all evidence that the building collapse in the desert had been anything other than an accident. A few well-placed calls to some very important people had undermined Bishop's credibility, gotten him shipped stateside to a Walter Reed psych unit and a one-way ticket back to Houston. Miller had hoped that Bishop would've learned his lesson, kept his curiosity in check and his mouth shut. Now he wondered if the man might just become another loose end he could ill afford.

Closing the army file, he picked up the intel his own people had just gathered covering the seven years since Bishop's return to the U.S. Though the doctor had joined Alcoholics Anonymous, his already rocky marriage soon dissolved. For months he stopped practicing cardiology, instead volunteering as a GP in recession-ravaged Houston clinics. Then, seemingly out of the blue, he was offered the post of chief of cardiology at Houston Medical. Given Bishop's history of alcoholism and breakdowns, that seemed surprising.

Miller read a little further until he discovered the nugget he'd been hoping for. *Well I'll be damned.* It wasn't just the glowing letters of reference from Donald Graves Senior that helped piece together the story. It was the yellowed photo of Frank Bishop, high school football star and his then-steady girlfriend, Julia Graves, along with the nineteen fifty-nine OB-GYN's note documenting a D&C perfomed on the girl. Obviously, eighteen-year old-Bishop had gotten sixteen-year-old Julia pregnant. In exchange for his silence about the pregnancy and his leaving town, he not only received no jail time for what could have been construed as statutory rape, but got recommendations from her rich father—first to West Point and then, years later, to the hospital board in Houston. Not quite seventeen, Julia Graves, post-abortion, became Mrs. Neil Prescott. From the notes in the file, it looked as though Julia had a hand in bringing Bishop to LAU Medical.

Well, adultery was definitely something he could hold over Bishop's head. Sometime tomorrow he'd give the good doctor a call to make that clear.

CHAPTER SEVEN

Near the end of another overnight shift, De'andray slowed his plain wrap to a crawl. The red MINI Cooper convertible had several parking tickets flapping on its windshield. De'andray nodded at his partner, and pulled his car behind the small vehicle. Parking on most Bel Air streets had been banned since the fires started and the neighborhood had gone on red flag alert. The two detectives stepped out into the predawn and walked over to check out the abandoned convertible.

"Wash me," Ortego said as he ran a finger across the sliding roof, leaving a trail in the ash that had covered the MINI Cooper like a layer of gray snow.

De'andray brushed off dust from the driver's window and peered in. An opened makeup kit was strewn on the floor of the passenger side, along with two round hairbrushes and a bottle of Fuze low-cal juice. On the backseat were a pair of New Balance running shoes with frayed laces and a can of spray-on tan. Nothing unusual for L.A.

He ambled over to the windshield and lifted up the wiper to grab one of the tickets. Shaking it clean in his hand, he strode back to his car and called in the license and ticket information. "Got a twenty-eight or twenty-nine on this plate?" he asked the dispatcher.

"Nada. Let's see if we can locate the owner's name and address."

He could hear the clicking of a computer keyboard as she talked.

"Okay, here we go. Car's registered to a Sylvie Pauzé, twenty-three twenty-five Ashland Street. No outstanding tickets."

"Thanks."

"Dee?"

"Yeah, hon?"

"I think I remember something. Let me check." More clicking. "Yep. That's the same address we sent the black-and-whites out on last night. For the girl that died in the fire."

De'andray whistled, turning to Ortego, whose brow was puckered. "Now that's something I didn't expect."

Leaning back in his chair with eyes closed, the guard nearly fell over when Sammy approached his desk a little before six a.m.. Obviously surprised to see visitors in the building this early—let alone on Christmas morning. But a call upstairs found her father in, evidently expecting her.

As the elevator accelerated skyward to his thirty-sixth-floor suite, Sammy's stomach lurched downward. Gravity or nerves? She couldn't honestly say as she stepped from the car and headed toward 3601. At the entrance to the suite, she hesitated. Part of her heart hoped her father was reaching out for reconciliation, the other, hurt so often before, just wanted to avoid more pain. She took a deep breath, then with feigned bravado, walked inside, past the deserted reception area into a long, heavily carpeted hallway. At the far end, she found the corner office belonging to Jeffrey Greene, CEO.

Through the half-open door she could see her father seated behind a large mahogany desk, his back to a wall of glass that framed the city, his head bent over in concentration. For several seconds she stood quietly at the door, studying him with a measure of skepticism and curiosity. It was just past dawn, yet he appeared to have rolled out of bed, clean-shaven, perfectly coifed and dressed to the nines, the cut of his dark suit obviously custom. And for a man of fifty, he had the trim build of someone much younger. Probably contoured by a personal trainer. Everything in the picture bespoke money, confirming what Sammy had just read online. *Dear old dad was doing very well*, Sammy thought with an unwelcome dash of bitterness honed by years of separation.

Without knocking, she strode inside and sat in one of two chairs facing the desk. "How'd you find me?" she demanded, her tone angrier than intended.

Jeffrey looked up and flashed a smile that Sammy guessed to be the expensive handiwork of some Beverly Hills cosmetic dentist. She didn't recall such evenly spaced, white teeth from her last visit as a college student.

"Is that a nice way to greet your father?"

"You didn't answer my question."

"Trina heard your show—"

"Trina." Sammy couldn't keep disdain from her voice. "Sounds exotic."

Jeffrey lifted a gilded frame from the corner of his desk and held it up to Sammy. "She's a remarkable person. Can't wait til you meet her."

The woman in the photo did indeed look exotic and, Sammy had to admit, beautiful. Dark haired with piercing dark eyes. She guessed Trina's age to be late thirties, though with the wonders of plastic surgery—especially in this town—she might be a decade or more older.

"Why didn't you tell us you were in L.A.?" Jeffrey asked. "It's been what? Two, three—?"

"Six years," Sammy corrected.

Jeffrey ignored the hostile edge. "Well, you look terrific."

Sammy felt her cheeks redden, "*Bubba meisa.*"

"Huh?"

"Yiddish for baloney."

"You sound like your grandmother."

"Well, she raised me," Sammy snapped.

Jeffrey rose and came around the desk to stand in front of her. "How about a hug?"

It would have been easy to refuse. For so long she'd grown accustomed to disappointments from this man. "It isn't necessary."

Jeffrey leaned against his polished desk. "Hey, Sammy. I know I haven't always been 'Mr. Father Knows Best.' I know an 'I'm sorry' won't cut it with someone as bright as you. But, we're both adults now. And I have changed. Really. I'm a new man."

"You mean you're a rich man."

"Yes, I've got money. Finally. But that's what we all needed. You make it sound terrible." He waved his arm around the beautifully appointed office. "Look at this, Sammy. I made it. I've worked damn hard for what I've achieved." With a look of contrition, he reached out to her. "Would it really hurt to give me another chance?"

Sammy stayed silent for a moment, searching his features for guile. It wasn't there. His remorse seemed genuine. She certainly wasn't ready to trust him, but she wanted so much to feel a father's arms around her that she found herself rising as he walked over and enfolded her.

"That was nice," he said, stepping back again. "Hungry? I know a twenty-four-hour deli on Fairfax where we can get some breakfast."

"No, uh, thanks," Sammy said, feeling off balance. "I've got to get ready for our station's food drive for the homeless."

"Yeah, that was one of the things I wanted to talk to you about."

"Oh?" Wary, Sammy's heart began beating faster.

Jeffrey walked over to a coffeemaker sitting on his credenza, poured some of the steaming brew into two mugs and handed one to his daughter. "Still take it black?"

Nodding, Sammy had to smile at the jogged memory. Though her short visit with her father the summer after her freshman year had ended badly, she'd returned to Ellsford with a shared love for java straight. It was a habit she'd yet to break.

Jeffrey sat back down behind the desk and opened his top drawer. "Until we heard you on the air last night we didn't know about your event. Nice thing you're doing, by the way." That winning smile again. "Sorry I didn't have time to browbeat any of my friends to help out. But Trina and I would like to provide some of the food. We'll have it delivered later this morning. And here," he said, handing Sammy a check, "is a small donation."

Sammy was stunned at the amount. "Ten thousand dollars! That's unbelievably generous." Hesitating for a moment, she folded the check and placed it carefully inside her pocket.

Jeffrey beamed. "It's the least I can do for such a worthy cause. Besides, our firm is doing the renovations on the Canyon City Hall site. Never hurts to give something back. Right?"

"I suppose," Sammy's response was tentative, her caution flag raised. Jeffrey Greene, an altruist?

"By the way, you know who helped finance the remodel of that old building?"

"No—"

"Congressman Prescott."

"Really?" Sammy squirmed, aware that her father was studying her reaction.

"Really. Neil isn't what you said on your show. He cares about those less fortunate."

"As long as they're not in his backyard."

Jeffrey chuckled, "I'm afraid Neil's let himself get a bad rap with the press. I'd love for you to get a chance to meet him and see what a mensch he really is." His expression brightened. "You know, I could arrange for you to have a private interview. You could do a story on Neil's 'Keep America Safe from Terror' bill that's in committee."

"You mean his 'Keep America Terrorized' bill? They've got us thinking Y2K will be another Hiroshima."

"That's just politics. Neil's a solid guy who loves his country. Like we all do." Jeffrey folded his hands in his lap. "Sammy, I wish you'd let me help you. I know how much you want a career in broadcasting. I've got the connections now to make it happen."

"I *have* a career in broadcasting." *Such as it is.* "Thanks, but no thanks."

"I guess we all have to find our own way. I just wanted you to hear the truth about Neil, *and* about me." Jeffrey sipped from a steaming mug labeled Greene Progress, and added, "We're here if you need us. Just say the word, and this," he waved his hand around the lush office suite, "can be your home."

Sammy smiled politely, and nodded, hoping her expression didn't reveal her true emotion. *I'm homeless.*

The moment Sammy left his office, Jeffrey dialed Trina.

"It's taken care of," he said, trying to conceal his hesitation.

"Did you read her the riot act?" Trina asked.

"Not exactly."

"What the hell does that mean?"

Jeffrey sighed. Trina's passionate, assertive nature was a thrill between the sheets, but could become overbearing outside the bedroom. Subtlety was not her strong suit. "In this case, you'll just have to trust my instincts."

"And they are?"

"When it comes to Sammy, you get a lot more flies with honey."

"Clear." De'andray slammed the trunk door of the MINI Cooper shut, and coughed as the dust flew into his face. He frowned at the sound of Ortego's laugh. "I don't see anything funny, Chico."

"That's 'cause you can't see *you*, Dee. You look snow white, bro."

Glaring at his partner, De'andray brushed the ashes off of his scalp and cheeks. "We could use a little snow around here. My son thinks Santa's sled's got wheels."

A flash of pain crossing Ortego's face reminded De'andray that his partner hadn't seen his own children for months. "Any word from the wife?"

Ortego shook his head. "Don't know where she is. Don't care."

"I hear you." Frowning, De'andray leaned against his unmarked car and rubbed his neck.

"I'll call in the tow," Ortego said.

"You don't think anything else is up? Same address as the dead burn victim. Could be a roommate. You read the report from the crew that checked out her apartment last night. Anything unusual?"

"Place looked like a trick pad. That's it. Bet this one," he nodded at the MINI Cooper, "ran for it when our guys paid their visit."

"Why didn't she take her car?"

"How the fuck do I know? Maybe she was working a job around here last night," Ortego chuckled, "and now she's turning tricks at the evac centers. Bad pennies, man. She'll turn up." He walked over to the passenger side door of his car and opened it.

"She'll have to do a good night's work to pay off all these parking tickets." De'andray slid into the driver's seat and started the engine. "I'll take you up on your offer. You call it in to parking services. Let them follow up with this Sylvie Pauzé. I'd love to crawl under the covers with my wife for a quickie before the kids wake up looking for their presents."

"You really been married to the same woman for ten years?" Ortego asked as he buckled in. "Don't know how you do it, Dee. Mine walked out the door a dozen times in less than three."

"Like a good wine, Chico. Better every year."

"Well, *amigo*, I wish you both *Feliz Navidad*," Ortego said, his stony expression hidden by the darkness of the predawn night.

"What chutzpah," Sammy muttered as she opened the door to her apartment. "The nerve of him."

"Something I said?" came a voice from the living room.

"What? Oh gosh, no, Gus, I'm sorry, not you. I was, uh—I didn't mean to wake you."

"It's almost eight. I've been up for hours." He turned on the light. Showered, shaved and dressed in a clean shirt, he'd tidied up the living room, and even folded the linens on the couch.

"Wow, you're the houseguest everybody dreams of." Sammy lay her satchel on top of the TV and settled on the couch beside Pappajohn.

"Want to talk about it?"

Sammy saw Pappajohn's pained expression, his sad eyes, the lines of worry carved into his brow. *He* was the one who should be asking for a listening ear, a supportive shoulder. "It's really not that important."

"I've sworn never to say those words again," he whispered. "What's the problem?"

Sammy sighed. "My father. I just got back from seeing him."

"Took my advice, eh?" Pappajohn prompted. "And?"

"And I—I don't know. It's been so long and there's so much baggage." She plunged into a full account of the meeting, including the generous donation.

"He's reached out to you. That's a big step," Pappajohn said. "Believe me, I know."

It hung there for a long moment. Between them. The empty space each longed to fill. In Pappajohn's case, Sammy understood, he was telling her it was too late for him and Ana.

"I guess I should give him a chance," she said. "Still, I can't help thinking the money's a bribe. I mean he practically warned me off digging up any more dirt on Prescott."

"He obviously doesn't know you very well." Pappajohn smiled. "Why not take his gesture at face value?" he asked. "By the way. I listened to your show last night too. Most people just talk. You're actually going out there and doing something for others today. I'd like to help."

"Really?"

The smile slid away. "So many young people on the streets. Alone, hungry, scared." He turned to gaze out the window. "How little I really knew her," he said, his voice cracking. "I realize I can't bring her back, but maybe I can reach out to some kid who—"

Sammy placed a comforting arm on his shoulder. "Thank you. We'd love to have you join us. But first," Sammy rose and grabbed her satchel, "my father recommended a deli on Fairfax. I bought fresh bagels, a little Nova, cream cheese, and a half dozen eggs. Give me a minute and I'll whip you up a nice omelet."

"I'm not hungry."

"You'll get sick if you don't eat." Sammy started for the kitchen.

"Did anyone tell you you're a pain in the tookas?" Pappajohn asked.

"That's *tuchas*," Sammy rejoined without turning around. "And yes, you did. Many times."

•   •   •

She was gone! Kaye couldn't believe what Yevgeny was telling her. Like a speck of ash swept away by these devil winds, somehow Ana had completely slipped through their fingers. Again. Along with the client list Sylvie stole.

"I looked everywhere. She's not with any of your girls."

"Did you check the house in Malibu?" she yelled into the receiver. It was a long shot, but Ana and Courtney Phillips had been roommates at Promise House, the expensive facility Kaye sent her girls for rehab. Sylvie had told her those two had gotten pretty tight, in the bonding sense, and that last summer the actress had invited Ana to a hideaway in the Malibu hills few people knew about.

"No one was there."

Kaye felt a growing sense of panic. She had to find Ana before Miller learned the girl was still alive. Unfortunately, it was becoming clear that Kaye had but one option left. So far, Yevgeny had proved absolutely useless. She would have liked to reach into the phone and wring his neck.

Instead, she hung up without a goodbye and began to punch in the number to her LAPD contact. Time to call in the pros.

The first rays of sunlight teased the manicured gardens outside her Malibu mansion. Courtney's bloodshot eyes, however, didn't welcome the brightness. Slipping on a pair of sunglasses and fighting off nausea, she stumbled into the living room to let in some air. The stench of her own vomit roiled her already unsettled stomach.

Straining from the effort, Courtney managed to open a front window just enough to allow a few breaths. But the air was hardly fresh, she realized, choking with every inhalation. The heavy smell of smoke from the fires to the southeast had made its way to Malibu. If only she were back home in Colorado, where everything had been so unsullied, so real.

Squinting into the haze, she spotted something lying in the azaleas a few feet from the house. A dog? No, human. And female. Was she sleeping? Or—

Courtney slammed the window shut and hid to one side, peeking out to discern if the body moved. After a few moments, the woman rolled over and curled into a ball. Now her face was clearly visible. And familiar.

"I need a favor."

"I thought that's what you did for *me*," the voice on the other end replied.

It took all of Kaye's self control not to tell the SOB to go fuck himself. But she'd long ago made her deal with this devil and there was no going back. Unless she regularly fed him information on her johns, she knew he would back off on Vice and she could end up in jail. So she bit her tongue. "I just heard about poor Ana Pappajohn."

"Name hasn't been officially released. How'd you get it?"

"Does the CIA tell the KGB?" she asked coyly.

"Which one are you?" When she didn't answer, he continued. "Okay so the girl's dead. What's the favor?"

"She had a kid. I'd like to make sure he's okay."

"I don't see you as the madam with the heart of gold."

"Nonsense. When it comes to children, I'm a soft touch. The boy has some kind of disability. Ana had to give him up when she was using. I'd like to find out where he is. Maybe buy him a Christmas gift. Can you get his address from Social Services?"

"You want me to deliver the gift?"

"That won't be necessary. Just find out where the boy lives, and I'll take care of the rest." *Like I always end up having to do*," she grumbled, slamming down the phone.

CHAPTER EIGHT

Saturday
Christmas Day, 1999

Smoke from still-raging fires had turned the Christmas morning sky over Canyon City into a sepia blur. City Hall was locked up and empty for the holiday, but the large parking lots on either side of the office building were packed with flimsy tents hastily erected by homeless activists hoping to embarrass a local administration blind to their needs. Strong Santa Ana winds blew hard against the tent flaps, exposing those trying to catch a few last winks of sleep on mattresses of canvas and asphalt.

Declared a historical landmark over twenty years before, City Hall's renovations to highlight the structure's classic Spanish-mission architecture had only recently been completed. Several hundred people marched noisily around the main two-story building, shouting slogans and carrying placards under the watchful eye of a few yawning officers who leaned on their motorcycles at strategic vantage points along the route. The police, tasked to keep the protest peaceful, stayed away from the last remaining construction zone—Greene Progress's restoration and seismic retrofit of the building's bell tower scheduled for completion by spring. Not really a difficult assignment when other units were out working the fire evacuations.

Two news helicopters monitored the marchers. Several protesters carried effigies of both the Los Angeles and the Canyon City mayors while others waved giant papier-mâché puppets of pigs at the TV cameras to protest corporate greed. The rotors of the copters added turbulence to the wind gusts from the Santa Anas, at times blowing the vulnerable tents and marchers completely off balance.

"Quite a scene," Sammy observed, as she laid out the escargot and the paté. She and Pappajohn, along with Jim and a few other station volunteers, had been working since just after breakfast, setting up serving tables for the midday meals. To her surprise, her father had kept his promise. Less than an hour ago, three shiny black Humvees had stopped by and delivered tray after tray of gourmet food. Not the kind of fare these homeless folks were used to, but, she had to admit, a nice gesture.

"More police here than people," Jim groused, ignoring Pappajohn's disparaging glare.

"What time is Jésus getting here with our eats anyway?" Sammy asked. KPCF's sales manager was bringing a more traditional holiday menu—turkeys, stuffing, and an assortment of pies, many donated by patrons of Sammy's radio show.

Jim smiled. "Give the guy a break. He was only born this morning."

Sammy blinked, momentarily confused. "Ha. Gee, Jim, I thought you were an atheist."

"I follow the teachings of Gautama Buddha, but I'll be the first to cheer when Jésus arrives. In fact, I think I see him coming now, hallelujah!" He bowed in the direction of the parking lot's driveway. "Edible food."

Sammy spied the station's rickety van with Jésus at the wheel. She waved for him to stop next to their tables and let the van serve as a buffer against the winds. Rolling her eyes at Pappajohn, she wrinkled her nose at Jim.

No one paid attention to the Canyon City police van that had arrived just behind the KPCF junker and parked facing the construction fence around the bell tower. Like the news vans, it only had windows beside the driver and front seat passenger. Two young, trim men with buzz cuts and blue Canyon City PD uniforms exited those seats, and, after scanning the area, leaned against the vehicle, immersed in conversation.

Inside, out of sight, Miller, Fahim, and al-Salid sat in front of a console of keyboards and monitors that filled the cargo area and resembled the cockpit of a 747. Unlike his urbane and expressive compatriot, the clean-shaven al-Salid was somber and restrained, his eyes darting from one video screen to another as they displayed a panorama of the entire scene, including an overhead shot of rooftops around the block.

Fahim gestured toward one TV. "You can see street numbers from that one."

"Our satellites can spot a fly," Miller said. "A good fact to remind the prince when you return."

Al-Salid motioned at another monitor displaying the tower and spoke a few sentences in Arabic to Fahim.

"Winds are starting to make the tower sway," Miller responded in Arabic, without turning to face his colleagues. "Normally, the computers managing the active seismic-control system in the apex should help counteract the wind's force. Normally."

"I did not know you spoke our language so well," Fahim stammered in English. "You are a man of many talents."

This time, Miller turned to face him, and replied in Arabic, "Another good fact to remind the prince."

Fahim pointed to the large machine that filled the back of the van's cargo space. "This resonator will make the control system's weights work in sync with the winds, so the tower's swaying and shaking becomes stronger." In Arabic, he added, "and falls."

"You get an A, Fahim," Miller said. "Okay, now that we're all set, let's warm her up."

As if on cue, the resonator whirred to life. The size of six desktop computers, the machine resembled the old mainframe computers with blinking lights and spinning disks commonly seen in 1960's Hollywood films. But these lights were LEDs, and the discs were laser-cut DVDs. Within minutes, the remote computer in the van was ready to transmit its binary Trojan Horse into the Canyon City tower's computers and take over control of the counterweights.

"They'll start serving food as soon as the bell rings twelve." Miller nodded at the tower centered on one of the monitors above his keyboard. "That's when we'll amp up. Target should be between 12:30 and 12:45."

Smiling at al-Salid, he spoke in perfect German, "And, as I said back in Munich, that's when the curtain will rise on Götterdämmerung."

"Here you go." Sammy scooped a hefty spoonful of mashed potatoes onto a little girl's plate. "Gravy?"

The child nodded and giggled as Sammy covered the mound of potatoes with the thick, brown liquid. Sammy watched her skip off behind her siblings, her plate overflowing.

"More turkey!" Jim's voice was muted by the winds.

"More ballast!" Pappajohn gripped an electric knife in one hand and with the other struggled to prevent his tablecloth from flying off and catapulting a twenty-pound roaster onto the gravel.

Sammy lugged over an untouched tray of raw oysters and dumped it on Pappajohn's carving table. "Don't think these are going anywhere."

"Damn winds practically knocked me over," grumbled Pappajohn as he filled a plate with slices from the enormous bird. "Amazing that thing doesn't get blown away." He pointed his knife at the creaking scaffolding surrounding the bell tower a few yards from their tables. "Look at that bell rock."

Clutching the tray of turkey, Sammy observed the bell's swaying and strained to hear it ring over the roar of the winds.

"What's that?"

Sammy turned back to two middle-aged women dressed in dirty denims staring at one of her father's epicurean dishes. "Salmon mousse. Would you like some?"

"Hell, no," one of the women said. "Don't trust that genetic stuff. Only eat one type of animal at a time. Just give me turkey."

Sammy forked a couple of slices from Jim's tray onto each of the ladies' plates, adding scoops of potatoes. She couldn't resist a chuckle as she watched the women move on and overheard one say to the other, "Who the hell eats moose anyway?"

Resuming her rhythmic dealing of spuds, Sammy stole a few glances at the bell. Was it her imagination, or had that last gust of wind made the tower visibly tremble for a moment? Sammy looked around to see if anyone else had noticed, but they were all too busy doling out food.

Another gust of wind blew Sammy's almost empty aluminum potato tray off the table. With her back turned to the crowd as she chased the rolling tray in the direction of the KPCF van, Sammy missed seeing the tall stucco bell tower creak and then, begin to sway.

Pressing a series of computer keys, Miller brought up screen after screen of equations and graphs. Fahim couldn't follow the numbers, but he was able to monitor the tower vibrations displayed as multiple wave signals on the oscilloscope.

"T minus thirty seconds," Miller reported. "Keep your eyes on the bouncing waves."

Whirring like a swarm of bumble bees rose from behind the men as the resonator continued beaming its instructions to the tower's computer sensors, magnifying the wind's forces by manipulating the movements of the counterweights. Fahim gripped the armrests of his seat. It wasn't the wind rocking the van that made his heart race. He gasped at the size of the enormous synchronized wave created on the oscilloscope when the multiple waves slowly merged into one green glowing tsunami.

"Lift-off imminent," whooped Miller, pointing to the TV monitor displaying the swaying tower. Shards of scaffolding began to break off and fall to the ground.

Fahim's jaw dropped as he watched a giant crack appear near the top of the structure and heard Miller's cry: "Thar she blows!"

• • •

The bell tower swayed precariously back and forth over the parking lot and the tent city, widening its cracks with each pendulum-like swing.

"Run!" Sammy screamed, racing toward the crowd, at the same time pointing up at the tottering structure. "It's coming down!"

Jim ran past her, shouting something, but Sammy couldn't hear his words above the wind and the cries of the protesters and homeless campers.

Chunks of wood and plaster dropped, shattering by her feet while she and Pappajohn tried to guide people from the path in which the tower appeared to be falling. Up ahead, Sammy spotted the little girl with the adorable giggle sitting with her brother. Just as the tower broke apart, she yelled, hoping to warn Jim to get himself and the children away before the structure came crashing down on the asphalt. But it was too late. Within seconds, the tower had slammed onto the parking lot, a giant dust cloud enveloping Jim and the two tots.

Breathless, Pappajohn ran up to Sammy. "You all right?" He was covered in white powder from head to toe. "We got as many out as we could."

Sammy coughed and gagged from the swirling dust. "Jim! The children!"

They both stared in horror at the dust ball where the tower had landed.

Like ghostly apparitions, two tiny figures emerged from the cloud. Dirty and frightened, but barely scratched, they raced into their tearful mother's arms. Jim staggered behind, coated in white powder, rivulets of blood streaming down his face and chest. With a grunt and a gasp, he collapsed, unconscious, into the bushes.

Taking advantage of the chaos and confusion, the Canyon City police van moved slowly away from the scene, wending its way through the hysterical crowds pouring into the street and dodging police cars and ambulances screeching to the City Hall parking lot. By the time the medical helicopter had landed on the grassy knoll beside the building to transport its first critical patients to LAU Med, Miller's van was long gone.

The phone beside his hospital bed rang just once before Prescott answered.

"The bell has rung," came a voice on the other end.

Satisfied with the message, Prescott clicked off without a reply, laid back on his pillows with his eyes closed, and smiled.

Bishop hung up the wall phone in the Cardiovascular Intervention suite and leaned wearily against the polished tiles.

"You all right?" his lead nurse asked.

Bishop stood erect and nodded. "Eccles just called a code one emergency. There's been a building collapse in Canyon City. Hundreds injured and on their way."

"Oh, my God." The nurse paled. "I'll get things ready here and see if ER needs help with triage."

"Good, and please page Dr. Wyndham. To come back in STAT."

Sammy didn't know where the past few hours had gone. After the tower's deafening collapse, the screams of the injured and the dying had merged with the blare of ambulance sirens and police bullhorns. And the wind—like a monstrous creature—kept howling at the horrific scene below. Sammy knew she'd never forget those sounds.

Now, as she paced nervously back and forth in the waiting area of LAU Medical's emergency room, she wondered how the collapse had happened. One minute they were serving Christmas dinner to thousands of hungry tent city denizens and the next the tower had just toppled, leaving a trail of dust, blood, and debris in its wake.

Sammy glanced over at Pappajohn, seated in the corner of the crowded room, trying to comfort the father of one of the injured protesters who'd just been taken to surgery. It was a tender side of Pappajohn he usually kept well hidden. This bear of a man presented himself to the world as a gruff and feisty loner, someone who tried to make you think he didn't need or care about anyone—not even his own daughter. Watching him, Sammy's heart ached, aware how rarely Pappajohn allowed this side of himself to be seen.

She felt a gentle tap on her shoulder and turned to see Reed, dressed in green scrubs, his features creased with concern. "Sammy, thank God you're all right."

"Reed, what are you doing here? I thought you were off today."

"Everyone available was called in. Code one disaster. Good thing we'd just been through the drill. We've gotten all the criticals and most of the injured. Community hospitals got the rest."

"How's Jim?" she asked. "Jim Lodge. My producer."

Reed wiped his brow. "Guy's a real hero, saving those kids. Considering what might have happened, he's a lucky man. Just a concussion and lots of scratches. No intracranial bleed. We're admitting him for observation, but he should be fine."

"Thank you." Sammy's lip quivered. She turned to indicate the slight man who'd been talking with Pappajohn. "What about his daughter? Carmen Moran?"

A scrub-clad doctor had approached the two men, shaking his head. "No!" the father shrieked, almost sliding to the floor. Sammy watched as Pappajohn helped the doctor lift the devastated man to his feet and lead him into one of the tiny rooms off the waiting area. Even with the door shut, she could hear the anguished cries.

"They couldn't save her," Reed said, his own regret clearly written on his face. "That makes at least four we've lost, I'm afraid."

"I don't understand it!" Sammy voice rose, her body trembled with rage and grief. "How could that tower fall like that!"

Everyone in the waiting area looked up.

"Not here." Reed put his arm around Sammy's shoulder. "Let's go into the staff room and talk."

Still shaking, Sammy allowed Reed to guide her into the doctor's lounge. Closing the door, he turned to face her.

"I know you're upset and—"

"Upset! I can't even begin to describe how I feel." She took a deep breath, desperate to control her emotions. "If I'd even had a clue that that building was dangerous, I would never—" She spoke in rushed spurts, her eyes brimming like a dam about to burst.

"Whoa! You're blaming yourself for this accident?"

"I'm the one who told all those people to come and serve food today."

"Sammy, the tent city has been there for weeks. That protest was planned before you even arrived in L.A." Reed stepped closer and wiped a tear from her cheek "You were just trying to do a good deed. You know you had nothing to do with what happened."

"I know," she sniffled, "but still—" Despite her best intentions, the dam finally erupted.

Reed put his arms around her and drew her in.

Surprised by the depth of her sorrow, Sammy laid her head against his chest and cried like she couldn't remember crying since she was a child. Even after the tears were spent, she remained protected in the warmth of his arms, listening to Reed's pounding heartbeat. When he pressed his lips to her hair, she lifted her face to him.

"Reed."

Before she could interpret the look in his violet eyes, she stood on tiptoe so their lips could touch, welcoming the kiss.

The door to the lounge was pushed open, breaking the spell.

"Oh, I—I'm sorry."

Reed jumped back, turning to face Michelle, who clutched a patient record to her chest. Ignoring Sammy, Michelle held out the chart, her tone professional, her expression neutral. "Dr. Wyndham. Dr. Bishop asked me to find you. He's just moved Mr. Prescott to the VIP ward to make room for one of the criticals."

"Thanks, I—"

Michelle didn't wait to hear what Reed had to say. The minute she'd handed over the record, she turned on her heels and left the room, slamming the door behind her.

"I guess I'm the one who should apologize," Sammy said when they were alone again. "That shouldn't have happened."

Reed studied her for a long moment. "No, I suppose not."

"Can you forget it did?" she asked softly.

"Can you?"

As their eyes met, the buzz of the intercom interrupted the charged silence.

Reed blinked as though unsure where he was. He walked to the desk in the corner and pressed the intercom button.

"Yes?"

Lou's brisk voice came through the speaker. "Hi, Doc. Is there a Sammy Greene in there?"

"She's here."

"Thought I recognized her from the other day," Lou chuckled. "You're a lucky dude, Doc. Can you tell her her father's on the line? She can grab the call out here at my desk."

"Sure." Wincing, Reed clicked off. "Lou's a real smart-ass."

"Guess I better take that call," Sammy said with a reluctant smile.

Nodding, Reed held open the door and followed her out of the room. Their moment of intimacy gone, questions still hanging between them, unanswered.

Lou pointed to a multi-line phone on his desk with several blinking lights. "Line three." He grabbed several charts and ambled off toward the nurses' station.

Sammy lifted the receiver and, after a moment of hesitation, punched the appropriate button. "Hello?"

"Honey, I'm so relieved you're okay."

Sammy was surprised by Jeffrey's concern. "I was lucky, but a lot of people weren't," she said, her voice cracking.

"Radio reported some deaths. It's awful. My attorney said three people—"

"Four," interrupted Sammy, unable to remove the mental picture of the devastated father. How many more anguished family members would hear tragic news before the day was done?

"A real shame. If only we'd had time to fix that ancient construction. Back in the fifties, they just didn't know how to bolster buildings the way we do now."

"Yeah, guess so." Sammy frowned, remembering the tall scaffolding. It sure seemed that Greene Progress had already begun their work. Could renovation efforts actually make a building more vulnerable? Something she had to research.

"Listen, I'm a little busy with some, uh, things right now, but how about joining me at Nate's for breakfast after your show tonight?"

"I'm not on the air—the weekend—and Jim is—" she choked back a sob. "My producer was injured. I'm going to hang at the hospital for a while. I'll call you. Maybe we can do lunch this week if you're free."

"Sounds good. Hey, why don't you plan on joining us for New Year's Eve? Friday night. We're having a big bash at the Newport house. You can finally meet Trina. Bring a date."

"I don't know—"

"Well think about it. We'd—oops, got another call, hon, gotta go, bye."

Jeffrey hung up, leaving Sammy standing stiffly at Lou's desk, still grasping the receiver.

Just outside the hospital room, Sammy peeked in. Jim lay in bed, gowned and scrubbed, his eyes shut, an IV hooked into his right arm. Observing his steady breathing for a few minutes, she was struck by how literally overnight she'd developed a certain fondness, if not outright respect, for this aging hippie. In his fifty-something years of life, Jim had weathered the ups and mostly downs of the radio business. Who could blame his resenting her? In town a short time and already handed a three-hour chunk of his air time? Saving the children today, without a thought for his own safety, was an eye-opener. Perhaps, as with her father, Sammy owed Jim a second chance.

His eyes flickered open.

"Thought you were sleeping," Sammy said.

"Just meditating."

"No atheists in foxholes, eh?"

"I said meditating, *not* praying." With his free hand, Jim waved her in.

"Well you look better than I expected." Sammy approached his bedside. Several angry red scratches along both arms and cheeks and a half dollar-sized bruise over his forehead were the only clues to his close brush with death.

"Can't say the same for you."

Sammy glanced at the mirror above the corner sink and checked her reflection. The strawberry mane she'd so carefully tamed that morning was now tangled and dotted with dust. She made a futile attempt at smoothing, then shrugged. "It's why I do radio." She turned back to face him. "How're you feeling?"

"My age. Everybody else okay?"

"Jésus and I got a lungful of asbestos, but we're doing all right. Pappajohn's Teflon. Not a scratch. He's in the ER helping some of the families."

"You realize we have to do a show on today's disaster."

"You shouldn't be thinking about work."

Holding up a finger, Jim grabbed the TV remote from the bedside table and clicked past several Christmas pageants before stopping at a local newscast: "A terrible accident at Canyon City Hall today—"

Jim pushed the mute button. "That's what they've been saying all day: 'a terrible accident.'"

"You don't agree?" Sammy asked.

"I say we need to investigate. That bell tower withstood a six point eight earthquake in ninety-four with only a couple of cracks."

"The Santa Ana winds *were* ferocious," Sammy countered. "Maybe the ninety-four quake caused some vulnerability and that's why they were going to retrofit."

"Going to?" Jim rolled his eyes and then winced. "Looks like they'd already started to me."

"They meaning Greene Progress?" Sammy wasn't sure why, but she felt defensive. "My dad told me they hadn't—"

His eyes half closed, Jim held up a hand. "Okay, okay. Stay cool. I said investigate, not accuse."

Sammy inhaled and forced back a retort. Hero or not, Jim was still irritating. "Fair enough. But right now you need to rest. *Especially* at your age."

"Can't argue with that," he whispered as he closed his eyes tighter and resumed his trance-like posture.

Sammy inched toward the door, almost missing Jim's quiet, "Thanks."

"Shit." Courtney removed her hand from Ana's burning forehead, afraid she might need serious help. Though she'd stopped gasping and coughing, Ana's breathing was still labored. Asthma? Pneumonia? A doctor would know. But getting her back down stairs in her condition would be difficult. And taking her outside might prove fatal.

Courtney peered through her bedroom window. Though sunset was still an hour away, it was dark as night outside. The winds had not only knocked out power in Malibu, they'd blown much of the smoke and ash from the fires toward the west and blanketed the beach view canyon.

Ana groaned and thrashed under the sheets before falling back into a troubled sleep. Arranging votive candles strategically around the room for light, Courtney wondered what else to do. Maybe Ana needed water. Or, better yet, a hot toddy. If the gas stove was working, she could make tea and add honey and a touch of brandy. That might help Ana come down from whatever high had made her so sick. And give Courtney a chance to pour herself some brandy too. Straight up.

Sammy stepped off the hospital elevator on the first floor and saw Pappajohn chatting with Lou at the front desk. "There you are."

Her maternal tone produced a look of annoyance from the older man. "Costanza here told me you'd gone up to see Jim. He okay?"

"He'll be his old self soon," Sammy said, studying Pappajohn.

His bleary eyes and dusty clothes reflected lack of sleep and accumulated stress of the past twenty-four hours, "How are you, Gus? That poor man." She indicated the adjacent room from which the father's muffled sobs could still be heard.

"Seen better days," Pappajohn said quietly, "but no point not accepting what you can't change."

Sammy nodded. Had he effectively convinced himself of that as well? "I'm sure that man appreciated your help. It's all just so awful."

Sammy felt a pair of arms on her shoulders, and spun around, shocked to face Reed. She still hadn't processed her emotions from their earlier encounter. Now she could only stammer like a foolish schoolgirl. "What are you—?"

Reed's glance gave away nothing. Instead, he looked past Sammy. "Things slowed down a bit in the ER. Thought I'd come out and say hi to Gus." He offered his hand and sympathies to Pappajohn. "Sorry about your daughter. Anything that could be done to save her, well, they tried."

Pappajohn nodded. "There will always be questions. But, I know."

"When the post is done, I think the report will reassure you that she didn't suffer."

"The report *is* done," Sammy interrupted. "The medical examiner told us that with the fires, they'd called in extra staff and—"

"I see."

Sammy thought she caught surprise in Reed's expression, although it was fleeting. Now he smiled gently at Pappajohn. "Well, if there's anything I can do—"

"Dr. Wyndham." The call sounded like an order.

Reed stiffened and pivoted to wave at Bishop, standing in the door to the entrance of the emergency room. "Sorry, folks, gotta go." He leaned over and air-kissed Sammy's cheek, shook Pappajohn's hand once more, then set off at a rapid pace toward his grim-looking chief.

Turning back to Pappajohn, Sammy hid her own surprise at

Reed's reaction, tucking it in her mental notebook for future con-
sideration.

Hours after they'd returned to the apartment, freshly showered,
Sammy found Pappajohn sitting in front of her computer, the screen
blank, his head in his hands. She came over and gently touched his
arm. "Gus?"

Blinking and swallowing, Pappajohn lifted his head. He turned
to see that Sammy had changed into sweatpants and an oversized T-
shirt. Her still-wet red mop was once again starting to sprout curls.
"Four a.m. in Athens. Too late to call Eleni, so I thought I'd e-mail,
let her know what happened." He shook his head. "But I just
couldn't. Not on Christmas. First time I've missed wishing Eleni
Chronia Polla."

Feeling helpless to comfort him, Sammy just nodded. She'd
never seen Pappajohn in so much pain, so vulnerable. And today's
tragic events only made everything worse.

Pappajohn's gaze drifted to the ceiling for a long beat, then
turned back to her. "I need to understand what happened to Ana
here. How she lived, who were her friends, what she was doing
the night she—" His voice drifted off again. "Tomorrow I'll make
plans for the funeral. And first thing Monday, I'm going to look for
answers."

"Let me help. I'm not due back on air til Monday midnight. Besides, you'll need a driver."

Pappajohn locked eyes with Sammy, considering the offer. "I
won't be putting you out?"

"Not at all. In fact, as I remember, we always did make a good
team," she said referring back to the murder they solved together at
Ellsford University.

A genuine smile flickered across Pappajohn's lips. "I think they
call that selective memory."

Sammy chuckled, glad for the banter. "So where do you plan
to start your search?"

"Her apartment. Then, the cops who took the report at the hospital. Then," he said, his voice quavering, "things should be ready at the morgue."

"It's been a long day. How about a bedtime snack?" Sammy grabbed Pappajohn's hand and led him to the kitchen like a child. "I'll make you a nice bagel and a glass of milk. You haven't eaten all day."

"You're turning into a Jewish mother," he said, taking a seat at her tiny kitchen table.

She produced a wry smile. "Now who's the pain in the *tuchus?*"

Bishop closed the medical journal, slipped off his reading glasses, and was about to turn out the light when his bedside phone rang. He picked up on the first ring.

"Colonel Bishop?"

The voice on the line had been electronically altered. Bishop strained, but couldn't identify the caller. "Who is this?" No one had addressed him as colonel since he'd turned his back on the army seven years before.

"That's not important. What I'm about to say to you, however, is."

"I'm hanging up." Angry, Bishop's tone was firm and unwavering.

"I wouldn't do that if I were you. Nineteen fifty-nine, a pregnant sixteen-year-old named Julia. No longer pregnant. Need I say more?"

Bishop froze. "I don't know what you're talking about."

"Oh, I think you do," the caller replied. "I must say, you and the little lady have worked hard to redeem yourselves. Shame to stir things up now."

"Who are you?" The tough tenor of Bishop's voice now had an audible tremor.

"Someone who'd like to see your reputation remain intact. As well as that unfortunate young woman's."

Bishop held his breath. "What is it you want?"

"Your silence. About the woman's husband. About his activities. About everything. In exchange for my silence. Clear?"

"I would never hurt Julia."

"Good, that's all I wanted to hear. As long as you don't decide to be a Boy Scout, no one has anything to worry about."

The disembodied voice clicked off before Bishop could respond. Temples pounding, he lay back against the headboard, trying to force his muscles to relax. Who was the caller? What did he really want? And how had he found out?

Old memories had come back to haunt him, memories that lurked and throbbed in his mind like a growing migraine. Finally, no longer able to tolerate the pain, he leaned over and shook out two tablets of Tylenol from a bottle on the nightstand. It was the only medication he allowed himself these days. Swallowing the pills, he switched off the light and lay back, praying for the salve of sleep to take away the headache and the memories for good.

CHAPTER NINE

DECEMBER 26, 1999
SUNDAY

Miller lay in bed, concentrating on the television set across the room. He kept changing stations with the remote, searching for the story he'd floated over the weekend through back channels cultivated during days as a field agent. Every news team in L.A. had covered the Christmas Day disaster at Canyon City Hall as a horrible, unfortunate accident—exactly how Miller wanted it played. National political shows focused on the homeless problem in general, barely mentioning the tower's collapse. Y2K was the only bogyman on their radar. Any connection to what was coming on New Year's Eve could be made after the fact.

Miller flipped past CNN, CNBC, and MSNBC where the fires and speculation about Courtney Phillips's whereabouts and condition filled the airwaves. Finally, on FOX, he found Mac Derbyshire looking directly into the camera, warning of imminent danger lurking in the Middle East. Through unnamed intelligence sources, the anchor claimed to have learned that recent foreign chatter suggested the real possibility of a terrorist attack by Y2K.

"Is our president on top of this?" he asked the audience rhetorically. "No, he's too busy smoking cigars. And the veep, our so-called Democratic candidate? He'll have you believe the world is one big *kumbaya*. Pay attention, my friends, or we could find ourselves defeated and under the thumb of a terrorist dictator."

The tirade ended with a menacing looking photo of Saddam Hussein in an Arab headdress, glaring angrily into the camera and, in close-up, directly into viewers' eyes.

From his hospital bed on the deluxe Schwarzenegger Hospital VIP ward, Prescott watched the same station on the wall-mounted flat-screen TV. An excellent touch, juxtaposing terrorist threats with the Iraqi leader's image. Planting the seeds of fear in the minds of the electorate should translate into votes for his party when frightened arms pulled those levers next November.

Despite Julia's admonishments to wait until he was fully recovered, Prescott had his press secretary bring in a crew to videotape his statement for that evening's news. The number of people required to film a thirty-second spot always amazed him. His spacious hospital suite quickly filled with scruffy invaders in T-shirts and jeans carrying boxes of equipment and a bevy of wires. His own aides dressed in suits and ties. Prescott handed one his prepared remarks.

The press secretary read them aloud. "As head of the House Armed Services Committee, I, like all of us in our party, take Y2K threats to our country and our citizens very seriously. Unfortunately, at a time when we are most vulnerable, this administration has hamstrung the military and squandered resources needed to defend America from twenty-first century enemies to our way of life. We need a president who will never leave his watch and duck out of his responsibility to protect the United States. Your safety is our first priority. Our party understands. May God bless America."

Nodding at Prescott, the press secretary handed the text to another suited assistant. "Put this on prompter. And get makeup in here. We don't want him looking like Death."

Prescott watched the hubbub surrounding him, delighted by the attention. He leaned over, turned off the monitors one by one, and began peeling off the adhesive clad electrodes that had monitored his vital signs. When the cameras rolled, he planned to project the image of a man in the peak of health.

Now, as long as he was out of this hospital before New Year's, everything should go as planned.

Sammy turned her car northwest, taking surface streets to reach the imposing Byzantine Greek Orthodox Cathedral, Saint Sophia, on the corner of Pico and Normandie.

As they drove up Vermont, a few families unwilling to stay inside despite the smoky air, stopped to bargain with equally stubborn street vendors hoping to sell churros, mangos, and buttered corn. From the passenger seat, Pappajohn read the signs on the mom-and-pop stores they passed. "Carniceria, Verduras, Frutas, Lavanderia." He shook his head. "Are we still in America?"

"*Latin* America. Anything East of La Brea and you need to learn Spanish."

"Neighborhood reminds me of Greece." As they turned left on Pico, Pappajohn pointed to a busy sidewalk café. "They even have tavernas."

"Only they're called *ristorantes*," Sammy explained. "Look at that." A large sign in classic font on top of a renovated building read BYZANTINE-LATINO DISTRICT.

Pappajohn actually smiled. "How—?"

"Saint Sophia's head priest must be a master of good neighborhood relations." Sammy turned left on Normandie and into the gates of the impressive church modeled after its Constantinople predecessor.

In contrast to the banged-up sedans and trade vehicles parked along the adjacent streets, the lot inside the church gates was filled with brand new luxury cars—a sign that these Greek immigrants had moved higher up the social ladder than the more recently arrived Latinos.

Sammy located a space near the back of the lot and waited for Pappajohn to ease himself out of the car. They walked to the front entrance of the massive church, past parishioners in their Sunday best milling about after the service. Ignoring them, Pappajohn strode somberly to the lobby, which held large gold leaf trays carrying dozens of flickering tapers.

Standing to one side of the large open bureau, Sammy observed Pappajohn reach into his pocket for a five dollar bill that he dropped into a slot box. From a nearby table, he selected a long candle and, blinking furiously to hold back tears, lit it from the tiny flames in one of the gold trays. After crossing himself, he pushed the candle into the sandy gravel holding up the other lights and moved over to an icon of Mary and a baby Jesus. Crossing himself again, Pappajohn brushed the figures with his lips.

A stern-looking older man in black robes and a priest's collar appeared at his side and extended a hand. Sammy watched Pappajohn bow to kiss it, noting the tears falling on the bearded priest's wrist. She couldn't make out what he whispered in his ear.

"My deepest condolences on your loss, my son," the priest said, his booming voice accented with a hint of Greek. "*Theos 'xorestina.*" *God forgive her.*

Pappajohn's voice cracked in response. "*To koritsaki mou.* My little girl."

"You may not understand it now, but some higher purpose has been served by this terrible tragedy." The priest placed an arm around Pappajohn's bent and trembling shoulders.

"Everything happens for a reason, my son. She is one with God now and safe in his arms."

Pappajohn nodded somberly. "They said I can pick up her body tomorrow. Can we make the arrangements for Tuesday?"

The priest slid a hand into his gown and drew out a card. "Call my assistant on Monday morning. She'll review everything." Smiling, he patted Pappajohn on the arm, then rushed away to greet a well-known Hollywood couple entering the apse.

Pappapjohn stopped by the gold tray for one last wistful look at Ana's flickering candle.

"You okay?" Sammy asked, taking his hand.

Pappajohn stared at her, his expression tight, his eyes dry now.

"No. Not until Ana is." He shook his head. "She will not be safe in God's arms until I have buried her."

CHAPTER TEN

DECEMBER 27, 1999
MONDAY

Sammy drove slowly along Ashland Street, straining to discern house numbers in the dawn's first light. After another restless night, Pappajohn had insisted on an earlier start than originally planned. His lumbering around the apartment provided Sammy's wake-up call well before six a.m.

Now, at six thirty, she found the beachside neighborhood eerily quiet for a Monday morning. No people jogging or walking their dogs. Just a few parked cars, each coated with a fine layer of ash from the fires still out of control a few miles away. The weatherman on her car radio predicted Santa Anas and red flag fire conditions through New Year's.

"Twenty-three twenty-five. This is the place." Sammy stopped the Tercel in front of the address listed on Ana's license. Pappajohn, who'd said little during the short drive from Palms to Santa Monica, grunted an assent. His eyes focused on the four-story apartment building where his daughter had lived. Sammy could only guess at the whirlpool of emotions churning inside his controlled facade. Maybe this hadn't been such a good idea.

"You okay?" she asked, shutting off the engine.

Pappajohn let out a deep sigh as if to expel the tension with his breath. "Yes." He reached around to the backseat for the manila envelope from the medical examiner and stepped out of the car.

Sammy followed him through the courtyard and up the stairs to the third floor.

"Locked," Sammy said after trying the doorknob to apartment 3B. "Promise not to arrest me and I'll pick it with my handy penknife." She'd used the skill learned growing up on Brooklyn streets more than once in her days at Ellsford.

"This should work." Pappajohn pulled a key from the envelope. "Ana's," he explained as it slid smoothly into the keyhole, unlocking the door with one turn.

Sammy and Pappajohn stood in the living room of the apartment in stunned disbelief. Chairs upended, sofa bed cushions slashed open, papers and books strewn about. The place was a complete mess.

"Looks like an earthquake," Sammy declared. Pappajohn said nothing. Sammy turned to look at the ex-cop and was surprised to see his demeanor had changed. No longer the weary devastated old man, Pappajohn stood stiff and poised like a foxhound, his piercing gaze scanning the room from corner to corner.

"They didn't find it."

"Find what?"

"Whatever they were looking for." His lips were pressed together, his expression tense. "Don't touch anything."

Sammy raised her hands up in a gesture of compliance, then stuffed them in the pockets of her jeans. "Should we call the police?"

"They've been here." Pappajohn pointed to a strand of yellow plastic tape peeking out of the kitchen trash can. "They didn't find it either," he added in a gruff tone. "Follow me."

Sammy tiptoed behind Pappajohn into Ana's bedroom. The "earthquake" had not spared this room either. Every drawer had been pulled open, clothes and shoes flung randomly on the carpet. A Payless shoe box lay on its side on the floor of the closet.

Pappajohn stood on a clear spot of hardwood and surveyed the chaos, in foxhound mode again. Bending over, he picked up a pencil he found lying on the floor and, turning it to extend the eraser end, began an examination of the room, lifting objects, then laying them down after studying them carefully.

Sammy watched as he wandered from item to item: a micro-skirt, a sequined bra, a pair of risqué panties minus the crotch, a pasty, a riding crop, some loose uppers and downers, leather hand-cuffs, and flavored condoms. All the while, Pappajohn remained stone faced, a detective investigating a case, not a father searching for clues to the path his daughter had taken since she'd run away from home.

That path was heartbreakingly clear to Sammy. Evidence sug-gested Pappajohn's daughter had chosen a less than respectable lifestyle. Sure he'd been aware that Ana hadn't opted for the high road, but to confront it here like this would break any father's heart. Sammy guessed the coldness reflected in his face now was willful, determined ignorance. *His* daughter, the little girl he loved, could never have called this place her home.

"Here!" Pappajohn stood by the smashed computer. "It was here." He probed the pieces of metal, plastic, and glass with his pen-cil. "Didn't leave forensics much to work with," he said, shaking his head.

Taking a step closer, Sammy nearly tripped over a couple of un-matched designer spikes. How could anyone wear shoes like that, Sammy wondered as she pushed them aside with her Vans and stooped to check size eight written in one heel and size six in the other.

"Did Ana live here alone?" she asked.

"I don't know," Pappajohn had to admit. "Why?"

Sammy strode over to the closet and began digging through the mound of expensive clothes piled on the floor. She shoved away the Payless box to get to the dresses. "Aha!" She held up a couple of matching outfits. "Unless Ana bought everything in twos, I'm guess-ing she had a roommate." Sammy pointed to the different sized shoes. "I doubt an eight could wear a six or vice versa." She reached another arm into the pile. "Oh my God!"

"What is it?" Pappajohn rushed over.

The pink silk handbag Sammy showed him was identical to the one Ana had with her when she died.

Pappajohn's face paled. The purse from the coroner was charred in the fire. This was pristine. He grabbed it from Sammy and reached inside. But there was no wallet, no credit card. Nothing to identify its owner except a dog-eared color photo of two smiling blondes, dressed in matching red and white sundresses. Pappajohn stared at the picture for a long time.

Peeking over his shoulder, Sammy saw that one girl was obviously Ana. But the other? "Gosh, they look like twins. If she's Ana's rommmate, *where* is she?"

"And," Sammy added, "*who* is she?"

Pappajohn's turned to her, his face expressing grim determination. "Let's get out of here. That's exactly what I plan to ask the LAPD."

"Aargh!" Sammy's cry brought Pappajohn running out the apartment door. In the hallway, Sammy's legs were trying to dodge the affectionate assaults of a very energetic canine whose long flowing double coat resembled a dust mop.

"Get over here, Princess. That's not Ana."

Pink bow, rhinestone collar, Princess was an apt name, Sammy thought. She watched the dog retreat toward a tall, skinny man who'd just exited the apartment next door.

"Are you her owner?" she asked.

The neighbor sported a two-day ration of beard stubble and appeared to be in his late thirties. Dressed in running shorts and tennis shoes, he carried a leash and plastic baggie. He erupted with a high-pitched laugh. "Princess is a Shih Tzu, a member of a distinguished breed that goes back a thousand years. She is *my* owner."

He swept the dog up in his bony arms, frowning at Pappajohn, who'd just finished closing and locking the door. "Are you cops? 'Cause with these fires, no one seems to care that we've been getting lots of burglaries in the building. I just moved in a few weeks ago and I'm thinking of breaking the lease. Luckily, Princess is a great alarm system."

The sweet-faced toy dog was wagging her furry tail, begging for attention. Pappajohn leaned over to pet her, then looked over at the man. "I'm Ana's father," he said. "She died in the fires."

The neighbor appeared genuinely upset. "Oh my God. That's awful. She is, I mean *was* such a nice person, wasn't she, Princess?" He scratched his dog's head and hugged her closer. "Princess loved her. I'm so sorry." He reached over to Pappajohn and, holding Princess in one arm, extended the other. "Name's Matt Henderson. I live next door."

Pappajohn accepted the handshake. "Gus Pappajohn. My friend, Sammy Greene. So there've been a lot of break-ins here?"

"Yeah, Mrs. Hernandez in One C had her TV stolen last month, and last week somebody smashed my car window and took my laptop right out of the backseat. Now I have to start all over on my screenplay."

Pappajohn nodded politely. "Yep, I've learned the hard way, too. Can't have too many back-ups. You didn't happen to see or hear anything unusual three nights ago, did you?"

"Sorry, I'm a pharmacy tech at Harbor. Between the fires and the holidays, I've been doing double shifts. Except to walk Princess, I get home, lock the door, and hit the sheets. But Mrs. Hernandez told me the cops were here."

"How about before that? In the evening?"

Henderson shrugged. "She didn't say anything else. But, she's hard of hearing. Keeps the TV really, really loud."

"We think Ana had a roommate," Sammy said. "Have you seen her?"

Pappajohn showed him the snapshot of the two girls.

Henderson rested Princess gently on the stained carpet and pulled the photo close to his eyes. "Yeah." He pointed to the blonde next to Ana. "Sometimes she goes out in the evenings, never comes back before I have to leave for work. Princess doesn't like her, so we've never really talked. She's not home?"

Sammy shook her head. "No. We were hoping to touch base, but—"

"Any other neighbors who might have been around that night?" Pappajohn pressed.

Henderson shook his head. "Not that I know of. This isn't a very friendly building. That's another reason I'm considering moving out. Mrs. Pascali on the other side of Ana's place is okay. Went to Phoenix last week 'cause her daughter just had a baby. And Dean Foster, he's not around so much any more. Hot and heavy at his girlfriend's place, you know. Wish I could help."

Princess was jumping up and down at Henderson's feet. "Okay, sweetheart, we're going." He snapped the leash on the dog's collar. "She's got to do her thing and I've got to get to bed," he said to Pappajohn. "Really sorry about your daughter, sir."

"Thanks," Pappajohn replied mechanically as he watched Henderson and Princess scamper down the stairs toward the street below.

Sammy yelled after him, "If you see Ana's roommate—" But the odd couple was long gone.

"You boys busy?" From the doorway, the desk sergeant leaned into the precinct break room and waved to De'andray and Ortego. Still in their dusty suits, the two detectives sat at a wooden table laden with Styrofoam coffee cups and a half-empty tray of donuts. Breakfast at eight a.m. after a long night on call.

Before they could respond, their sergeant stepped aside and introduced Pappajohn. "Gus here's retired Boston PD, on the job twenty-five years," he said, in an obvious effort to establish instant camaraderie. "His daughter—" He looked at Pappajohn, at the same time wrapping an avuncular arm around his shoulder: "Anastasia?"

Pappajohn nodded confirmation.

"The vic from the fire."

Standing behind both the sergeant and Pappajohn, Sammy winced at the cavalier use of the word vic, though she guessed that as an ex-cop, Pappajohn was inured to this kind of shoptalk.

"Gus has some questions. I'll keep the rest of the squad out while you guys talk with him and—" he turned to Sammy.

"Sammy Greene. I'm a friend."

"She's with me," Pappajohn's sharp tone prohibited challenge.

The desk sergeant nodded. "Okay, then. I'll leave you two in good hands."

As soon as he'd departed, the detectives pushed their chairs back and came over to shake Pappajohn's hand.

Mutt and Jeff, Sammy thought when the two introduced themselves.

"Damn shame what happened," Ortego said with genuine sympathy. "Sorry for your loss, Gus."

"Likewise," De'andry repeated, though Sammy thought his flat tone seemed less than sincere. Frowning, De'andray spun to focus on her. "Have we met?"

From his lofty six foot two the officer made the barely five-foot Sammy feel like a small child. "Not that I know of." Her laugh was forced. "I haven't been in town long enough to get in trouble."

De'andray's serious ebony eyes continued to probe. "No, no. I'm great with faces. No it's—wait a sec. What's your name again?"

"Sammy Greene."

"That's it." He nodded to his partner. "That night radio chick. Saw your picture on a couple of benches at the bus stops this month." He brushed some dust off the front of his jacket, adding with evident sarcasm, "Mother Teresa of Canyon City."

Sammy gritted her teeth. Was he accusing her of something? Feeding the poor wasn't a crime.

"Coffee?" Ortego interjected, an apparent effort to defuse the tension. He found a couple of folded bridge chairs in the corner and carried them over to the table.

"Nothing, thanks," Pappajohn replied, sitting down.

Her stomach growling, Sammy eyed a cruller. "I wouldn't mind a donut." She reached for one from the tray and took a bite. They'd left so early that breakfast had not been on Pappajohn's schedule.

De'andray closed the door on the din in the main office and joined them at the table.

"So," Ortego said, "how can we help?"

"I understand you both took the report at the hospital?"

Ortego nodded. "It was all pretty routine, Gus. We're so sorry."

"I'd like to see it."

Ortego raised an eyebrow. "Any particular reason? I thought the ME had shared his findings with you."

"Yeah, but I'm trying to get a picture of what exactly happened that night. Where Ana went, how she ended up in that fire."

Ortego's expression didn't change, but De'andray scowled.

"When did you two last talk?" Ortego asked.

Pappajohn exhaled. "It'd been a while. We'd, uh, lost touch after my wife died and Ana ran away." He rubbed his temples. "I probably should've been home more, but my job—"

"We probably should be home from our jobs, too," De'andray hinted with another dose of sarcasm as he pointedly checked his watch.

"And how long ago was that?" Ortego continued, ignoring his partner.

Pappajohn hesitated, "Eight, nine years." He added quickly, "but, we'd e-mail once in a while. And Ana used to call Eleni, my sister, for birthdays, Christmas."

Sammy thought she saw his eyes mist again.

"Said she was working as a waitress. Saving up money to become a nurse."

"Nurse? Well, she *was* working, all right." De'andray snickered. "You knew your daughter was into drugs, didn't you?" He pulled a notebook from his jacket pocket. "Let's see." He flipped through the pages, "Misdemeanor drug possession in ninety-six. Second arrest last year." He looked at Pappajohn with palpable disdain. "As an ex-cop, you got to know L.A. is a mean mother of a town for a kid on her own. How come you refused to fly out for her arraignment?"

Pappajohn reacted as though he'd been physically wounded. "I . . . I thought a little tough love might teach her a lesson." His voice trailed off. "Besides, the officer I spoke with out here said she'd be sent to mandatory rehab. No jail time."

"Promise House?"

Pappajohn appeared confused.

"The state sends druggies to some outpatient clinics downtown. Promise House is luxury Malibu. Sea views, catered meals, massage and yoga overlooking the Pacific. Rehab to the stars," De'andray explained. "Any idea where she'd get the cash to pay for that?"

Though Pappajohn shook his head, Sammy knew he'd figured out the truth already. He'd lost Ana in this city of dreams and nightmares. Sammy also knew how much he blamed himself. Having to suffer De'andray's obvious scorn seemed unfair. She glared at the tall detective.

Ortego leaned forward and gripped his partner's forearm to cut him off. "Look I know it hurts," he interceded. "Dee here's a dad. I'm a dad too. But, we've got to face it, your daughter wasn't such an innocent."

"What happened that night?" Pappajohn sounded close to the boiling point.

"She was found on Roscomare near the bottom of Benedict Canyon, probably running from the fire—"

Sammy didn't know why, but Ortego looked over at her.

"—in high heels and tripped. Hit her head. Knocked unconscious and—well, you know the rest."

"She didn't have a car?"

"Not according to DMV records." Ortego glanced over at his partner as if to see if it was okay to reveal information. "There seems to have been a roommate. Sylvie Pauzé. She owned a car, so maybe they drove together."

"This her?" Pappajohn handed Ortego the snapshot he'd just found.

"Where'd you get this?" Ortego asked after studying it for a moment.

"At her apartment." Pappajohn explained that they'd gone there that morning to see where his daughter had lived.

De'andray exploded. "Jesus Christ, man. That's a crime scene. You of all people should know better."

"The only police tape was in the trash, *inside* the apartment. *Which* I entered with a key," Pappajohn shot back. "And I was careful not to disturb anything, just in case forensics wanted a second look. I assume you guys know the place was tossed."

De'andray shook his head in disbelief. "Second look? You have any idea how overloaded the system is with these fires? Not to mention relocating all those homeless squatters." He aimed his obvious disgust at Sammy as if she were somehow responsible for what happened yesterday. "Homicides, armed robberies, freeway riots. Pauzé had a rap sheet even longer than your daughter's. Looting a trick pad's got to take a backseat to real crime."

"You don't think someone was looking for something?"

"Sure, coke, meth, pootie tang—"

Pappajohn jumped out of his chair. Sammy grabbed his arm, whispering, "Gus!"

Pappajohn wrenched free and glared up at the taller De'andray, unbridled anger oozing from every pore.

Sammy interrupted, "At least tell us where we can find this Sylvie. She might know where Ana was that night, how she came to be by herself in the fire." She appealed to Ortego. "You certainly can appreciate that a parent needs closure."

A tense silence followed as Ortego looked from Sammy to Pappajohn, and then to De'andray. Finally, he rose and left the room, returning minutes later carrying a manila file from his desk. "We've told you all we know. It was an accident. Accidents—well, they never provide closure."

Pappajohn grabbed the folder from Ortego's extended hand, then sat back down and started leafing through the pages, with Sammy peeking over his shoulder.

Sammy read through the officers' interviews with EMTs and hospital ER medical staff. *Severe third degree burns over most of her body and an occipital head injury.* The story on paper was straightforward and consistent with Ortego's narrative. Only one item caught Sammy's eye. Michelle's comment that Ana had "temporomandibular instability." She'd have to ask Reed what that meant. Maybe that was what he'd hesitated telling her.

Pappajohn lingered on the few photos of his daughter in the file. Ana on her driver's license, looking beautiful as a blonde. Ana on the gurney, her charred face hidden by an oxygen mask and breathing tube, her long bleached-blonde hair scorched and singed. Sammy turned away after a quick glance. What a horrible way to die.

The one-page DMV report included a smudged black-and-white photocopy of the registration and title to a 1990 red MINI Cooper convertible found abandoned on Anzio Road at 5:45 a.m. on December 25. The duplicated license of its owner, Sylvie Pauzé, had just the minimal data—age: twenty-nine, hair: blonde, eyes: blue, height: five feet three. Same pretty face as the girl in the picture they'd discovered in the apartment.

The statement on the break-in had even less to add. Officers called to investigate that busy night found the place trashed and abandoned. Sammy read through the sketchy notes: *Bedroom ransacked, computer knocked over, multiple pills on nightstand (note to forensics), clothes and shoes dumped on closet floor.*

No obvious clues. Nothing to indicate who might have done the job or why. Maybe De'andray was right—just looters taking advantage of the chaos brought by the devil wind that night.

When he'd finished his review, Pappajohn threw the file onto the table. He rose and stuck out his hand to shake Ortego's, adding a curt, "Thanks. You'll let me know when forensics does their job?"

"Sure, leave us where to call."

Sammy scribbled her cell number on a slip of paper from her satchel and handed it to the stocky detective.

De'andray frowned. "Hey, Gus," he said coldly, "when did you come in anyway?"

Pappajohn returned the icy gaze. "Christmas Eve. *After* noon."

He pulled himself up to his full five foot ten inches. "Too late." Waving to Sammy to follow, he spun on his heels and strode from the room.

At the door, Sammy glanced back. Ortega had grabbed the remaining donut, but De'andray was watching her, his dark eyes narrowed, his expression grim.

Can you believe that *momzer?*" Sammy declared when they were back in the car. "Bastard actually accusing you of—" She couldn't finish the sentence.

"It's his job. I would've done the same thing." Pappajohn's voice remained even. "It's the part of their job they're not doing that pisses me off."

"You mean not investigating the break-in?"

Pappajohn, who had been staring out the passenger-side window, turned to her, his face now etched by pain and resignation. "And they won't," he said with a weary fatalism, "because deep down, they don't think Ana matters."

"Then we'll make them. We'll go and—"

Pappajohn spread out his hands in a gesture of defeat. "I know you mean well, Sammy, but I'm tired. Right now I need to make arrangements to bury my daughter."

Sammy looked at him with concern. Clearly the last two hours—the last two days—had taken a great toll on her old friend. "Okay, Gus." She started the engine and backed out of the LAPD lot. "Let's do that."

This time the middle-aged clerk at the medical examiner's office greeted Pappajohn by name. "Didn't you get my message?" she asked as she spotted them in the hallway. "I called the number you left with Dr. Gharani."

"What message?" Sammy's phone hadn't vibrated.

The woman's umber features reflected genuine regret. "With Saturday's accident and all the fires, everything's even more backed up than before Christmas. Dr. Gharani said to tell you he's sorry, but it could be another day or two before we can release your daughter's body."

Pappajohn simply nodded, though from the way he clenched his jaw, Sammy knew he was upset. She reached out a hand, but he pulled away, heading for the bench and a moment alone.

"What about the final autopsy report?" Sammy asked when he was out of earshot.

"At least a week. Most of our transcription staff is off until after New Year's. The government's worried about the computers. You know." The clerk lowered her voice in a conspiratorial whisper. "Y2K."

Sammy did her best not to roll her eyes. "Yeah. So, how'd you get the short straw to work on a holiday?"

"Don't matter to me. Chanukah was real early this year. I'm glad to fill in over Christmas."

Well what do you know, one of the lost tribe. Patting the clerk's arm, Sammy wished her *a gut yor* before rejoining Pappajohn.

Two hours later, Pappajohn was fast asleep on the living room couch. Though he'd balked at the bowl of canned chicken soup Sammy insisted he eat, he'd finished it all, then like an exhausted child, retreated for a nap. Watching his deep rhythmic breathing, Sammy guessed he'd be out for most of the day.

Just as well. Yesterday, after taking him to the church, she felt the need to spend time with him. They'd talked until late in the night, sharing memories of those they'd lost—Pappajohn's wife and daughter; Sammy's mother. The adversarial tone that had marked their relationship early in Sammy's junior year had evolved into mutual admiration and friendship when they'd joined forces to uncover a university scandal and solve an honored professor's murder. Now their losses had helped them forge an even stronger bond. In some ways, Pappajohn had become the father Sammy had longed for in Jeffrey Greene.

Tiptoeing to her bedroom, Sammy closed the door and sat down at her computer. Glad for the quiet time, she decided to investigate the Canyon City tower collapse for tonight's show, to get a clearer picture of Prescott's connection with her father.

Where to start? Normally she'd begin with primary sources—checking original permits and plans, looking for possible code violations or other shenanigans. But she'd been too busy today to visit the Office of Building and Safety. Tomorrow she'd go downtown and see if Jim's suspicions about the tower's structural integrity might bear fruit.

Right now, she'd have to settle for what she could learn by surfing the web. She closed her eyes for a moment, trying to strategize her search. First rule of good reporting: when in doubt, follow the money. Though part of her hoped her father sincerely wanted a relationship, that his check was a genuine show of altruism, her experience argued for a hidden agenda behind his gesture.

What had her father said? That Neil Prescott had helped finance the renovation of the Canyon City tower? Why, she wondered? His stomping grounds were in Orange County and Beverly Hills. She doubted his motives had anything to do with caring about the unfortunate protesters either. Despite Jeffrey's assertion that Prescott was a mensch, so far Sammy had found no evidence that he championed artistic or humanitarian activities or initiatives. In fact, she recalled, the man was usually front and center as an advocate for aggressive military expansion, both at home and abroad.

Your father and Congressman Prescott are pretty tight...where there's rumor, there's a fire—Jim's words.

Did Jim know something specific or was he just pointing her toward a possible story? She'd already discovered that her father was one of the congressman's biggest fund-raisers. While Sammy hated the idea, that was no crime.

She opened her eyes and jotted down what she knew so far. Prescott was somehow involved in the Canyon City City Hall project. How? Why? That was one trail to follow. As she clicked on the Netscape icon, Sammy wondered if her questions about the tower's collapse would eventually lead to answers she'd rather not know.

For the first fifteen minutes, she carefully reviewed all the material she had already collected on Prescott, including the fact that he led the powerful House Armed Services Committee. One small article named the congressman as an investor in America First Communications, the national broadcasting empire that syndicated practically every top right-wing talk show host in the country. *That* would have gotten him on Jim's radar. But, the deal just sounded like business. Not her politics, true, but not illegal.

Frustrated by the lack of web-based information on the man, Sammy pulled up her address book on the screen. Once a much lengthier list, she'd deleted most of the Washington crowd who'd turned their backs on her the moment the network let her go. Only her buddy Vito, sage of the network's assignment desk, had been willing to stick his neck out and help her get the L.A. job. Luckily, he was home and happy to catch up. He was sorry about the fires, sorrier still about the horrible building collapse, and relieved that Jim was okay. Sammy and Vito were soon joking about how the hippie producer was an acquired taste.

"One of the few old-timers who's managed to stay in the business and still keep his integrity," Vito said. "Getting harder and harder each year." The result? Jim was still at the bottom of the news food chain. Sammy didn't bother to say she was there with him.

Instead, she changed the subject, explaining that she was digging into Congressman Prescott's past and wondered what background Vito could share. With a warning to stay out of trouble, her old friend reluctantly promised to get back to her soon.

Hanging up, Sammy checked e-mail. Only one new message in her in-box. She recognized the sender as her father's second wife, the one person who'd showed kindness when she'd last spent time here as a college student. Typical of Susan, her message was brief and to the point. *Heard you on the radio. Welcome to L.A. Call anytime, 714-555…*

Area code 714. Orange County. It'd be nice to see her again. Maybe Susan could offer some perspective on the changes Sammy had observed in her father. And his burgeoning career. Sammy copied the phone number into her book with a note to set up a visit the next day.

Shutting down her computer, she stretched her neck, trying to remove the kinks. Resting her eyes, she reviewed the morning's run-in with the two detectives who'd been so unsympathetic, so callous. Was this the real L.A.? A city with no heart? A city indifferent to those who lived beneath the radar? Like Ana? Like the thousands of homeless she'd tried to help yesterday? Maybe Ana hadn't followed the straight and narrow, but didn't she deserve some modicum of respect as a human being?

The more Sammy considered it, the less she was willing to let it go. Ana was dead. Sammy couldn't bring her back. Ana's roommate could hold the keys to the poor girl's last hours. Maybe Sammy could learn something that would help Pappajohn make peace with the reality of Ana's death.

Where was Sylvie anyway? Why had she abandoned her car—and her roommate? It wasn't hard to disappear in a city as big and anonymous as L.A. But why would Sylvie be hiding unless she was involved—or afraid?

Knowing it was a long shot, Sammy grabbed the ragged yellow pages next to her desk phone and made a list of hotels and motels between Benedict Canyon and Santa Monica. After a dozen calls she gave up. If Sylvie Pauzé had checked into any of those establishments, she hadn't used her real name. Another dead end.

Sammy stared at the phone for a long time, an idea tickling the edge of her brain. On impulse, she picked up the receiver and dialed LAU Medical.

"ER. Costanza."

"Hey, Lou, Sammy Greene, Dr. Wydham's friend."

"Red, how could I forget *you*? You gotta promise me if you two ever break up, I'm next."

"You're number one on my waiting list," Sammy forced herself to banter. "Listen, I need a favor."

"Your wish—"

Sammy nudged a smile into her voice. "I want to send Reed a surprise birthday card. Believe it or not, I don't know his zip code. Can you check your computer?" she asked, adding, "shhh, just between us, of course."

"My lips are sealed," he said in a conspiratorial whisper. "I'm bringing it up now. In the Marina, right?"

"Yeah, that's it." She tried to sound definite. "Been there many times, but never paid attention to the address."

"I hear you. Don't even know my own cell number." His voice brightened. "Got it. 11645 Admiralty Way, right? 9B. And the zip is 90292."

"Perfect. Thanks, Lou, you're a lifesaver."

"Any time, beautiful."

Sammy gently laid down the receiver. Poor Lou. Hope he finds the girl of his dreams someday. Another girl. Meanwhile, *this* girl was going to look in her closet for something really, really nice to wear.

Sporting just a bath towel, his thick waves of sandy hair tousled and wet, Reed opened the apartment door on the third knock.

"Very nice," he said, admiring Sammy's form fitting sheath and high heels. "And the dress is a winner, too."

A faint flush exposed Sammy's secret pleasure that he'd noticed her efforts. She'd last worn this dress at the spring correspondents dinner in D.C.

"Cool digs." She peered past him at the spacious loft with its floor-to-ceiling view of the marina. Today, the Pacific was a froth of waves caused by the Santa Anas. "Didn't realize residents lived this well."

"Fellow."

"Huh?"

"Cardiology fellow. Three years internal medicine residency, one year chief resident, now I'm a fellow."

"That you are." Sammy's appreciative look lasered onto Reed's half-naked body. Though she teased him, she was well aware that

Reed had paid a heavy price, rejecting his family's banking legacy to become a doctor. He'd worked hard and he'd done it all on his own. It was something Sammy had always admired.

"Aren't you going to invite me in?" She held up a paper bag. "Blueberry bagels. For old times' sake." Her green eyes twinkled at the reference. When they'd first met at an Ellsford University party more than four years ago, Sammy just assumed her Brooklyn Jewish working class roots precluded a serious relationship with the blond-haired, New Hampshire WASP. But Reed had pursued the perky red-head until they'd become a steady couple. And though he'd learned to like brisket and chicken soup, he tenaciously held onto the blue-berries in his bagels.

Now he raised an eyebrow. "Why does the phrase 'beware of Greeks bearing gifts' come to mind?"

"Friends of Greeks," Sammy parried.

"How is Pappajohn?"

Sammy's smile faded. "Actually that's what I wanted to talk to you about," she said, walking through the half-open doorway into the apartment. "He's having a rough time."

Reed shut the door. "I guess I can put off sleep for a little while longer." He rubbed his eyes. Holding up his towel with one hand, with the other he pointed past the kitchen alcove to the main room. "Have a seat, I'll be right back."

"Don't dress up on my account," Sammy said as he padded off barefoot toward the bedroom. With his demanding schedule, how did he ever have time to keep working out?

Alone, in the large open area, Sammy wandered around, step-ping over medical books and journals stacked in every corner, search-ing for a place to settle. Despite the magnificent view, the loft's décor could only be described as minimalist: a couple of beanbag chairs, a low glass coffee table, and a plain leather couch. Nothing on the sterile white walls. Doubtful Michelle, or any female for that matter, had had a hand in the selections. Sammy knew she no longer had a claim on Reed. Still, she found that observation oddly satisfying.

Minutes later, Reed returned looking handsome in tight jeans and a button-down shirt. He sat down on the couch and motioned for her to join him. "Okay, what's up?"

Trying not to miss details, Sammy told him what she and Pappajohn had found at Ana's apartment and the reaction of the detectives. "They're not investigating the break-in. They're not even looking for Sylvie."

"Sylvie?"

"The roommate. Said they're too busy with more important cases. Can you believe that?"

Reed shrugged. "I know from what's been going on at the hospital, there's been a rash of violent crime since the fires. These crazy winds have caused all kinds of fallout, not to mention yesterday's accident at Canyon City. And then there's Y2K. Everybody's got their hands full this week—doctors, firemen, LAPD. I guess they feel a case like Ana's can wait until things die down a little."

Sammy shook her head. "LAPD will never take her death seriously. Even Gus said so. You should have seen how they treated him. Made him feel like two cents. Here the poor guy's just lost his daughter and this one cop—named, uh, De'andray, practically called him a lame father to his face." Sammy smiled sadly. "I know from lame fathers. Maybe Gus should have tried harder when Ana ran away, but he didn't abandon her as a kid." Sammy paused. "Anyway, I thought maybe you could help him get some closure."

"How can I help?"

"A small favor."

Reed's eyes narrowed. "I knew I should never have answered the door."

"I just need a copy of Ana's autopsy report. What's the big deal?"

"Can't Pappajohn get it from the medical examiner?"

"The clerk says it won't be off the computer for a week." Sammy snorted. "Y2K."

"I thought the ME told him the results."

"Claimed her death was an accident, but something you said. Or rather," she looked at him intently, "something you didn't say, makes me wonder if there's been a cover-up."

Reed exhaled, exasperation visible in his face. "I know you love conspiracies, but what could I have said—or not said—that could possibly suggest a cover-up?"

"In the hospital morgue, when I asked if the fires caused Ana's death, you hesitated."

"Only because the ME has to make the call, based on the autopsy," Reed explained.

"And how long do autopsies usually take?"

Reed didn't answer.

"Don't tell me you weren't surprised when I told you the autopsy was done and the case closed in less than twelve hours?"

"I admit it was faster than usual, but I just told you everything's mixed up this week. No doubt the coroner rushed some cases to get their stats up by the New Year. Like it or not, the ME's office serves the city. Without the numbers, the powers-that-be won't approve next year's budget."

"So if they rushed, they might have missed something?"

"Like what?"

"TMJ dislocation."

"Where'd you get that?"

Sammy told him what she'd read in the detectives' report. "Could that mean she was beaten?"

Reed looked away for a moment as if considering how to answer. "Michelle wasn't sure. The jaw dislocation and the skull fracture could be related to her fall. Like I said, the medical examiner makes the final determination. Not an ER resident. Or a cardiology fellow."

"The report of Ana's apartment break-in didn't mention a skull fracture," Sammy declared as if it were an "aha" moment. "It's got to be a cover-up."

Reed ran a hand through his thick waves. "Why are you doing this?"

"What do you mean?"

"I mean what's this *really* about?"

"I want to help Gus. If Ana was assaulted, he needs to know the truth."

"How can that possibly help him?"

"If someone murdered her, don't you think he'd want to get the killer?" She took his hand in hers. "My God, Reed, when you lose someone you love, you spend a lifetime wondering what you could have done to save them." Reed had been so supportive as she'd struggled to come to terms with her mother's suicide. "It takes years to let go of the guilt. Doing something—anything—helps."

Reed pursed his lips. "Guess you're right."

"Then you'll get the report?"

"I'll try. I'll check with the ME's office when I go in to the hospital tomorrow morning."

Sammy leaned over and kissed him on the cheek. "You always were a good guy."

"Yeah, I know," he said. "I'm a *gitina shima*."

She was caught in a dark forest of kindling bursting into flames all around her, stoked by winds that knocked her off her feet onto the sizzling brush tickling her legs. Wind and fire all around her, no matter how fast she ran, she was unable to escape. Filled with smoke, her lungs felt as if they'd burst. "Help me!" Her throat had been rubbed raw from screaming. Finally, too exhausted to continue, she lay down on the ground and prayed. "Please don't let me die! Save me!"

"It's okay. I'm here."

A pair of cool hands reached out for her, pulling her upward. "That's it. Sit up slowly."

Ana blinked open her eyes. No fiery inferno. She was in a dark bedroom, bathed only in pale moonlight. Tree shadows swayed on the lacy curtains next to the soft, warm bed.

"It's me, Courtney. You're in my house. In Malibu."

Ana forced herself to focus. Squinting, she saw that it was her erstwhile rehab roommate. The slim brunette was wearing only a thong and torn T-shirt.

"You *are* here." Ana's whisper became a wheeze and then a cough. "I rang the doorbell, but—"

"Power's been out. And I wasn't exactly sober until after Christmas."

Ana sat up straight. "What? After Christmas? How long have I been here?"

"It's Monday evening. Found you in the bushes Saturday morning. You were really out of it. Fever, coughing, like asthma, and you could barely walk. Took me almost an hour to lug you up here."

Courtney leaned over and felt Ana's forehead. "You're cooler now. All night you were talking in tongues. Almost thought you were a goner."

"Three days?" Like a curtain rising, the memories returned. Sylvie burned and fighting for her life at the hospital, the trashed apartment, her narrow escape from Kaye's thug, jumping over the wall here, and then blacking out. "I'm in trouble."

"Using again?"

"No," Ana said, reality crashing in on her with the force of a tidal wave. "I'm running. For my life."

Courtney grabbed a mug filled with amber colored liquid from the night table. "Hot toddy. Brandy and honey cures everything. Have a few more sips, and then you can tell me the truth."

"Blueberry bagels and macaroni, bacon bits, and cheese," Sammy chuckled. "Grandma Rose would be spinning in her grave."

"I don't eat at home very often," Reed admitted. "But trust me, this beats the hospital cafeteria chow."

"Don't doubt that." Sammy laughed. "And the company can't be beat."

"Why am I not surprised that you ruffled the network suits?" Reed asked after Sammy had caught him up on her career. "Ever since the OJ trial, journalism has become more entertainment than news. Woodward and Bernstein are out."

"Corruption, graft, and cronyism are not out," Sammy said. "We still need guys like them."

"People get complacent when they're not hungry. Even Woodward and Bernstein are well paid these days. And the suits now control the paychecks. It's hard to walk away from the good life."

"You did, choosing medicine over your family's money."

"I'm not exactly on the street." Reed waved toward the moonlit window and the starlight view. "You might have been."

"That's why I wanted so much to help." Her eyes began to fill with tears. "We should all help each other."

Reed slid his chair closer to hers and put a comforting arm around her shoulders. "I'm here to help anytime. You know that."

Sammy looked up into his gentle eyes once again. The invitation was clear as their lips touched. Her arms circled his muscled chest, pressing him close, their embrace so natural, so much like home. She'd forgotten what a wonderful feeling that had been. And why it hadn't lasted.

With food scrounged from the pantry in her belly, a lukewarm shower, and a borrowed pair of jeans and T-shirt, Ana was beginning to feel well enough to share her story. She walked back into the bedroom where Courtney was seated on the plush pile carpet, knocking down shots of brandy.

"Ready for more?" Courtney held up the almost empty bottle before pouring herself another glass.

Ana shook her head. "Maybe you shouldn't."

"It's the holidays." Courtney's face set in a pout. "My present to me."

Ana's expression held a note of pity. She'd read in the tabloids that Courtney's battling divorced parents had both flown to New York last month for her kid sister's rehearsals in a Broadway revival of *Little Orphan Annie*. Neither returned to L.A. when Courtney had been rushed to the hospital. Looked like she and Courtney *did* have a lot in common.

"Holidays suck," Ana agreed, stuffing the money left on the armoire when she'd changed clothes into her new pockets. She picked up the thick orange disk from the bureau.

"What's that?"

"I'm not sure." Ana explained the dangerous game Sylvie had been playing lately, handing Kaye information on the johns, while working with LAPD to get dirt on Kaye.

Courtney whistled. "And I thought I lived on the fucking edge."

Ana told Courtney how Sylvie had laughed the night of the party. "Said she had a plan to break away from Madam Kaye." She held up the disk. "There could be compromising photos. Or video. I wouldn't put it past Sylvie to tape some of her clients. It'd be nice to find out, but it didn't fit in the computer at the library." She handed the disk to Courtney. "I think it's what Kaye's goon was after." Ana hugged herself, chilled by the horror of the past forty-eight hours. "I'm desperate for a way out myself."

Courtney turned the disk over in her hands. "I think I know what this is. Wait a sec." Jumping up, she dashed out of the bedroom and stumbled down the stairs.

Ana sat down on the edge of the bed, fighting off the shivers. Courtney's brandy on the carpet seemed to beckon, the half full glass of alcohol promising to numb her growing fear. She reached for it, then pulled her arm back. She had to stay clear-headed and strong. To stay alive. For Teddy.

"Got it. My accountant used one of these." Courtney stood at the doorway holding a small gray box from which dangled a few loose cables. "He called it a Jazz drive. Holds about a gig, costs about a thou. Said he needed it to run my TV revenues."

"Does my—Sylvie's—disk fit?" Ana asked, daring to hope.

"It's already in this drive." Courtney took a seat at her desk near the window. "As soon as the power comes on, I'll try to wire it up to my computer and we can see Sylvie's show."

The sound of the wind battering the window jolted Sammy from sleep. Night had fallen. She felt the cool sheets against her bare skin and relished their softness for a moment before realizing she was in Reed's bed. She patted the warm space beside her. "Reed?" He was gone. She sat up and flipped on the light switch above the bed. The alarm clock on the end table read 10:59 p.m. "Jeez, my show!" She had less than an hour to make it to the studio.

The alarm went off as she leapt out of bed, nearly falling over the table, trying to silence it. That's when she saw the note lying beside the clock. Sammy grabbed it, squinting to make out Reed's chicken scratch. Doctors!

> *Set the clock for eleven. You seemed exhausted. Got called
> into the hospital tonight. Next time hope you will stay. Reed.*

As she slipped on her dress and heels, she thought about the cryptic note.

He'd come back into her life. Or more correctly she'd come into his. He'd overcome her hesitation by reassuring her that, despite testing the waters, he hadn't made a commitment to anyone else. Was that because he still had feelings for her?

Next time hope you will stay.

Next time. As she hurried out the door, she wondered if next time she would.

CHAPTER ELEVEN

December 28, 1999
Tuesday a.m.

Sammy smoothed the wrinkles from her dress and opened the studio door at 11:59, expecting a new producer for her show.

Instead, a familiar voice greeted her, "Now that's more like it."

She was surprised to see Jim in his usual seat. "If I'd known you were coming, I'd have brought chicken soup. I thought the doctors sent you home to rest."

"I hurt too much to lie down. Figured I might as well work."

Sammy rushed over, reaching out for a hug.

Jim held up a hand. "Everything's sore." He pointed to the clock. "You're on in one. No time for sentimental reunions."

"Nonsense. Grandma Rose used to say, there's always time," Sammy leaned in and encircled the air around him with her arms. "An air hug for a true hero."

Jim gave a tentative head shake, his grimace suggesting that even that movement was painful. "Nah, it was just like being back in Nam. You act or you die."

"You fought in the Vietnam War? I thought you were a pacifist."

"There are no warmongers in foxholes. It's the chicken hawks in Congress that never saw combat we should worry about. Just ask your buddy Pappajohn. He was a veteran, too. Thirty seconds."

Sammy raced into her booth, flipping on the television as she sat in her chair, and pulled on her headphones. The TV screen played a montage of the day's disasters, fires out of control in the Santa Monica mountains near Malibu and the Canyon City tower collapse. The crawl underneath listed the number of dead now as six. A dozen homeless victims were still in critical condition.

On Jim's cue, Sammy began, "This is Sammy Greene on the L.A. Scene. I'd like to wish my listeners happy holidays, but tonight, I can't. Looks like Santa brought our city a giant lump of coal this year, with one natural disaster after another." She paused to clear her throat.

"Saturday, the Santa Ana devil wind brought down the old Canyon City Hall tower. Down on the backs of its poorest and most vulnerable citizens. Six people dead, hundreds injured, many hospitalized in critical condition. Among the victims, one infant and one college student volunteering at the tent city. Carmen Moran sacrificed her holiday break to help those in need and now her family faces the heartbreak of her loss. Our thoughts and our hearts go out to everyone who suffered in that horrible accident and their loved ones and friends. If you're the religious type, send them your prayers. And, while you're connected with God, ask him 'Why?'"

From the corner of her eye, Sammy saw a thumbs-up from Jim. The phone lines were already blinking. "I haven't been around that long myself, but long enough to see that human error, negligence, hubris, and hatred have brought more death and destruction than any natural disaster. Was there a human hand behind the tower's collapse yesterday? Devil's breath? Or poor construction, faulty engineering?

"If Neil Prescott hadn't led that initiative to clean up Beverly Hills, those men, women, and children would never have been in Canyon City. I'll tell you this, it may have been the Santa Anas that blew down the tower, but Congressman Prescott sure gave it a strong push. Fifteen after."

●   ●   ●

Jeffrey winced. *Poor construction, faulty engineering, human error. Negligence.* His lawyers would have convulsions hearing those terms bandied about. And by his own daughter, no less.

Trina glowered at the radio. She'd insisted they stay up for Sammy's show to learn if she'd backed off of her vendetta against Prescott. Jeffrey knew this segment had just confirmed Trina's worst fears.

"So *this* is your 'flies with honey' approach?" She turned to face him, her tone cold as ice. "You realize contacts like Neil Prescott are why Jeffrey Greene is no longer some two-bit salesman, but a real estate tycoon. I don't know what Prescott is up to and I don't want to know. But we have to shut your daughter down. *Now.*"

Jeffrey let out a deep breath through puffed cheeks. Perhaps Trina was right. If Prescott got pissed, he might try to deep six the Playa Bella deal and leave Jeffrey holding the bag. Family was family, but it seemed Sammy had inherited a hefty dose of Bubbe Rose's genes and didn't know when to stop. "So what do you suggest?"

"I'll take care of it," Trina said. "I'm sure I can convince her to keep her big mouth shut."

"You wouldn't do anything to hurt her, would you?"

Trina laughed. "Of course not, *carino.* She's your daughter. But she's more likely to listen if she truly understands the consequences of continuing down this road. For us and," she muttered sotto voce, "for her."

"Apocalypse!" the caller cried. "A sign from God. America is headed for terrible doom. You can laugh, but you'll see. Welcome the Lord Jesus as your Savior because time is running out!"

"Believe me," Sammy said. "I'm not laughing. But my rabbi would be a little upset if I took your advice without proof. How do you know?"

"It is written. The Book of Revelation, I'm warning you. The Lord has commanded seven angels to pour seven vials of the wrath of God upon the Earth! The new millennium will bring us Armageddon!"

Sammy cut off the caller. "Looks like your calendar's a bit off, sir. Y2K may become Armageddon for IBM, but the new millennium isn't til 2001. Mike in Downey, you have a comment about Y2K?"

"Hi. This is Mike."

"Yes, Mike, we know, go ahead."

"Am I on?"

"Yes, Mike, we're all waiting breathlessly."

"Okay. Hi. Haven't you seen all the warnings on the news?"

"About?"

"Terrorists. The USS *Cole*, the bombings in Kenya. And now Y2K. Take your money out of the bank, stock up on canned food and water, and buy lots of MREs."

"Wait a minute," Sammy interrupted. "If you're talking about the military ready-to-eat meals, they say it's illegal to sell them. Right on the package."

"But it isn't. We've been pushing them on eBay and the Pentagon can't do a thing. There's no law on the books against it. So, go on eBay, type in Mike's MREs and be prepared—"

Sammy cut him off in mid-sentence. "Folks, we love advertising here. Just call our sales associates Monday through Friday and pay for it! Stella in Hermosa Beach on the Canyon City tragedy." She clicked on the next caller.

"It wasn't the winds, you know."

"No?" prompted Sammy.

"No. The tower fell because Mars and Jupiter were in alignment. Your callers are right to worry about Y2K. My charting shows an exact conjunction between Pluto and Chiron, at about eleven and a half degrees of Sagittarius, the twelfth degree of the sign. The Sun and Moon occupy similar degrees of the prior and succeeding signs to Sag, Scorpio, and Capricorn, or in other words the conjunction is semisextile to both luminaries. This means the Pluto-Chiron conjunction is very much emphasized, brought to rational and emotional awareness, being at the Sun-Moon midpoint as they sextile each other."

"Let's keep this show G-rated," Sammy said as she hung up on the caller, "And, reality-based, people. Please. The stars had nothing to do with the tower's fall. Humans built it, and humans are most likely responsible for what happened. It's up to us to find out why, and then make sure this never happens again. Twenty-eight after."

Distracted by Sammy's show blasting on Lou's boombox, Bishop stopped writing the ER consultation note to listen. Unbidden thoughts drifted back to the battlefields of northeast Iraq, a place he'd tried so long to forget. The collapse of a five-story apartment building during a vicious sandstorm had killed more than thirty innocent men, women, and children.

And one young soldier dying in his arms, the winds echoing his words: *resonator . . . murder . . .*

And Bishop's words that had soon followed: *We need to investigate, uncover the cause, make sure this never happens again.*

"Dr. Bishop, we're ready to move your patient to the CCU. Can we have the chart, sir?" The dark-haired orderly spoke politely, with a faint, unplaceable accent.

Startled, Bishop focused again on the unfinished record. "Of course." He scribbled a few notes before handing it over. "Just thinking about the case."

The long-forgotten case.

"Radio's dead and we're out of batteries," Courtney said. "My manager told me to get a generator."

"All that horrible news was creeping me out, anyway." Ana said. "These candles kind of remind me of camping with the Girl Scouts."

Courtney sat down on the couch beside Ana and raised her glass in a toast. "Or in my case, the Boy Scouts." In the flickering candlelight, she was glad to see Ana's pale, drawn features melt into a smile.

"The mayor of Canyon City refuses to comment. We'll keep you updated as events progress. In other tragedies," Sammy pulled over a piece of paper for reference, "it looks like the fire's moved west through parts of Brentwood and the Palisades, and has now killed three people and destroyed over two hundred homes. Another ten thousand have been evacuated from Mandeville Canyon and Temescal Canyon tonight. Firefighters are working to keep the flames from Topanga. Power is out from Malibu to Oxnard. DWP is on the job, trying to bring things back online in West L.A. County. Hope you all have your flashlights and batteries working. This is earthquake country and we better be prepared."

Sammy hesitated. Would she be going too far if she asked? Jim looked tense through the glass, waving a finger for her to speak. Her pause, known in the radio business as "dead air," would make listeners reach for the dial in confusion or frustration. More than a few seconds of silence was unprofessional. She had to make a choice.

"One of the fire's victims died on Christmas Eve," she finally began. "A young woman with her life ahead of her. I knew—I know her dad. I just want to help. I've never had kids, but I lost my mother when I was seven. Your world just ends. You want to understand what happened and why." After another brief pause, she added, "What could I have done to prevent it?"

Sammy sighed. "Ana Pappajohn was twenty-seven. Her father would like to answer those questions too. We know she died alone, in the hills of Bel Air, but if anyone can tell us more, we want to hear from you. If you're a friend, or her roommate," she checked her notes, "Sylvie Pauzé, please call us. Ana's father would just like to know how she spent her last hours, her last days. Our number is 310-555-KPCF. 310-555-5725. Forty-six after."

Pappajohn switched off the radio. He had no appetite for more of Sammy's show tonight. While he knew she meant well, he could no longer see the point. If only he could rewrite his life, create a new, happy ending. A tide of despair swept over him without warning and he wept. He was doing a lot of that lately. Weeping for his beloved Effie, his darling Ana, for everything he'd lost, let slip through his hands, beyond his reach.

Tomorrow, he would call the church and finalize the plans for

Ana's funeral. If the coroner released her body, maybe they could have the service by Wednesday. Once he'd buried his daughter, he'd leave this hellhole of a city and go home. Alone.

Wondering if he could ever sleep again without his dreams tormenting him, he rested his head on the pillows and blankets he'd piled on one end of Sammy's couch. Shutting his eyes tight, he whispered a prayer to the one who wasn't there for him, who didn't protect him from such pain. *Please, God, don't let me wake up. Ever.*

Ana blew out the candles in the bedroom while Courtney connected the wires of her accountant's drive to her computer. The power had returned, but with the ferocious winds, who knew for how long?

Courtney sat down at her keyboard and waited until the monitor flashed the message, *Equipment Recognized, Removable Disk F.* "Show time!" she yelled. With Ana leaning on her shoulder, she double clicked to open the Jazz drive, revealing several files labeled in French. "No videos," she said after scanning the list. "Just Word files."

"Wait!" Ana pointed to a file labeled Deneuve. "Open that one." Cathérine Deneuve had been Sylvie's favorite actress. She'd watch the classic film Belle de Jour over and over on the VCR when she got depressed.

Courtney clicked and opened a long list of names with notes beside each. Famous names and compromising information.

"They're all Kaye's clients!" Ana said.

Scrolling through the columns, Courtney shook her head. "You know how many careers would be six feet under if these names came out? No wonder your madam is ready to kill." She turned and looked up at Ana. "You *are* in deep shit, girl."

Kaye cursed as she turned off the radio. That talk-show bitch was stirring up what should have been laid to rest days ago. Not only was she after Ana's history, but now she'd started looking for Sylvie. And that was the last thing Kaye needed right now. Reaching over, she picked up her cell phone. Time to call Yevgeny once again.

• • •

The elderly woman on the gurney had been gasping for air for the better part of an hour before Reed was able to remove the excess fluid from her congested lungs. She was the third cardiac patient he'd treated today, all pushed into pulmonary edema and heart failure by the added stress from the city's smoky air.

He adjusted the IV and increased the oxygen in her nasal cannula. "You'll feel better now," he promised the woman. Exiting the cubicle, he handed the chart to one of the ER nurses with orders to transfer the patient to the CCU and shuffled toward the doctors' lounge.

At two a.m., the room was vacant, though from the near-empty level of the coffee in the community pot, it was clear that he was not the only one substituting caffeine for sleep tonight. Even Bishop had stayed to help with consults.

Exhausted, Reed poured himself a half cup of sludge, then settled down on the couch for a moment of contemplation. What had happened this afternoon? Sammy showing up at his door, looking so hot. The green color of her tight-fitting dress accentuating her emerald eyes. Her red hair, wind blown, falling in soft curls against her shoulders. He smiled at the memory. The five-foot pixie he'd met more than four years ago at Ellsford University had morphed into a beautiful, sexy young woman.

Reed shook himself. They'd been down this road before. Had anything really changed? Sammy was still the intrepid seeker of truth who couldn't let go of a challenge until she'd conquered it. And, then?

Was her appearance today manipulation, or had their lovemaking meant as much to her as it had to him? Each time he'd gotten really close before, she'd managed to back away.

The door opened and Michelle marched in, brusquely tossing a couple of charts onto the counter.

"Were you called in too?"

"I'm a resident. I never go home. That's probably why I've missed *your* calls."

Chastened, Reed looked down at his feet. "Sorry, I've been so busy—"

"Who hasn't been?" Michelle's voice softened. "Literal black clouds raining patients down on us." She approached him and leaned in for a kiss, then stepped back, sniffing. "Jasmine?"

"Huh?"

"New perfume?"

Reed felt his cheeks redden. "Must be the soap in the men's john."

"Really." Michelle's face tightened. She pulled over a rolling chair from the counter, sat, and grabbed a few papers from her pile.

"What are you doing, Reed?" Michelle held out two faxes on L.A. County Medical Examiner's letterhead. "I'm only a first-year resident, but even I know you can't order a final autopsy report without special permission. If Bishop finds out, you'll be in big trouble."

"He won't find out," Reed's voice had a hint of pleading. "I had to do it for Sammy and Gus."

"Sammy? She's the reason you're sticking your neck out?" Michelle shook her head. "I thought you said the two of you were through."

"We were. We are."

"Were or are?" Michelle asked, her tone pure ice. "Maybe you and I need to take a break until you get your tenses straight." She handed him the report. "Here's the chart you asked for." She slapped it down on the table, rose, spun on her heels, and strode out of the lounge without another word.

Damn, Reed cursed when he was alone again. Things had been going so well before Sammy came riding into town. Michelle was right. Ana Pappajohn wasn't his patient. If Bishop learned that he'd poked around the records of someone not under his care, he'd have his ass. In fact, HIPAA threatened to criminally prosecute health professionals who violated its strict rules of confidentiality. Lying about being Ana's doctor and pressuring the poor substitute clerk at the ME's to release the information could jeopardize his license. Thank you, Sammy. It better turn out to be worth it.

With the deed done, Reed now skimmed the faxes, searching for something that might be of interest.

```
Date of report: December 24, 1999
Time of report: 10:00 a.m.
Name of Decedent: Anastasia Pappajohn
Age: 26
Date and time of death: December 24,
    1999. 2:15 a.m.
```

Less than eight hours from the time Michelle had called the code until a report was posted. That alone was odd. Normally reports took at least two or three days. Unless, as he'd told Sammy, cause of death was so clear-cut, the ME figured he might as well finish the report and get home for Christmas.

Reed read through Dr. Gharani's descriptions. Third degree burns over 80 percent of the victim's body as well as a frontal skull fracture. Assessment of the internal organs showed an enlarged liver, probably from chronic alcohol abuse. Reed skipped to the lab report on the second page where the toxicology screen listed a blood alcohol level of .18—well above the legal limit. The screen was positive for cocaine and Ecstasy as well. It certainly seemed clear to Gharani. An intoxicated young woman panicked and ran blindly down a dark road to escape the flames. She tripped and fell, cracking her skull and losing consciousness, helpless before the oncoming flames.

```
Cause of death: Burns
Manner of death: Accidental
```

Tragic, but hardly suspicious, Reed concurred.

He reached for the chart Michelle had tossed to his side. It was the first and only LAU Medical admission for Anastasia Pappajohn. He thumbed through the few pages until he found Michelle's notes. She'd identified the frontal skull fracture and third-degree burns. However, unlike the ME, Michelle had also documented a TMJ dislocation, buccal mucosa lacerations, and zygomatic arch instability, which, she wrote, "may have been caused by impact trauma, possibly secondary to assault and battery." Suspecting a crime, Michelle, like all licensed health professionals, was required to report her findings to the police. A record of her call to the West L.A. Precinct was appended in the chart's Plan section.

The cause of the injuries Michelle listed would be up to the police to determine. Reed wondered why an experienced ME like Gharani had failed to identify them. Incompetence? Negligence? Or cover-up? If so, of what? Assault, battery, drugs, murder?

Damn! He was thinking like Sammy again. Sighing, Reed walked over to the lounge phone and dialed her cell number. He'd just report the conflicting findings in the two records. Let Sammy come up with conspiracy theories. Stirring up controversy was one of her many talents.

"Thanks, Reed." Sammy ended the conversation, clearly disturbed. Even Jim moved his pained facial muscles into an expression of concern. Shaking her head, she pointed to the clock and slipped on her headphones.

"Breaking news. Just came to my attention. There may be reason to believe that Ana Pappajohn, the victim of the Christmas Eve fire in Bel Air, was murdered," Sammy announced, struggling to control her emotions. The police had been in such a hurry to label her death an accident, to sweep her life under the rug with the ashes from these Godforsaken fires. "So it's even more important for anyone who has news of Sylvie Pauzé, Ana's roommate, to come forward. If our lines are busy, please keep trying. We have to find out what happened."

Slipping her pen back into her purse, Sammy spied her father's check. She hadn't had time to deposit it. On impulse, she made a decision. "In fact," she continued without missing a beat, "we're offering a ten thousand dollar reward for anyone with information leading to the discovery and arrest of Ana's murderer. Our number is—"

•   •   •

De'andray spewed out a spray of his coffee. *"Damn!* I knew that girl was trouble."

Ortego slid into his seat on the passenger side of the unmarked car and rested a bag of donuts on the dashboard. "Who?"

" 'Sammy Greene on the L.A. Scene'!" De'andray pointed to the car's radio. "Accusing us of burying a possible homicide! Now she's put up a reward for anyone with information on the girl's death. And on her roommate, the one with that car." He shook his head. "All of a sudden, everybody's a detective. Probably got that Boston blue behind her, pulling her strings *and* ours."

Ortego sat staring at his coffee.

"Hey, dude. You asleep?"

"Not asleep, Chico. Just wondering why the roommate hasn't turned up. We've had an APB out on her for over a day."

"You think she's got something to do with this Ana chick's death?" De'andray raised an eyebrow. "Hiding out?"

Ortego shrugged.

"Aw, man. *You're* thinking it wasn't an accident?"

Ortego took a sip of the steaming coffee before responding. "Anything's possible."

Sitting on the can, Miller had made a note to congratulate Prescott in the morning on revving up the terrorism chatter just in time for Y2K. It was important to use the press to shape the message: *be afraid.* Hadn't he told Fahim about the study of fear? Making others afraid was a powerful tool Miller had learned as a boy, but honed as a man. Now even callers to that pinko commie radio station expected the Apocalypse in the next few days.

He chuckled. Armageddon, the eons old conflict between good and evil was due to end in the epic battle on Mount Megiddo, Har Mageddon in the Ancient Hebrew. God would fight Satan and emerge victorious. In a way, Y2K would launch that heroic saga in the new millenium. The resonator was the sword that would lead Miller and his loyalists to victory on that figurative mount. It was, after all, as Fahim had so poetically put it the other day, the Hand of God.

Returning to his study, Miller picked up the remote for his Bose radio, ready to switch off KPCF and retire to bed. His finger remained frozen, hovering above the *off* button.

Murdered? How in hell did she figure that? Dropping the remote, he reached for his cell phone and dialed a number. The last thing he needed with D-day so close was the cops sniffing around after Ana Pappajohn, Fahim, or himself.

Sounds of "My Way" wafted through the bungalow's bedroom in West Hollywood. It took three rings before a hairy wrist reached over from silk sheets to answer.

"Yeah?" Gharani mumbled sleepily. Who would be calling at this hour? He cocked an eye and glanced at the dial on his beside clock radio—2:20 a.m.

"Burn her." The gravelly voice didn't mince words.

"What?"

"You heard me. Ana Pappajohn. Cremate her and have it done by morning."

The call ended abruptly, leaving Gharani no choice. Slowly, he eased out of his warm, comfortable bed, wondering if the tightness he felt gripping his neck was just his imagination. He cursed in Farsi as the terrible truth dawned on him. His bridle was all too real. Miller's calls would never stop coming, and he'd never again be free.

Courtney pushed her chair back from her computer. Another hour of exploring Sylvie's disk had turned up little more. Bank accounts, calendars, and schedules, a few surprisingly sentimental poems, and a couple of ear-splitting music files, courtesy of Sylvie's musician boyfriend.

"Sylvie's Plan B has to be the dirt on these johns," Ana said. Renowned clients and their innumerable peccadilloes. City councilmen, state assemblymen, congressmen, including Neil Prescott. Even the former mayor. Business leaders, celebrities, the crème de la crème of Los Angeles, and the über wealthy from other parts of the U.S. and abroad.

Ana understood why the madam needed those names for protection. The mere threat of public revelation would silence a difficult client. If Sylvie had been feeding anything on Kaye's list to the cops, Kaye could find herself in as much trouble as her customers.

Had the madam discovered that Sylvie worked both sides? Set her up for a beating? Or worse? *Damn you, Sylvie,* Ana silently cursed, wishing her friend had heeded her warnings not to play dangerous games.

Courtney handed the ejected disk back to Ana. "There's more than enough to use to—negotiate. Why not give it to your madam and call it a deal?"

"This isn't Hollywood. She'll get rid of the disk *and* me." Ana could almost feel Yevgeny's grip on her arm.

"Hey, I'm not stupid. I uploaded everything onto my computer. And I'm making a backup disk. Tell Kaye if anything happens to you, a copy's going to the cops *and* the fucking *L.A. Times. That's* your Plan B, girlfriend."

Sammy's offer of reward money attracted a bevy of callers. Not one line remained open for the rest of her show. Unfortunately, most callers had no clue, figuratively or literally. By three a.m., Sammy had begun to regret her impulsive decision.

Discouraged, she stuffed her papers under her arm and entered Jim's booth as he hung up his phone.

"We may have a bite." He held up a phone number and Hispanic name. "Taxi driver thinks he gave Sylvie a ride home the night Ana died."

"Just add him to the list of alien sightings," Sammy said wearily.

"Claims she carried a bright pink purse. "

"You're kidding." Sammy snatched the paper, folded it into her pocket and threw Jim a kiss. "I'd give you a real one, but I know you're hurting. In fact, why not go home and rest? I can finish your show tonight."

"Nah, I can rest pretty damn well on the air." Jim clicked on his mic and, with a wink, began his hypnotic broadcast.

Sammy nodded and waved goodbye as she exited the studio. She really was starting to like the guy. An acquired taste, she thought. Like blueberry bagels.

Rushing to her car to avoid blasting winds, she failed to register the parked Escalade, its muscled driver hunched low in his seat. Nor did she notice the pair of headlights a block behind that followed her all the way home.

Courtney eyed the haze outside her bedroom window. "Looks shitty." She aimed the remote at her big-screen TV in the corner. "Let's check on the fires. We almost burned out here last year." She clicked past cable station infomercials to a local network where an L.A. metro area map displayed at least a dozen tiny flames.

"Santa Ana winds continue to spread the Southern California firestorms. Due to rapidly changing conditions, residents are urged to stay away from threatened communities. Evacuations continue in Sherman Oaks, Studio City, and Tarzana. Eight firefighters have been seriously injured around the city. One is in critical condition."

None of the flickering flames overlayed Malibu. "At least we're safe for now." Courtney turned down the volume as the scene switched from the burning hills to the LAU Medical Center.

Ana pointed to the TV where an ambulance was unloading the screaming actress. "That's you!"

Courtney rolled her eyes. "Turn it off. I know what I look like. Hey, that's *you!*" Now she was pointing to the screen.

Stunned, Ana saw that the camera had caught her crouching behind the EMTs. The shot passed quickly, but anyone paying attention who knew her might realize that Ana Pappajohn was alive and well at LAU Medical the night Sylvie was burned.

Courtney turned up the volume again. "As of this hour, still no news on the whereabouts of Courtney Phillips. Her manager's keeping mum, but rumors have it that she's left the country for a self-imposed 'holiday' to recover from 'exhaustion.'" The anchor added the quotes with a smug intonation. "I'll bet the $100,000 a month Hope Rehab Center in the Bahamas is where our reporters will find Courtney next."

Courtney poured herself another glass of brandy. "Yeah, more like where their reporters would like a working holiday." She grabbed the remote and aimed it at the TV.

"Wait!" Ana gestured at the graphics.

"Another sad note. Police have confirmed that the Christmas Eve victim of the fires in Benedict Canyon has died. She's been identified as Anastasia Pappajohn, age twenty-six, a resident of Santa Monica. And, in yesterday's Canyon City tower accident, the number of dead and injured is mounting as—"

Feeling faint, Ana clung to Courtney for support.

"Sorry, girlfriend." Courtney clicked off the TV. "I know you two were tight."

Ana gasped and struggled for air between sobs. Sylvie dead? It was too much. She fell onto Courtney's bed, her tears drenching the fine silk duvet.

Now even the police believed Sylvie was Ana Pappajohn. Only she and Kaye knew the truth about the mix-up. So why hadn't Kaye told the police? Ana's heart began pounding as she considered the possibilities. The client list! Kaye must somehow believe that Sylvie had shared it with Ana. She'd obviously stop at nothing to get it back. Her Russian goon had failed. What could Kaye do now to draw Ana from her hiding place?

Oh, my God. Teddy! Though Ana had only told Sylvie about her son, Sylvie and the madam had been close. Much as Ana hated to admit it, it was more than possible that Sylvie had betrayed her secret. If Kaye knew about Teddy, she might try to find him and use him as bait.

Terrified, Ana jumped up and dried her tears on her sleeve. "I've got to call Mrs. Darden. Make sure my son's safe. Can I use your phone?" She pointed to the cell she'd brought with her. "Batteries are dead."

"Sure. Okay." Courtney traded Sylvie's phone for her own pink studded mobile, and added in a gentle voice. "'Course he is. I'll recharge yours in the kitchen while I find us something to eat."

Sammy tiptoed quietly into the apartment at three thirty a.m., past a snoring Pappajohn. Glad he was finally sleeping deeply, she took care not to wake him as she hurried down the hall to her bedroom.

Sitting on her bed, she reached in her pocket for the paper from Jim and punched in the telephone number on her cordless handset.

"*Hola.*"

"Hello. May I speak to Porfirio Sandoval?"

"*Si, Porfirio,*" the woman responded with a heavy Hispanic accent. "*Es trabajando. No esta aqui.*"

Wishing she'd studied high school Spanish instead of French, Sammy guessed that meant her husband was still working. "When will he be home?"

"*No entiendo. No hablo ingles.*"

"*Quand retourner?*" she improvised. "*Um, cuando est il a la casa.*"

"*El va regresar manana. Lo puedo llamar a les siete, de la tarde. Gracias.*"

"Siete" had to be "seven," Sammy thought as she replaced the cordless in its cradle. She'd call during the day tomorrow and set up a face-to-face. If the cabbie *had* given Sylvie a ride the night Ana died, Sammy would get him to ID the photo. Maybe he could tell where she'd been going and where she might be found.

Sammy eyed her bedside clock. Four a.m. A few hours of sleep would do her a world of good. Stretching the kinks from her tired muscles, she ambled over to the window to lower the blinds. The smoky fog outside was too thick for Sammy to see the dark Escalade now parked down the block outside her building, or the black Lincoln staking out the other side of the street.

•   •   •

Courtney turned from the open refrigerator to see Ana standing in the kitchen. "Everything okay?" She pulled out a carton of orange juice and poured some into a tall glass half filled with a clear liquor.

"Teddy's fine. Mrs. Darden, his foster mother, took him up to the Bay Area to visit her relatives. I talked with her husband."

"You didn't tell him who you were?"

Ana shook her head. "I didn't want anyone listening to know it was me. I used that Québécois accent Sylvie taught me. Said I was a friend of Ana Pappajohn's. That she'd asked me to bring Teddy a video game from Canada when I came to L.A."

"That's creative." Courtney returned the juice to an empty shelf and shut the refrigerator door.

"Thank God, Teddy's out of town. I wouldn't want him to hear our local news and think his mother might really be dead. They'll be back in L.A. on Thursday." Ana leaned against the sink. "By then, I hope everything'll be taken care of."

"That gives us a few days to make a plan."

A Celine Dion tune stopped them in their tracks. They both turned to search for the source.

Courtney pointed to the cell she'd plugged into the wall charger. Sylvie's phone. "You gonna answer it?" Seeing Ana's hesitation, she added, "Don't worry, I did a TV cop show where they took at least five minutes to trace the call. Just hang up quickly."

Hoping Courtney was right, Ana grabbed the phone and flipped it open. "Text message," she said in explanation, before gasping and dropping the phone on the tiled floor. "Oh, my God!"

Courtney rushed over. "What? What?"

"The message. I never checked it. It's from Sylvie!"

Ana stared at the text Sylvie had sent the night of the fire. Date: December 24, Time: 12:05 a.m. The message she'd ignored in the panicked rush to the LAU Med ER and ignored in her frenzied escape. A few hours later and her friend was gone forever. Seeing the message in black and white now made Sylvie's tragic death heartbreakingly real. If only Ana had called Sylvie back, might she have been able to save her?

"This makes no sense." Ana showed the screen to Courtney.

"Eyes only, al-Harbi. Op. Y2K 34.058710–118.442183. Beats me."

"Look, more numbers," Ana said, pointing. "31, 12, 99, 23, 59. Think it's a code?"

"Dunno. Sylvie must have been trying to tell you something. An address, a phone number?" Courtney grabbed a piece of paper and copied it all down. "Could be a phone number. Seven digits and an area code."

"It's not written like one. And L.A. is 310, not 311." Ana motioned to Courtney. "Give me your phone."

Ana dialed the numbers, and, to her surprise, heard the phone ring. She put the call on speaker.

"Los Angeles Citywide Services Directory. Routine and non-emergency City Services and L.A. Fire Department. How can we assist you?"

Ana switched off the call, confused. "Fire Department? Why wouldn't she call 911?"

Courtney shrugged. "Any other text messages?"

Ana punched the keys on Sylvie's phone once again. "Just a couple of voicemails. 323 area code. Let me try." She entered 123 and listened for the voice mail ring.

"You know her password?"

"Maybe." When cued, Ana tried *Sylvie* knowing Sylvie used it for her e-mail. The entry failed.

"How about her last name?" Courtney suggested, taking a long sip of her screwdriver.

Ana tried Pauzé. "No luck." When the system gave a third prompt, she scratched her head, thinking of her last conversation with Sylvie. *Plan B. Payless shoes, Remember*—Could that be it?

Ana entered *Payless* and within seconds, a male voice was shouting at them through the speaker: "Hey, what happened? Where the fuck are you?"

Ana saved the call and pressed the button for the second message. Same voice, a few hours later. And, this time, much more abusive.

Even Courtney seemed offended by the string of expletives. "Shit, that guy is pissed! Recognize the voice?"

"It's not Kaye's goon, for sure."

Courtney grabbed the phone from Ana's hand.

"What are you doing?"

"Shhh." Courtney retrieved the number on the cell and pushed *call*. She held up the phone on speaker mode so they could both listen. After three rings, the call was picked up. *"You have reached LAPD West Los Angeles Precinct Main Office. If you know your party's extension..."*

"Oh my God!" Ana reached over and pushed *end*.

"Why'd you do that? Don't you want to find out who the guy is?"

"I'm supposed to be dead. *Sylvie's* dead and *I've* got her phone and her ID. You want me to talk to the cops? They'll arrest me. And I've got a record!"

Courtney, unsteady on her feet, draped an arm around Ana's shoulders. "Hey, I do, too. Only mine went platinum," she giggled.

Ana pushed her away. "Damn it, I'm in trouble, Courtney. I need help. And *you*, you're drunk." She began to pace. "Guess I have no choice. Tomorrow, I've got to get word to my father."

CHAPTER TWELVE

Holding her head down to avoid the rain of ash whipped up by sudden Santa Ana gusts, Sammy hurried inside the six-story L.A. Department of Building and Safety the moment the security guard unlocked the front door. She'd crept out of her apartment an hour before, careful not to wake Pappajohn. A part of her was grateful for the delay. She didn't know how he'd take the news that Ana might have been murdered.

"You're an early bird," the guard at the main entrance said. At half past seven, she was the only one waiting to pass through the metal detector. Holidays and fires obviously made for a slow day.

"Looking for worms," Sammy replied, then asked for directions to *Permits*.

"One ten. First floor."

Sammy located the room at the end of the hall and went in. A heavyset, older woman with a faint mustache hunched over her computer behind the long counter. The name tag on her desk said "Ethel Fitzgerald." The other two desks were unoccupied.

"Sorry to bother you. Ms. Fitzgerald."

At the sound of her name, Ethel looked up. "Yes?"

"I'm looking for information on the Canyon City renovation project."

"What kind of information?"

"Well, I'd like to know if the renovation had actually started, when the contractor got the permits approved. That sort of thing."

Ethel eyed her with suspicion. "And you are?"

"I'm an investigative reporter." Sammy opened her purse and pulled out her press ID. "Do you listen to KPCF?" she asked, producing a charming smile. "I have a talk show. 'Sammy Greene on the L.A. Scene.' Midnight to three."

"That's a leftie station." Ethel wasn't impressed. "And I'm asleep by nine."

"Sounds like a wise choice," Sammy began, as her eyes caught the rosary beads sticking out from a pile of papers on Ethel's desk. "I just have to say that KPCF owes so much to the Catholic Charities of Los Angeles for their donations of food and clothing for the homeless tent city survivors. So many lost everything they had with the tower's collapse."

"What a horrible accident. All those poor people. May God save their souls," Ethel agreed, her features softening. "I give to Catholic Charities every year, you know."

"L.A. has its own Mother Teresas, that's for sure. We are so grateful."

Smiling now, Ethel turned to her computer. "You wanted to know if the tower renovation had been started?"

"I was told that it hadn't, but I did see scaffolding there."

"Let me check." Ethel pressed a few keys on her computer. "The main City Hall building was approved in July ninety-eight. Construction was supposed to start in January ninety-nine. But you wanted the tower, right?"

Sammy nodded as Ethel continued to search.

"Seismic retrofit. That's a totally different application. Here we go. Number CC000102453. I'll need to go in the back for the file." She pushed herself away from her desk and headed for an exit at the far end of the room, returning several minutes later with a thick legal-sized manila folder. "Canyon City Hall tower renovation." She laid the folder on one of the unoccupied desks and gestured for Sammy to have a seat.

Sammy watched Ethel settle into her chair and resume typing before she sat down at the empty desk and began thumbing through the file. The initial project permit request was dated September 23. The form listed Greene Progress, LLC as the general contractor and Newport Savings & Loan as the construction lender. She pulled out her notebook to jot down the bank name and address in Newport Beach, Orange County, wondering if there might be a Prescott connection. Didn't her father say that the congressman helped with the financing?

Page after page of construction plans and multiple permit forms. Demolition, electrical, mechanical, plumbing, roofing, sandblasting. The specifications meant nothing to Sammy. She was looking for something, anything that might jump out at her. Finally, she found one inspection report labeled SEISMIC CODES AND PROVISIONS. Language about adequacy of tower stability. Two ruptures in structure. Request for additional plans to stabilize with active seismic control system. Sammy searched for the inspector's name, but where the signature should have been, there was only an APPROVED stamp and date: November 23. She flipped through the file two more times, but could find no evidence that additional plans had been submitted.

"Excuse me. Ms. Fitzgerald?"

"Yes?"

"It looks as though the project was approved in two months. Is that typical?"

"Not for a complex project like the City Hall renovation. Permits and plan checks through normal city bureaucracy could easily take three times as long."

"So how do you go from six months to two?"

Ethel's long silence along with the troubled look on her face suggested she was waging some internal conflict. Though they were alone in the room, Ethel did a one-eigthy to make sure no one might be listening, then spoke, her voice barely above a whisper. "Connections."

"Excuse me?"

"Case Management. It's a little known unit set up two years ago to fast-track projects that are supposed to benefit the city."

"I guess the Canyon City City Hall buildings would qualify."

"Maybe," Ethel said with a smirk. "But after twenty years in this office, I can tell you that's not always how it works."

"What do you mean?"

Her eyes narrowed. "You won't quote me?"

"This is strictly off the record."

Ethel took a deep breath and lowered her voice again. "No standards. If you checked whose projects get expedited through the Case Management Unit, it's always the contractors with political connections."

Like Greene Progress.

"By sidestepping the usual permit process, these big developers avoid delays that could cost them millions," Ethel added.

"Was the Canyon City renovation project tracked through that unit?"

"You'd have to talk with Lawrence Graves. He's head of the Case Management Unit. He'll be back from vacation next week. Third floor, room three seventeen."

Graves? Why did that name sound familiar? Sammy took out her notebook and jotted it down, then handed the folder back to Ms. Fitzgerald. "Anything else you can tell me?"

Ethel put a finger up to her lips. "Don't let him know you're a reporter."

As soon as Sammy stepped into her car, her phone rang. It was Vito with news about Prescott.

"You were right, kid. But I really had to dig for this one. Around a year ago there was buzz on the wires about a hotel collapse in Orange County. That's what you probably remembered. Seems the congressman was a major investor in the project through a local savings and loan. Original plans called for a brand-new luxury hotel on the site, but the Orange County commissioners declared it a historic landmark and refused to allow a complete tear down. Somehow during the renovation, the whole thing just fell down like a bunch of LEGOs. The DA started a criminal investigation into the collapse, citing possible negligence, but it got dropped. The final report ended up calling it accidental and the story died. Prescott was off the hook."

"How convenient," Sammy said. And how coincidental. Two buildings Prescott was involved with had literally collapsed.

"By the way," Vito added, "the general contractor was Greene Progress. Didn't you say your father was in real estate? Any relation?"

"Distant," Sammy said, cringing. "Why'd the DA drop the investigation? Are we talking hush money?"

It sounded as if Vito was shuffling papers. "Nope. Marshall Taylor, age fifty-six, died in a car accident last February in the San Joaquin Hills, on Route Seventy-three. Seven twenty-six p.m., it says here. Dark, foggy, and rainy. Visibility was poor. Seems an eighteen-wheeler was going very slowly and the DA couldn't stop in time. Killed instantly. Anyway, nothing came out on Prescott. Or this *distant* relative of yours."

Sammy took a moment to gather her thoughts. Too many coincidences. Too many connections. She finally said, "Thanks, Vito. You've been incredibly helpful. As always."

"You going to follow up on this?"

"Of course," she said. "I'm a reporter first." *And a daughter second*, Sammy thought when she'd ended the conversation. With one eye on the road, she scrolled down her address book and speed dialed Susan's Orange County number.

Pappajohn's call to the funeral home had been heartrending, reviving painful memories of saying goodbye to Effie years ago. Hard enough to bury your wife. You were not supposed to bury your children.

The call to Eleni would be just as difficult. His sister had doted on Ana as a child. He dreaded telling his only surviving relative the horrible news of Ana's death. Sitting at Sammy's bedroom desk, his hand hovered over the phone before he decided to check e-mail.

Staring at the computer, the black monitor reflected his haggard features with a ghostlike distortion.

It had been years since he'd bought his first Apple IIe. Computers now were half the size and had a thousand times the capabilities. As compared to aging, old aficionados like himself who were twice the size and had half the capabilities of fifteen years before.

Still, his IT buddy Keith McKay of Pueblo Software Systems had considered Pappajohn's skills sharp enough to hire him as part-time consultant on Y2K preparations in Boston. Pappajohn's income in the last six months had far surpassed what he'd earned in eight years as campus cop at Ellsford University. He'd even begun teaching Eleni basic computer skills, after convincing her that e-mails could save a fortune in long-distance calls from Greece. Now he wondered if she might have sent an online holiday message.

Ignoring his depressing reflection, he pressed the keyboard and the screen whirred to life. He clicked open the Eudora icon and entered the data for his own e-mail account, then downloaded his accumulated messages, cursing the spam clogging his in-box. Sure enough, scrolling through the queue he found a note from Eleni wishing him a Merry Christmas and wondering why he hadn't called.

He allowed himself a small smile. Guess the tutoring *had* worked. But the idea of having to answer her renewed his pain. Should he tell her he was in Los Angeles? And why? Pappajohn rested his fingers in his lap. Finally, he typed a short reply, assuring her that he was fine, promising to write more in a day or two, and congratulating her on her computer skills. Ana's passing was one piece of news that should not be delivered online. Best to finish his good-byes to his daughter here, then consider a flight to Athens to tell Eleni in person and mourn by her side. With no one left for him in the U.S., he might just move there himself.

About to log off, he spotted a new e-mail wedged between the spam. At first the sender didn't register. Then, the ID nearly took his breath away: `AnaP, December 24.`

His hand shook as he clicked it open.

```
Dear Baba. Don't worry, I'm okay. I've been
clean for over a year. I have more news. I'll
try to get in touch as soon as I can. Merry
Christmas.
```

```
                              Love, Ana
```

He stared at the screen, his stomach churning, his body numb. Like a message from a world beyond, his daughter's words taunted him from the Internet ether.

I'm okay. Love, Ana.

But she was not okay. His precious Ana was gone forever. He'd lost the chance to make amends for his stubbornness, his stupidity, to tell her that he loved her too. He'd buried his sorrow deep within him to get through the day, but now it surfaced like a gusher of grief.

"Too late." he said, his eyes welling with tears.

"Too late for what?" Sammy's voice came from the open doorway.

"Just checking e-mail," Pappajohn's voice quavered, "and I...I found one from Ana."

With a sharp intake of breath, Sammy raced over to the desk. She rested a hand on Pappajohn's shoulder in a gesture of comfort, at the same time glancing at the open message. "My God."

"Yes, it's—"

"Wait a sec." Leaning over him, Sammy grabbed the mouse and scrolled up to the date. "This can't be right. December 24."

"Must have written it sometime after midnight, just before she—"

"Not the date. Look at the time. Ten fifty-five a.m."

Pappajohn squinted at the figures.

"That's in the morning, hours later. Ana was already—" Sammy stopped herself before saying the word *dead*.

Pappajohn and Sammy turned to each other, in shock.

"Come on, Aunt Eleni. Pick up!" Ana's voice reflected growing agitation. It was the third time in a few hours she'd dialed the Massachusetts number. She had to get word to her father. Eleni would know how to reach him. Right now she didn't care what Gus thought of her. Teddy would be back in L.A. in a few days. Ana needed her father's help to keep him safe from Kaye.

"No voice mail?" Courtney's slurred words made it sound like 'voyshmail.'

Ana snapped her cell shut and shook her head. "Aunt Eleni's not much on technology."

Courtney shrugged. "How about e-mail? Now that power's back, I could see if my modem's working."

"I don't think she's ever even been on a computer. Besides, I already sent my father an e-mail." She looked at Courtney and her face dissolved into tears. "Teddy's coming back on Thursday. The police think I'm dead and Kaye wants to kill me. What am I going to do?"

"There's got to be an answer," Sammy declared. "When I was at the TV network, e-mail went down one day. When it came back up, all the e-mails had the same date and time. Maybe something like that happened."

"It's the simplest explanation," Pappajohn said.

"Could the discrepancy be some virus related to Y2K?" It was a question Sammy figured Pappajohn could answer since she knew he was something of an amateur hacker. His computer skills had saved her life years ago at Ellsford University.

Pappajohn shook his head. "Not likely. This whole Y2K panic is just trumped up hoo-hah. A bonanza for IT companies. Last summer I actually got work consulting in computer security." He forced a smile. "Guess they needed us geezers who know how to work the old machines."

"I'll lay odds this Y2K stuff is all about the election. Give the people something to fear, and they'll vote for God, guns, and Republicans," Sammy said. "It's certainly scaring the callers on my show." She half expected the conservative Pappajohn to come back with a snappy retort, but he didn't seem to be listening. The lines in his forehead were deeply furrowed, as if he was trying to capture a thought.

"Okay, then how *do* you explain it?" she asked. The difference between Ana's time of death in the ME report and an e-mail supposedly sent by Ana hours later. If not a virus or a computer glitch, what did it mean? Sammy had no idea. But something certainly wasn't kosher.

Pappajohn's gaze drifted to the ceiling for a long beat, then turned to her. "I honestly don't know. Unless there's modems in heaven, it's either a software bug or a cruel prank." He checked his watch. "It's afternoon in Boston. My buddy Keith McKay at Pueblo Software Systems may still be in the office. By tracing back the ISP and IDing the IP address, he can identify which computer sent this message. And if this *was* a date error, Keith will be able to tell that too."

"If not?"

"Then I want to talk to whoever's pretending to be Ana."

Sammy sat on the edge of her bed, her expression somber, wondering how to word the additional shocking news she had to relay. "Did you happen to catch my show last night?"

"Only the first hour." Pappajohn sat up straight, stretching his legs. "Didn't quite have the energy, honestly." He yawned. "Got seven hours sleep. That's a record since, uh, Ana—"

"Then you didn't hear?"

"Hear what?" Pappajohn frowned. "Is your producer okay?"

"Yeah, the guy's pretty awesome. Came and worked my show last night." Sammy clasped and unclasped her hands. "You remember Reed. My boy—ex-boyfriend? He called at the station around two," she finally began. "I'd asked him to get the preliminary autopsy report and compare it to the evaluation at LAU Med."

"And?" Pappajohn pressed, not chiding her for violating protocol.

"I'm so sorry, Gus. The autopsy record doesn't mention the jaw injuries the resident noted on the police report and the chart. Or the loosened teeth, or the cuts on the inside of Ana's mouth. One of the molars actually penetrated her cheek and Reed thinks—"

"Somebody belted her," Pappajohn finished. "You're saying she was murdered?"

Sammy hesitated, avoiding eye contact. "It's possible. Otherwise, why bother to whitewash the autopsy report?"

Pappajohn sat staring at his hands, his expression grim.

"And then there's the tox screen."

Pappajohn looked up at Sammy. "Drugs?"

"Afraid so. Positive for cocaine and Ecstasy." She couldn't miss the look of pain that flashed across Pappajohn's face. Their eyes were drawn to Ana's message on the computer screen.

```
I've been clean for over a year.
```

"Rehab is a crock," Pappajohn said as he picked up the phone and dialed Boston. "Tox screens don't lie, people do."

Reed placed the stethoscope in his ears and pressed MUTE on the TV remote. "Can't hear over the news," he said, resting the diaphragm on Prescott's chest and bending over to listen to his heartbeat.

"Is my husband okay?" Julia asked when Reed stood up again. He knew she'd been spending the better part of every day sitting on the couch in the suite, to all appearances the doting wife.

"If the latest labs are normal, we plan to send him home this afternoon."

"Not soon enough." Prescott grabbed the remote and revved up the volume. "Hey, look, Jules, they're replaying the statement I taped yesterday." He pointed to the wall-mounted screen. "Not bad looking for a man in a hospital bed, wouldn't you say, honey?"

As head of the House Armed Services Committee, I, like all of us in our party, take Y2K threats to our country and our citizens very seriously—"

"Well done, Neil. You said what had to be said."

Reed wondered if he imagined the hint of bitterness in her voice. The betrayal of unhappiness. The unhappiness of betrayal. Why *would* such an attractive and independently wealthy woman stay with a man who'd cheated on her? Why had his mother stayed with his father? Fear perhaps? The fear of loss? For other women like Sammy the fear of loss led them to leave rather than risk abandonment. To strike out on their own because there was no trust given to lose.

"Yet another victim in the Canyon City tower collapse," the news anchor now reported. "Although an official investigation has not begun, last night one of our local radio talk show hosts suggested this horrible accident might have been prevented. Sammy Greene on the L.A. Scene named U.S. Congressman Neil Prescott—"

"What the—?" A chorus of monitors began beeping as Prescott's face contorted into a spasm of agony. He made a fist across his chest and gasped, "Hurts."

Two nurses rushed in wheeling a crash cart.

"What's happening?" Julia cried, jumping up from the couch.

Reed squinted at the EKG monitor. The S-T changes indicated myocardial ischemia. He placed a nasal cannula in Prescott's nose and attached the other end to the wall oxygen unit. "Morphine IV, stat!" he ordered one nurse. "Get Dr. Bishop! He's down the hall," he directed the other.

"We may need to do another angioplasty, Mr. Prescott," he said, forcing a calm tone. "Your blood vessels have gone into spasm again."

"Oh, my God." Julia sat down, her face ashen. "Another heart attack?"

Within seconds, Bishop ran in, listened to Reed's report, and nodded. "We'll take care of him, Julia. Don't worry."

Prescott grunted through his pain, "No! Not a heart attack! Can't! Have to go home!"

No one seemed to be listening as two orderlies arrived to move his bed from the room toward the elevators.

Sammy marched into the West L.A. precinct and found De'andray buried in papers at his desk.

"Not you again!" the detective groaned, looking up. "One of these days I'd like to get out of here before noon."

"Not until my daughter's murder is investigated," Pappajohn boomed from the doorway.

"Gus," whispered Sammy, aware that the roomful of police officers were all staring.

"I don't give a damn," he growled, as he headed for De'andray. "I've had enough. Ana may have been a working girl, but she had a father. A father who wants to know who beat her up and left her to die alone in the street."

De'andray stood up to his full six-foot-two height, towering over both Sammy and Pappajohn. "How about we take this private?" Without waiting for assent, he led them into a conference room whose walls and whiteboards were decorated with crime-scene photos and mug shots. No pictures of Ana anywhere, Sammy noted, with a measure of puzzlement and relief.

De'andray opened the folder he'd carried in with him and removed a fax. "The autopsy report. Just came in this morning." He tossed it onto the table, took a seat, and pointed to two chairs on the opposite side.

Pappajohn picked up the document while Sammy drew her own chair closer so she could read over his shoulder. As Reed had relayed to her, the report showed no mention of injuries beyond the frontal skull fracture that had supposedly knocked Ana out.

De'andray leaned back and shrugged his shoulders. "Nothing suggesting murder there."

Sammy shook her head. "We know the ER doctor had concerns about a possible beating. That's why she made a police report. Yet the injuries documented in Ana's ER chart aren't in this autopsy report." She grabbed her notebook from her purse and flipped it open. "Nothing about jaw looseness, teeth embedded in the cheek, fracture of the, um, xylophonic arch." She wasn't sure she'd gotten all the terms Reed had mentioned exactly right, but her point was to highlight the discrepancy.

De'andray's dark eyes narrowed. "How did *you* happen to see the ER chart?"

"I didn't see it." Sammy was reluctant to implicate Reed. "I … uh … my source is reliable."

"Your source! You think 'cause you have a damn radio talk show, you're a detective? Offering a reward for leads to a possible suspect? You're pushin' it, honey. We don't cotton to vigilantes in *this* part of the West. Even if it's all to boost your ratings."

"Now, hold on," Sammy sputtered. "I'm an investigative reporter, and, I know the law. According to the fourth amendment, I have a right to investigate. Including murder."

"Better put the word *alleged* in your dictionary then, or you may need a lawyer when you're hit with a libel charge." De'andray turned to Pappajohn, "And *you*. You used to be a cop. You should know better. We can't have civilians running around town playing policeman. The medical examiner says right here," he tapped the autopsy report, "cause of death was accidental. Case closed."

"No, sir!" Pappajohn banged his fist on the table. "Sammy's right. Those findings reported by the ER doctor were missing from the ME's version. Damn well sounds like a cover-up to me!"

De'andray's deep exhalation was an obvious display of frustration. "Why? Why would he go to all that trouble just for a—" he didn't finish his sentence.

"Say it!" Pappajohn shouted, jumping out of his chair. "For a *prostitute*. Say it!" He rose and strode toward De'andray, fists clenched.

The door opened and Ortego stepped in between them. Nodding toward the hallway, he gestured at De'andray. "Call for you on line two."

De'andray seemed about to speak, then stood and walked out without a word.

Ortego turned to Pappajohn. "Sorry my partner upset you. He's been pulling extra duty for a week now with the fires and the homeless and all. His wife's pissed that he's not around for the holidays. You know how that goes."

"Yeah, I do." Pappajohn sat down again.

"Maybe I can help," Ortego said gently, taking the seat his partner had vacated. "How 'bout you tell me what's going on."

Sammy quickly itemized the disparities between the two examinations they'd discovered.

Ortego frowned. "That does sound strange. Honestly, though, the ER doctor never said anything to me about loose teeth. Or that xylophone thing you said."

"Then why call you in the first place?" Sammy asked. It wasn't routine for police to be called in on accidental deaths.

Ortego nodded. "I hear your concerns. Did she knock herself out and die in the flames? Or did she die first from something else, and then get burned? Wasn't a question the docs in the ER or the police were qualified to answer. Frankly, after the fire did its work, I don't think anybody really could. In the end, it's the ME's report we have to rely on."

Pappajohn clasped his hands tightly in his lap. Ortego reached over and gave his arm a comforting squeeze. "We're all really sorry. I appreciate what you're going through. But, as a fellow cop, you know what you're asking is almost impossible. We've searched the site where she was found and the nearby area. We've interviewed the kids who called it in. We've talked to her doctors. We got a damn fast report from the ME. There's nothing left roadside for us to gather. Everything was burned out by the fires. Only residual drainage in that gully kept her from dying on site."

Pappajohn remained stone-faced and silent.

"Tell you what, "Ortego said. "I'll give, uh—" he turned the autopsy report over, "Dr. Gharani a call. See if he can reexamine your daughter's face and teeth. Just in case he did miss something. You never know." He rose from his seat, indicating the meeting was over.

Pappajohn stood and shook his hand. "Appreciate that, Detective."

"Emilio."

Pappajohn nodded.

"Good, then, Gus." Ortego began ushering them through the precinct.

"Oh, one more thing," Pappajohn said when they'd reached the exit. "Were you able to locate the roommate?"

"APB's been out for two days, but nada." Ortego threw up his arms. "Vanished into thin air. Not a clue." He turned to Sammy with a disapproving glance. "In the meantime, senorita, you don't have to do our job for us. We'll find her. Okay?"

Sammy merely smiled. *Sometimes investigative reporters could open doors closed to the police*, she thought. Like the cabbie. If he panned out, she'd send him Ortego's way. If not, no harm, no foul. No point in further provoking De'andray. Instead, she waved good-bye and watched Ortego disappear back inside.

"So, what do you think?" she asked Pappajohn as they walked to the car.

Pappajohn took a long deep breath and then stared at her, his expression transformed from one of resigned despair to fierce determination. "They're right. They *should* be able to do their job. But I'll be damned if that'll stop me from doing mine. I have to know if Ana was killed. If Dr. Gharani's going to take a closer look, he's going to do it with me standing right there beside him."

"What's the name again?"

The caller sounded impatient. "Anastasia Pappajohn. We don't know the kid's name. First foster placement through Social Services should be in nineteen ninety-five. Just check your computer."

"As soon as the department servers are up again. They're doing the Y2K refit this week," the clerk explained.

"No paper records at all?"

"Sure, but I can't get into the file room. The Omni lock to the place is on the computer system. I'll have to ask my supervisor for a special key."

"Get him on the phone. I'm sure he'll be happy to help the police"

"Can't. He's in Hawaii til Thursday. Better call early. We'll have to go through a stack of card files. If this Anastasia's anything like our typical clients, she's probably moved a lot since ninety-five. Without those welfare checks coming in any more, they keep getting evicted. It's awful, really. We have to go out and pick up their kids, find foster homes, go to court and—hello? Officer? Are you there?" the clerk shouted into the receiver,

But the connection was broken, the caller having long ago hung up.

With a short stop for lunch, it was a little past two p.m. when Sammy turned into the parking lot at the L.A. County morgue. Pappajohn had called the funeral home and asked to delay Ana's pickup until the next day, hoping Dr. Gharani could reopen the autopsy and investigate their concerns. Pappajohn didn't wait for Sammy before heading down the stairs to the basement level.

An Indian woman in a white coat over a colorful sari stopped them in the hall. Sammy guessed the doctor was in her mid-thirties. Probably just out of residency. "Sorry sir, the public's not allowed down here."

"I have an appointment with Dr. Gharani," Pappajohn told her.

"The doctor was called out this morning. Some kind of family emergency."

"Well, maybe you can help me," Pappajohn read her name tag, "Dr. Mehta." He quickly told her why he'd come, that he needed to have someone in the ME's office reexamine the body.

"I'm pretty new here. I—"

"Please, doctor. Ana was my only child. If she was murdered, I have to know."

His appeal had the desired effect. "Okay, have a seat in here," she said ushering them into a tiny cubicle off the sterile hallway. "Let me see what I can find out."

Less than five minutes later, Dr. Mehta returned with the same African-American clerk who'd helped them before. Instead of a smile, now she appeared anxious. "Mr. Pappajohn, I don't understand."

"Understand what?" Pappajohn asked, rising.

"You called to have your daughter cremated. That's what Dr. Gh—"

"Cremated?" he screamed, slapping his forehead with his hands. *"The-eh mou! Ochi! Einai amartia!"*

Sammy took Pappajohn's hand and gently urged him into the chair. Shaking his head and muttering in Greek, he finally looked up, his expression pure anguish, his face wet with tears. "You don't understand. We don't cremate in the Greek Orthodox Church. The body is God's creation and cannot be burned. It's a mortal sin!"

Clearly distraught herself, the clerk apologized. "We're so very sorry. We didn't know that. Dr. Gharani said he spoke to you."

"I would never consent to cremation!" Pappajohn insisted. "And I haven't spoken to Gharani since I was here last week." Pappajohn buried his face in his hands. "I'd hoped Ana's path to heaven would be free of struggle."

Sammy turned to the two women. "Give us Dr. Gharani's address. We've got to find out how this horrible mistake happened." It was as much demand as request. How much more should Gus have to endure?

The clerk chewed her lip. "I don't have his address. Only his emergency number. I could call and see if you could talk to him."

"I have his address and his cell phone number," Dr. Mehta interjected, her eyes moist at the sight of Pappajohn. She raised a hand at the clerk. "I know it's not protocol, but I respect traditions. And this man needs to find out why Dr. Gharani didn't."

"Okay that should do it." Bishop quickly deflated the balloon in Prescott's right coronary, removing it along with the catheter. "No muscle damage. Looks like our patient dodged another bullet." He slipped off his gloves, putting one over the other, and tossed them neatly into the trash bucket.

Reed found himself exhaling a deep breath. Throughout the thirty-five-minute procedure, he'd been second guessing his actions the night Prescott had come into the ER. Between little sleep and his shock at hearing Sammy's voice after so much time, he wondered if he'd been too distracted, perhaps had missed something. "That artery was barely occluded when I did the original angio," he stammered.

Michelle, who'd been allowed to observe the procedure, looked puzzled. An unwritten rule residents all learned early was not to call attention to mistakes. However, Bishop's mentoring had taught Reed that owning up to errors produced better patient outcomes, even if one's reputation lost a bit of shine.

Expecting criticism, Reed was surprised that Bishop merely nodded. "Obviously flipped another clot. Happens more than you know." He strode over to the door and pulled off his mask and surgical gown "All yours, Dr. Wyndham. I've got to run to an Emergency Operations committee meeting. Hang a heparin drip and get him back to CCU. Looks like he won't be going home til after Y2K."

"No, Op...Y..." Prescott muttered, shaking his head.."Home. Friday. Y2..."

"He's coming out of it," Bishop said. "Let's keep him sedated for the next twelve to twenty-four hours. And no TV," he added as he left the procedure room.

Twenty minutes later with Prescott settled in the CCU and Michelle headed back to the ward, Reed pressed the button for the express elevator down to the first floor, lost in thought. Prescott's mumbling had reminded him of the conversation he'd overheard the other night outside the VIP suite between Prescott and another man. Reed hadn't recognized the voice then and he never saw the man's face. But he had caught some of of his words.

Op ...Y...Home, Friday...Y2.

Thinking back, Reed was certain the man had mentioned Prescott getting discharged before Friday and something about an Operation Y2K.

Thick clouds of smoke blowing south from the Cahuenga Pass made the stop-and-go freeway traffic unbearable, so Sammy decided to exit and take Sunset Boulevard to the medical examiner's home. For her, the long thoroughfare that cut a twisted swatch from downtown's Olvera Street Latino district westward to the Pacific near Malibu and its lavish ocean view villas was a study in contrasts that no words could describe. She'd traveled it only once since she'd come to live here, amazed by the changing landscapes along the winding boulevard's twenty or so miles.

Today her route ended in West Hollywood, a diverse region of apartments, homes, restaurants, and boutiques. Rich and not so rich mingled in its inclusive borders that were much more welcoming for Sammy than the opulent mansions and wide, treelined avenues of Beverly Hills or Bel Air. To Sammy, those neighborhoods looked plastic, like an upscale Main Street at Disneyland.

In West Hollywood, the character was more eccentric. Many of the homes were vintage bungalows from the 1920s, others were modern and gleaming with glass and steel. The streets, even on a smoky, windy day like today, were filled with seniors and young families, refugees from Europe and the Middle East, straights and gays. A careful observer would note a polyglot of languages, an assortment of lifestyles. Almost like Sammy's memories of Brooklyn in her childhood.

Sammy drove by several trendy-looking shops and nightspots before she found Westbourne Drive. Slowing the car, she rolled down her window to stop a couple of handsome men stylishly dressed in muscle shirts and low-cut jeans strolling arm in arm. Both wore paper face masks, presumably as protection against the effects of the smoky air. "We're looking for 3148. Around here?"

They pointed toward the end of the block.

Sammy parked in front of a weather-beaten bungalow. The rusty mailbox bore a hand-printed *Gharani*. The lawn displayed a prominent *For Sale* sign. *This won't sell anytime soon*, Sammy speculated, eyeing the chipped paint and loose shingles of the tiny house.

Sammy glanced at Pappajohn. On the surface he appeared composed, but she had little doubt he was holding back his fury. Both she and Pappajohn were now convinced Gharani possessed the key to the mystery of Ana's death. Otherwise, why bother to whitewash the autopsy, then eliminate all evidence that might prove his daughter was murdered? "Ready?"

Pappajohn nodded.

They got out of the car and walked over the cracked pathway to the front of the house. Sammy searched for a bell, but saw only a few ragged wires sticking out of a hole by the door. She knocked several times.

No answer.

Pappajohn tried rapping more loudly, then banging with his bulky fist. Still no response. They peeked through the front windows, but the house inside was dark. And there was no sign of activity in the yard.

Pappajohn waved at Sammy, then took off around the house. A few minutes later, he returned, shaking his head. "Looks like no one's home."

"The clerk said he had some kind of emergency. Maybe we should call," suggested Sammy, pulling out her phone. Shortly after punching in the first number, a traditional ring trilled from the house. Sammy let the phone ring for several minutes before giving up. Frustrated, she tried Gharani's cell. After a few rings, she snapped her phone shut. "Not in service at this time."

"I'll wait," Pappajohn said tersely.

"I know how you feel, Gus, but, Gharani could be gone for a long time. Even out of town." She sighed. "I'd stay here with you, but I promised my stepmother I'd meet her for dinner in Orange County. If the traffic earlier was a hint of rush hour, I'll just have time to drop you off at home and hit the road."

"Okay, but we're coming back tomorrow," Pappapjohn said, following her to the car.

As they drove off, neither noticed the black Lincoln parked at the other end of the block whose tinted windows hid the two men who'd been following them all day.

•   •   •

Ignoring the plumes of smoke rising from the hills outside his panoramic window, Miller sat at his desk, concentrating, meticulously going over every phase of the operation, making sure there were no loopholes, nothing that could go wrong. His thoughts were interrupted by the buzz of his phone.

"We've found the girl. MILSTAR traced her to a location in Malibu. We've ID'd the house as belonging to a Courtney Phillips."

"Well, I'll be damned," Miller said, genuinely surprised.

"Beg your pardon, sir?"

"You boys close?"

"ETA twenty minutes, unless we hit road closures. You want us to bring them in?"

"Yes, indeedy. That I do." Miller's voice dropped several decibels. "And here's how it's going to go down."

Sammy walked into the living room just as Pappajohn was hanging up the phone. She'd only had time for a quick shower, but she had to get the stink of the smoke and the morgue out of her hair. A speedy blow-dry, a long sleeved blouse, and a clean pair of jeans, and she was ready for her reunion with Susan.

Pappajohn sat staring at his hands, his expression frozen in sadness. "The priest says we could do a modified service next week." Though his voice was soft, Pappajohn's tight fists betrayed his anger. "So at least her soul can rest in peace."

Sammy nodded. She knew how hard it had been for Pappajohn to make that call.

"But, it's still not..." Pappajohn struggled for the word. "Kosher."

Despite the pressure of her ticking clock, Sammy sat down on the edge of the couch beside him. "I've never been terribly religious, but I've always believed that if there is a God, he'd understand and welcome people to heaven who tried their best."

"I appreciate the thought, but neither Ana nor I fit in that group. We both screwed up. And God's not giving us a second chance." He looked at Sammy. "Does your God believe in regret?"

"You kidding? We've got a whole day for it. Yom Kippur. The Day of Atonement. We've got enough guilt to work on for a lifetime."

Sammy was glad to see a glimmer of a smile. "You going to be okay tonight?"

"Yeah. Go see your stepmother. I'll be fine. Might even be a good time to catch up with my friend, Keith. See if he's got any information to help."

Sammy stood and raised a finger. "Speaking of, I finally connected with the cab driver who claims he drove Sylvie the night of the fire."

"And?" Pappajohn prompted.

"I made a date to meet him when he gets off shift at seven tomorrow. I want to show him Sylvie's picture. See if he can identify her."

"I'm coming with you."

"Of course," Sammy said, grabbing her purse. Feeling a rush of affection for this big man who'd lost so much, she gave him a quick peck on the cheek. "There's roast chicken in the fridge. Got it fresh from Whole Foods Market this morning on the way back from Building and Safety. Promise me you'll eat and get some rest."

"Promise me you'll drive safely. *Kai ta matia sou thekatessera.*

Sammy raised an eyebrow.

"Old Greek expression. Meaning *make your eyes fourteen.* In other words, watch your back."

Sammy winked. "Always do." She closed and locked the door behind her, warmed by Pappajohn's paternal warning and wishing her own father would have been as demonstrative.

As she slid into her car, Sammy shook her head. Pipe dream. Jeffrey Greene had never cared about anyone other than himself.

Waking from an alcohol-induced nap, Courtney discovered the lights dimmed, the TV on MUTE, and Ana staring at herself in the bedroom mirror.

"Shee-it, girl. What's with the Elvira hair?"

"I found a bottle of Revlon Midnight Black under the sink."

"I can see that. But Halloween was last month."

"It's not far from my natural color." Ana turned to face her, "I want Teddy to recognize me—you know, before—Besides, everyone's looking for a blonde."

Courtney noted her own unkempt hair. "Shame I don't have honey blonde dye. I've got enough people chasing *me*." She pulled a few straggly strands from her face. "Or I could shave it off."

"You're not *that* drunk," Ana said. "And," her voice softened, "I'm glad."

"I'm not," Courtney muttered, though she didn't reach for the nearly empty bottle of brandy.

A loud buzz made them both jump.

"What's that?" Ana cried.

Courtney frowned. "Intercom. I'm not expecting anybody."

"Whoever it is may not be here for you." Ana ran over to the window.

"Get away from there!" Courtney ordered in a whisper. "And keep quiet." She switched on a video screen mounted above her bed. "I have a security camera at the front gate."

"Malibu Patrol!" boomed the voice over the intercom. "Open up."

Courtney adjusted the picture. At five forty p.m. it was already dark outside, making it difficult to see details, but the fact that two stocky men dressed all in black stood at the entry was clear enough.

"Recognize them?"

Trembling, Ana shook her head.

"Open the gate, please. There's a mandatory evacuation of everyone in the area."

"No, I just heard the last report," Ana said, lowering her voice. "This area's still safe."

"We have orders to check every residence. This isn't voluntary. Open the gate!"

Staring at the video screen, Ana's eyes widened in fear, "Look, that one's got a gun!" The glint from the object in the man's hand suggested she was right.

"Okay, we have to improvise." Courtney pressed the intercom

speaker and affected a lazy drawl. "Sorry, officer. I was fast asleep. Can I help you all?"

While waiting for a response, Courtney grabbed a blonde wig from her closet and slipped on a pair of jeans and tennis shoes. "Take the Jazz drive and the copied disk," she told Ana while she tied her shoes.

"There's a fire, lady. You've got to evacuate. We'll escort you out. Open the gate."

Courtney flipped a switch on the wall panel sending bright arcs of light over the front of the mansion including the entry. Both men, built like prizefighters, were now clearly visible. And so were their guns.

"Hey!" One of them held a hand over his face as a shield from the blinding light. His partner whispered something that sounded enough like "Let's just shoot the damn lock open and get that Sylvie bitch" to make Ana panic. It took her every bit of self-control not to scream. She looked at Courtney, terrified. "We've got to get out of here!"

Courtney pushed in the speaker again and reprised her southern damsel. "Why you all just hold your horses, there. After I buzz you in, stay on the path to the house. I'll meet you at the front door." She opened the gate.

"Are you out of your mind?" Ana hissed.

In response, Courtney flipped off every light and dragged Ana from the bedroom. "Just follow my lead. I've got a plan."

"What do we do?"

"We're going to sneak out the back and run like hell!"

Susan was seated at a back booth of the Souplantation in the middle-class Orange County town of Costa Mesa when Sammy entered a little after seven. She returned Susan's wave and hurried over. "Sorry I'm late. The 405 was a parking lot."

"It's like that even without the fires." Susan stood and gave her a genuine hug, which the motherless child in Sammy happily reciprocated, momentarily transported back to her freshman summer when she'd last visited Susan *and* her Dad. It hadn't taken long then to realize it was her stepmother who'd wanted to forge a reconciliation, not Jeffrey.

Pulling back from the embrace, Sammy studied Susan. Though she still had the slim figure and lovely face that had once attracted her father, the new lines around Susan's eyes and mouth mirrored the wear and tear she'd been through the past six years. Unlike Trina, the trophy wife, who Sammy'd guessed, based on her photo, kept Beverly Hills plastic surgeons in business. "It's really good to see you again," Sammy said.

"And you look gorgeous! I love what you've done to your hair."

Unaccustomed to compliments about her appearance, Sammy merely blushed. "Should we get in line?" She pointed to patrons sliding trays along the soup and salad stations. Not the posh fare of Beverly Hills, this was a reasonably priced restaurant that catered to families. Lots of salads, muffins, pizza, and pasta. And the best clam chowder on the West Coast. Comfort food.

As they traveled through the line, making their selections, Sammy shared the reasons she'd ended up in L.A.

"It sure sounds as though you've landed on your feet," Susan said. "But that doesn't surprise me." She poured oil and vinegar dressing on the vegetables neatly arranged on her plate. "You know, my neighbor insisted I turn on your show. Said it was the best talk radio in town. I've been listening every night since. And," she laughed, "missing precious hours of sleep."

"Sorry."

"Nonsense. I couldn't be prouder of you." They'd reached the cashier. Susan told Sammy to put her wallet away. "Your father may not have been the most generous man, but he didn't leave me destitute. Besides, I made enough profit on the Encino ranch to buy a condo down here and still have a little money left to live on while I finish my degree at UC Irvine." She paid the tab and followed Sammy back to their table. "One more semester and I'll earn my MBA."

"Mazel tov."

"So," Susan began once they were both seated. "there was something you wanted to ask me?"

"There's a lot I've wanted to ask you," Sammy said. "Why don't I start with an easy one. Do you think my Dad has changed?"

Susan raised an eyebrow. "That's an easy one? What do you mean 'changed?'"

Sammy explained how after all these years—decades, actually—of showing no interest, Jeffrey had tracked her down at the station, insisting they meet. "Said he was sorry we'd never been close. That he really wants a relationship now."

Susan remained silent, but the way she lifted her other eyebrow seemed to echo Sammy's own surprise at Jeffrey's gesture.

"I just don't know if I can trust him," Sammy said. "It's not something I *have* to do."

Susan sat back. "Look, Sammy. Your father's not a bad man."

"But?"

Susan exhaled. "But, he's a man with certain . . ." She seemed to be searching for just the right word, finally settling on "challenges," then described how Jeffrey had been struggling with one failed business idea after the other when they'd first met in Los Angeles. Her solid skills as a CPA complemented his dynamic, larger-than-life enthusiasm, and, together, they built some successful investments. "Looking back, I often wonder about the attraction. Guess his energy and ambition was the aphrodisiac."

Susan took a sip of water. "When we married, I introduced Jeffrey to real estate. It was exciting back in the eighties. We could buy houses with little down, fix them up, then flip them—sell them—as their value soared.

"Unfortunately, what the experts say is true: 'what goes up must come down.' Jeffrey refused to believe me when I thought the market was too hot, that we ought to take our winnings and sit on the sidelines for a while. Instead, he started taking on bigger and bigger risk, leveraging real estate buys like a monopoly player.

"I got nervous. Told him I wouldn't go along. That really made him mad. I think he felt I was standing between him and his dreams of great wealth. That's when he started 'working late at the office,' going on 'business trips,' and hitting parties with 'investors' without me."

She lowered her voice as if masking her shame. "I never imagined he was cheating on me at first. When he'd come home smelling of other women's perfume, I actually believed he was wining and dining investors. The thought that it might be something more did cross my mind, but I rationalized, figuring that if he was having affairs, they meant nothing, that he needed to build his empire. And his self-esteem."

Susan summoned a tenuous smile. "Then he met Trina. She tried to put him into a few dirty deals I was sure would cause trouble with the real estate board or worse, but he went ahead anyway. That's when I said enough. The minute our divorce became final, Jeffrey married the woman."

"I'm really sorry."

"Don't be. I learned my lesson." She reached out and patted Sammy's hand. "And I got to have you in my life. I always wanted a daughter."

Sammy put down her fork and looked directly into her stepmother's eyes, "And I've always needed a mom."

They ate for several minutes, focusing on their food.

Finally, Sammy broke the silence. "Do you know anything about Neil Prescott?"

"The congressman?" Susan frowned. "He's an institution in his district. I'm certain you probably picked up a lot of buzz when you were in D.C."

"I gather he's not your cup of tea?"

"Not his politics," Susan replied. "Lower taxes, less government. But he does speak to a lot of voters in Orange County. This is a pretty conservative area."

"My father seems to be one of them."

"I'm afraid so. Jeffrey and Trina are among his biggest fund-raisers."

Sammy nodded. "I got that from searching the Internet. Lots of pictures of Dad and Prescott looking chummy." Sammy pushed some peas around her plate with her fork. "A hotel Dad's company was renovating collapsed about a year ago?"

"The Palacio Real. The old queen of Newport Beach," Susan said. "That was one of those crazy deals I was talking about. Jeffrey bought it anyway. Prescott arranged for financing through his brother-in-law's savings and loan. Frankly, if it hadn't been for the accident, Jeffrey would have lost his shirt. After the building collapsed, with FEMA funds and insurance, he was able to build the Montagne Olympus and turned a tidy profit. For a year's tuition, I can treat you to dinner there some time." She sighed. "But, it did buy Jeffrey his suite in Fox Plaza, and an estate on the Newport coast."

"I heard there was an investigation. The DA suspected something criminal?"

"That you'd have to ask your father," Susan said. "I will tell you this, if there's one man I definitely wouldn't trust, it's Neil Prescott."

Courtney slid open the glass doors facing the wide backyard and grabbed Ana's hand. "Run!" she shouted. With the lights off and the moon obscured by the fire's smoky haze, she knew they had cover. If they could reach the hill at the far edge of her property, they'd be okay.

Warm winds whistling past them could not dampen the loud curses of the two men as they stumbled in the darkness, trying to find the front path.

"They're going to kill us!" Ana panted from exertion and fear.

At a cluster of trees two-thirds of the way between the back of the house and the hill, Courtney signaled to hunch down to rest. "Just a little farther."

"What is?" Ana asked.

"The hill. I figure it's another fifty feet. When we get to the edge, there's a low wall and a steep path we'll have to manage. So be careful."

"I can't see a thing."

"Hold on to me."

They heard a bang followed by the sound of the front door being kicked in.

"Oh my God, Courtney, they're in the house."

Both girls watched the lights inside the mansion flip on. First the living room, then the bedrooms upstairs.

"What are we going to do?"

Without a word, Courtney pulled Ana up and, hand in hand, they sprinted toward the hill. They were within a few feet when the backyard floodlights burst on, exposing them.

"Jesus, they found the control panels. Hurry." Courtney pointed to a three-foot brick wall that bordered the hill.

Ana lifted one leg over, hoisted herself up to straddle the wall, then hopped down onto the first flat, narrow level of a steep terraced path on the other side.

Courtney was ready to take her turn when a chunk of brick exploded right beside her.

"They're shooting at us!"

Without looking back, Courtney put two hands on the wall, vaulting over it, and tumbling to the other side in a heap. "Duck!" she yelled as two more shots reverberated, sending pieces of brick in the air.

Ana dove head first onto the hard dirt.

"You okay?"

Ana pushed herself onto her knees, careful to stay huddled behind the wall. "I think so," she gasped. Except for a few scrapes on her head and arms, she seemed to be in one piece.

"Follow me," Courtney ordered. Using her arms as support, she slid on her backside down the first few steps of the terraced path until sure they couldn't be seen by the men who'd now found their way out of the house and could be heard bounding toward them. As soon as Ana reached the same level, they both stood and rushed down the remaining steps to the street below.

Breathless, Courtney whispered, "This is how I sneak onto the property, when I'm not supposed to be here. And this," she said pointing to a red Vespa parked nearby, "is our ticket out." She motioned for Ana to take a seat on the back of the scooter while she hurried to the side of the last step and flipped a switch, engulfing everything in total blackness.

A loud thud, high above them indicated that one of the men had tripped on the wall. His screams of pain were accompanied by dual curses.

Courtney inched her way over to the Vespa and jumped on. Turning the ignition key, she kicked down on the starter pedal until it coughed to life. "Hold on," she shouted as another volley of shots rang out. Without a backward glance, Courtney gunned the throttle, rocketing the scooter toward Pacific Coast Highway and south to Santa Monica, their pursuers far behind.

A half hour into her drive north on the 405, Sammy hit gale-force headwinds that blew drifts of thick smoke and cinders across her windshield, obscuring her view. The sluggish pace of the Tercel's old wipers only accentuated the problem. The fact that it was a moonless night didn't help either. The car's headlights illuminated no more than a few feet ahead, forcing her to slow to a crawl. Just like the time she'd driven a drunk Pappajohn home through a Vermont blizzard, except that this snow was black, not white.

When several cars passed her, she decided to move over to the safety of the farthest right lane. Even so, two fire trucks, sirens blaring, rushed by, nearly sideswiping her. *Where were they headed?* Five days and there seemed to be no let up to the outbreak of wildfires across the southland. The minute one blaze was extinguished, another took its place. Bel Air, the Hollywood Hills, Malibu, Topanga Canyon.

As much as Sammy wanted to rage at the LAPD's apparent indifference to investigating Ana's death, she knew the area's police and firefighting resources were strained to the limit. Even Reed was working overtime, caring for patients made sick by the fire's residue.

Sammy anxiously switched on the radio, hoping to catch updates, but the whine of wind hissing against her windows drowned out the news and she shut it off.

Leaning forward, she squinted into the night. Ahead the rear lights of the few cars appeared as ghostly halos in the gloom. Behind, there was only darkness. With the radio silent and the air filter closed to keep out the stench of smoke, she couldn't help feeling an eerie isolation in her four-wheel cocoon. Perhaps the callers to her show weren't so crazy after all when they imagined monsters in the night.

After fifteen minutes of tense driving, she spotted a road sign for her exit. CULVER BOULEVARD, TWO MILES. Thank God.

Glancing into her rearview mirror, she noticed a pair of bright headlights weaving in and out of the lanes behind her. Either the driver had trouble seeing the reflector lane markings or he was drunk. Either way, he was an accident waiting to happen and she was glad she'd be off the freeway soon.

A sudden gust buffeted the car with such ferocity that she had to wrestle the steering wheel not to get pulled out of her lane and lose control. "Shit!"

Struggling to stay within the faded white lines of the highway's right margin, Sammy didn't notice the headlights closing in. It wasn't until she felt the first bump that she checked her rearview mirror and saw a huge SUV emerge out of the ashy darkness like a phantom. The impact pressed her back against the seat.

What the—? Crazy L.A. drivers! Sammy rolled down her window to hurl a few choice words, but the SUV had retreated several car lengths behind.

Stunned, she watched as seconds later, the five-thousand-pound machine barreled forward, swerving into her lane, and shoving her car sideways, onto the freeway's shoulder. Despite the darkness, she sensed that she was dangerously close to the guardrail and the drop-off beyond.

Sammy screamed when the SUV slammed into her driver's side a third time. The son of a bitch was going to run her off the road. Frantic, she tried moving out of the giant vehicle's way. She could never hope to outrun the behemoth. And if she accelerated, she was likely to miss her exit. Her intended turnoff was barely visible through the gloom a few feet ahead. She jammed on the brakes when the SUV came up alongside yet again. Not expecting her to slow down, the Suburban passed her car and the exit.

Adrenalin pumping, Sammy jerked the steering wheel to the right, and swung onto the off-ramp. Alone for the next two miles, Sammy sped through the streets of Canyon City towards KPCF, checking the rearview mirror as she drove, but all she could see around her was the darkness, shielded by a curtain of ash.

By the time she reached the radio station, she'd convinced herself that while the driver had been crazy, it was more than a little paranoid to assume he'd been after her.

CHAPTER THIRTEEN

"I see what you mean," Sammy said to Jim, "the lines haven't stopped blinking." She waved away his offer of coffee and grabbed a bottled water. After her close call on the 405, she wouldn't need caffeine to stay alert tonight.

"Amazing what a ten-thousand-dollar reward will draw out of the tar pits," Jim returned. "Maybe I should put on a blonde wig and say *I'm Sylvie!*"

"You're too good looking," Sammy teased as she rolled her neck and shoulders to work off her tension. "If you could screen out the UFO people and the Y2K freaks, I'd be eternally grateful."

"That would eliminate almost everyone."

Sammy rolled her eyes as she flipped on her mic.

"We're back. Thanks to all who've provided clues or leads about Sylvie Pauzé. Please, though, before anyone else calls, remember, the reward is only for information that leads to actually finding Sylvie, in person, with confirmed ID. We're not paying out just because your brother dressed up in a blonde wig and says he's Sylvie, okay?"

Sammy winked at Jim. "Or, if we have to fly to Neptune to meet her. If you have a legit lead, keep trying to get through. We really want to talk to you. Steve, in Alhambra?" She pressed the button to patch in her caller's voice.

"I don't have a clue about this girl you're looking for," he began.

"Thanks for your honesty. And you're calling because?"

"I think everyone's too casual about Y2K."

Sammy groaned silently.

The caller continued, "Do you know how much we depend on computers? Air traffic, street lights, banking, even your grocery store?"

"So, maybe we do a little arithmetic for a few days. And use cash. You're talking like Y2K will bring nuclear winter."

"You really think our computer systems are secure?"

Sammy had to acknowledge his point. "Maybe not enough."

"That's an understatement. What happens if terrorists decide to hack into our Defense Department systems?"

"I liked *War Games* too," Sammy countered, "but, I'm sure the government has done everything it needs to protect us from Matthew Broderick."

"Make your jokes. Me? I'd like to wake up on January first. Alive." He clicked off.

Sammy whistled. "*That* was scary. Why don't we go to a break and hit the fridge for some comfort food, okay? After all, if we're doomed in three days, we can afford a few extra calories, right? Sixteen after."

She turned off her mic and buzzed Jim. "I take it back. Give me the UFO folks, *please.*"

"I can't entirely disagree with him. You really trust our government to do what needs to be done?" Jim shook his head. "With blowhards like Neil Prescott out there stirring up fear, instead of really doing something to keep us safe."

"Is that why you're pissed at Prescott?"

"You *do* know he's trying to buy this station."

"I know he's with America First Communications."

"America First syndicates almost every top radio talk show in this country," Jim explained. "Every conservative radio talk show."

"Sadly, I know that too."

"Did you know that America First owns almost every top radio station in the major U.S. markets?"

Sammy shook her head. "Isn't that illegal? I thought you couldn't own more than one station in each market."

"The rules have changed. America First is the largest communications conglomerate in the United States, and it intends to use its ample budget to get out its message. Its very conservative message." Jim rubbed his temples. "And we—KPCF—are in the way."

The satellite phone's ring interrupted Miller's new nightly vigil of Sammy's broadcast. Finally. Enough time wasted tracking Sylvie Pauzé. He swiveled his chair to view the Santa Monica Mountains adorned by the glow of flickering fires like a necklace of red Christmas lights

"You got her?"

"No, sir. Lost her. Place has more security than the White House."

"What?" Miller banged on his cherrywood desk. "Where the fuck is she?"

"We don't know, sir. She left her phone at the house. They had a Vespa in the back. Went down the hill through the trees. We couldn't follow."

"A *Vespa?*" Enraged, Miller clicked off, reached over and pushed a button on one of his office lines. "Get me a trace on a cell phone for a Courtney Phillips," he told an assistant. "Yes, *that* Courtney Phillips. Now!"

"You okay?" Ana whispered as she lay back on the cot lined up among the hundreds of others in the gymnasium of Santa Monica High.

Courtney, still in her blonde wig and now hiding behind large sunglasses, scanned the sea of cots filled with refugees from the fires in the Santa Monica Mountains. "It ain't the Ritz."

"You think they can find us here?" Ana worried aloud. "How'd they track me to your house anyway?"

"Must've been your cell phone. Good thing we left it behind."

"Did you bring yours? I can try Aunt Eleni again."

Courtney shook her head. "Too risky. I shut mine off and removed the battery. If they could trace your phone, they can figure out who owns the Malibu house and trace mine. We'll find a safe place to make a call in the morning."

Leaning on her elbow, Ana sat halfway up on the cot. "How bout the library? I can send another e-mail to my dad from there. It opens at nine."

Courtney nodded. "Fine with me. If your father was a cop, maybe you should send him Kaye's client list and that code, too." She tossed her blonde hair. "Those guys were obviously after something Sylvie had. Where's the disk and the copy?"

Ana patted her pelvis.

"Good job, girlfriend."

In the dim light, Ana didn't see Courtney's wry smile.

Kaye's girls might be ladies of the night, but the madam was generally in bed by eleven. At her age, insufficient sleep could visibly overcome expensive monthly botox. Yet, here she was, forced to stay awake, listening to that nosy reporter until three a.m. What trouble would she stir up next?

Broadcasting allegations that Sylvie—Ana—was murdered to all those listeners night after night did not please Kaye. Though perhaps the reward might draw Ana out of hiding. For the past twenty-four hours, Yevgeny had tailed Sammy Greene with no results. If Ana didn't make contact, her LAPD friend better come through with Plan B.

Kaye's cell phone vibrated the moment Sammy broke for commercial. Miller again. "Has she called you?"

"No." Good. Miller didn't have her either. But his persistence implied he was after something big. Something worth killing for. What had Sylvie stumbled on while servicing that stupid arms dealer?

"Call off your bulldog. He's as discreet as an elephant and keeps getting in our way." Miller's tone had a threatening edge.

"I'll pull him on one condition," Kaye said.

"Go on." They both knew Kaye would blow the whistle on Fahim for murder if it served her interests.

"If you get her, I get back what's mine. No questions asked."

"Deal." Miller agreed, adding, "*When* we get her."

Kaye felt confident enough to let irony seep through her reply. "Isn't that what I just said?" She laughed and clicked off.

With one ear focused on the radio now that Sammy had returned, she speed-dialed Yevgeny. Her message was short. "They've made you, you asshole," she shouted in Russian. "Stay farther back. Hide!"

Not long after Sammy began her show that night, and hours after Medical Examiner Gharani had returned home and fallen asleep, the black Lincoln reappeared on Westbourne Drive. Hot blasts of smoky air had chased the hip residents of West Hollywood indoors, leaving the street deserted when the two occupants of the sedan stepped onto the sidewalk and quietly walked around to the back of Gharani's bungalow. With the expertise of accomplished burglars, they jimmied the lock on the door and tiptoed inside and up the stairs to the bedroom.

One man grabbed a pillow and before Gharani could awaken, covered his face. Despite a reflexive struggle against suffocation, Gharani was dead within minutes. The killer replaced the pillow while his partner slipped on latex gloves, removed a cigarette from a plastic bag, and lit one end from his lighter. Leaving the lit end open for air, he used the plastic bag to protect his lips and DNA while he puffed. Once the smelly tobacco had burned down a half inch, he carefully positioned the unfiltered cigarette inside Gharani's sagging lips to allow smoke to settle into the dead man's oral cavity. Then he placed the cigarette against the sheets and, motioning for his colleague to open the windows and let in the gusty winds, waited until the bed ignited.

Unobserved, they quickly returned to the car and sat watching through the tinted glass, only pulling away from the curb when the entire house was engulfed in flames.

•   •   •

The escape from the mansion had left Courtney jumpy and anxious. Unable to sleep, she abandoned her cot and wandered from the gym into the smoky gloom outside. Hoping she wouldn't be recognized in her blonde wig and shades, she settled down near a half dozen fellow insomniacs listening to weather updates on the radio. According to the announcer, a new fire had just broken out in West Hollywood, and a couple of her favorite clubs on the Sunset Strip were being evacuated. *Bummer.* She wondered how much more of the city would burn before this nightmare ended. Closing her eyes, she rested her head in her arms.

"Hey turn on KPCF," someone suggested. "That new girl's giving the man a hard time about kicking us out of Beverly Hills."

Courtney heard the sound of radio static until it stopped at the requested station.

"Sammy Greene on the L.A. Scene," the host was saying, "Back with hour three. Two renovations, two collapses. The Canyon City tragedy on Christmas Day. Rush job or con job? And, is there a connection between the Canyon City tower and the Palacio Real Hotel that collapsed less than a year ago? Maybe, and Neil Prescott may be that bridge."

"Yeah you tell 'em, Sammy," a voice near Courtney chimed in.

"First, though, just letting you know we're still taking tips that'll lead us to Sylvie Pauzé. Ten-thousand-dollar reward if we find her. Call our producer, big Jim, at 310-555—"

Courtney sat up straight. Whoa! Why were they looking for Ana's roommate on the radio?

"Man, I could use ten thousand dollars," laughed a toothless woman in a ragged housedress seated next to her shopping cart.

"I could use ten thousand anything. Damn, I wish I knew that Sylvie chick," a bearded man in a dirty sweatsuit said. He looked at the woman. "You wanna tell them you're Sylvie and we split the ten?"

"You don't think they're gonna check? Man, you're stoo-pid."

Courtney waited to hear more from Sammy Greene, to learn

why she was looking for Sylvie. But the talk show had drifted back to comments about the homeless protest in Canyon City.

Guess she'd have to test the waters herself, Courtney finally decided, spotting the pay phone on the corner. Ana was too scared to make the call. But Sylvie Pauzé could. Playing the part would give Courtney a chance to practice her French accent. She'd find out what Sammy Greene's game was and whether it was safe for Ana to play.

Pappajohn nearly fell off his chair when the phone rang. He'd been sitting in front of Sammy's computer, the radio tuned low to her show. Jim's sonorous voice at three a.m. must have lulled him to sleep. No surprise. The past few days had been exhausting and filled with untold grief, though now it was overlaid by a profound determination to take action, to find out who had killed his daughter. Hurrying over to the bedside table, he grabbed Sammy's cordless.

"Hi, Gus."

Pappajohn checked his watch—3:35 a.m. in L.A., 6:35 a.m. in Boston. "You're up early."

"Promised I'd check on that ISP," Keith said. "We're on the homestretch for Y2K at Pueblo. Deadlines looming. Haven't been able to get to it til now."

"I understand. Learn anything?"

"Well, I can't tell from here who literally typed in the message, but I did figure out when and from where it was sent and who logged in."

Pappajohn held his breath as the sound of keyboard clicks filled the background.

"ISP is Adelphia in Santa Monica, IP address is Santa Monica Library at six-oh-one Santa Monica Boulevard, and time sent is ten fifty-three a.m. 24 December. But—" Keith paused.

"But what?" Pappajohn pressed.

"The login's not Ana."

Not Ana.

With the phone pressed to his ear, Pappajohn lay back on

Sammy's bed and closed his eyes. He'd expected that answer. No last chance—for either of them.

"The system has a record of all the logins," Keith reported. "This message comes from an account whose login is assigned to a Sylvie Pauzé."

Jim was surprised to see a line blinking on the business office phone. He had a few minutes before the news ended, so he pressed the button. "KPCF."

"Finally." The woman's whispered voice sounded impatient.

Jim increased the input volume. "Can I help you?"

"Yeah, heard about the reward."

Another opportunist. "Sorry, business office is closed. Call back tomorrow after nine. Or call on the request line tomorrow night at midnight for Sammy Greene." He moved a finger to click the caller off.

"Yeah, good luck getting through. Been trying for hours. Don't you want to find Sylvie Pauzé?"

Something about the woman's tone kept Jim from hanging up. "Yes, we do." He waited.

"Then tell Greene to meet me at the California Science Center, IMAX theatre, three p.m. show. I'll be the blonde sitting inside. No cops."

The call was disconnected, leaving Jim staring at the phone for a few moments before pulling out his cell and dialing Sammy's number.

Pappajohn scribbled the information on the pad on Sammy's night table. "Thanks Keith. I owe you one. And more."

"Don't mention it. Hey, Gus?"

"Yes?"

"How are you doing?"

Pappajohn let out a long, deep breath. It was a question he'd been asked over and over the last few days. "I'm doing," he said.

"Well, let me know if there's anything else you need," Keith offered. "And, remember, there's a job waiting for you here when you get back."

Pappajohn replaced the handset in the charger and walked back to the desk with renewed determination. Sitting down at the computer, he clicked on his e-mail account. With no new messages in his in-box, he opened the saved one from Ana. For a long time he simply stared at the words,

```
     Dear Baba. Don't worry, I'm okay.
I've been clean for a year. I have more
news. I'll try to get in touch as soon
as I can. Merry Christmas. Love, Ana
```

I have more news.

Maybe that was the key. If Sylvie had sent this, perhaps she was asking Pappajohn to find her. And finding her would unlock the mystery of Ana's death.

CHAPTER FOURTEEN

At seven fifteen a.m. Sammy and Pappajohn stood on the sidewalk outside her apartment watching Sandoval wedge his yellow Checker taxi into a tight parking space, bumping cars on both ends. Stepping out of his cab, the beefy forty-something man reminded Sammy of how Pappajohn must have looked a decade earlier—when his bushy mustache was still dark. They were even the same height.

"Mr. Sandoval," Sammy said, offering a handshake. "I'm Sammy Greene."

"I'm too late," he responded. "Fires, fires, fires. Sunset, Wilshire, Santa Monica. All closed. *Maldita* wind! Nobody going out this week. My business is screwed." Unlike his wife, Sandoval spoke fairly good English, albeit still lightly seasoned with the accent of his native El Salvador.

Sammy brushed back wisps of hair from her face. "No problem. We appreciate your coming by."

"You got the ten thousand?"

"Not til we find our girl. We hope you can help us." She nodded at Pappajohn. "This here's my buddy, Sergeant Pappajohn."

Sandoval's eyes narrowed. "What's the deal?" He pointed to his chest with obvious pride. "American citizen. Fifteen years."

"He's a cop, not INS," Sammy explained.

The wariness remained. "Hey, my taxi license, all my papers, they're up to date."

"We're not interested in you," Pappajohn assured him. "We want to know if you picked up a young blonde last Friday night."

"Christmas Eve." Sandoval pulled a much-used hankie from his pocket and wiped his forehead. "Sí. I remember 'cause of the fires. Sunset was closed and Wilshire was jammed with cars. We had to take Santa Monica." He smiled at Sammy. "We listened to you on the radio. Like I told the guy at the station."

"Okay," Sammy said. "And what time did you pick her up?"

"After midnight. Maybe two or three o'clock."

"Can you check your log?" Pappajohn asked.

Sandoval opened the front door of the cab and leaned in to unlatch the glove compartment. He pulled out a ratty spiral notebook and flipped to a page, "Here it is. Two thirty-seven, Wilshire Boulevard, Westwood. Three forty-two, Ashland Street, Santa Monica. One hour to go five miles! *Maldita* fires!"

Sammy and Pappajohn stared at each other, acknowledging the street where Ana and Sylvie lived.

Pappajohn let out a deep breath and produced the snapshot of both girls. "Think you could identify the young woman?"

Sandoval took the photo and held it at arm's length as he pulled out a pair of drugstore reading glasses from his pocket. Squinting, he studied the image of the two blondes. "Twins?"

"No," Sammy replied, "but they do look alike."

"Did you give a ride to one of these girls?" Pappajohn demanded.

Sandoval's finger hovered over the picture, until, finally, he chose Ana. "I think it was this one."

"Jesus," Pappajohn mumbled, shaking his head. He pointed to Sylvie. "You sure it wasn't this one?"

Sandoval scratched his chin for a long moment, then bobbed his head up and down. "Sí, that's the one I gave the ride."

Pappajohn leaned back against the cab and closed his eyes as Sammy gently probed. "Okay, you took her to Ashland. What address?"

Sandoval checked his log again. "She told me twenty-three twenty-five. But I remember. She jumped out a block away. Gave me a lousy two dollar tip for my trouble," he grumbled. "Had to drive all the way back to LAU Med for another fare."

"You said you picked her up in Westwood?"

"Promenade Towers on Wilshire. The doorman, he calls me, you know, we're partn—" Sandoval stopped himself when Pappajohn opened one eye and turned in his direction.

"Anything you can tell us about her condition?" Sammy asked.

"She seemed *muy nervioso*, nervous. Could have been high," Sandoval speculated. "I think maybe she was a *pu*—working on the streets, you know, very tight dress, high heels, and pink purse." He looked at Pappajohn, waiting for a reaction and when none came, continued. "Didn't talk much. Looked like she had a bad night. Arms, legs, all scratches. Even got blood on my backseat."

Now Pappajohn stood up straight and opened the rear passenger door, triggering the roof light. A few streaks of blood stained the cloth seams where the girl's calves must have rested.

Sammy winced at Sandoval's lack of hygiene, but Pappajohn had already pulled out a wad of bills from his pocket, along with a Swiss Army knife. "Gus?"

"Three hundred dollars, and we take this patch. Get it reupholstered, or at least washed, okay?" Pappajohn thrust the bills at the driver, then reached over and started dissecting out a large swatch of the bloody upholstery. "Damn," he cursed as he cut his finger and a couple beads of his own blood dripped onto the fabric. Ripping the sample into two sections, he handed them both to Sammy "Just hold the bottom. The evidence may already be degraded, but if we get this out of the sun and into paper bags right away, there's a chance they contain enough DNA to make an ID."

"Of course," Sammy replied. If Sylvie had an arrest record as De'andray claimed, her DNA should be in the system. What better way to confirm that she'd left the area where Ana was killed than by placing her in this cab? Carefully balancing the samples, Sammy hurried up to her apartment, at the same time conjuring up a backup plan of her own.

"Police station, right?" Sammy aimed the Tercel north on Sepulveda, anticipating Pappajohn's next move. She figured he'd want Ortego to run the blood sample, confirming Sylvie as the passenger in Sandoval's cab.

"No, let's go catch that creep ME, first. I don't want to miss him again."

Sammy nodded. Time for Gharani to explain his actions in what clearly seemed a cover-up for Ana's murder.

West Hollywood's clubs and restaurants blossomed in the night, and woke up slowly in the morning, but even at eight fifteen, Sunset Boulevard was unusually deserted. Though the winds had taken a short breather, the stench of smoke still kept most people indoors.

Sammy was about to turn onto Westbourne Drive when she noticed the entrance to Gharani's street cordoned off with orange cones. A uniformed policewoman stationed behind a wooden barricade held up a palm to block both vehicle and pedestrian traffic. Nevertheless, a small crowd of gawkers, some dressed as if they'd just rolled out of bed, huddled nearby.

Sammy parked on Sunset and flew out of her car to ask what was going on. Pappajohn followed behind.

"Fire in the middle of the night. Woke us all up," a grey-haired woman in a bathrobe complained.

"Damn Santa Anas. Every fucking year. Lucky it was only one house." A tattooed man pointed toward the end of the street. Where the weather-beaten bungalow on the corner lot had once stood, was now a pile of blackened ashes. Yellow tape attached to one of the two standing pilings fluttered loosely in the hot breeze.

A coroner's van was just pulling away from the curb.

"That's Dr. Gharani's," Sammy cried. She raced up to the officer and flashed her press pass.

"Sorry, no one's allowed until fire and police finish their investigation."

"I was supposed to interview Dr. Gharani this morning."

"You knew the victim?"

"Victim?" Sammy blanched. "You mean—"

"They just removed the body."

"But how?" Sammy swiveled to see Pappajohn, breathing heavily, standing behind her.

The policewoman shook her head. "They don't call these 'devil winds' for nothing. All around the city we're seeing it. One house stands, another goes up—literally—in smoke. Terrible accident." She shifted her attention to a neighbor about to cross the barricade. "Hey!"

Pappajohn, hovering on the brink of rage, waved Sammy over to an empty spot on the nearby sidewalk. His eyes were glued to the smoldering ruins now overrun by LAFD's Arson Investigation Unit. "I don't care what anyone says. This was no accident." He nodded at the investigators. "And I'll bet they don't think so either."

"Should we talk to them?" Sammy asked, looking for a way past the policewoman.

Pappajohn shook his head. "This loose end's been tied up. Our only hope is to track down Sylvie." He checked his watch. "Almost nine. Let's see if we can follow her trail at the library."

"Wake up." Ana nudged Courtney's shoulders. "Courtney, wake up."

"Shhh!" Courtney lifted her head from the cot, her face registering a wave of nausea. It had been over twelve hours since she'd had a drink. "I'm Sylvie, remember?" she whispered.

"Right," Ana swallowed the lump in her throat. "Sorry."

"Why'd you wake me?" Courtney rubbed her temples, "What time is it?"

"Just before nine. The library opens in a few minutes. I want to send an e-mail to my father."

Courtney groaned. "Why don't you take the Vespa and let me sleep?"

"You don't mind?"

"I mind not sleeping. And pick me up a few bottles of Korbel on the way, okay?" She rolled over on her side and covered her head with her sweater.

Seeing no choice, Ana took the scooter's key from Courtney's purse along with a few dollars.

"Mission accomplished." Miller heard the caller say this time. "Smoking kills."

He allowed himself a smile. "Any luck finding the girls?"

"Trail's cold."

"Not entirely," Miller said. "Our tap of the radio station got us a bite. California Science Center at three p.m. IMAX Theatre. I'm betting it'll be either Courtney or Sylvie."

The Santa Monica library is a stately building just a few blocks from Ocean Avenue and the Pacific beyond. Today, its proximity to the ocean's breeze provided an oasis of respite from the smoky haze hanging over the rest of Los Angeles. Sammy relished taking deep gulps of fresh air for the first time in days. Even Pappajohn seemed to breathe more easily.

"Keith tracked the IP address—the computer's name, so to speak—to this library," Pappajohn explained as they entered. "They probably have a bank of public-access computers Sylvie could have used."

The young man at the information desk confirmed Pappajohn's deduction, directing them to the second floor. Though the library had just opened, every PC in the Computer Center was already occupied. Pappajohn walked over to the front desk where a stern-looking, elderly librarian sat reading a book.

"Good morning."

The librarian looked up. "ID, please."

"Uh, no," Pappajohn said. "I'm a police officer. I'd like to ask a few questions."

"Santa Monica police?"

"I'm working with the West L.A. precinct of LAPD." Pappajohn flashed his badge so quickly that only Sammy recognized the Ellsford University logo.

The librarian peered at both of them over her glasses. "What do you need?"

"We're looking for a young woman, blonde, about five four, mid-twenties, who might have been here the morning of December twenty-fourth," Pappajohn explained.

"You expect me to remember every single person who walks in this room?"

"Of course not." Pappajohn produced a smile so charming that even Sammy was wowed. "But I expect you've got a sign-up sheet and log before you let anyone use the computers."

The charm worked. The librarian's sharp features softened. "As a matter of fact, I do." She reached down to open a large drawer and removed a thick spiral notebook. "December twenty-fourth, let's see. Do you know what time?"

"Between ten and eleven," Sammy said.

The librarian leafed through the pages. "Here we are. Friday morning, December twenty-fourth, we had three women come in. Loretta Magid, Sylvie Pauzé, and—"

"That's the one, Sylvie Pauzé," Sammy cried, causing nearly every computer user to turn a head her way.

The librarian frowned. "Has she committed a crime?"

"No, ma'am. She may be a witness to one." Pappajohn lowered his voice. "Do you have an address, a phone number? Some other contact information?"

"Well, they do have to show ID," the librarian said. "I vaguely remember her, come to think of it. A blonde, right?"

"Right," Pappajohn responded. "Did Sylvie say anything to you? About where she was going, what she wanted to do?"

"No, just that she needed to use the computer." The librarian seemed lost in thought. "I do remember that she fell asleep on one of the chairs in the back. Must have been there most of the day. We were closing early 'cause of the fires and—"

"Did you see any scratches on her legs?" Sammy interrupted.

"No, I believe she wore trousers. Slacks, jeans."

Pappajohn reached into his pocket and produced the photo of Ana and Sylvie. "She was one of these two, right?"

The librarian pulled her head back, straining to study the images. "I need a new pair of glasses. My arms aren't long enough any more." She squinted to focus. "They look so much alike. It's hard for me to see, but I believe that is she."

Pappajohn and Sammy did a double take. For the second time that morning, a witness was pointing to Ana.

"That's the one you want, isn't it?" the librarian asked.

Pappajohn's voice quavered. "You're certain this is the girl you saw?"

The librarian shrugged. "I see so many people here. No, it could be either one. I'm not sure."

Pappajohn nodded, thanked her, and headed out with Sammy at his heels.

"Look, Gus, we *will* find Sylvie," Sammy tried to comfort him. "Jim got a call this morning from a woman who says she knows where Sylvie is. I'm going to meet her at the California Science Center at three in the IMAX theatre. How about I take you to the police station so you can drop off the blood sample while I have lunch with my father. Take a cab when you're done and meet me at the theatre. Hopefully, we'll get answers from somewhere today."

"I'd been hoping for answers here this morning," Pappajohn said. "Now all I have are more questions."

Ana pulled the Vespa into a space just vacated by a blue compact. The car was too far away to be sure of the make, but it looked like a Toyota Tercel, a model she'd been saving for back when she'd planned for a better future. Or any kind of a future for that matter.

Courtney's cognac bottles rattled in the storage bin of the scooter as Ana dismounted and set up the kickstands. Who would have thought the liquor store would be so crowded at this hour of the morning? Seemed as though everyone wanted to try their luck with the lottery today. The Super Lotto pot had grown to nearly seventy million dollars.

Ana had spent some of her time in the checkout line imagining the wonderful life she and Teddy could have if she became the lucky winner. She'd even bought a ticket, just for the heck of it, knowing the odds of winning were less than being struck by lightning. Like Sylvie's her bad luck had been a lightning strike. Wasn't it time for a little good luck?

Pushing open the doors to the computer center, she headed for the check-in desk where she handed over Sylvie's driver's license.

The librarian glanced at the ID, then back at Ana, her forehead creasing.

"Something wrong?" Ana felt her pulse quicken.

"Would you mind taking a seat over there?" The librarian pointed to an empty chair in the corner. "I need to check something with my supervisor." She reached for the phone, then turned her back as Ana started to walk away. "West L.A. precinct?"

Although the librarian spoke in a whisper, her words were loud enough for Ana to hear. The police! By the time the librarian glanced back, Ana had grabbed Sylvie's license off the counter and disappeared.

De'andray was headed out of the building when Sammy dropped Pappajohn in front of the West L.A. precinct station. The tall detective rolled his eyes as he watched Pappajohn climb out of the car. "Man, thought I'd finally get out of here on time today. What do you two want now?"

"Just me." Pappajohn's tone was all business. He held up a brown paper bag. "Got something for you. Let's go inside."

The detective followed Pappajohn back into the building as Sammy drove off. At De'andray's desk, Pappajohn pulled over an adjacent chair and sat down. "So, you got any news for me? Have you found Sylvie?"

De'andray pressed his lips together. "No and no. We *do* have other priorities right now." He pointed to the window where haze from the fires had colored the sky beige.

"Finding a murder witness was always a priority at Boston PD." Pappajohn laid the brown paper bag on the officer's desk. "The cab driver who picked up Sylvie in Westwood said her arms and legs were all scratched. He dropped her off in Santa Monica—*after* the murder. I got some blood samples from the taxi for you to confirm her DNA."

"Look, Gramps, don't you know what retired means? You're not a detective anymore. Stay the hell out of police business."

Pappajohn shot to his feet and leaned on the desk with both arms. "You want me to take this public? LAPD refuses to investigate a murder?"

"You and your bigmouthed radio friend have already done enough damage," De'andray responded. "Get it through your thick head. Your daughter's death was an accident. Get out of here or I'll have you busted for interfering with an active investigation."

"*Active?*" Pappajohn sputtered. "What investigation? You're doing *nothing*, and *that's* criminal!"

"Hey, hey." Ortego stood at the door of the conference room. "In here. Both of you. Now."

De'andray smirked, shrugged, then rose and went inside.

Pappajohn grabbed the paper bag before following.

Taking seats at opposite ends of the table, Pappajohn and De'andray continued to glare at each other like prizefighters in a ring, while Ortego, the referee, tried to make peace. "So, how can we help?" he asked.

Pappajohn quickly brought him up to speed, handing him the blood sample "We know Sylvie was in Santa Monica the morning after the murder. If she was a witness, she may be hiding from the police. Or the murderers."

Ortego nodded. "Of course, Gus. We'll run DNA on the sample. I'll ask the lab to rush it. But, if Sylvie was picked up in Westwood, how'd she get there? Her car was parked in Bel Air, not far from where your daughter's body was found, actually. Why didn't she use that to get away?"

Pappajohn threw up his hands. "I don't know. Maybe the, uh, murderer kidnapped both women, and dropped Ana's body—" His voice cracked. "If he heard Ana was still alive at the hospital, he may have gone there, and, in the crowd, Sylvie could have made a run for it?"

Another smirk from De'andray, "You're grasping at straws, Pops."

Pappajohn shook his head. "I know Sylvie was in that cab. The driver ID'd her. How and why she got there is your job to figure out."

"You're right, Gus," Ortego said. "And we will. Why don't you come with me? We'll drop the blood off at the lab. Let Dee here go home and get his beauty sleep, okay?"

Pappajohn nodded as he stood. "I just have one thing for you to think about," he said to De'andray. "The ME cremated her—against my religion and my wishes. *You're* the detective. Ask yourself why. And while you're at it, ask why that same ME just happened to end up a burn victim himself."

"Hey, miss, you can't go in there!"

Ignoring the triage nurse who'd jumped up to follow her, Sammy barged through the double doors into the emergency room's care area. She looked past patients moaning on gurneys, doctors shouting orders, and technicians delivering supplies, and waved at Lou seated at the central nurses' station.

"Hey, Red!" Lou broke out in a broad grin.

The triage nurse wasn't so happy. "Look, lady, I said, you can't—"

"It's okay," Lou intervened. "I've got her. She's Dr. Wynd-ham's—"

"Good friend," Sammy finished the introduction. Whether her status with Reed was more at this point remained to be seen, but there was no doubt that they *were* good friends. She'd figure out the rest later.

The nurse pointed at Lou's ID. "Visitor's badge then. You know the policy." She spun around and thrust open the double doors to exit back toward the triage desk.

"Sure do," Lou handed Sammy a pink visitor's pass from the drawer, and started penciling in her name. "That's Greene with an 'e,' right? By the way, I've been following your show. Any luck on finding the missing roommate?"

"Actually, that's why I'm here," Sammy said. "Could you page Reed, I mean Dr. Wyndham? I need to talk to him."

"No problem. You can wait in the doctors' break room."

Thanking him, Sammy headed toward the lounge. Pushing open the door with her shoulder, she collided with Michelle coming out, scattering charts on the polished linoleum floor. "I'm really sorry," she said, stooping to help.

"Sorry for bumping into me or sorry for driving Reed crazy?" Michelle grabbed the charts from Sammy's hands as they both stood.

"What are you talking about?" Sammy hoped the rising heat she felt on her cheeks wasn't a blush. Had Reed said something about the other night?

"You're kidding, right?" Michelle glared at her. "I don't get it. Weren't you the one who broke up with him years ago? Now you storm back into his life and start messing with his head again."

Sammy tried to suppress her bubbling anger. "Messing with his head?"

"He hasn't been himself lately. And it's affecting his work." Michelle grimaced with impatience. "Don't you care about him?"

"Of course I care."

"Then why can't you let him move on?"

He has moved on. At least that's what Reed had told Sammy. That he was now officially playing the field. *Had he neglected to tell Michelle?* Sammy took a deep breath and forced herself to remain calm. "I don't know what he's said to you, but Reed and I are still friends. And as far as moving on—well, I think that's his decision to make."

Sammy marched over to the other end of the room, grabbed a journal from the magazine rack and plopped down on the lumpy couch. Ignoring Michelle, she leafed through the tattered copy of JAMA. As far as she was concerned, the conversation was over.

She didn't look up until she heard Michelle leave, slamming the door behind her. Alone, Sammy laid the magazine on her lap and closed her eyes, pondering Michelle's accusations. She thought back to that weekend two years ago in Boston when she and Reed decided to call it quits. They'd had a good run. But the show was closed by bitter words, said in anger. And fear.

It wasn't exactly true that *she'd* ended the relationship. Though they'd ultimately both agreed, it was Reed who'd pushed her buttons with his upsetting question. *What are you afraid of?*

Afraid of being abandoned the way her father had abandoned her? But Reed was not Jeffrey Greene. Unlike her father, Reed had always been there for her, offering himself in a way that was both selfless and self-assured, and totally consuming.

Reed's words so many years ago: *I thought we had something special.*

Of course we do. We—

Not special enough to deserve your full attention.

Now that's not fair. We both have lots to do.

True, but I'm at the bottom of your to-do list.

Was that it? Sammy wondered. Was her ambition standing in the way? Was she afraid of somehow losing herself in total commitment? All her life she'd worked hard to appear unflappable, becoming the self-assured, tough kid, keeping emotions bottled up, the paragon of self-control. Then she'd met Reed. He'd poked beneath the surface, sensed her vulnerability, and tried to help her understand there was nothing wrong with leaning on someone once in a while, that it wasn't so bad to lose a little of that control.

She smiled, thinking of the other night when they'd made love. She'd done just that—lost control. Reed was right, it wasn't so bad. In fact, it felt wonderful falling asleep next to him again.

Sammy sighed. It had taken many years, but she'd finally gotten over the guilt of her mother's suicide. How long would it take to get over her fear to commit?

"Earth to Greene."

Sammy opened her eyes. "Reed, I didn't hear you come in. I was daydreaming."

"Since you were smiling, can I assume it wasn't a nightmare?" He settled into a space next to her on the couch.

"Definitely not a nightmare," she said, studying his face. His thick shock of sandy hair needed a trim, his eyes were red and bleary, probably from all the extra duty he'd been pulling since the fires. She'd gotten used to that look, his near-constant state of exhaustion. She just hoped Michelle wasn't right—that his work was suffering—and worse, that she was the cause. "Hey, it's good to see you."

"Me, too," he replied. "So, Lou called me. What's up?"

Sammy reached into her purse and pulled out a paper bag.

Reed raised an eyebrow as she handed it to him. "My lunch?"

"Blood sample. We think it may be Sylvie's. Ana's roommate."

"We?"

"Pappajohn and me." Sammy began to relate what had ensued since the night Reed had called with the autopsy report.

"My God, cremated?" Reed ran his hand through his hair. "I can't believe it."

"Believe it," Sammy said. "You were right. There's no doubt of a cover-up now."

"Hold it. I never said— How'd you jump to that conclusion?"

"We tried to talk to Dr. Gharani yesterday. The people at the morgue claimed he'd left with some kind of family emergency. So we drove out to his house."

"And?"

"And he wasn't home."

"You said he had an emergency."

"Today, we went back for answers." Sammy paused for effect. "Gharani's house burned down last night. With him in it. He's dead, Reed. I'd say that was a pretty convenient coincidence."

Reed whistled. "Wow. What do the police say?"

"I think they're finally paying attention. At least Detective Ortego seems to be. Gus is at the precinct now dropping off a blood sample we found for forensics."

Reed opened the brown bag and looked at the irregular piece of beige cloth. "And where did you get this?"

Sammy told him about the cabbie's response to her on-air request. "We know now that he picked up a blonde from a Westwood high-rise and took her to Ana's apartment. That's got to be Sylvie."

"And this is her blood?"

"Evidently the young woman had scratches on her arms and legs. She bled on the backseat of the cab. Pappajohn cut out a couple pieces figuring we could get a DNA match."

"And here the *we* means *me?*"

"Uh, well—"

"You said Pappajohn was taking a sample to the police."

"True, but honestly at this point, you can't blame him for losing faith in the system. On the other hand, I have complete faith in you."

"I don't know, Sammy. I can't just order a DNA screen on someone not checked in as a patient."

"I thought you could do it yourself. I mean you worked in Dr. Palmer's immunology lab at Ellsford. Didn't you do genetic screens there?"

"Sure, but that was different. It was a research lab. Everybody did their own thing. It'd look awfully strange to have a cardiology fellow doing tests in the lab here. Besides, I'm up to my eyeballs in work. We've had a run of patients with heart disease exacerbated by the fires, not to mention Prescott's relapse."

"Relapse? What kind of relapse?"

Reed sighed. "I guess I'm more tired than I realized. You didn't hear that from me."

"Hear what?"

"Off the record, okay?"

Sammy made a crossing motion over her heart.

"Last night the congressman had another episode of coronary spasm. Dr. Bishop put in a second stent. Luckily there was no heart damage." Reed shook his head. "But I can't help second-guessing myself. Maybe I blew it the first time."

"Is it unusual to have a second attack like that?" Sammy tried to sound sympathetic.

"Not necessarily, if there's some precipitating factor." Reed's eyes narrowed. "Come to think of it, Prescott was listening to a TV anchor's report. Seems a certain local talk show host claimed he might be involved in the Canyon City tower collapse."

"Now *I'm* responsible?" Sammy felt her temper flare. "Maybe a heavy dose of guilt was the 'precipitating factor.'"

"I didn't intend to imply—" Reed appeared contrite. "Frankly, I don't know if the man's capable of guilt."

"Meaning?"

"As long as I'm speaking off the record, Prescott's got an unbelievably devoted wife and yet I'm told he was brought to the ER by a young blonde."

Sammy's eyebrows rose to attention. "Shall I hazard a guess? Mrs. Prescott's not a young blonde?"

"Not a blonde at all. Though she's a very attractive and elegant brunette. In her fifties."

"Why am I not surprised?" Sammy reached into her purse for her notebook and a pen.

"*Sammy!*"

"If I can check the security cameras in the ER bay, I won't need you as a source."

"We don't have cameras out there. With Y2K, internal security for the Schwarzenegger Hospital has been the administration's priority. The ER's part of the old hospital and hasn't been wired up yet."

Sammy started to put away her notebook. "Wait a sec, that was the night Courtney Phillips came in as a patient, right?"

"Yeah?"

"Well, paparazzi, TV cameras were all over the place. Maybe Jim, my producer, can get some of the B-roll. Before radio, he worked at a local TV station." She jumped up and kissed Reed on the cheek.

"What was that for?"

"That," she explained, "was for always being there for me." She leaned closer, this time kissing him on the lips. "And *that's* for checking the DNA," she said as she sprinted out of the lounge.

Signal beeping, the large white van backed carefully toward the Schwarzenegger Hospital loading dock where al-Salid, clipboard in hand, stood with two of his men. All sported Facilities uniforms.

Fahim, wearing a shirt that matched the Alabaster Chemical Supply logo on the side of the van, hopped out of the driver's seat and opened the rear doors. Quickly, al-Salid's men moved in with a heavy-duty dolly and loaded a sofa-sized crate with hazmat labeling marked FLAMMABLE, FORMALDEHYDE. In less than fifteen minutes, the crate had been deposited in the morgue's storage room, and the van's space yielded to the linen service truck's daily delivery.

Sammy raced into Massimo's popular restaurant in Beverly Hills, as always, at least twenty minutes late. She knew her father was a stickler for punctuality and hoped he wouldn't be angry. He hadn't answered his phone when she'd tried to call to explain her delay.

Jeffrey Greene was sipping a Chardonnay, immersed in the *Wall Street Journal*, as Sammy slipped into a seat across from his at their table. "I can't believe this traffic," she complained. "And I thought D.C. was bad."

Jeffrey looked up with a wan smile. "You need to allow an extra half hour to get anywhere around here." A waiter came over with two plates of food. "Hope you don't mind. I ordered us both the linguine allo scoglio."

Sammy nodded, noting the dish had a variety of seafood, including shrimp. Keeping kosher was one tradition they'd both rejected after leaving Grandma Rose's sphere of influence. Sammy reached for a slice of warm bread and dipped it in the peppered olive oil between them. "So, I'm glad we were able to meet."

Silence from Jeffrey.

Sammy swallowed a second piece of bread before trying again. "You said I could talk to you about Neil Prescott."

Jeffrey nodded. "I wish you would."

"The Palacio Real. Tell me about the collapse."

"What about it?"

"Was it an accident?"

Jeffrey took a bite of shrimp before responding. "Of course. There was a full investigation."

"I heard it was dropped after the prosecutor died," Sammy said in a neutral tone, waiting to gauge the effect on her father.

Leaning forward, Jeffrey's hazel eyes bore into her own. "What the hell are you implying?"

"Nothing. I'm just trying to get some background."

"Let me explain something. Everyone in this town wants to be rich, and everyone who's rich wants to be powerful. First it's show biz, and then it's politics. That late prosecutor planned to throw his hat in the ring for Neil's congressional slot. Hoped to build a straw case that would get his name in the running. Tried to dig up dirt on Neil and me, but he couldn't. Nothing. Sammy, you're barking up the wrong tree. Neil Prescott is a good man."

"Is it true his brother-in-law's savings and loan financed that project?"

"Listen, kid, you haven't been here long enough to understand how this town works. Connections. The only way to succeed. I needed financing to renovate that hotel. Neil Prescott's brother-in-law owns a savings and loan. That's not a crime. Donald Graves gave me the best deal."

Graves? Frowning, Sammy pulled her notebook from her purse and flipped through the pages until she found what she was looking for. "Is he any relation to a Lawrence Graves who heads the city's Case Management Unit?"

"They're cousins. How'd you know about that?"

"I'm a reporter." Sammy read from her notes. "Case Management, a little known unit set up two years ago to expedite certain projects." She looked at her father. "Now I understand how the

Canyon City remodel got the green light so fast. By sidestepping the usual permit process, big developers like Greene Progress avoid delays that could cost millions."

"You don't think the mayor of Canyon City might want to promote a quick renovation? I don't see a damn thing wrong with cutting through layers of bureaucracy."

Sammy opened her palms. "Can't argue with that. But the plans for the, uh, seismic-active system never got turned in. Or reviewed."

"You mean the active-seismic-control system? We did turn them in. Probably weren't filed in the right folder."

"Aren't those systems supposed to keep buildings up?"

"They should. If the ground starts to shake, they counter the quake forces and stabilize the building. But seismic control isn't relevant to Canyon City. There wasn't a quake when the tower fell."

"But the system had been installed, right? I thought you said the tower renovation hadn't been started?"

Jeffrey coughed into his napkin. "I was referring to the structure itself. You saw how cracked it was. Even an operational seismic-control system couldn't prevent an unstable tower from falling, and ours hadn't even been tested yet. Maybe if we'd had time to work on the tower's framework, strengthen the unreinforced masonry, things might have turned out differently."

Sammy returned her notebook to her purse. "It's just curious. Two tall structures, both financed by Newport S and L, both renovated by Greene Progress, both collapse unexpectedly. Neil Prescott was one of the common elements, the other was—"

"Me?" Jeffrey's tone was cold. "You certainly don't pull your punches. Rose's granddaughter to the core." He wiped his mouth with his linen napkin. "I may have been behind the eight ball twenty-five years ago, but I run a multimillion-dollar business now. And it's a clean shop. Renovations are tricky. Greene Progress has a terrific construction record. Go to Building and Safety and check it out."

"I have," Sammy said. "And it is. Except for these two cases."

Jeffrey laid his napkin on the table and took a deep breath.

"Before you go running to your listeners, blaming your own father for the deaths of those poor people, understand the reason we moved so quickly. That tower was at risk. We just weren't fast enough." He cleared his throat, seemed genuinely sad.

"Look, I'm not out to get Greene Progress," Sammy said. "Or you. But—"

"You are out to get Neil Prescott." The voice came from behind Sammy. She spun around to see a tall, slim, impeccably dressed brunette walk up to her father and peck him on the cheek. "Hello, *carino*."

Her accent was exotic. *Italian, Spanish, French?* wondered Sammy.

"Trina, glad you could join us." Jeffrey stood up halfway and pulled out a chair for his wife who sat down gracefully, at the same time extending a hand to her stepdaughter.

Close-up, Trina appeared to be a very young forty-something despite obvious traces of botox and plastic surgery. The giant diamond on her finger might be real, but Sammy was sure those oversized breasts straining against the tight silk blouse were enhancements.

Sammy politely pulled her hand from Trina's strong grip. "It may seem that way," she explained, "but I'm actually after the truth."

"How utterly charming. And naïve." Trina's laugh was low and throaty. She turned to Jeffrey and stroked his cheek. "Reminds me a little of you when we first met. Must be in the Greene genes."

In deference to her father, Sammy held her tongue.

"Samantha, dear, I've wanted to meet you ever since Jeffrey told me you'd moved here to do your little radio show."

"My name is Sammy, not Samantha. And 'my little radio show' is doing quite well, thank you."

Trina smiled warmly at a server who brought her a glass of Chardonnay. "So what were we saying, Samantha? Oh, yes, I've been telling Jeffrey, now that you're in L.A., we should help you make friends, dear. Friends who can help you. Like Neil Prescott."

"Prescott's not someone I want as a friend," Sammy said. Unable to control her growing irritation at this insipid woman, she added, "And neither are you. Dear."

Trina's dark eyes narrowed, while her tone maintained neutrality. "That's certainly your choice. But seeing as you're Jeffrey's daughter, you do need to respect his choice too."

"Excuse me?" Sammy was genuinely puzzled.

"Neil Prescott is our friend. Don't make him your enemy," Trina said quietly. "Don't make us have to choose between our friends and you. That would be a very big mistake." Resting her hand over Jeffrey's, she stared directly at Sammy. "Have I made myself clear?"

Sammy stared back. "Perfectly." She stood and placed her napkin near her plate. "I think I've had about enough. Bye, Dad, I'll be in touch," she said with a modicum of warmth. Toward Trina, her tone turned frosty. "Nice meeting you, Mom."

Eager to avoid a second bone-crunching handshake, Sammy grabbed her purse and left. A glance at her watch revealed it was almost two. Barely time to make the drive downtown for her three o'clock meeting with Jim's mystery caller.

Ana resisted the impulse to share Courtney's cognac. She'd raced back to the shelter, nervously checking the Vespa's mirrors for evidence of a tail. As tempting as a chemical relaxant might be, she needed to keep her head clear.

Now she watched Courtney standing in front of the bathroom mirror, brushing the knots from her blonde wig. "Think I'll pass?" Courtney asked, adjusting her sunglasses.

Ana studied the reflection. "You're taller than Sylvie, but with the wig and glasses, you don't look like Courtney Phillips either."

"I might just go blonde after this is over. Doesn't make my skin seem so washed out." Courtney pulled a lock of hair over her chin.

"What are you going to tell Sammy Greene?" Ana was eager to get back to business.

"Got any breath freshener?" Courtney asked, as she ran a wet finger over her teeth. "First, I'll scope out the place, make sure I'm not followed."

"They're handing out toothbrushes."

"If Greene's by herself and I can trust her, I'll say I'm Sylvie.

See what she wants from there." Courtney shrugged, "I was always good at improv."

"Maybe I should come with you."

Courtney slung an arm around her shoulder and gave her a squeeze. "You're safer here. No one knows who you are, and no one can find you."

"Nice of you to do this," Pappajohn told Ortego as the detective aimed his red Mustang north on Sunset Boulevard at the entrance to Bel Air. After the scrap with De'andray, Ortego had offered Pappajohn a ride to the California Science Center. Because the site where Ana's body had been found wasn't far out of the way, Ortego suggested making a quick stop there first.

"No problemo." Ortego scratched his buzz cut. "Dee doesn't like to bend the rules. Even for a good cause. But sometimes you gotta do what you gotta do. That was something we all learned in Desert Storm."

"Same in Vietnam," Pappajohn agreed. *Only turned out not to be such a good cause after all.*

"This is it." Ortego stopped his Mustang on a side street near the bottom of the canyon and pointed to a charred dune nestled in a blackened forest. The dust brown chaparral snapped and crackled like cornflakes beneath Pappajohn's feet as he stepped out of the car. The stench of smoke hung in the air like a heavy, cheap perfume.

Pappajohn leaned against the car and closed his eyes, imagining his daughter's voice. Crying for help as she'd raced down the hill, running from the flames. In her final moments, had she been desperate and alone? Or had someone been chasing her?

Ortego interrupted his nightmare. "Report said she was found in the gully here by a group of kids fleeing the fire."

Pappajohn opened his eyes to see where the detective was pointing. Rivulets of water still drained down the ditch.

"That's probably how she survived at all," Ortego said. "The flames must have hopped over her some."

A gust of hot air brushed past his cheek as Pappajohn surveyed the burnt acreage. The few homes hidden in the charred brush were far enough away that the ferocity of the Santa Anas screaming through the canyon that night would have masked Ana's cries for help. Some of these million-dollar dwellings had themselves been victims of the devil wind, their ghostly frames now twisted and stooped like blackened skeletons of old men.

Ortego looked around. "Perfect place to dump a body."

Pappajohn took a deep breath and nodded. He slowly paced the perimeter of the area, traces of Pappajohn-the-cop suppressing the pain of bereaved father. Unfortunately, days of fires, winds, and water trails had long since erased all traces of footsteps or tire tracks. After a careful search, Pappajohn returned to the car, disappointed. "Nothing."

Ortego was sympathetic. "Maybe your lead on the roommate will pan out. In fact, why don't I come with you? If it is this Sylvie, we'll bring her in for questioning. Finally get you some answers."

Pappajohn's big shoulders rose and fell. "Sure." He clapped his new friend on the back. His voice was hoarse when he added, "Thanks."

"Did I wake you?" Sammy held her cell phone by one ear as she used her free hand to turn the wheel onto Exposition Boulevard. Driving past the University of Southern California's imposing brick buildings, she couldn't help thinking how different this campus was from the isolated, bucolic grounds of Ellsford University where she'd spent her college days. USC was its own city, surrounded by an even more giant metropolis. How nice of the landscapers to plant a few trees among the ivory towers.

"Yeah." Jim's monotone interrupted her sightseeing. "So what's the good reason?"

"You used to work in TV, right?"

"Not a good reason," Jim muttered.

"You still know people in TV news, don't you?"

"Yeah."

"Can you get me some B-roll from the night Courtney was admitted to LAU Med?"

"You woke me up for Courtney Philips? Forget—"

"Don't hang up!" Sammy pleaded. "Neil Prescott was admitted the same night as Courtney."

"And the connection?"

"My boy—uh, my friend, Reed, says Prescott was brought in by a young blonde—not his wife, by the way—who sounds a lot like the woman the cabbie described." Sammy summarized her early morning conversation with Sandoval. "It might be a long shot, but he picked up Sylvie less than a mile from the hospital. If we can get a shot of her on B-roll, maybe we can pick up her trail through our favorite politician."

"The dead girl's roommate was screwing Prescott?" Jim's voice had lost its grumpy edge.

Sammy smiled, imagining him sitting up at her news. "Exactly," she said. "And just maybe, Sylvie can tell us what happened to Ana that night."

"As much as I'd love to help your friend Pappajohn, this really does sound like a wild-goose chase," Jim told her, "However, it would be nice to ID Prescott's chippie."

"Chippie?"

"Old timer's term for working girl."

"Ah." Sammy had reached the science center and pulled her car into the parking lot. "Got to go," she said. "If you could have that for me ASAP, I'd be ever so grateful."

"You get something solid on Neil Prescott, and *I'll* be ever so grateful." Jim laughed before Sammy disconnected the call.

Her car's clock read 3:05. Sammy locked the door and hurried off toward the modern science museum, anxious to meet the woman she hoped would finally lead her to Sylvie.

Yevgeny found space for his Escalade in a far corner of the science center's lot, then jumped out and surveyed the area until he spied his quarry. Darting between rows of parked cars, he observed the petite redhead running toward the modern brick buildings that housed the museum and IMAX theatre. The thick, smoky air had obviously kept the crowds away. Missing were the usual snaking lines wrapped around the circular movie palace.

Yevgeny stepped behind a bushy ficus for cover when Sammy stopped at the ticket counter. As soon as she entered the theater, he rushed over to purchase his own entry pass.

The woman in the glass booth pressed a button activating a microphone. "Like I told the young lady, show's already started. Next one's in forty minutes."

"It's okay," Yevgeny said. "I just want to find a place where I can breathe."

"I hear you on that one." She slid open the door of a plexiglass slot, pushed through a ticket, then shut it again, insulating herself from the outside air. "Inside and to your left."

Yevgeny walked into the lobby and found the theatre, its marquee advertising a nature film about undersea predators. *How appropriate*, he thought, as he entered the darkness where a pair of hammerhead sharks swam across the giant movie screen. Waiting for his eyes to accommodate in the dim light, he failed to notice the two dark-suited men leaning against the back wall, intent on finding prey of their own.

From an end seat in a middle row, Sammy tried to avoid looking at the giant shark, swimming, it seemed, directly toward her. Except for the rare trip to Coney Island, growing up in Brooklyn hadn't provided much opportunity to feel at home with the sea.

A moment before, the theater door had opened, sending a wave of light across the cavernous room, exposing the fact that it was at least a third empty.

Scanning the auditorium, Sammy caught sight of a familiar balding salt-and-pepper pate in the front row where she'd told Pappajohn to sit. Good. She was glad he'd managed to get to the theater on time. She strained to peer around a tall teen in front of her, but if her eyes didn't deceive her, the man sitting beside Pappa-john looked a lot like Detective Ortego. Sammy smiled. Guess the two finally bonded during their time together today. It might help to have another cop around if the woman they were meeting made a run for it.

So where was this mystery caller? She'd refused to say exactly where she'd be seated. Just that she'd be somewhere inside.

One of the sharks on the screen lunged toward a school of bass, its wide, sharp jaws about to snap shut on as many as it could snare. Turning away, Sammy spotted a solitary blonde seated several rows ahead, opposite an exit sign. Sammy rose, and slipped into a seat directly behind her. Leaning towards her ear, she whispered, "Are you Sylvie?"

"Greene?" the blonde whispered back.

"Yes."

The blonde twisted her neck to check out Sammy. "I'm not Sylvie, but I know the truth about Ana and—" She stopped in mid-sentence, looking past her, alarm blooming on her face. "I told you no cops!"

How did she—? Sammy turned to where the blonde was staring. Two suited men, who could have been G-men from central casting, were moving quickly toward her row. "They're not—"

The blonde wasn't listening. She'd flipped open a cell phone and pushed one button. Obviously speed-dialing someone. "I'm outta here." Erupting from her seat, she made a direct run for the exit.

At the same time, a burly man in a black Nike sweatsuit charged down the far aisle to the front row, dashed across and out the door, followed by the two G-men.

Stunned, Sammy stood and called out to Pappajohn. "Gus!"

"Hey lady, keep it down!" someone in the audience yelled.

The reprimand was moot. Pappajohn and Ortego had already reached the exit seconds ahead of Sammy who raced to follow them into the lobby and out to the parking lot.

Years of chasing crowded New York buses compensated for

Sammy's short strides. She soon passed Pappajohn whose wheezing made it hard for him to keep up. Ahead, she could see the blonde scurry between parked cars with the G-men and Ortego only a few feet behind. She'd lost sight of the burly man during the chase.

The blonde aimed for a red motor scooter hidden between two enormous vans. With a graceful leap, she hopped onto its seat and started its engine, accelerating onto the sidewalk, avoiding her pursuers as she fled back onto the pavement and toward the exit to the street.

Sammy heard a screech of tires as a black Escalade straddled the driveway. The driver turned out to be the burly man who now jumped from his truck and ran toward the blonde, just as Sammy and the G-men approached from the other side. Ortego and the G-men fanned out along the asphalt to limit the woman's escape, then encircled her.

Believing the blonde was trapped, Sammy slowed her pace. But a moment later, she stood openmouthed as a line of SUVs, trucks, and motorcycles carrying men and women holding photo and video cameras, swooped onto the grounds of the science center.

With the flourish of a striptease artist, the blonde slid off her sunglasses and wig, revealing brunette locks and her true identity. Courtney Phillips! Sammy held her breath while Courtney swerved her scooter onto an open stretch of sidewalk and weaved through the photographers. Laughing, Courtney hung a reckless left onto Figueroa Boulevard, narrowly missing an oncoming bus. Amid a chorus of angry horns, she sped off, leaving even the paparazzi on motorbikes unable to follow.

Cursing in what Sammy thought to be either Polish or Russian, the burly man reached inside his jacket for what looked like a gun and pointed it in Courtney's direction. Ortego gestured for Sammy to stay back. The G-men pulled out their guns and approached him from both sides, shouting to drop his weapon. The gun clattered to the asphalt.

For a split second, it appeared he might make a run for it, but he lost his chance as Ortego crept up from behind, and, in one swift motion, grabbed the man's thick arms and cuffed him. One of the G-men patted him down and removed another handgun from the waistband of his sweats, then checked inside his wallet, Sammy assumed, for ID.

After several minutes of agitated discussion between Ortego and the G-men, inaudible to Sammy, Ortego threw his hands in the air and stepped away. Shaking his head, he joined her on the sidewalk. They watched the G-men haul off their quarry, shoving him into a parked van.

Panting, Pappajohn caught up with Sammy and Ortego. "What's happening? Feds?"

"INS," Ortego said.

"What are *they* doing here?

Ortego appeared sheepish. "My partner called them."

"De'andray? Why?" Pappajohn asked between wheezes.

"Seems Sylvie had overstayed her visa. It's not really LAPD's gig to do the work of *La Migra*, but, like I told you, Dee's got a rod up his ass when it comes to rules. When I told him where I'd be today, he alerted immigration. Just in case we got lucky."

"So who's the guy in the sweatsuit? And why was he after Sylvie?"

Ortego shrugged. "I'd guess Russian mob. We'll find out more after they process him and I can do some questioning." He shook his head. "If Dee hadn't called them in, we'd be interrogating *el bastardo* right now."

"Damn it!" Pappajohn cursed. "And on top of that, we've lost Sylvie!"

"She wasn't Sylvie." Sammy said. "I'm sorry."

"You talked to her. What'd she say?" Ortego asked.

Sammy looked at Pappajohn, whose face betrayed disappointment. No point in upsetting him further. "Nothing. It was all a publicity stunt."

Or was it? Sammy wondered as she accompanied Pappajohn back to her car. Courtney had seemed sincere, though she *was* an actress. An actress who didn't need more publicity. *I know the truth about Ana—*

Sammy was now as desperate as Pappajohn to learn that truth.

"What's taking so long?"

Sammy turned from her computer to face Pappajohn standing in the doorway of her bedroom. Anxious to continue her research on the tower collapse, she'd insisted on coming straight back to the apartment from the science center, and waiting there for Ortego's call. The detective had promised to let them know when he was ready to interrogate the Russian. "You asked me that an hour ago," she said, shifting her attention back to the screen.

Pappajohn walked over and sat behind her on the bed. "What's so riveting?"

"A website on seismic safety. It describes base-isolation and active-seismic control systems," she said, scrolling down the pages. "New ways to keep buildings up in an earthquake."

"Oh?" Pappajohn stood to peer over Sammy's shoulder.

"Yep. Says here base isolation's like a pillow that cushions earthquake waves so buildings shake less. Computers in the top floors move giant counterweights that oppose an earthquake's force. Pretty amazing."

"It works."

Sammy looked up at Pappajohn. "You know about this?"

"We had time to kill before the meeting. While Ortego grabbed some lunch, I took a tour of the science center museum. One of the rooms had an exhibit where kids could build towers out of blocks, then knock them down with a button that shook the table. They were having a blast."

"I used to love building sandcastles at Coney Island. When I was done, I'd run and jump right on top of them." Sammy smiled at the childhood memory.

"The museum had a poster explaining this base isolation thing. And a video of a computer-generated building showing how it stays up in a quake."

Sammy pulled up a Quicktime file on her PC and clicked PLAY. "You mean this one?"

"Looks like it," Pappajohn said. "The control system has sensors that read the quake forces and then send large weights in the opposite direction to keep the building from swaying. That'll save a lot of lives someday."

"*If* it works right. But seven people are dead from the one that didn't work in Canyon City. She clicked on a photo of the Palacio Real renovation. "It didn't work there either. I wish I knew why."

Pappajohn furrowed his brow. "Keith and I were in the army together in Nam. He was a civil engineer before he became a rich computer CEO. How 'bout I give him another call and see what he thinks?"

Sammy nodded, and returned to her research. At least Pappajohn had something more to do than wait.

An hour later Pappajohn was back with a thumbs-up. "Keith'll look into it for us. He's got a couple of buddies at MIT who work in earthquake safety."

"Great. I'll order in some Chinese for us before I leave for the station and—"

The phone jangled. "That was quick."

Pappajohn grabbed the cordless. "Hello?" His expression registered surprise. As he listened, his features became a montage of shock, anger, then desolation. "Dammit to hell." He shook his head. "Yeah, thanks," he added, before slamming down the phone.

"What happened?" Sammy asked.

Pappajohn sat on the bed, hands between his legs, his head sagging on his chest. "The Russian at the INS? He's dead. Suicided in his cell." He looked up at Sammy. "Suicide, my ass!"

Kaye erupted in a string of curses when Miller told her what had happened to Yevgeny.

"I warned you. Your Russian goon interfered with my operation. We need to find Sylvie Pauzé."

"Yevgeny was close. He'd been following that Sammy Greene. She was—"

"Yevgeny screwed up. The contact wasn't Sylvie. Don't you watch the evening news? It was all a publicity stunt by that so-called actress, Courtney Phillips. The paparazzi that didn't take off after her got far too interested in my men. Lucky for us, Yevgeny gave them good cover and they could claim to be INS. So I guess I should thank *you* in some circuitous way," Miller observed.

Kaye felt confused, her bravado waning. "I didn't see Yevgeny on the news. Or your boys."

"Thanks to a few calls to friends in high places." Miller's tone became ironic. "Shall I assume you don't want his body back?"

Kaye gritted her teeth. How much she hated this man. "No." She'd tell her cousin that his nephew had disappeared. Bodies always led to questions, and quests for revenge.

"Unfortunately, not only did we lose Sylvie," Miller said, "now we've got the dead girl's father and that chatterbox radio talk show host on our backs. I'm not happy."

Kaye envisioned her empire crumbling before her very eyes. Miller's "calls to high places" could quickly put *her* out of business. And in prison. "I think I have a way to flush out the girl."

"Go on."

Kaye did a quick calculation. If she shared her scheme with Miller, she'd have to admit to deceiving him about Ana. At this point, she couldn't risk it. He'd never forgive the double cross. On the other hand, whatever Sylvie had managed to steal from that Arab must be pretty important. If she could find it first, she'd not only have her client list back, but Miller's treasure to hold over his head.

"I need to do this alone," she finally told him. "Sylvie trusts me. I can get her for you."

"All right," Miller agreed. "You have twenty-four hours."

CHAPTER FIFTEEN

"—from the Federal Emergency Management Agency, FEMA. Many of the families have been relocated to trailers in downtown Los Angeles with food, clothing, and other supplies provided by L.A. County working with the Red Cross and other charitable foundations. If you'd like to make a donation, please send a check to the American Red Cross. Twenty-eight after."

Sammy clicked off her mic and shook her head. "Too little, too late," she muttered. "They wouldn't have been in Canyon City if people had bothered to care before the tower collapsed. A dozen are still in the hospital."

Jim's voice came through the intercom. "Speaking of hospital, my buddy from channel two is dropping off a dub of the Courtney Phillips parade outside the LAU Med ER."

"Thanks. Though if I never see or hear of Courtney Phillips again it'll be too soon."

"Maybe she does know something about Ana. After all, they were in the same hospital on the same night," Jim said. "Why not ask her to meet you at the station? I'll keep goon watch."

"Maybe I should. But if it was just a publicity stunt, she won't bother to come." Sammy glanced at the clock and leaned over toward her mic, switching it back on. "Wake up, L.A., it's only night-time. Winds've died down a bit, and LAFD has let most of the residents of the Santa Monica Mountains return to what's left of their homes. Latest tally, over three hundred homes totaled, and four deaths from the winds and the fires. FEMA should set up a permanent presence in this town.

"We'll take your calls in a minute. Got some updates first. We're still looking for Sylvie Pauzé to help us learn more about fire victim Ana Pappajohn. If you can lead us to Sylvie, please call tonight. 310-555-KPCF. Ten thousand bucks to whoever brings us the prize. Courtney, think how many hours in rehab that'll buy you," Sammy added, only half joking.

"And, remember to send your checks for the Canyon City victims to the Red Cross. By the way, I've done a little research on the City Hall tower. Turns out the renovation was financed by none other than Mr. Get-the-homeless-out-of-Beverly Hills himself, Congressman Neil Prescott. Through his brother-in-law, Donald Graves of Newport Savings and Loan. My guess, these big *machers* helped grease the bureaucratic wheels to expedite a go-ahead on the project. Looks like they'd already started retrofitting something called an active-seismic-control system without final plan approval from Building and Safety. Now *that's* efficiency. Or is it a crime? Forty-four after."

Agitated, Dr. Bishop switched off the radio by his bed. Since hearing Sammy question the Canyon City tower incident on her show the other night, he'd been drawn to her coverage, fascinated by her suppositions. Her research had provided some intriguing information. Active-seismic-control systems could keep buildings up. That he knew. But could a poorly designed or implemented control system have the opposite effect? Accidentally or on purpose?

He massaged his temples in a vain attempt to reduce the pounding pain. Headaches he'd hoped had finally stopped, lately recurring with greater intensity. Just as they had right after— Shutting his eyes, he flashed back to a desert night eight years ago. Hot winds blowing then too when, shortly after midnight, he'd been awakened to care for a critically injured young soldier. The search-and-rescue team had said an apartment house in southern Iraq collapsed, trapping hundreds of civilians. Faulty construction, they'd claimed, though much later he'd discovered that the building had been brand-new and thought to be earthquake safe.

The soldier's whispers long buried in Bishop's memory now rose like an ethereal moan. *Murder.* His last gasps, desperate pleas that someone hear the word he struggled to repeat. *Resonator.*

Bishop's calls to headquarters had been stonewalled. Warned to drop it. Everything about that mission had been classified. All he'd been able to learn was that weapons tests had been conducted in the neighborhood of the collapse. A neighborhood far from the battle lines.

Through his pulsating pain, Bishop thought of the disembodied voice on the phone four nights ago.

What is it you want?

Your silence—As long as you don't decide to be a Boy Scout—

Resurrecting old fears. Bishop wondered if he wasn't going mad, imagining conspiracies that were never there. He drew a deep breath, considering what to do. One thing was certain. He'd need to be careful. Last time he'd demanded an investigation, it had ruined his career and nearly cost him his life. This time, he'd have to be sure of his facts before making accusations.

At a little past midnight, the fire shelter was more than half empty. Most evacuees had returned home; only the truly homeless now remained resting on the uncomfortable cots. Unable to sleep, Ana and Courtney sat in the facility's lounge, listening to Sammy's show on the radio.

"We've got to get you to Greene," Courtney said. "Someplace where there'll be no cops. Maybe at KPCF?"

"Too dangerous." Ana lowered her voice. "Teddy's coming back tomorrow. Whoever's after me will be watching the station. I can't risk getting caught,"

"You can't keep running. Eventually, they'll find you. Even here. Sammy Greene can help you get to your father."

Ana sighed. "I know, I know. But, I'm scared, Courtney. I just want to pick up Teddy and leave this town. Once and for all."

"And go where? Those guys at the theater had big mother guns. They're not playing hide-and-seek."

"You're right," Ana said. "Guess I don't have much choice."

Courtney glanced over at a skinny man dressed in a dirty shirt, baggy pants, and a woolen ski cap covering his eyes, sitting on the floor in the far corner of the lounge, rocking back and forth, muttering to himself. She leaned closer to Ana. "I've got an idea. Give me twenty minutes to change into costume and Courtney Phillips will be ready for her next act."

Trina carried two glasses of Pinot Noir back to the bedroom, surprised to find Jeffrey looking worried. He'd turned off the radio, and was furiously surfing through the TV news channels.

"What did she say this time?" Trina asked as she handed Jeffrey his glass.

"That our seismic-control system caused the Canyon City tower collapse." He shook his head. "Dammit! Why not plant a nuclear bomb in the Greene Progress offices? Would've achieved the same effect!"

Trina's dark eyes narrowed. "She said that?"

"Pretty much. And that my collaboration with Neil Prescott led to fraud and negligence." Jeffrey looked directly at Trina. "I thought I could handle this myself."

Trina sat on the edge of the bed and placed her hand on his arm, just as Prescott's face appeared on the TV screen. Jeffrey turned up the volume to listen to the congressman's taped warning of the dangers of terrorism in the new millennium.

"He *is* good," Trina said. "If we get a new regime in the White House, I could see him in the cabinet."

"From your beautiful lips." Jeffrey shook his head.

Prescott's photo, displayed behind the headline news anchor, drew their eyes back to the TV. "According to LAU Medical Center Chief of Cardiology Franklin Bishop, Congressman Prescott had a setback in his heart attack recovery yesterday and is now in the Coronary Care Unit of the Schwarzenegger Hospital."

Jeffrey slammed his fist on the mattress. "Shit! If Neil doesn't make it, neither will Greene Progress."

Single file, Courtney and Ana jumped off the bus a few blocks from an all-night Internet café on Montana Avenue. Afraid the Vespa might be recognized after its star turn on the evening news, Courtney had insisted they ride public transportation from the shelter. True to her word, she had completely transformed herself. For twenty dollars and a half-empty bottle of Korbel, the homeless man was more than willing to exchange his rags. Her slim frame hidden in the baggy pants, the ski cap covering her dark mane, Courtney was easily mistaken for one of the denizens of the night. The stench emanating from the clothes only added to the authenticity of the part as the few bus passengers moved as far away from her as possible. Even Ana chose a seat across the aisle.

"Okay," Courtney said once they'd arrived outside the café. "You go in and send your e-mail. I'll hop on the next bus to Canyon City and catch Sammy Greene when she leaves the station. We'll meet back here around five. You gonna be okay?"

Ana looked around the almost deserted street and nodded. "I think so. You?"

"You kidding? You're not the only pro, you know. After all these years playing airhead teeny boppers, I finally get to stretch my instrument with a meaty character role." Seeing Ana grin, Courtney waved and turned to go.

"Wait," Ana reached her arms back behind her neck and unclasped her necklace. She placed the gold cross in Courtney's palm and guided her fingers closed. "Tell Sammy Greene to get it to my father. If he doesn't believe the e-mail, he'll know this is from me."

"Good idea," Courtney said, secreting the necklace in her pocket.

"I guess it's kept me alive this long. Maybe it'll bring you luck too." Ana glanced around to make sure no one was watching before giving Courtney a quick hug. "P-U. Now go out there and break a leg."

Sammy was relieved when the clock on the wall displayed 2:57 so she could sign off for the night. If only her pleas for leads to Ana's murder had paid off tonight. Instead, "Sylvie sightings" burned up the station's phone lines, like a three-alarm blaze. By the end of her show, twenty-two new tips had come in, none of them promising.

Shuffling into Jim's booth, she shook her head in disappointment.

"Patience is the greatest of all virtues. Cato the Elder," he said gently as he clicked from the commercial into the news. He reached over to the side of his counter. "I have something for you."

Jim picked up a videocassette and extended it to her. "Dean dropped it off while you were on the air."

The B-roll from the TV cameras. The night Courtney was brought to the hospital. Sammy leaned over to give Jim a hug, but he held up a hand. "Not yet, I'm still achy."

Sammy backed off, placing the tape in her bulky purse. "Thanks."

"Anything I can do to help." Jim nodded at the speaker broadcasting news of the congressman's relapse. "Seems Prescott's having a rough time of it lately too. Maybe facing mortality will give him a new perspective, soften him up a bit, and," Jim waved his arm around the studio, "save our skins here."

"Now that really would be a mitzvah."

Jim winked, and, with a small salute, turned back toward his mic.

Sammy slowly pushed open the station exit door and peered into the darkness before stepping outside. Tonight it wasn't the Santa Anas that made her pause, it was fear of who might lurk in the shadows that had her on edge. After the scene at the science center, she'd been on 24/7 high alert. Like being back on the streets of Brooklyn as a kid.

In the dim light of the parking lot, she could barely discern the outline of a homeless man curled up, fast asleep on the ground near one of the large recycling bins. Otherwise, the area appeared deserted. Considering whether to wake the poor man and invite him into the station for shelter, she decided she might as well let him be.

It was almost dawn. Knowing Jim, he'd make sure in the morning that the man had a hot meal and a couple of bucks to start the day. The stench carried on a draft of wind as Sammy rushed past to her car, made her think Jim ought to offer the KPCF shower facilities to the poor guy as well. Just to be sure, she'd call him when she got home.

Sammy reached her car, and slipped her key into the lock, quietly opening the door. Turning to sit in the driver's seat, someone leapt out of the gloom and pulled her back up. Startled, it took her a second to recognize the homeless man, his fetid breath reeking of alcohol, just inches from her face. With a force that belied his slim build, he held his arms around her, pinning her against the car.

Not again. Terrified, Sammy flashed back to the day five years ago when she'd been attacked on the streets of a New York slum. She refused to be easy prey this time. Struggling against the malodorous man, she tried slipping from his grasp. Cries of "Help!" were forming in her mouth when a female voice ordered her to "Shut up, I won't hurt you!"

Staring directly into the face of her assailant, Sammy realized that the smooth skin and delicate features of her assailant belonged to a woman. And, once the shades and ski cap were removed, Sammy knew which woman. Courtney Phillips!

"Are you meshuga? You scared the hell out of me!" She stepped back a foot and brushed her clothes with her hands. "*And* yanked my chain earlier today."

"Hey, sweetie, you're the one that screwed me," Courtney said, keeping her voice low. "I said no cops and you brought the fucking cavalry."

"I wasn't the one who called the—" Sammy started to protest.

"I don't have time to chat," Courtney interrupted. "I'm not here for me. I'm here for Ana Pappajohn. She's alive."

Sammy felt her pulse race. "How do you know Ana?"

"Long story. We were in rehab together a few years back." Courtney did a one-eighty glance around the lot. "Listen, the girl's in trouble." She quickly explained how Sylvie had grabbed Ana's purse with ID at the party, that she'd gone into hiding. "Ana needs to talk to her father."

Sammy shook her head. "You've already sent us on one wild-goose chase. I'm not setting up Gus Pappajohn for another disappointment."

"He's in L.A.?"

Sammy nodded.

Courtney fished in her pocket and pulled out a shiny object. "Then show him this." She handed Sammy the necklace with the gold cross. "And tell him to check his e-mail."

Sammy gazed at the pendant, glistening in the dim light, trying to remember. Hadn't Pappajohn mentioned something about Ana's cross missing among the personal effects from the morgue? Maybe, this *was* hers.

"Then what?" Sammy palmed the necklace and slipped it in her own pocket.

"We meet somewhere, you and Ana's dad. No other cops. I'll arrange for a reunion."

Not entirely convinced, Sammy still agreed. "Nate's Deli, Beverly Hills, at noon. Lots of crowds, we can stay under the radar."

"Twelve it is."

"How'd you get mixed up in this?" Sammy asked Courtney just as the station door cracked open.

"You all right?"

Sammy stepped away from the car and turned to see Jim standing in the doorway. "Yeah, just giving a donation," she shouted. "Everything's fine."

"Okay," Jim said. "Saw the car still here and wanted to check."

Sammy smiled. Nice to have someone watching your back. She

waved at Jim, then swiveled around expecting to finish her conversation, but somehow Courtney had managed to slip away without a sound.

Manipulating the joystick to scan the electron microscopy display, Reed was concentrating on the fractured patterns of chromosome 11 on the video monitor, when the door to the lab quietly opened.

"What in God's name are you doing in the genetics lab at four a.m.?"

Reed spun around, nearly falling off his stool. "Michelle? How did you find me?"

"Lucky I did and not Bishop," she said, coming over to where he sat. "If the chief knew you were hogging the EM, he'd have your head."

Reed's grin reflected sheepishness. "Can it be our secret?"

"So this isn't a work-related project?" She frowned as she eyed the DNA analyses on the screen.

"As a matter of fact, it has to do with Ana Pappajohn."

Ana Pappajohn? Reed was doing this for Sammy Greene! The redhead might stand only five feet tall and maybe a hundred pounds soaking wet, but she clearly had a stranglehold on Reed's heart. Michelle found her face growing warm, irritation bubbling up, and she struggled to push it back. As much as she wanted to lash out, to demand *why her and not me*, she resisted now. Instead, she asked, "You're still on that case?"

Obviously relieved to avoid another row, Reed told her about the discrepancies between her own ER exam and the autopsy. "Sammy and Pappajohn now feel Ana's death was no accident."

"That's why you wanted the medical examiner's report." Her eyes focused on her late patient's chart that lay open next to Reed's elbow.

Reed nodded. "Sammy's using her radio show to track down Sylvie, Ana's roommate, hoping she'll tell them what happened, or at least why."

"Isn't that a job for the police?"

"You know how busy they've been with these fires. Yesterday, Sammy got a call from a cabbie who claimed he drove Sylvie home the night of the fire. Apparently she'd been bleeding—enough to leave a sample on the seat. Pappajohn cut a wedge from the cushion and Sammy asked me to do a DNA analysis. See if I could identify this Sylvie."

"Did you?"

"Well, that's just it. Pappajohn cut himself while he was getting the sample," Reed picked up a ragged cloth with a pair of forceps "A few drops of blood came from a male. Blood type, B negative. Only two percent of the population have it."

Michelle nodded. "Okay, let's assume that sample belongs to Pappajohn. What about the other?"

"The other was female and AB negatuve," Reed said.

"Even rarer, right?"

"Only about one percent," Reed said. "Now suppose Pappajohn's wife was type AA or AO."

"Their child could be AB negative." Michelle raised her eyebrows. "You trying to say the roommate and Pappajohn are related?"

"It's medically possible. But, socially, it doesn't make sense. Unless—unless the roommate is actually Pappajohn's daughter."

"Now *that* doesn't make sense." Michelle pointed to the chart. "What's, uh, Ana's blood type there?"

"A."

Michelle nodded. "Her mother could be AA or AO and father BO. That would work, too. What's her RhD antigen?"

"Positive," he muttered. "I know, I know, RH positive is dominant and common. But if a recessive allele from Mom was RH negative then the taxi sample—"

"That's a stretch, Reed."

"Fine, okay, but how do you explain this?" He tipped his head toward the screen. "The two samples from the taxi. Chromosome 11, what do you see?"

Michelle shrugged. "The elecrophoretic patterns look similar, but this is out of my pay grade. Intern, remember?"

"I've only used the Quad technique so far," Reed explained, referring to a method of analyzing small areas of DNA. "It seems like a close match, but I'll need to do a more advanced analysis to be sure. That'll take at least another day. But, both of these samples seem to show a mutation in one of the Beta alleles of the HBB gene. That's a marker of the trait for beta thalassemia. Otherwise known as Mediterranean anemia."

"Which is hereditary," Michelle finished the thought. "My God, you don't really think Ana Pappajohn might still be alive?"

Reed yawned. "It's a leap. Tell you the truth, right now I'm so tired, I don't know what I think."

"So get some sleep and tomorrow give Ana's father a call. See if he knows his wife's blood type."

Reed sighed. "If only I had a tissue sample from your ER patient to verify that she was or wasn't his daughter. I'd hate to be the one to get the man's hopes up, only to—"

Michelle leaned in and caressed his cheek. "Sammy's a lucky girl. I hope she knows that."

Reed's eyes met Michelle's, mirroring real regret. "I'm so sorry."

Michelle held up a palm. "I overreacted today. We never made any promises. I had no right to presume anything. Besides, I've always believed there's more than one person out there for all of us. Another bus'll come down the road soon enough. It's not terribly romantic, but, then again, maybe it is. Think of all the possibilities we have in life for love. Good things happen when you take a chance."

"So you're telling me I need to move to the next bus?" Reed asked, gazing at her intently.

She shook her head. "No. *I* do." She gave him a gentle peck on his cheek and added with a rueful smile as she started for the door, "I'm off for a few days. Going to see the folks in Santa Barbara. Clear my head. You have a good New Year."

"See you after Y2K?"

"Sure. After Y2K," Michelle repeated without looking back. She didn't want Reed to see her lips quivering.

• • •

Sammy was glad to find Pappajohn fast asleep on the couch when she entered her apartment at half past four. Since Courtney's claim that Ana was alive, she'd been mulling over possibilities. What if it was true? What if it was Ana in that cab and not Sylvie? Then who'd the ambulance bring to the ER the night of the fire? The ID belonged to Ana Pappajohn, but the girl was burned so badly. Couldn't see her face.

Ana and Sylvie looked like twins. The cabbie and the librarian both had trouble telling them apart. Even had the same pink purse. What if Courtney was right and they'd traded IDs? That would explain the e-mail message Pappajohn received from Ana *after* she was supposed to be dead. In the morning she'd call Reed to see what he'd learned from the DNA. In the meantime, was it wise—or right—to express her suspicions to Pappajohn without being absolutely sure?

Tiptoeing into her bedroom, she pulled out the tape from her purse, and slipped it into the VCR under her TV. She pushed PLAY and lowered the volume, then settled down on her bed to watch. The display that appeared on the screen was dark and grainy and seemed to have been filmed from the erratic perspective of a race car driver's tour of Los Angeles. Sammy guessed the Channel 2 cameraman had been leaning out the window to get his shots. Every time his vehicle turned to follow the speeding ambulance, the frame shook.

The nighttime darkness was illuminated only by the red strobe of the ambulance and the flashing blinkers and brake lights of the TV station's van as it tried to follow. Sammy could hear the howling winds and see the blowing ash and dust across the dimly lit path, reminding her of a blinding New England snowstorm.

The camera moved wildly once more as the van swung into the hospital's emergency room driveway and screeched to a halt. The cameraman jumped out to join the paparazzi filming EMTs unloading a gurney. His close-up zoom identified a disheveled-looking Courtney Phillips whose loud expletives made Sammy lower the volume on the VCR. After a minute or more of tight shots, the cameraman slowly panned the area for a long shot. Sammy saw another ambulance in the ER driveway, along with what appeared to be a high-end Mercedes.

"Don't find too many of those in my neck of the woods. S600— easily six figures."

Sammy whipped around. Pappajohn, dressed only in an undershirt and boxers, hovered at her door. She paused the tape. "What are you doing up?"

"Bathroom break. One of the perks of my age." He pointed to the screen. "That the tape your friend Jim promised?"

"Yeah."

"See anything?"

"Not yet."

"Mind if I watch?" Without waiting for permission, he sat down on the bed.

With some reluctance, Sammy restarted the tape. "That fancy car is probably Prescott's," she said as she thought she saw the Mercedes's dome light come on and then extinguish. "Did you see that?" She stopped the tape and rewound a few frames. Again the light was on and—"Look, the car door is opening." Instead of staying on the Mercedes, the video abruptly cut to a new montage of Courtney before focusing on another patient on a gurney.

Sammy gasped and put her hand to her lips. It was the burn victim. She turned to see Pappajohn pale as he must have realized the EMTs were working on the girl he assumed was Ana. Sammy reached for his hand while they watched the gurney disappear through the double doors of the ER.

Then the camera and its light shifted away to illuminate some of the gawkers. Most appeared to be Goth/Grunge groupies, costumed as Courtney courtesans. But one young blonde seemed out of place. Though the camera closed in on her stricken face for a mere second or two, it was enough.

"*The-ooli mou!*" Pappajohn cried out. "That's Ana!"

•   •   •

Waiting for the elevator, Michelle replayed the scene with Reed. Nothing different she could do. He was still in love with Sammy. She'd have to settle for being friends.

The elevator doors opened and she entered the car, pushing B2 instead of lobby. No reason she couldn't help a friend. She'd make one stop before heading for the parking lot and home. If Reed needed DNA from the ER patient to compare to the blood samples from the taxi, perhaps she could find a hair or a piece of tissue in the drawer where the body had been stored.

At B2, she stepped out into a dark, deserted hallway. She'd been down in this shadowy subterranean world a few times before at night, but somehow now, with each footstep echoing off the tiled floor, Michelle felt a strange uneasiness. It was as though she was being watched by unseen eyes. She hurried toward her destination without looking back.

Entering the morgue, she heard Salsa music coming from the portable radio on the floor, but saw no sign of the night tech. The sound of running water in the adjacent bathroom suggested he'd emerge soon. Taking advantage of the moment, she quickly flipped through the I and O log, scanning the page for December 24, until she found the name Anastasia Pappajohn written next to drawer number 23. Fortunately, no other body had been signed into that slot in the days since. Less likely that tissue or hair samples she retrieved would be contaminated.

Checking that the bathroom door was still closed, Michelle found the drawer and pulled it open. To her surprise, it was filled with barrel-sized machinery including multicolored wiring and a functional timer. Leaning down to get a closer view, she could see some kind of lettering on the container that she guessed to be Arabic. An LED panel on one rim flickered with a sequence of colors.

Startled, Michelle jumped back and into the arms of a scrub-clad night duty tech. Struggling against his tight grip, she craned her neck to determine if she knew him, but realized that she'd never seen this swarthy man with a trim beard before. "Hey, I'm Dr. Hunt."

The man seemed unconvinced, even as Michelle tried to free

an arm to show him her ID. "What you doing here?" he growled in a thick Middle Eastern accent.

"Looking for one of my patients. Ex-patients," stammered Michelle, pointing to the drawer. The machine's LEDs flickered through a series of colors again that reflected off the screen of an unlit clock. "Is that a timer? Wait, that's a—" In that instant she felt the tech's hands move from her waist to her neck, slowly tightening around her windpipe. *Oh, my God, he's trying to kill me!* Gasping for air, she scratched, clawed, and kicked with all her might. But she was no match for her assailant, and, in a few desperate seconds, the darkness closed in.

"You're sure it's her?" Sammy asked after they'd replayed the scene many times. She knew Pappajohn hadn't laid eyes on his daughter for nearly a decade. The features of the girl on the video were grainy and distorted. Could he be seeing Sylvie, wanting so much to believe it was Ana instead?

"The blonde hair, she does look different," Pappajohn said, shaking his head. "But your child, you never forget."

Sammy let out a deep breath. "Gus, I need to tell you something, and I want you to try to be objective."

Pappajohn's brow creased. "Something about Ana?"

Sammy nodded, and plunged into a full account of the encounter with Courtney. "She wants to meet at noon. Says as long as we're alone, she'll take us to Ana."

For a long beat, Pappajohn was quiet, staring at his hands.

"I'm sorry, I had to tell you."

To Sammy's surprise, Pappajohn didn't behave like the grieving father clutching at newfound hope. Turning to her, once again he became the professional detective, unwilling to jump to conclusions without cold, hard proof. "What exactly did she say?"

"That Ana and her roommate had mixed up their purses at a party in Bel Air the night of the fire."

"That fits. The pink purse in the apartment matched the one that was burned."

"Ana kept Sylvie's ID and tried to stay in hiding until she could contact you."

"So the e-mail *was* from Ana."

Sammy nodded. "Courtney told me to have you check your e-mail again." She pulled the gold cross from the pocket of her jeans. "And to give you this."

At the sight of the gift he'd bought his daughter long ago, Pappajohn's cool cop exterior vanished and like a great dam bursting, the mourning father's tears overflowed once more. He grabbed the cross from Sammy and clutching it tightly to his chest, cried out, "She's alive! *Zee!*"

The bedside phone rang several times before Fahim sat up to answer it. Recognizing the number, he spoke in his native tongue, "Hello."

"A complication," the caller said in Arabic. "But we fixed it."

Annoyed, Fahim placed the cordless back in its cradle and pressed SPEAKER, checking the clock on the end table. Four forty-five a.m. He grabbed the glass of Scotch he'd emptied just a half hour ago, a few unmelted pieces of ice still at the bottom, and placed it like a compress on his forehead. "What kind of complication?"

"One of the doctors stumbled onto our equipment. We had no choice but to neutralize her."

Fahim cursed. "Why call me?"

"The body's still in the morgue. We need Alabaster Chemical Supply to come and do a pick up. We'll put her in our empty crate."

Knowing he too had no choice, Fahim responded coldly. "I'll need at least forty-five minutes to get the truck, another fifteen to reach the hospital. I should be there before six. Have your men keep watch." Without waiting for assent, he slammed down the receiver.

Eyeing the packed bags in the corner, he knew his plans to be far from L.A. before New Year's Eve were off. Missing his morning flight to Las Vegas was bad enough. The thought of having to inform Miller made his blood run cold.

•   •   •

Pappajohn had regained his composure, though the roller coaster of emotions he'd ridden since arriving on Christmas Eve had taken its toll. His eyes were still red from crying, the lids drooping from fatigue, and, though Sammy had pestered him not to skip meals all week, he was beginning to lose his paunch.

Now, bundled in Sammy's oversize terrycloth robe, he sat in front of the computer on Sammy's desk, while she watched from over his shoulder. Double clicking on the Eudora icon, he entered the data for his e-mail account. Five messages sat in his in-box—the saved e-mails from Ana and Eleni and three new ones. With a trembling hand, he opened the first of these.

```
Dear Baba,
```

Sammy heard Pappajohn's sharp intake of breath. "Gus?"

"*Baba.*" He pronounced the word in the Greek, with the accent on the last syllable, explaining that it meant *Dad.* "Anastasia hasn't called me that since—" his voice cracked, "since her mother died."

"That means it *had* to come from Ana," Sammy said, excited by the implication. "What does it say?"

Pappajohn cleared his throat and read aloud:

```
   I'm sorry for the pain I've caused
you. I am in major trouble. I think
Sylvie was killed for something she
knew. I'm forwarding the messages she
sent the night she died. Please do not
go to the police. They may be in on
it. I hope to see you soon, Love, Ana.
```

•   •   •

"So this must be Sylvie's." Sammy pointed to the second unread e-mail with "PLAN B" on the subject line and a file attachment named *Catherine Deneuve*. "Who's that?" she asked.

"French actress. My generation." Pappajohn frowned, clicking on the file. "I doubt Ana's heard of her." Within seconds, it revealed a long list of names.

As Pappajohn scrolled through, Sammy recognized several well-known celebrities, businessmen, and politicians. Beside each were various comments: *Coke, crack, meth, E, threesomes, domination, soixante-neuf.* "It's a client list!" *And their drug and sexual pleasures*, she thought, mentally translating the French. One famous actor favored tall, model types, a dot-com mogul preferred natural-no silicone, while someone called Fahim wanted blondes only, no Arab girls. Beside his name was an asterisk and the word sadist.

"Whoever trashed the apartment must have been after this list."

Sammy had to agree. How many careers would end if it went public? How many might kill to prevent it?

Pappajohn nodded at the screen. "Looks like Congressman Prescott was a regular."

Sammy leaned in, surprised there were no particular preferences beside his name. If it *was* Ana on the video, she must be the blonde who'd driven Prescott to the hospital that night. Sammy shook her head. Seemed the congressman was hiding more than just banking and real estate shenanigans. As soon as Reed released him from the CCU, she planned to get an interview.

Pappajohn had already opened the third message and started reading.

```
Eyes only, al-Harbi.
Op. Y2K
34.058710,-118.442183
31, 12, 99, 23, 59.
```

Sammy grabbed her notebook to jot it down. "What do you think it means?"

"Got me. *Eyes only* can be top secret. *Op Y2K*, Operation Y2K? I don't have a clue about the rest. Phone number, address, safe deposit box, combination? Could be anything." Pappajohn stared at the screen for a long time. "This one was forwarded first to a blind e-mail, then to Sylvie Pauzé, and then to me. I can't determine the original source."

"Any way to trace it?"

"Not from here." He clicked FORWARD, typed a short note, then pushed SEND. "But Keith and his buddies in Boston might."

Sammy checked her alarm clock. 5:50 a.m. Six hours to the meeting. "There's nothing more you can do now, Gus. Better get some sleep. You want to be rested and alert when you meet your daughter."

Miller sat next to Fahim in the back of his parked Lincoln, listening with growing irritation. One day from his goal, and he'd been forced to take this predawn clandestine meeting in the underground lot of LAU Medical. This was not part of his carefully strategized plan.

"You disappoint me, my friend," he said, anger crawling into his voice. "I thought you'd learned your lesson. The whore's death was bad enough, but now a doctor?"

"It couldn't be helped," Fahim tried to explain. Perspiration rolling down his neck belied his calm tone. "The woman discovered the bomb."

"Where's the body?"

Fahim pointed to the Alabaster Chemical Truck parked nearby. "I'll take care of disposal."

Bowing his head as if in prayer, Miller was quiet for a long time, considering contingencies. He'd already planted "evidence" that would soon implicate Fahim al-Harbi as the terrorist leader behind the "horrible bombing that brought down the hospital on New Year's Eve." The phone message, the watch list notification, the money he'd wired to Dubai. He'd made sure the entire trail would be traced back to the Saudi. He'd even arranged for Fahim's arrest the day after Y2K in Las Vegas.

Best laid plans. Perhaps he could find another use for this patsy. A smile curled his lips as he raised his head to look at Fahim. "Okay, here's the new plan. First, my men will help you dispose of that women's body and her car. Then I want you and that truck back here at eleven p.m. Just when the night shift starts. You're going to make another pick up. Understand?"

"But Las Vegas?" Fahim's voice had become a whine.

Some gambler. Miller sneered, "I'm afraid you've just thrown snake eyes."

CHAPTER SIXTEEN

Ana met Courtney outside the Internet café as the first rays of sunlight cast a pink glow on the smoky sky. She was surprised to learn
that her father was in Los Angeles. "Guess I had to die to finally get
his attention," she said with a measure of sadness.

"At least *yours* came at all. As long as I brought in the money,
mine never cared what I did."

Ana gave Courtney a hug. "I care. No charge."

A sudden softness flashed in Courtney's blue eyes then retreated
behind her actor's mask. "Did you send the e-mail?"

"Yeah. Along with everything Sylvie had copied that night."

"Good." Courtney followed Ana onto the bus that would take
them back to the shelter. "I'm ready to crash for a couple before I
meet them." They slid into an empty bench at the back. "Noon at
Nate's."

"In Beverly Hills? Isn't that too high profile? What if they're
followed?"

Courtney gestured at her homeless disguise. "I'll scope out the
territory first."

Ana shook her head. "Maybe you shouldn't bring them to the
shelter. How about the diner on Lincoln and Broadway? I can hide
in a booth until I'm sure it's safe."

Courtney made a face. "That place is rank."

"It's homey, it's walking distance, and I can call Mrs. Darden from their pay phone. Teddy should be back in town this morning."

Courtney shrugged, "Okay, but I was really looking forward to ditching these threads."

"Not as much as me," Ana said, pinching her nose.

By nine forty-five a.m., the police officer calling in to the Department of Child Protective Services had persuaded the supervisor to trace foster home records for the name and whereabouts of Ana Pappajohn's son.

"Here we are," he said when he'd come back on the line ten minutes later. "Theodore Pappajohn, age ten. Mother, Anastasia Pappajohn; father, unnamed. Mother voluntarily surrendered the boy into the system in nineteen ninety-five. Hmmm."

"What?"

"It says here Theodore's a special-needs kid. CP. Cerebral palsy. No wonder his file's so thick. Hard to find foster parents who'll take on the responsibility. Seems he's been moved from home to home in the last four years."

"Where's the kid now?"

"Let's see. He's with the Dardens. Good solid family. No children of their own, but these folks have taken in a dozen with special needs since nineteen eighty-nine. Right now Theodore's their only one. Lucky kid."

Lucky indeed, the officer thought, jotting down the address before disconnecting. As he dialed Kaye's private line, he couldn't stop wondering why she was so interested in a dead whore's son. Bait to flush out Sylvie? Nah, Sylvie didn't seem the type to care. It had to be something else.

Determined to discover the real reason, he finished his call to Kaye, then picked up his jacket and, waving to colleagues, headed out to his car.

Forty minutes later, Courtney hopped off the bus at San Vicente. With her cap set low over her head to shield her from the warm

Santa Anas, she walked south toward the twenty-four-hour deli-catessen in the busy shopping district of Beverly Hills. Hardy socialites used umbrellas to block the soot and ash that flew by their delicately nipped and tucked faces as they made the rounds of Tiffany, Gucci, and Ferragamo.

Courtney leaned against one of the stores' faux brick walls, stole a swig from her brandy flask, and observed the parade. Dressed in threadbare clothes, she was invisible to the same women who normally begged for autographs. Capping her flask after a few sips to take the edge off her withdrawal nausea, she set off back into the wind toward her destination.

Rounding the corner, she encountered an unexpected procession of homeless people crowding the middle of the next block, spilling into the street. Many carried makeshift banners and signs that read: EXILE AND MURDER, TAKE BACK BEVERLY HILLS, and HOMELESS RIGHTS, NOT WRONGS! Some shouted epithets, "Murder, Genocide!" and "We're back and we're not going away!" A police car skidded around the turn a few feet from Courtney and sped toward the gathering.

The mob pushed into the center of the boulevard, forming a human barricade that stopped traffic. More policemen appeared from each end of the block. Frustrated drivers of late-model luxury cars began honking horns. Some even rolled down their windows to curse or make rude gestures as the homeless approached.

Fascinated, Courtney neared the slow-moving group, just when a half dozen uniformed men jumped from a Beverly Hills Police Department van that had pulled over to the curb. A gray-haired officer used a megaphone to order everyone out of the street. Unyielding, the protesters continued their march while additional cars backed up and added to the cacophony of horns and cries.

One homeless woman a few feet ahead of Courtney picked up a chipped brick and hurled it through the window of a jewelry store, setting off the security alarm and triggering police whistles. Courtney turned as two policemen jogged up, shouting instructions inaudible amidst the chaos. She tried to step aside, but felt her shoulders and arms pinned back, and her body knocked to the ground.

Handcuffs? She was being arrested! "Wait!" she cried, when the two officers lifted her up and shoved her toward the paddy wagon. "I'm not one of them, I'm Courtney Phillips!"

"Yeah, and I'm Britney Spears," one of the officers snickered, shoving her through the open van doors, alongside a few equally unwashed companions.

Within minutes, the van filled with demonstrators under arrest, none sympathetic to Courtney's protestations. It jolted as its driver backed out of the melee, using the sidewalk to take the first wave of prisoners to the Beverly Hills courthouse and jail. Knocked off her feet, Courtney rolled into a corner of the van.

Cursing her bad luck, she knew it would be hours before she could call her lawyer. Sammy Greene and Ana's father would assume she'd stood them up. *Again*.

Ana used the diner's pay phone to call Teddy's foster mother. "I spoke with your husband. I'm Sylvie, Ana Pappajohn's friend," she said, affecting Sylvie's Quebecois accent.

"That poor girl. So young," Mrs. Darden cleared her throat, "I didn't have the heart to tell Teddy."

Ana hated the ruse, but she had no choice. "Um, I was wondering if I could come by this morning and see my—see Teddy."

"You just missed him. The social worker came by—"

Ana felt her stomach tighten. "Social worker?"

"A family wants to adopt him." Mrs. Darden sniffled. "It's all so sudden. If we were younger, we'd adopt him ourselves. We love the boy. I asked if he could stay until New Year's, but the social worker said the family expects him today. I only had time to pack a few clothes. We forgot his Game Boy."

It took all Ana's self-control not to shout into the phone. "What was her name?"

"The social worker?" Mrs. Darden blew her nose. "Gosh, I don't remember. But I'm pretty sure her accent was Russian."

Russian? Ana dropped her own faux accent, screaming, "Oh, my God!"

"Where the hell are they?" Pappajohn finished his second round of coffee and waved for the waitress to refill his cup.

"They'll be here. It's only ten after." Sammy said. "Go easy on the caffeine, okay?"

Pappajohn glared at her. "This actress. Fool me once—"

Sammy nodded, weary. "But the cross?"

Pappajohn laid the cross on the Formica table. It glistened under the fluorescent lights. "Shame on me," he muttered.

"She's alive! Then who's in the ashcan?"

"Sylvie Pauzé, according to CODIS. Looks like you got punked, bro."

Miller slammed down the receiver, his fury mounting. It was the second interruption that morning. First the Arab's screwup and now Kaye. This call had confirmed his suspicions. Maybe the madam could pull the wool over the eyes of others. But swindle him? Dean of Special Ops? Not a chance. And certainly not now, with the future of the country at stake. He'd waited eight long years for the chance to help his world vision find a home in the White House. Offense, not defense. Preemptive tactics. That was the way to keep enemies at bay. Why couldn't those soft-bellied Washington elites understand? Well, no matter. By the strike of midnight tomorrow they would all be uniting in the call for military revenge.

In the meantime, he had to deal with yet another complication, eliminate certain loose ends. Otherwise his plan could literally blow up in his face. He picked up the phone again. Still, nothing to lose sleep over. To Miller, it was the necessary cost of getting the job done. After all, in any war, one had to expect collateral damage.

Sammy frowned as she exited Nate's with an angry Pappajohn in tow. Red lights flashed in the distance, a line of cars were backed up for blocks. "What's going on?" she asked, handing her parking stub to the valet.

"Homeless protest." The attendant stamped her ticket and asked for eight dollars. "Cops arresting everyone."

Momzers! The Canyon City tower collapses and the rich of Beverly Hills still can't open their hearts to show a little real charity. Sammy shook her head, thinking she'd report this tonight on her show. A good follow-up to her focus on the homeless.

The buxom policewoman shoved Courtney into the holding cell with a dozen other women from the protest.

"I get a call, bitch. I know my rights! My lawyer will have your balls!" Courtney shrieked as the door slammed shut.

"I'll put you on the waiting list," the policewoman laughed on her way down the hall.

Courtney kicked the bars in frustration, grimacing at the pain in her toes. How had she ended up here? Her last album had made *Billboard's* Top 10. They'd even taken her cell phone. And left her to rot in this stinkpot with—these people. This game wasn't fun any more.

There was no room for Courtney on the benches, which were bolted to the concrete floor. Not that she wanted to be too close to any of these women. She chose a corner spot where she could feign a sense of privacy and think. Dammit all, she'd really messed up. Now Sammy Greene would never believe she'd told the truth about Ana. Ana would be waiting at the diner, maybe with Teddy, and no one would come.

Fucked up royally. She reached for her flask. Jeez, they'd taken that, too. Not only would she be stuck here for who knew how long, but she'd be stuck here sober.

A wave of panic washed over Ana like a tsunami. Teddy gone? She had no doubt the social worker with a Russian accent was Kaye. Why had she ever told Sylvie—a pipeline to Kaye—about her son?

She closed her eyes, breathing in and out, forcing calm. She needed to think.

Trembling, she checked the diner's wall clock—12:05 p.m. Even if her father agreed to come, he wouldn't arrive for an hour. She couldn't wait. Who knew what Kaye was capable of? She'd already tried to have Ana killed. What if she was behind Sylvie's death?

Fishing in her pocket for the phone card she'd purchased, Ana dialed the memorized number. When the call was finally picked up, she didn't wait for a greeting, but blurted into the receiver, "I know you have my son. Let's make a deal."

"Now what?" Sammy asked, maneuvering away from the Beverly Hills traffic. She glanced over at Pappajohn, sitting stone-faced in the passenger seat. Still clutching the cross in his right fist, his steely expression belied the pain in his tired eyes. How could Courtney have been so heartless? What could she possibly gain by such a cruel hoax?

"Reed might have the preliminary DNA. Shall I swing by the hospital to check?"

Pappajohn shook his head. "Can you take me to the West L.A. PD? Ortego promised he'd have the lab rush the results."

Nodding, Sammy executed a U-turn on Wilshire, then swung a left onto Santa Monica Boulevard.

They arrived at the police station twenty minutes later only to learn that Ortego had already gone off shift. "Where I'd like to be," De'andray said, still working at his desk. He lay down his pen. "Winds've picked up and I'm seeing another wave of double duty coming. How long you two gonna stay on my case?"

"As long as you're not working on *our* case," Pappajohn replied. "We need the DNA results from the taxi. Emilio said they'd be ready today. Courtney Phillips insists Ana's alive."

De'andray rolled his eyes. "Look, can't you see you've been conned? Assuming the girl you met *is* Courtney Phillips, she's hardly a reliable witness. Who knows what game she's playing."

"Do you have the results?" Sammy interrupted.

"As a matter of fact, I do." De'andray pulled a single sheet from under his stack of files. "According to CODIS," he read, using the acronym for the Combined DNA Index System, "one sample belonged to Costas "Gus" Pappajohn." He looked up and added, "still alive to harass me."

"And the other?" Pappajohn demanded, not smiling.

"Sylvie Pauzé."

Pappajohn's exhalation sounded like a deflating balloon.

"Look, Pops," De'andray said, "I'm sorry for your loss, but, Emilio had no business wasting county resources on this nonsense. The sooner you accept your daughter's death, the better off—"

Shaking his head, Pappajohn spun on his heels and marched out of the station.

Sammy watched him go, then looked back at De'andray, furious. "Are you trying to destroy the man?"

"I'm doing my job," De'andray said, his tone defensive.

"With the incompetence I've seen around here, I wouldn't be surprised if someone screwed up those results," Sammy said. "Right or wrong, a young woman died on Christmas Eve. Ana Pappajohn or Sylvie Pauzé. Burned to death. Murdered, according to the evidence. Yet you've decided *neither* deserve your attention because of the lives they lived. You think Gus Pappajohn's a bad father, so you give *him* short shrift. Even though he's a fellow cop, a man who took two bullets once doing *his* job." Barely stopping to draw a breath, Sammy threw up her hands. "When we finally got close to finding Sylvie, Ana, whoever, you had to go and mess that up by calling in the INS. Lucky for you, your partner's willing to take up the slack, but—"

De'andray sat back in his chair, crossed his arms, and frowned. "Listen here, Greene."

"You know what?" Sammy said, glaring. "I'm done listening." With that she turned and strode off, leaving a wary-looking De'andray behind.

Outside she found Pappajohn waiting by the Tercel, one hand rubbing his upper abdomen.

"My gut's telling me De'andray's off base," Pappajohn muttered, his jaw set tight. "I think I would like to have a talk with your friend, Reed."

Even before Sammy had pulled off the West L.A. PD lot, De'andray was on the phone, calling his contact.

"You have something I want and vice versa," Kaye said, obviously expecting Ana's call. "I'm sure we can make a trade."

My darling Teddy! "Where can we meet?" Ana asked, frantic to get Teddy back and end the nightmare. Let Kaye have her stupid client list. Teddy was all that mattered. Her father had been right. It's the choices we make. Nothing was worth Teddy's life.

"Huntington Pier. I'll pick you up at two thirty." Kaye was off the line before Ana could argue.

Ana's eye caught the old analog clock hanging precariously on the diner's wall—12:20. Just two hours to run back to the shelter where Courtney had stashed the Vespa and drive it forty miles south to the seaside rendezvous. Nodding at the friendly waitress, Ana stepped out onto the sidewalk and was hit by a sharp gust of warm wind. Santa Anas were back with a vengeance. She prayed they wouldn't blow the Vespa right off Pacific Coast Highway.

Teddy was growing nervous. His cerebral palsy may have led the other kids to call him a "gimp," but the condition didn't mean he was dumb. In fact, Mrs. Darden had told him his IQ tested at 140. "You're a genius," she'd marveled.

He'd really liked the older lady who'd been his foster mom for the past year, had hoped this time to make a permanent home with her and her husband—at least until his mother took him back. Someday.

Ana. He liked saying her name.

"I'm finally getting my act together," she'd told him on her last visit. "No more drugs."

"What about—the other stuff?" Streetwise beyond his years, Teddy guessed the nature of his mother's work.

"No more of that either," she'd promised. "I'll get a real job and take you home."

So why hadn't his mother come? Even if she wasn't ready to have him live with her, he'd expected a holiday visit. He wanted to thank her for the Game Boy. Thanksgiving they'd had turkey at the local IHOP—Ana and the Dardens. She'd made him promise not to open his Christmas package early. The Game Boy was cool, but he would gladly trade it for her being there, feeling her arms around him. And, now, in all the rush, he'd left her gift behind.

Teddy scratched his head. Why had this social worker come to take him to another family today? Mrs. Darden had hugged him tighter than she ever had before, kissed his head, and handed him over without any real explanation. "I'm so sorry," was all she'd said as she'd waved goodbye. Something in the kind woman's face had made him leery. She looked sad. And worried.

And, now, swerving down the freeway with this dark-haired stranger driving, Teddy was really confused. First there was the car. Teddy had made a hobby of knowing every model of automobile on the road. This woman's brand new Porsche had to cost a whole lot more than most of the L.A. County social workers he'd met could afford.

And then there was her accent. At Mrs. Darden's she'd sounded like Natasha, Boris's evil sidekick from the Bullwinkle show he used to watch on Nickelodeon. Now she was on her cell talking to someone in a soft voice, with hardly an accent at all. Was she an actress too? And where the heck was she going? They were passing Long Beach going south. The next exit would take them into Orange County. That didn't make sense either. He was supposed to stay in L.A. Better let her know she'd gone too far. "Excuse me."

"*Ta guile!*" she yelled. Teddy had no idea what language she spoke, but the accompanying slap to his cheek knocked his glasses off, and nearly took his breath away, making any translation pointless.

•   •   •

Lou must have read Pappajohn's anguished expression because there were no jokes and no smiles. Without even his usual wink at Sammy, he paged Dr. Wyndham STAT and ushered Sammy and Pappajohn into the empty doctors' lounge.

"Everyone's hustling today. Santa Anas are stirring up again. Just heard that more fires broke out in South Coast and Laguna Hills. We may have to pick up the slack if those beach communities get evacuated," Lou said. "UC Irvine Hospital is already shipping non-criticals to Long Beach Memorial." He shook his head as he closed the door, leaving them alone.

Sammy sat on the couch, but Pappajohn paced like a bear with a briar stuck in its paw. Back and forth, up and down, round and round.

A few minutes later Reed entered, looking as haggard as Sammy had ever seen him. "So what's up? Lou said it was an emergency."

His no-nonsense tone made Sammy wonder if she was right to have barged in on him, but one look at Pappajohn's agonized features removed doubt. Pappajohn needed answers. And closure.

"Here's the thing." Sammy quickly reviewed most of what had happened since she'd left the sample with Reed, including her early morning encounter with Courtney outside the station, the video-tape from the night of the fire, and the new e-mail message from Ana. "It all pointed to Ana's being alive. Then this morning, Courtney was a no-show and now that *shmendrick* Sergeant De'andray says the blood belongs to the roommate, Sylvie Pauzé. So, either Courtney is lying, or De'andray—"

The creases in Reed's forehead deepened as he listened. "De'andray compared the sample from the cab to the CODIS database?"

"So he claims."

"If Sylvie's ancestry was originally European French, it's possible. Beta thalassemia is not uncommon throughout the entire Mediterranean basin."

At that, Pappajohn, stopped pacing. "Mediterranean? I'm carrying that anemia thing—trait."

Reed nodded. "I know. Your blood confirms that one of your hemoglobin genes is mutated. You have what's called the thalassemia trait. But, the other blood in the taxi had a beta thal trait pattern, too."

A glimmer of hope arose on Pappajohn's face. "My doctor said it runs in families. If Ana got the trait, could the blood have been from her?"

Reed scratched his head. "Look Gus, my results are probably not as accurate as the county lab's. They use the latest techniques. I haven't done DNA testing since med school. I only had time last night for a quick check. And I can't even access CODIS."

"I understand," Pappajohn interrupted. "But what did it show?"

"The two blood samples appear to belong to a male and female who share the same mutation for beta thalassemia," explained Reed.

"So Ana could be alive," Sammy said.

"Or Sylvie could have the same trait. Do you happen to know your wife's blood type?

Pappajohn replied without hesitation. "Double A. I know because one of the guys on the force donated blood after her cancer surgery since I couldn't."

"That fits," Reed said. "Anyone tell you whether she was Rh-positive or negative?"

Pappajohn shook his head. "I don't think so. Is it important? Her doctor died a few years after she did. I'm not sure how to get hold of his records."

"It's a holiday weekend anyway," Reed said after a delayed silence. "Let me finish running the taxi samples today and see if I can find any other matches."

Pappajohn sat down on the couch, closed his eyes and bent his head as if in prayer. When he looked up again, his cheeks were wet.

Reed sat down beside him. "Honestly, I'm as confused as you are. If you had a sample we could confirm as Ana's DNA, it might clarify things."

Reaching into his pocket, Pappajohn handed Reed the necklace with the gold cross. "I gave her this when she was a little girl. She wore it all her life."

Reed nodded. "I'll have to look under the microscope for embedded skin or hair. If there is, I can probably do a DNA test. I won't have time until things quiet down around here."

"Thank you." Pappajohn caught Reed in a bear hug.

Not wanting to provoke another painful slap, Teddy kept his mouth shut. By now he was convinced that the driver was no social worker, but he had no idea who she was or what she was doing with him. He just felt it couldn't be good.

Sitting as far from her as he could manage in the compact Porsche and holding his eye glasses lest she slug him again, he pressed his nose to the passenger window, trying desperately not to cry. Once they'd exited the freeway in Seal Beach, the passing signs were unfamiliar.

He tried to glean clues about his situation from the two telephone calls the woman received. Unfortunately, her end of the conversations were mixtures of foreign words he'd guessed were curses, stuff like: "I know my time's almost up—" "Don't worry, you'll get what you want—" "I knew you'd call—" "You have the list—"

By the time she'd completed the second call, they'd arrived at a long, gated road. A key card admitted the Porsche. Teddy could smell the sea before he saw it. Stealing an anxious glance at the fake social worker, he slipped his glasses over his ears and turned his gaze outside as the car rolled by rows and rows of sailboats and motorboats. The wind was kicking up and the massive vessels bobbed up and down in the marina like bottle corks.

They drove past the docks, then down a dirt road until they stopped near a wooden pier at the end of which was a white and silver cabin cruiser named *Lucky Lady*.

"Is that yours?" Teddy blurted, too awed by the size of the boat to stop himself.

For the first time, the woman smiled at him. "All mine," she said. "Isn't it beautiful?"

Teddy nodded.

"Would you like to see it?"

Teddy stared at her, expecting another trick, but she continued smiling, so he gave a quick headshake.

She came around to his side of the car and helped him out.

Standing on the pier, Teddy inhaled the salt air and marveled at the beauty of the ocean. In all his years living in Los Angeles, he'd rarely seen it. There were some outings to the beach when he lived at the group home, but it always seemed as if he was putting the staff out by requiring special attention. His wheelchair took up extra space, and not all the kids could fit in the van. Feeling guilt, he'd feign indifference, electing to stay behind with the babies. Perhaps that was why, despite his doctors' pronouncements to the contrary, he'd struggled so hard to learn to walk. His crouched gait with knees flexed may have earned him the nickname *pigeon*, but it gave him mobility and independence that was worth ignoring a few unkind remarks.

Clutching the railing, Teddy haltingly, but proudly, followed the woman up the dock onto the boat.

As soon as Pappajohn had excused himself to make a pit stop, Sammy turned to Reed. "I want to thank you too," she said. "I know how busy you've been. I shouldn't have asked you—"

"I never could say no to you." Reed pulled her toward him in an embrace, gently brushing her lips with his. She reached her arms around his neck and rose to meet him on tiptoes just as his beeper went off. Sighing, they both lingered for a moment, drawing apart so Reed could check the source of the call. "CCU. Got to go."

"Guess I'll take a rain check," Sammy said. "Any interest in a New Year's Eve party at my father's? I'm told his place in Newport has an awesome view of the Pacific." She smiled. "I'll even dress up again."

Reed reached out to smooth a few copper-colored tendrils from her forehead. "Unfortunately, I'm on call until Y2K. With the fires, the freaks, and the terror alerts, I'll be up to my eyeballs in work here on New Year's Eve. But, I'll take that rain check for the first."

Sammy stood on tiptoe once more to give him a quick good-bye kiss on the lips. "It's a date. We'll start Y2K together."

Sammy glanced over at Pappajohn as they drove back to her apartment. Since meeting with Reed, his sullen expression had turned pensive. "I know that look. What's bugging you?"

Pappajohn took a deep breath. "All these discrepancies. The blood results. The autopsy. And, did you notice that the police report had Sylvie's computer on the floor—but not smashed? Someone's gone to a whole lot of trouble to cover up this murder."

Sammy realized Pappajohn hadn't mentioned Ana's name, as if invoking it now might undo the possibility of her being alive.

"I'll bet dollars to donuts, Gharani's death was no accident either."

Sammy couldn't disagree. Even if the cops were simply dragging their feet, the discrepancies, the unauthorized cremation of the girl's body, the mysterious deaths of the ME, and that Russian thug suggested something sinister. "Ana's e-mail said Sylvie was killed for something she knew. The answer's got to be in the messages she forwarded. If it's the client list, every one of the men on it could be a suspect," she said. "Except for Congressman Prescott of course. We all know where he was that night." And with whom.

Pappajohn nodded. "And that *eyes only* message. Something tells me there's a clue there too."

"So what do we do now?" Sammy asked, pulling into a parking space in front of her apartment.

"First, I'm going to catch up with Keith. And then I think I'll give Emilio a call. Ask what he thinks about those DNA results." In a much softer voice, Sammy heard him say, "I need to know, one way or another,"

"Gus? Glad you rang," Keith said as soon as he heard Pappajohn's greeting. "I've got some interesting stuff for you. First, on this seismic safety business. I sent you the background. Check your e-mail. Cc'ed a copy to your friend Sammy."

"Will do. Hold on, I'll put you on speaker, so she can hear this." Pappajohn punched the speaker button, placed the cordless phone in the cradle, and waved Sammy over to his seat on the sofa.

"Hey, Keith," Sammy said, settling down next to Pappajohn.

"Am I speaking to the famous Sammy Greene?"

"Infamous is more like it." Sammy made a face at Pappajohn, who merely shrugged.

"Believe me, with Gus, that's a good thing," Keith said. "Anyway, I understand you've been researching seismic safety measures."

"I'm trying to understand why they didn't work in two projects out here in California." Sammy mentioned the collapse of the Canyon City tower and the Palacio Real Hotel. "They both had active-seismic-control systems yet they still fell down."

"Two options," Keith said. "Either, construction was poor and the buildings so destabilized that any ground vibrations or winds could topple them. Or, the forces were so incredibly strong—like a huge quake—that they overwhelmed the seismic-control sensors' instructions to the counterweights."

"There were no earthquakes in either case. You think these Santa Ana winds are strong enough to bring down a building?" Sammy asked.

"Theoretically if they were gale force. Most likely I'd go with option one," Keith said. "Poor construction."

"Any other info?" Pappajohn asked, ignoring Sammy's frown.

"Yeah, that *eyes only* message? Whoever sent it has maximum-grade security. I worked for hours and still can't figure out where it came from. I'm on deadline with my Y2K clients, so I've had to let it sit for a while. I'm going to send it over to a buddy at the NSA first thing in the morning. Meanwhile, let me give you some advice, Sammy."

"Yes?"

"Deep waters. Watch your step."

• • •

"Que paso?"

Courtney opened her blue eyes to face several pairs of brown ones peering at her with concern. She was shivering, despite the windbreaker someone had thrown over her. Teeth chattering, she said, "I don't speak Spanish. *No hablo español.* Shoo! Go away!"

"You are sick?" one of the women asked in strongly accented English.

Courtney hugged herself and shook her head. "No sicko. Okay? Go!"

Another homeless woman removed her shawl and laid it gently on top of Courtney's shaking body. "*Es muy frio aqui.*"

Courtney rolled her eyes. "Grassy ass, okay? Now leave me alone." She surveyed the packed cell, filled with women of all shapes, sizes, ages, and colors. The few who were well-dressed were easily identified as streetwalkers, though, unlike Ana, they seemed outfitted for the low-rent district. Most of the others wore plain clothes that they'd probably found at secondhand stores.

"Dee-a-beh-tes?" the first woman asked Courtney.

"*Quieres un poco a comer?*" another probed.

"No." Courtney held up two shaking hands. "Nothing. *Nada.* Kapish?" *All she needed was a drink.* Maybe someone had managed to sneak in a little alcohol. Courtney gestured with one hand as if sipping from a cup.

Two of the women looked at each other, obviously confused. Finally, one nodded, reached inside her billowy housedress and pulled out a small plastic baby bottle, half filled with formula, from between her pendulous breasts. She extended it to Courtney with an apologetic expression.

Courtney shook her head, and gently pushed the bottle back. "Where's your baby?"

"*No se.*" Teary eyed, the young woman pointed at a uniformed guard walking down the hallway. "They take."

Courtney patted the mother's arm. "Bastards."

All the women nodded. The word didn't need translation.

•   •   •

The moment Pappajohn ended his conversation with Keith, he left a message on Ortego's cell. He told Sammy he wanted the detective's take on the conflicting DNA results as she retreated to her bedroom to check her own e-mail. She had two messages waiting— one from Keith and another from her Washington colleague, Vito.

Opening Keith's first, she spent fifteen minutes reviewing the background information he'd sent. No matter how she considered the facts, she couldn't find a way to mitigate Greene Progress's responsibility in the buildings' destruction. The winds alone couldn't have toppled that tower. Either faulty installation of the active seismic-control systems had contributed to the buildings' collapses, or there'd been active negligence in their operation.

She clicked open Vito's e-mail next and found a note with an attachment. "Read summary first. This is really big!" The attached document, titled "Playa Bella Partnerships," was thirty pages long so Sammy scrolled to the end where she found three pages summarizing two specfic real estate deals involving land sold by the military— one in 1994 and one still pending.

Playa Bella Partnerhsip #1 involved a large tract of undeveloped land in Newport Beach bought from the Marine Corps by Greene Progress for twenty million dollars, then sold two years later for ten times that amount. An asterisk next to the twenty million referred Sammy to the bottom of the page listing the assets on the property. What she saw there was a shock. Palacio Real Hotel sold to Mulholland Real Estate in 1993. The old hotel had been built on land leased from the Marines. Back to the top, she saw that the president of Mulholland Real Estate was none other than Jeffrey Greene.

Playa Bella Partnership #2 involved two Navy golf courses sold to the city of Mission Alto. The plan was to build a world-class resort on the property. Apparently the city had solicited bids and Greene Progress was poised to get the deal.

The second summary page listed the investors in both deals. At the top of the list was Neil Prescott. Another asterisk explained that Prescott had sat on the House Armed Services Committee for the past ten years with access to insider information about military-owned land available for sale. In addition, all loans made to Greene Progress came through the Savings and Loan owned by Prescott's brother-in-law, Donald Graves.

As Sammy read what amounted to a picture of corruption, cronyism, and criminality, the reporter in her grew excited by the notion that she was on the verge of exposing a real web of deceit. The daughter though, was sick at heart. For it was a web in which her father was clearly enmeshed.

Almost worse than the fact that Prescott's tips about military land sales were certainly unethical if not downright illegal, was the very real possibility that her father had built his mega fortune on substandard operations.

Sammy leaned back in her chair, struggling with her conscience. Eight people had died in Canyon City, dozens injured, many more homeless families devastated by the tower collapse. To ignore their story would be tantamount to abandonment. She couldn't do that. But if she blew the whistle, any hope of reconciliation with her father would be crushed. And he was the only family she had.

She was tempted to ask Pappajohn for advice. He'd encouraged her to reach out to Jeffrey. But burdening the poor man with her problems when he struggled with his own crisis was out of the question. Better to call Jim. Now that she'd gotten to know him, she valued his wisdom. Maybe he'd know how to do the right thing.

Sammy dialed the numbers to Jim's cell on her cordless. It was too early for him to be at the station for tonight's show. As soon as he picked up, Sammy launched into her spiel.

"I got it," she said, breathless with excitement. "I got the break I needed. Vetted by civil engineers from MIT. Enough to nail Prescott's *batzim* to the wall tonight. But I need some advice."

"Sammy?" came a groggy voice. "Whoa. Slow down."

"You're not still sleeping, are you? We have a show in six hours."

Jim grunted. "Give me a sec."

The sound of a deep inhalation, a held breath, and a slow exhalation produced a vision of the aging hippie smoking a joint. "Aren't you celebrating Y2K a little early?" Sammy asked.

"I'm medicating. Just got the news an hour ago."

"What news?"

"You haven't checked your messages?"

Sammy looked over at her answering machine. "Nothing, why?"

"Right before the close of trading today, they made the announcement. America First Communications is buying KPCF.

Sammy gasped. "No way!"

"Way. The program director called me right after. We're out. *Sammy Greene on the L.A. Scene* is fucking cancelled. Finis." Jim accented his announcement with another audible toke. "We're being replaced by Frank Feral." He added morosely, "And yeah, I'm celebrating—"

"Dammit! And *I* was worried about protecting my father!" She leaped from her chair. "Stay sane, friend, I'm not taking this lying down. I'm going to go see dear old dad and make him take us back!"

"What are you talking about?" Jim sounded confused. "This has Prescott's fingerprints all over it!"

"Prescott's still in the CCU. No, it's my father. He said he could help me with my broadcasting career. I didn't take his carrot, and I'm not standing for his stick!" Without waiting for a response, Sammy clicked off and dialed Jeffrey's office.

"Mr. Greene just went home to Newport," his assistant told her. "The Laguna Hills fire is spreading north. He plans to be back in the office tomorrow. Would you like me to page him?"

"No thanks." Sammy hung up and grabbed the notepad where she'd jotted down her father's address. Newport Beach. South about thirty-five miles. If she left now, she might get there—with L.A. traffic—in an hour and confront the son of a bitch. Grandma Rose was right when she'd called Jeffrey a *gonif*. Her father *was* a thief—

not just in business, but in life. She'd wanted so much to believe in him again, but now he'd stolen that from her too. And that loss was something Sammy could never forgive.

Franklin Bishop found Julia Prescott dozing in a chair in the patient waiting room. Even asleep she was as beautiful as he remembered the fresh-faced sixteen-year-old. Living up to the promise he'd made to her father years ago, he'd stayed away, though it broke his heart. He'd never gotten over the fact that he hadn't stood by her when she'd been pregnant, but Donald Graves, Sr., was not a man he'd been able to fight in his teens. By the time the Army had put some guts under his belt, it was too late. Julia had already become the wife of Neil Prescott. He never forgave himself for letting her go.

A fortuitous meeting when he'd returned from the Army, a broken man, had changed his life again. Julia had convinced him to consider returning to work. He always knew the jobs at Baylor and then LAU Med hadn't come his way by chance. Now he woke Julia with a gentle tap on the shoulder.

"Oh my God, Franklin, is Neil—?"

"Neil's doing fine. But you look exhausted. Why not go home, get a real night's sleep? Neil's getting the best attention here."

Julia's smile was thin. "After all these years, I've become the quintessential devoted wife."

Something in her tone made him blurt out the question. "How devoted?"

She hesitated, as if groping for an answer. "I'm married to one of the most powerful men in the U.S. Congress, Frank. I'd be lying if I said I didn't enjoy the perks. Makes the commitment bearable." She looked directly into his eyes. "Devoted enough."

"I am sorry," Bishop said softly.

"We were young." Blinking, she looked away.

Bishop nodded, leaving regret unspoken. He sat down on the chair beside her. "You've heard the accusations about the tower collapse."

"Of course."

"You think it was an accident?"

"What are you suggesting?" A scowl furrowed her brow.

"Just wondering." He told her about his midnight caller.

"Probably one of Neil's handlers," Julia said. "They watch out for anything that could tar Neil's reelection with innuendo, especially now. Besides, if Neil goes down, so could his party—and that wouldn't be good for the country. If you watched his TV spot, you know that Neil's obsessed about national security. He's convinced this administration is too lax. We need change at the top."

Bishop rubbed his temples. "Those are talking points. Is that what you really think?"

"Me?" Her laugh was bitter. "Like I said, I'm just the dutiful wife. I'm not paid to think." She brushed her hand against his, then pulled away. "Maybe thinking is what they were warning you against. Sometimes it's better, safer, not to."

Before she hit the freeway Sammy left a message with the LAU Medical operator to have Reed call her as soon as he got the DNA results. She hoped his news would confirm what she and Pappajohn now felt to be better than even odds: that Ana was alive.

Driving south on the 405, she was surprised to see how few cars were traveling in her direction. She passed a sign for Huntington Beach and realized she'd almost reached her destination in under thirty-five minutes. A new record for a freeway that at rush hour, often resembled a parking lot. By contrast, northbound traffic was bumper to bumper, many of the cars and trucks loaded with household belongings.

Switching on the radio, Sammy heard the weatherman report heavy winds and new fires along the Pacific coast north from Laguna Beach to Newport. The governor had declared Orange County a disaster area, warning residents in the fire zones to evacuate. Even in the dim light of dusk she could see distant plumes of black smoke and wondered, watching the northbound caravan, if she'd been wise to attempt this trip tonight.

Radio static made her scan the stations, searching for a stronger signal. The only one coming in loud and clear was a national talk show. A conservative talk show. A caller from Alabama was hysterical about warnings filling the news all week—that a major terrorist attack in the U.S. was imminent.

"The FBI is sitting on this," the caller's voice was high pitched. "But it's gonna happen, I can see the signs. I'm heading for the hills before Y2K. Got a bunker in North Carolina. Filled up the place with enough food and water to last a month."

"Federal Bureau of Incompetence, they are," the host agreed. "We have to protect ourselves, become freedom fighters, because our government isn't going to do it for us. Kevin in Sacramento, what's the word?"

"America for Americans. We didn't have these problems before the president opened our borders. If we make it through Y2K, next November we'd all better vote for a God-fearing leader with some real values."

"Amen to that," said the host. "The whole world is holding its collective breath until midnight tomorrow. Will two thousand be the start of Armageddon, or can we make it instead, the new American century?"

Despite what to Sammy was repellent politics, the program, from a broadcast professional's standpoint, provided significant entertainment. She listened in disgusted fascination as the host fielded a few more calls. He encouraged the fears and prejudices of his audience on the air reminding her of a polished evangelical snake oil salesman out to prey on the unsuspecting—and the oversuspecting—for a buck. *When did our airwaves devolve from freedom of speech to freedom to spew?*

"America for Americans. The clock is ticking, and you better pray I'll be back with you tomorrow night. This is Frank Feral, the man who is to the right of Rush and to the left of God, signing off."

Frank Feral! This manipulative SOB was replacing her show? Not a chance, she vowed, flipping the radio dial to off. Flooring the accelerator, she sped into the wind.

Ten minutes later Sammy barreled through an open gate, and,

skidding on the gravel with each turn, maneuvered her way up a long, steep driveway. At the top of the hill, she came to an abrupt stop in front of her father's three-story sprawling modern glass-and-wood mansion. Every light in the place seemed to be on, making the structure appear like an unearthly temple against the dark night sky.

Stepping out of the car, she was assaulted by the stench of smoke carried on powerful wafts of wind. Although she knew her father's home overlooked the ocean, as she stood at the glass paneled front door waiting for her knock to be answered, all she could see on the horizon beyond was a wall of murky blackness created by fires she knew were heading this way.

A knock at the door woke Pappajohn from a half sleep. Too keyed up since learning that Ana might be alive, he'd laid down on the couch, ticking off possible suspects and motives for Sylvie's murder. The effect must have been like counting sheep, Pappajohn realized as he rose to answer the door. It was quarter after six on his watch and pitch dark outside. He'd been asleep since five.

Pappajohn peeked through the peephole. "Emilio? I left you a message on your phone," he said, opening the door to invite him in.

"Yeah, I got it and decided to swing by. I live in Venice. Not too far."

"De'andray said you were off today." Though Ortego was dressed in casual clothes, Pappajohn caught a glimpse of his pistol in the shoulder holster beneath his windbreaker.

"Actually, Dee's the reason I'm here." Ortego rubbed his buzz cut like a genie and let out a long, loud breath, "Jeez, it pains me to say this, Gus. Honestly, I trusted the man. Like a brother. But, I can't deny it any more. He's dragging his heels on this investigation. What I'm not sure of is why."

Pappajohn's eyes narrowed. "You have a theory?"

Ortego nodded. "I think someone's paying him off."

Pappajohn noted Ortego's tortured expression and felt an instant camaraderie. Years ago, as a Boston cop, a colleague he'd depended on had betrayed his trust. When Pappajohn had discovered a couple of narco officers squireling away part of the take from their drug busts and selling the stuff on the street, he and his friend, Chief Donovan, had launched a sting to catch the bastards. Except that Donovan had been in the game up to his eyeballs. The sting had been a setup that caught Pappajohn unaware. He'd ended up with two bullets in his gut and a reputation as a stool pigeon, forcing him to take early retirement from the Boston force.

Now Pappajohn gave Ortego's shoulder an avuncular squeeze. "I've had bad vibes from the guy, too, but you'd better be sure before you turn him in. Shit happens."

"That's why I came to talk to you before I do anything. I think I've caught a break in your daughter's case, and I'd like to take you with me. I'll explain everything on the way." He looked around the tiny living room area. "Where's Sammy? She's been a part of your investigation. She might as well come too."

"She's gone to see her father," Pappajohn said, grabbing the house key she'd left him. "We can catch up with her later."

Ortego smiled. "Sure thing." He wrapped an arm around Pappajohn as together they left the apartment and headed for his car.

Between the holidays and the fires, the hospital genetics research lab was as deserted this afternoon as it had been during the night. Reed walked over to the corner where three hours earlier he'd left the gel electrophoresis apparatus plugged in. Good. The blue tracking dye had migrated to the bottom of the shallow dish, indicating that the separation of DNA fragments from the single hair root he'd found embedded in the chain of the gold cross was complete.

It didn't take long for Reed to appreciate the findings. The DNA from the cab and the hair caught in the necklace were identical.

Reed had to tell Sammy. He picked up the wall phone to request an outside line.

"Dr. Wyndham?"

"Yes?"

"There's a message for you from a Sammy Greene," the operator reported. "She said not to disturb you while you were busy."

Reed smiled. Sammy Greene changing her ways? "That's it?"

"No, let me read this," the operator replied, rustling the paper on which she had written the message. "Going down to Newport to see my father. Call my cell if you get the results today."

A minute later a single ring was followed by: *Due to the Santa Anas and the fires we are experiencing a number of outages in the area. Please try your call later.*

Wondering whether to wait until Sammy returned from Newport, Reed decided it might be wise to let the police know they needed to double check that CODIS report.

Hanging up, he asked the operator for the number of the West L.A. police precinct and another outside line. This time the call went through and Reed found himself talking to Detective Montel De'andray.

Jeffrey Greene opened the door, a legal-sized file in one hand, a look of surprise on his haggard face. Though his warm-up suit was Gucci, tonight he looked less crisp, more frazzled than usual. "Sammy? I was expecting Trina. She should have been home hours ago."

"And I'm glad to see you too, Dad," Sammy said, barging into the vaulted foyer without waiting for his invitation.

Jeffrey shut the door and turned to his daughter. "Of course I'm glad to see you. But didn't you hear the news? The fires from Laguna are heading up this way. I was just trying to get my important papers together to store in the safe on my boat. Governor's already declared a disaster—"

"*Shtup* the governor," Sammy retorted. "I've got my own disaster. The one *you* declared!"

Fahim stood on the steep buff overlooking Zuma Beach, watching the last rays of smoke-muted sunlight dip below the horizon, listening to the crashing of waves on the Malibu shore sixty meters below the craggy rocks. The wind rose in sudden, impetuous gusts, whipping up swirls of surf here and there until the ocean's surface resembled threatening storm clouds in a winter sky. The waves would typically have been an irresistible temptation for young, muscled swimmers on surfboards. But now, with the smoke from the nearby mountain fires blanketing the coast, the beach was deserted.

Enveloped in darkness, Fahim heard a car whip around the hairpin curve off Pacific Coast Highway and pull into the scenic turnout where he'd parked the Alabaster Chemical truck. Miller's men driving the dead doctor's Honda Civic. The sound of heavy footsteps approaching made him turn.

"Ready?"

Fahim nodded at the two stocky men wearing latex gloves and dressed all in black. Other than the fact that one sported a blue Dodgers baseball cap, while the other was hatless, they could have been twins. Neither smiled. Without a word, the hatless man handed Fahim a pair of latex gloves to put on before following them both back to his truck.

Together all three unloaded the body al-Salid's men had hidden inside a wooden crate. The woman was bigger and heavier than the whore he'd killed, and despite the assistance, Fahim found himself out of breath and covered with sweat by the time they'd laid her down on the ground near her car. As he unrolled the hospital sheet in which she'd been wrapped, he couldn't avoid gazing at the blonde's long, shapely legs and fine-boned facial features. Beautiful even in death. An American Amazon. For his next sexual rendezvous he'd have to ask for one like this. He supposed there were many in Las Vegas.

"Let's get the show on the road," the Dodger fan said. He got into the Civic, started the engine, and drove it out of the turnout and up and just to the very edge of the precipice. Leaving the car in neutral, he helped Fahim lift the body into the driver's seat.

Satisfied that he'd positioned the dead woman with her foot on the accelerator, he reached into his back pocket, removed a flask filled with whiskey and poured it over the front seats. Then he moved the shift knob to *drive* and shut the door. Just before joining

Fahim and his partner at the rear of the car, he tossed in a lighted match, igniting the interior. With one concentrated shove, they all pushed, sending the flaming compact somersaulting downward. In seconds, it slammed into the rocks and brush near the bottom of the cliff and exploded, a giant ball of fire.

"Well that went a whole lot smoother than that DA we ran off the road last year," the Dodger fan said, slipping off his latex gloves.

His partner agreed. "Much easier when they're already dead." They both began the walk back to the truck.

Fahim stayed behind for a moment, mesmerized by the conflagration. From high above he felt its heat. Yet he shivered in the darkness, wondering how Allah would judge him at *yawm ad-din*. True, he'd killed the whore, but it was an accident, truly. He was no cold-blooded killer. Not like these men who seemed to relish death. Miller. Al-Salid. All of them driven by some obsessive need to control the world. Fahim was just a man who wanted nothing more than to enjoy its fruits, a warm female body and a cool drink. The money Miller was fronting for al-Salid should have been in the Dubai account already. But Miller didn't seem to want to let go of the reins yet.

"Coming?" one of them called out. "You gotta drive us back to the hospital for that eleven o'clock pickup."

With a last look at the flames below, Fahim returned to the truck and slid into the driver's seat. As he pulled onto Pacific Coast Highway heading south, he had one realization. No matter how much he wished otherwise, Miller would keep him in this scheme until the very end.

"Sammy, listen to me," Jeffrey said. "I had absolutely nothing to do with your show being cancelled. Please believe me. If you want, I'll call Neil in the hospital. He'll know how to fix this."

"Yeah. He sure knows how to put in the fix all right. Like he did for your Orange County land deal. Like he did with Donald Graves at the S and L." Sammy's eyes filled as she stared at her father. She thought she'd pushed her yearning for family down where it would never rise again. But seeing him now was another reminder of all the pain and disappointments she'd endured because of him.

"Grandma Rose tried to make me see you for the bastard that you are, but I refused to believe her, tried making excuses for your leaving me as a kid. Well, now I have my own proof that you're a crook." To hide her tears, she turned away from him and faced the bay window of the elegantly paneled home office. The churning Pacific beyond the marina echoed the churning in her soul.

Jeffrey came over and laid a hand on her shoulder. "Baby, you've got it all wrong. All I ever wanted was to build a future that would make my family proud. That would make *you* proud."

Sammy choked back sniffles with a wry laugh. "Oh, right, you did this all for me. The luxury suite in Century City, the trophy wife, the mansion, this view." She waved an arm at the 180 degree panorama of the wind-battered marina and the turbulent ocean below.

Jeffrey tightened his lips and handed her a box of files on his rosewood desk. "Look, Sammy, just help me get these papers down to the boat, and I promise you, I'll get you back on the air as soon as—tomorrow." He opened his wall safe and removed several more documents, laying them on top of her box.

"The fires seem miles away," Sammy said, squinting at the hills to the south.

"Bradley Farnsworth just called from Corona Del Mar. Less than a mile. Said his guesthouse is gone." Jeffrey took a framed black-and-white photo from his desk, and placed it gingerly on top of a box filled with ledgers, disks, and other paperwork by his feet on the floor.

Curious, Sammy glanced at the portrait. To her amazement, it displayed a scowling middle-aged Grandma Rose holding a laughing curly haired toddler in her lap. Behind her, stood a young couple—her father, tall and handsome, and her frizzy-haired pixie mother with that lopsided grin Sammy'd almost forgotten, leaning her head on his shoulder.

Clearing his throat, Jeffrey lifted the cardboard container and nodded at Sammy to follow.

Blinking back her own tears, Sammy balanced her box on one hip and followed him out the door to his car.

Teddy awoke in confusion. Everything around him was blurry. And rocking. He reached around for his glasses, at the same time fighting the urge to shut his eyes and go back to sleep. Touching his face, he was surprised to feel his glasses still on his nose. Where was he? As his blurred vision slowly cleared, he scanned the wood-paneled room. He seemed to be in a small cabin on a bed.

That's when Teddy remembered. The boat. The fake social worker with the fake smile. He'd thought she was being nice, showing him around the beautiful cabin cruiser, then offering him a glass of milk and chocolate chip cookies. She'd even told him to call her Kaye. He'd washed down a cookie with the milk, and then she'd said something about his taking a nap. But he'd told her he wanted to go home. Didn't he? How did he end up here? And how long had he been asleep? In the dim light, he couldn't tell if it was night or day.

Forcing himself into a sitting position, he waited for a wave of nausea to pass before attempting to stand. Everything was rocking up and down, back and forth, aggravating the drumming in his abdomen. Trying to maintain his balance, he staggered over to the door and turned the knob. It wouldn't budge. He was locked in! A prisoner. Why? Though not a particular fan of fairy tales, he couldn't help thinking of Hansel and Gretel—with Kaye, the fake social worker, as the villainess of this story.

Gripped by fear, he leaned against the paneling for balance, heart pounding. How could he escape? Think! Didn't Mrs. Darden say he was a genius? He had to be able to figure some way out. He looked around the room, but there seemed to be no other exit. He'd have to wait until someone opened the door. Then he could push it closed and knock them against the jamb. No good, he realized. They'd catch him the minute he tried his getaway. Though he'd learned to walk, he still couldn't run.

But he *was* strong. He'd gotten his mother to buy him a set of barbells last year so he could strengthen his arms. He never really explained that he wanted to prove his grit against a bully at school. It still made him smile to recall the shocked look and the bloody nose on the kid after he'd managed a sucker punch.

Now he searched for a weapon. Every bit of furniture seemed to be bolted to the floor—the bed, a small table, even the chair. In the corner, however, he spotted a square, ridged ashtray. Expecting it to be glued down, he was surprised he could lift it, though it was really heavy. If he could hit someone hard enough in the stomach to knock the air out of them, maybe he could get away. Without a better idea, it was worth a try.

Through the ceiling vents, he thought he heard angry voices. Too muffled to make out the words, they seemed to be moving closer. Quickly, Teddy hobbled over to the door, gripping the glass, waiting. Within minutes his muscles had cramped and he was close to vomiting from the rocking. Just as he was about to put the ashtray down again, footsteps approached. With renewed effort, he held the glass close, hoping to launch it like a discus the second the door opened.

The handle jiggled and the door was unlocked. Teddy held his breath, aiming for his target. But instead of Kaye, his mother faced him. Shocked, he dropped the ashtray. Before he could speak, someone shoved her into the room, knocking him backward onto the floor.

Ana rushed over and knelt to take him in her arms. "Sweetheart. Are you okay?"

"I think so," he said, then screamed, "No!" when he saw Kaye standing in the open doorway, pointing a gun in his direction. Her neat dark hair had been tangled by the wind, her brown eyes, once kinder, were wild with fury. To Teddy, she could easily have been the Wicked Witch.

"How very maternal." The witch laughed. "For a whore."

Ana stood and straddled Teddy, placing her body between his and Kaye, her arms spread to shield her son. "Let my boy go. I said I'd give you what you wanted."

Kaye pointed the gun directly at Ana. "First, hand over what Sylvie stole from me."

Ana lowered one arm to reach into her jeans pocket.

"Try anything and I'll kill you both." Kaye waved her gun from Ana to Teddy.

Slowly, Ana pulled out the Jazz drive and, holding it between two fingers, extended it toward Kaye.

Aiming the gun with her left hand, Kaye grabbed the disk. "It's all there?"

"Whatever *it* is," Ana said with a casualness Teddy knew to be false. "Sylvie called it Plan B, but she never said what it was. And I couldn't fit it into the computer—"

"Plan B! I gave that girl everything and this is how she repaid me? By stealing my list of clients?" Kaye held up the Jazz drive. "And *you*," she glared at Ana. "You couldn't leave well enough alone? Yevgeny turned your apartment upside down that night."

"You've got what you wanted." Ana grabbed Teddy's hand and started toward the door.

"Not so fast." Kaye pointed the gun directly at Teddy's heart. "Aren't you forgetting something?"

Ana moved in front of him. "I don't know what you're talking about," she stammered.

"I think you do. Miller doesn't send his men out on foxhunts unless he's after a fox. Whatever Sylvie managed to steal from that Arab must be pretty important."

"I don't know who Miller is, but if you mean this text message, it's here." Ana reached into her pocket and handed over the copy she'd made. "It's just gibberish, Kaye. You don't have to worry. We won't tell anyone."

Kaye glanced at the jumble of letters and numbers, then slipped the paper inside her cleavage. "Oh, I'm not worried."

To Teddy, the smile she produced was pure evil. *This was no fairy tale*, he thought as he heard the click of the handgun's release. This was a real live nightmare.

•   •   •

"So what makes you think De'andray's dirty?" Pappajohn asked Ortego. They'd been driving for fifteen minutes and so far the detective had just made small talk. Pappajohn was anxious to hear his theory and share his own.

"You, amigo," Ortego said, stealing a glance at Pappajohn before turning his attention back to freeway traffic.

"Me?"

"Yeah. I thought you were like all those parents who won't believe the truth about their kids." Ortego eased the police-issued Grand Am out of the carpool lane and headed toward the right. "Even after you'd pointed out the ER report that didn't match the autopsy. Figured it was typical county fuckup. Especially when I never got a call back from that ME. Too many coincidences, even for this crazy town. The ME cremates the body without your okay, then burns to death in a house fire?" He expressed his derision with a grunt. "Asked one of my fireman buddies to give me the four eleven on the ME's *casita*."

"Arson?"

"Not that you could prove in court." Ortego lowered his voice to a whisper, "Devil wind." He laughed. "My homeboy says they found a piece of a filter tip in the rubble. In the bedroom. Just one. You ever know a smoker that didn't have a couple of packs stored up for emergencies?"

"They could've burned up in the fire," Pappajohn countered. "But, I suppose it might be a plant. Knock him out, make him look like he fell asleep smoking? Did they check for nicotine levels at the post?"

Ortego shrugged a shoulder as he headed for the upcoming exit. "Body was ashes. No bone damage ID'd, no tox screens done." He shook his head. "Just smells like murder. You know that feeling in your gut?"

Pappajohn unconsciously laid a hand on his abdomen. "Still doesn't explain where De'andray fits in."

At the stop sign, Ortego checked for oncoming cars before easing onto Route 1. "Every time I told Dee things weren't adding up, he dug in his heels. That's not like him. Your daughter, the ME, the Pauzé girl's car, the taxi. Told me he didn't want to rock the boat, just doing his job."

Ortego turned west onto a side road. "He always used to talk to me. About everything. The last time he and his wife had sex. Then, all of a sudden, a couple of months ago, nothing."

"No more sex?" Pappajohn offered.

"No more talk. He'd sneak into another room to answer his phone. Started going through my files when he thought I wasn't looking. Shit like that."

Pappajohn nodded. The behavior sounded familiar.

"So, I thought I'd do a little detecting myself. Turns out, he's been phoning this call girl."

"My daughter?"

"No. Her roommate. Sylvie Pauzé. Dee made sure the charges were dropped the last time she got busted. Maybe she's giving him something in return. I think he was squeezing her to get through to her madam. For a cut of the business. Or blackmail info on their rich clients."

Pappajohn whistled. "Why didn't you say something?"

"I wasn't sure about any of this til today," Ortego explained. "I started tracking Dee after he pulled that INS stunt with that Russian. According to my amigo in Vice, he was an odd-job man for a high-priced escort service run by a madam named Kaye Ludmilev. And, Sylvie Pauzé was her top girl."

"Wait a sec. You just said *was*. As in past tense. You think it's Sylvie who died in the fire and not Ana?" Pappajohn caught his breath.

Ortego smiled. "That's why I'm here, amigo."

"But what about the CODIS hit on the DNA?"

"What about it?"

"I was at the precinct today. De'andray told me blood sample in the taxi belonged to Sylvie."

"Man, he really is covering his tracks," Ortego muttered. "I got that report early this morning before I left the station. The blood in the cab was Ana Pappajohn's. Dee must have altered it."

Pappajohn felt his fists clenching. "Why? Why would he want me to believe my daughter was dead?"

"You ask, amigo? Does a dirty cop want another hungry detective sniffing on his back? Wouldn't be surprised if he'd do anything to get you out of his way—permanently."

Ortego stopped the car at a gated road. His beams illuminated a sign marked NEWPORT BEACH MARINA. "We'll have to walk the rest of the way." He unbuckled his seat belt and turned off the engine.

Engrossed in their converation, Pappajohn hadn't paid attention to their route. "What's here?" he asked, stepping into the darkness.

"If I'm right," Ortego responded, his voice almost lost in the noise of the wind, "at the end of this road we'll find your daughter."

"Trina!" Jeffrey stood in the open cabin doorway, stunned. What was she doing? Pointing a gun at a young woman and a boy?

Momentarily distracted by Jeffrey's outburst, Trina swiveled and Sammy rushed toward her, tackling her to the floor before the gunshot could find its mark. The bullet went wide, slamming into the ceiling. Sammy scrambled to grab Trina's arm and knock the gun from her hand before she could fire another round.

Immobilized by disbelief, Jeffrey could only watch, ashen-faced.

With feline grace, his wife slipped out of Sammy's grip, rolled into a crouch and aimed her gun directly at Sammy's head. "Jeffrey!" she barked, "move away from your daughter. Now!"

Sammy inched back a few steps toward the door.

"Trina, please," Jeffrey begged, his voice cracking. "Put the gun down." He shook his head, unable to comprehend. "Have you gone mad?"

"Trina?" The young brunette pushed the boy behind her to shield him, confusion playing across her face. "That's Madam Kaye."

"You shut up, Ana," Kaye hissed, keeping her eyes on Sammy.

"Ana?" In the dim light, Sammy squinted at the oddly familiar young woman huddled in the corner of the cabin, recognition dawning. "Ana Pappajohn?"

"Yes."

"You're her madam?" Sammy asked Trina. "I thought your name was—"

"My name is Katrina Ludmilev. I am the madam to the rich and famous. They all know Madam Kaye." Her soft cosmopolitan cadence morphed into a thick Russian accent as she glanced at Jeffrey, whose face registered horror.

"Don't you look at me like that," she snapped, her dark eyes filled with anger. "You think *you* were poor?" She almost spat the word. "You always had food to eat, a roof over your head.

I was eight when my father sold me for the first time in Moskva. With every trick, I swore someday I'd never have to whore again to survive. I came to this country penniless. Today, my business reaches to the halls of Congress. It helped build your real estate empire."

"I don't understand. How didn't I know?"

"You're like everyone else, Jeffrey. You see what you want to see," Kaye replied with renewed venom. "Without the money I laundered through your company, and contacts like Neil Prescott tipping me off to those military land deals, you'd just be another run-of-the-mill Newport realtor. I made you who you are, Jeffrey Greene. *I* did. And then *she* had to interfere." Kaye waved her gun at Sammy. "Too bad it's come to this, but I have no choice."

"God, no, why?" Sammy cried.

"I tried to warn you. I wasn't going to let you take us down. I even got Neil to buy your station to get you off the air. But you wouldn't quit." Kaye's finger moved on the trigger.

"No!" Sammy took a step back and lost her balance as the yacht began rocking again.

Jeffrey leapt forward to stop Kaye, a second before she fired the bullet.

The quarter-mile trek down the dirt road ended at a dock where a dozen sailboats and motorboats bobbed in the black water. There were no lights anywhere. The whole place seemed deserted. Probably, Pappajohn figured, in anticipation of the fires expected to move this way. The tiny sliver of moonlight was obscured by smoky ash, slowing their progress. Every few yards, Ortego struck a match to illuminate the path ahead, but the flame lasted mere seconds as warm winds whistling through the masts extinguished it.

At the far end of the dock, Ortego pointed to the slip where the *Lucky Lady* was moored. "Here we are." He drew the Glock from his shoulder holster and motioned for Pappajohn to follow him on board. Santa Ana winds were in full fury, and it was all the men could do to maintain balance as the cabin cruiser rocked and rolled in the choppy waters of the marina.

Inside, it was dark and silent. With deliberate slowness, they tiptoed through the ninety-foot yacht. In the galley they found a plate of cookies and an empty glass on the counter. Someone had been here recently. Pappajohn hoped they were still here.

Ortego carefully opened the door to the main cabin. In the dim light filtering through the porthole, Pappajohn could see a couple of cardboard boxes filled with files on the inlaid teak floor next to an empty safe. All four walls were paneled with the same expensive wood, the large bed was covered by what Pappajohn guessed was a mink duvet. *Nothing too good for Madam Kaye.*

Two smaller forward cabins were equally opulent and empty. Passing through the marble-paneled lounge, Pappajohn nearly tripped over the piano in the darkness. His heart pounded as he tried not to cry out.

Through the silence, he thought he heard voices coming from below. He motioned to Ortego, pointing at the deck with his index finger to indicate a lower floor. Ortego nodded and tiptoed out of the lounge with Pappajohn staggering behind.

On the bottom deck, the voices were louder, but still muffled. It was the shout of "No!" that galvanized them into action. Ortego released the safety on his revolver and held it ready in his right hand as he and Pappajohn sped toward the sound. At the end of a long hallway, a cabin door was partially open, and a woman was aiming a gun.

"Sammy!" Pappajohn screamed as the gun went off. Before he

could see what had happened, Ortego pushed past him and took his own shot.

A second later, Pappajohn found Ortego standing over a dark-haired woman's supine body, one bullet through the forehead, her eyes wide open, staring at the ceiling. A pool of blood formed around her head like a crimson halo.

"The madam," Ortego said in a monotone. "Not as pretty dead as her mug shot." He pulled out his cell. "I better call it in."

While Ortego was on the phone, Pappajohn turned his attention to Sammy who lay on the floor, not far from the dead woman.

"You okay?" he asked, helping her to sit up. Though she nodded, he noted her eyes were dilated with unspoken fear.

"Trina! Trina is Madam Kaye! She tried to kill me, Gus!" Sammy gasped in ragged staccato. "My father!" Sammy indicated the middle-aged man writhing in pain beside her. "He saved me." A red stain had begun to blossom over the right shoulder of Jeffrey's tan running suit. "Is he—?"

"Just a bad flesh wound," Pappajohn said after a quick assessment. "What the heck were you doing here?"

Sammy pointed to the dimly lit corner where Ana was still cowering. "Gus, Ana's alive!"

Pappajohn glanced at Ortego who had dropped to one knee, checking the pockets of the dead woman's slacks, Pappajohn presumed for positive ID. "Emilio, you were right!" he cried as he rose and stumbled over to his daughter.

"*Baba.*" Ana's voice sounded tentative, as if afraid of his reaction.

Pappajohn couldn't believe his eyes. Her hair was back to its natural color, she was older and thinner, but she was here, now, *his Ana.* Tears overflowed as he hugged her close. "Forgive me," he whispered.

"Forgive *me.*" She stepped away to reveal her son who'd been hidden behind her. Her own tears tracked down her cheeks as she introduced him. "Baba, meet Teddy. Theodore, your grandson."

Pappajohn looked from Ana to Teddy who offered up a sad smile. "Have you come to take us home?"

Choked by emotion, Pappajohn pulled the boy into a bear hug. "Theodore, my gift from God," he said hoarsely. "If your mother is willing, I would love to bring you both home with me."

Ana nodded. "Teddy and I almost died tonight for some crazy code my friend stole from an Arab john. I never want to see this town again."

"Is this it?" Ortego asked, holding up the Jazz drive.

"That's the client list Sylvie took from Kaye." Ana explained Sylvie's double-dealing, how she'd copied Kaye's client list as insurance in case she got caught. "The night she died, she was spying for Kaye. I think she was killed because of the text message she sent from the Arab's phone. He may have tried to stop her."

"You still have it?" Ortego demanded.

"The message? No, I gave it to Kaye," Ana said. "She hid it inside her blouse."

Oretgo rushed over to the dead woman and fished between her breasts until he found the paper and put it in his chest pocket.

"Poor Sylvie," Ana said. "She didn't deserve to die."

"That bitch Sylvie got exactly what she deserved!" Ortego's tone and expression had turned ugly.

Pappajohn felt the hairs on the back of his neck rise with a sense of foreboding. The sudden change in Ortego was the same kind of transformation he'd seen just before his former colleague, Donovan, had shot him in the gut.

Ana paled. "You're the cop on Sylvie's voice mail. The one she was working with!"

Pappajohn realized his intuition had kicked in too late. Ortego had already pulled out his Glock and was pointing it at Jeffrey and Sammy. "You two move over there with the family reunion."

Sammy glanced at Pappajohn as if to ask what she could do, but he just stared straight ahead. With obvious reluctance, she helped her still bleeding father limp over to the bed.

Pappajohn glared at Ortego. "So it was you. Not De'andray. *You* were the dirty cop."

"Bingo. Sylvie Pauzé kept me up to date on the latest dirt from her clients and I kept her out of jail. Tit for tat." Ortego's voice was calm and cold. "Kaye thought she had me on her payroll. Never even guessed I was making an extra killing from her top whore."

"So you knew all along it was Sylvie, not Ana who died." Pappajohn shook his head.

"Not til you started playing P.I., amigo. Even Miller didn't know. Wish I could've seen his face when I told him. Anyway," Ortego tapped his chest pocket, "he'll be glad to get his info back. Can't have military secrets floating around Southern California now, can we?"

Sammy turned to catch Pappajohn's eye again. This time he shook his head imperceptibly. Too dangerous to try an attack. Ortego was young and a veteran. And the only one with a gun.

Ortego must have read his thoughts. "That would be stupid, Gus. Tell you what. I really am a nice guy. You promise to keep your mouths shut and maybe you can get out of here," he said as he backed toward the cabin door, his gun raised. Stepping over the threshold, he saluted, adding, "Or not." Then, with a scornful laugh, he slammed the door shut and locked it.

Under a storage bench in the galley, Ortego found what he was looking for. A dozen signal flares. He carried them into the forward cabin nearest the engine and arranged them on top of the two cardboard cartons sitting on the teak floor. After opening the porthole to provide a flow of oxygen, he struck a match, igniting the top edge of each carton. Within seconds, the flares began sizzling, showering a spray of embers into the air. Once the papers caught fire, the Santa Anas swooping in would fan the flames already licking at the walls. With luck, long after he was gone, the gas line would rupture and blow them all to hell.

The fury of the winds outside was so deafening and Ortego so intent on his task, that he never heard the cabin door slam shut, automatically locking him inside until it was too late.

The silence was broken only by Jeffrey's heavy breathing. Pale and weak, eyes closed, he lay on the bed, his uninjured arm nursing the blood-soaked bandage improvised from Pappajohn's shirt.

After tending to Jeffrey, Pappajohn stood up to listen for signs that Ortego was in the vicinity. Nothing. With the boat swaying erratically, Pappajohn staggered like a drunk to the cabin door and tried opening it. As expected, it was locked. He muttered a Greek curse.

"I wish I still had my cell phone," Ana said. "We could call for help."

"Mine's in the house," Sammy sighed. "I never thought I'd need my purse for a quick trip to the boat." Gazing up at the ceiling vents, she gasped, pointing. "Gus!" Black smoke was pouring in, making visibility in the already dimly lit cabin impossible. "The boat's burning!"

"Ortego must have set a fire," Pappajohn wheezed. "We have to get out of here! Fast!"

Sammy's eyes were tearing.

Everyone had begun to cough and gag.

Clutching Teddy, Ana sobbed with fear. "*Baba,* I don't want to die!"

Out of the smoky darkness, Jeffrey whispered, "In my pocket, I have a key."

Ortego was trapped inside the forward cabin. The door wouldn't budge. Several blasts from his revolver could not dislodge the bolt lock. Flames had begun to consume the teak walls of his prison. In desperation, he tried closing the porthole, hoping to keep out the oxygen fanning the fire, but the metal and glass was too hot to touch. Painful blisters formed on his hands when he pulled them away.

As the fumes began to make breathing more labored, he

clutched his chest, knowing it was just a matter of minutes before the carbon monoxide rendered him unconscious. Then the flames would incinerate him. Even if what his LAFD buddies had told him was true—that death from fire is usually quiet and painless—he refused to wait. Praying for mercy, he placed the revolver next to his temple and fired the last shot.

Ana and Teddy stumbled from the cabin, with Sammy and Pappajohn supporting Jeffrey. The boat's violent rocking slowed their progress as they felt their way toward the hazy light of the emergency exit sign. The smell of smoke was everywhere. They all choked, but Pappajohn's wheezing sounded like agonal gasps. Moving toward the upper level, they heard the crack of a single gunshot.

"He's shooting at us!" Ana screamed.

"Shh!" Pappajohn ordered, his voice low and hoarse. "Stay down. Footsteps."

The sound of heavy footfalls approaching was now unmistakable. They pressed against the walls, hoping Ortego had not returned.

"Sammy Greene?" A familiar voice.

"De'andray?" Pappajohn called. "Over here!"

Like a dark angel, the tall detective appeared out of the murky gloom. "Hurry!" he shouted. "We don't have much time."

A sudden lurch of the boat caused Teddy to lose his balance and fall headlong onto the deck. De'andray swept the young boy in his arms. "I've got him," he yelled to Ana. "Let's go!"

With De'andray's help, they reached the upper deck, and, within a minute, stood on the dock. "Time to breathe later. Move!" De'andray continued to urge them forward until they'd left the pier for a grassy knoll beyond. "Hit the ground," he ordered as he gently put Teddy down on his side next to Ana.

Lying prone on the grass, Sammy couldn't resist sneaking a backward glance. The *Lucky Lady* was enveloped by flames.

"Cover your heads," De'andray yelled, as, with a loud, resonating blast, the yacht blew into smithereens, some pieces of its fiberglass hull landing and fizzling out a few feet short of their resting spot.

Pappajohn, still struggling to breathe, was among the first to stand and canvas the scene. Teddy, Ana, Sammy, Jeffrey. All okay. He offered De'andray a handshake and an expression of gratitude. "I don't know how to thank you. How did you—?"

De'andray smiled and nodded. "My job." He looked at Sammy. "You really owe your thanks to your friend, the doctor. Reed Wyndham."

Two hours later, Sammy was darting between cars like a New York cabbie. Traffic was still thick on the northbound 405 since the Laguna/Newport fires had spread up to Huntington Beach. Even from the South Bay she could see their bright glow against the night sky behind her. No wonder everyone in Orange County seemed to be joining her flight.

Impatient to reach the hospital, she weaved her way into the carpool lane and accelerated to seventy-five miles per hour. De'andray had expedited their questioning by the Newport cops and firemen responding to the marina blast, verifying their story, then remaining at the crime scene to help with the evaluation, but the delay had made Sammy anxious. She glanced at her father slumped in the passenger seat, his eyes closed. With no available ambulances, and hospitals south diverting patients, Pappajohn had suggested she get him to LAU Med. "You okay?"

Jeffrey's lids fluttered open. "Just drive. I'll be all right."

"I guess I should apologize. For what I said earlier."

"That I was a rotten father? You're right."

Sammy reached over and squeezed her father's hand. He offered a weak grin, then shut his eyes again.

Wheezing from the backseat made Sammy peer into her rearview mirror where she saw Pappajohn snoring like a hibernating bear between Ana and Teddy, his thick arms tightly hugging them as they slept against his chest. *Maybe you can teach an old dog new tricks.*

Pulling into the LAU Medical emergency room lot, it occurred to her that the story had come full circle. A week ago she'd been here to learn the identity of the Bel Air fire victim. Now she'd solved one mystery, only to discover another. They still didn't know who'd murdered Sylvie or the signficiance of the text message that may have led to her death. Some kind of code? Ortego had mentioned military secrets.

Whatever it meant, solving that puzzle would have to wait until her father's wound was treated. Pappajohn's wheezing was growing louder, too. Parking the car, Sammy's only thought as she raced inside the ER, was getting care for her family—Jeffrey *and* Gus.

At eleven p.m., the late shift CCU nurses were too busy taking report to pay much attention to the uniformed ambulance driver in the Dodger cap who'd come to move Prescott to an outside rehab facility. As far as they were concerned, the congressman hadn't required the unit's specialized attention for the past two days. He was out of the woods and doing fine. It was only his VIP status that had kept the hospital risk manager from demanding his bed be vacated for a more acute patient. And since no one had questioned the order, no one considered Prescott missing until the day shift—hours after the Alibaster Chemical truck had picked him up and delivered him to safety.

CHAPTER SEVENTEEN

At three a.m., Miller turned off his radio with a satisfied smile. Not only had the pickup gone smoothly, but thanks to American First Communications, Sammy Greene's show was officially off the air. And the best news of all had been the reports of the massive explosion on the luxury yacht in the Newport Marina.

No survivors. According to police, names of the deceased would not be released before family notification. That was routine. No matter. If Ortego had followed orders, every one of those loose ends would have gone down with the *Lucky Lady*.

No point in waiting up for confirmation. Not with all the cell phone outages in North Orange County due to tower damage in the fires. Ortego had called him that afternoon, the moment he'd learned of Kaye's duplicity—that the bitch knew all along it was Sylvie not Ana who'd died in that fire.

Nothing to worry about now. Less than twenty-four hours to go. Miller glanced at the clock on the bedstand, smiling as he imagined the director's consternation. Years of preparation, two dress rehearsals, all aimed at a single midnight performance—one that would make this nation understand what chauvinistic advocacy alone could never convey—that they must be afraid. Very, very afraid.

•   •   •

Reed cursed as he stubbed his toe on the desk in the darkened call room.

"Thought you said you'd wake me tomorrow," came a groggy voice from the lower of the two bunk beds.

"Today *is* tomorrow, Sammy," Reed said, flipping on the light to locate his white coat and stethoscope "I'm late for morning rounds. Then I've got an ER shift. You go back to sleep."

"It's all right. I'm awake." Sammy sat up, bumping her head on the top bunk. "Ow!" She gave a dazed laugh. "Think I can see my father now?"

"Best to wait til the afternoon. It'll be a few more hours before the anesthesia wears off. At least the surgeon got all the bullet fragments out of his shoulder."

"And Gus?"

"Still wheezing, but he sounds better. He's got some mild S-T elevation on his EKG."

"Heart attack?"

"Don't think so. Could be coronary vasospasm from all the stress or the smoke inhalation. Troponins are normal so far."

"And that's a good thing?" Sammy asked, confused by the medical jargon.

Reed nodded. "But just to be sure, I'll ask Dr. Bishop for a second opinion when he comes in for evening rounds."

"Your chief's working New Year's Eve? I'm impressed."

"He's head of Medical Services for our Emergency Operations team. With all the Y2K panic, he wants to watch over the unit tonight."

"I'll be glad to put this ridiculous fear behind us."

"Amen to that," Reed said, buttoning his white coat. "Listen, I've arranged for your father to share a room with Pappajohn in the step-down ward. Peds wants to keep Teddy one more day to make sure his hip is stable. Tomorrow he can go home for sure."

"How do I thank you for saving our lives? Again?" Sammy asked.

"Aw, shucks, ma'am. 'Twas nuthin," Reed said, coming over to sit down on her bunk. He leaned in and kissed her on the mouth, at first gently, and then with passion. "You're welcome."

Raised eyebrows reflected Sammy's surprise when he pulled away.

"Someone told me good things happen when you take a chance," Reed replied as explanation.

"Someone I know?"

"Actually it was Michelle."

Sammy's face registered disappointment. "Are we, uh, you, should we—?"

"It's okay," Reed said, "Michelle and I are officially just friends. By mutual consent. But, I've got to thank her for one thing. She's the one who made me see that I still love you."

For once Sammy was speechless.

"Is that so hard to believe?" Reed asked softly.

"I…" Sammy stammered, staring into his eyes as if searching for guile. "You're sure?"

Reed nodded, his eyes serious. "The question is, are *you* sure?"

Sammy exhaled the breath she'd been holding and put her arms around his neck "Yes," she said, her expression no longer tentative. "Yes. Finally."

The L.A. County Sheriff's patrol car arrived at the scene less than an hour after the Coast Guard put in the early morning call. The carcass of a Honda Civic lay on a craggy rock, lathered by the surf's foam with every wave. Vultures and seagulls rested on its roof, flapping their wings, then rising into the air to avoid the ocean's spray.

The charred skeleton in the front seat was identified as a female by the Ventura County coroner. Six females in the missing persons database might have fit the description of a tall, young woman, but crime-scene investigators resolved the mystery of this Jane Doe before the ME completed the autopsy. The license plates had melted, but the car's VIN identified its owner as Michelle Hunt, age twenty-seven, of Montecito and Los Angeles, missing person number five.

The preliminary report included the ME's assessment and was shared with family. Michelle was the eighth victim of the devastating L.A. fire season. Smoke from the mountains had likely blocked her visibility, and disoriented, she'd driven off the road to her death.

"Where's the congressman?" Reed asked the charge nurse as he was finishing CCU rounds. "There's another patient in his bed."

"Transferred to rehab last night."

"On whose orders?"

The nurse sorted through the morning report until she found the note. "Eleven p.m. verbal order, transfer request from Dr. Bishop."

"Guess he forgot to let me know," Reed said with a shrug. "First-year cardiac fellow. Low on the food chain."

Since she couldn't see her father for a few hours, Sammy took the opportunity to drive home for a quick shower and a change of clothes. On the way she called Jim with a follow-up on everyone's progress. She'd contacted him last night from the hospital with news of what had happened at the marina and the promise her father had made to help get their show back on the air. Until Jeffrey was discharged, they'd have to settle for a forced vacation, she told him, wishing him a happy New Year.

"No worries," Jim had replied in a mellow voice that suggested he'd already begun his partying.

The moment Sammy locked her apartment door, she stripped and jumped into the shower, turning on the water full force. Rotating slowly, she let the needlelike jets crash down on her head, rivulets of warmth running along both sides of her body, relaxing tight muscles. Spending the night in the call room with Reed had allowed her to suspend her deepest feelings about everything that had happened yesterday—finding Ana and Teddy, Trina's duplicity, Ortego's betrayal, the boat explosion, her father's sacrifice. The thought of how close they'd all come to dying rolled over her now with the force of a rogue wave. Overwhelmed, she was racked by sobs of sadness and relief. At least the danger was over. Spent at last, she closed her eyes, emptying her mind of everything but the pure pleasure of the shower. And her new future with Reed.

"About time," Courtney grumbled as the guard led her to a cubicle where she could make her phone call. "Your ass is grass," she added sotto voce.

"Hey, love, you hibernating or what?" her manager asked when he heard her voice. "You've missed some sweet parties."

"It's been a real party for me. Listen, get my lawyer down to the BH county lockup. Bring a couple of legal assistants. We're in stir."

"Jail? Beverly Hills? Whoa! And who's *we?*"

"Me, and a roomful of friends."

On the drive back to the hospital, Sammy had her radio tuned to a local news station. "Folks, the elusive Courtney Phillips has been found," the announcer was saying. "According to our source in the Beverly Hills Police Department, Ms. Phillips was arrested yesterday while participating in a homeless protest that blocked streets and held up traffic for hours. Word has it she's not only posted bail for herself, but for several dozen fellow protesters."

Guess that explained why Courtney missed their meeting yesterday. Ana would be glad to know her friend was safe. Sammy'd never figured Courtney Phillips for the altruistic type, but had to give her credit for making a move in the right direction. After all the dust had settled with her father's business, perhaps Sammy could talk him in to another donation to help those struggling in the land of plenty.

Pulling into the LAU Med parking lot, Sammy listened to the weatherman announce one more day of dangerous Santa Ana winds. "With continued threats of fire and Y2K concerns, anyone who can, should plan to stay indoors tonight."

Just as well, Sammy thought, as she locked up her car and headed into the hospital lobby. Given the fact that everyone she loved would be here tonight, this was where she'd be welcoming in the new millennium.

From his seat at the ICCC console, al-Salid focused on the B3-level security camera monitors. At a few minutes past eight p.m., he observed the last man on the day shift exit the morgue. Security Chief Eccles had already left. Said he wasn't about to hang around New Year's Eve when champagne was flowing freely at La Brasserie three blocks and a quick page away in Westwood Village. Holidays in hospitals were usually dead zones. *An apt description after the stroke of midnight*, al-Salid had thought as he'd waved goodbye to his soon-to-be former boss.

Two of al-Salid's men had just come on duty to man the twelve-hour Y2K night shift. Hidden in the pockets of their trousers tonight were the false IDs of the purported Iraqi terrorist bombers they were to scatter at ground zero before flying the coop. Evidence to be discovered and used by the postexplosion investigators seeking scapegoats for the dirty bomb attack.

At eight thirty, right on cue, al-Salid pressed *send* on his cell phone and watched the monitor to be sure his men staffing the morgue picked up the text message, the signal to begin the bomb's transfer from the morgue to the two-story mechanical room at the base of the Schwarzenegger Tower's elevators.

As soon as al-Salid saw the older man nod and give a thumbs-up, he zoomed his camera out to view the entire morgue suite one floor above. This way he could monitor his team's progress from upstairs while continuing to inject Miller's worms into the ICCC computers. Between now and midnight, each of these self-replicating computer programs would activate and shut down the hospital's operating system. Lighting, power, oxygen, elevators, dumbwaiters, monitors. The ventilation system worm would have the opposite function, however, amping up the internal vents, so that the radiation released by the bomb explosion would blanket the entire building and poison everyone within.

How fitting that the hospital named after Arnold Schwarzenegger, the action hero he'd admired as a teen, would soon end up being the terminator of lives.

The evening news was blaring when Sammy walked into the hospital room now shared by her father and Pappajohn.

"Can someone turn off that noise?" Pappajohn pointed to the TV mounted from the ceiling between the two patients.

Jeffrey nodded at the remote on the table by the right of his bed with his left hand. "Can't move my right arm with all the bandages."

"I'll do it," Sammy took the remote and pressed *off*.

"Thank you," Pappajohn said, "Fires, Y2K, impending terror attacks. It's enough to give you a heart attack."

"Well, this is the place to be for that," Jeffrey returned with a crooked smile.

"If it bleeds, it leads. Cardinal news rule." Sammy laughed. "Hi, Gus. Hi, Dad. Glad to see you're both feeling better."

"Be even better if I could get out of here. Spend some time with my daughter and grandson. Ana came by earlier, but they won't let Teddy on this floor."

"I just stopped in to see him."

"He's okay, isn't he?"

"He's fine. They want to watch him one more day. He's already up with crutches, making friends on the children's ward." Sammy went over and gave her father a kiss on the cheek. "How are you doing? Reed said they removed all the bullet fragments."

"It's all still a dream," Jeffrey replied with a deep sigh and a wince. "A very bad dream."

Sammy gave his good hand a reassuring squeeze. She knew he must be devastated by his wife's horrible betrayal, but decided this was neither the time nor place for that discussion. She'd save it for later. "You know, none of us might have woken from that bad dream if not for Reed and Detective De'andray."

"My ears are burning," a familiar voice boomed from the open doorway.

"Speak of the devil," Pappajohn waved. "Dee, come join the party."

"Only a minute. I've got a mound of paperwork waiting back at the station, and a wife who wanted me home two hours ago." De'andray walked over and stood by Pappajohn's bed. "Glad to see you're not wheezing."

"Lucky to see me at all," Pappajohn said. "A miracle you found us yesterday. How'd you track us down?"

De'andray shrugged. "Once Dr. Wyndham called with his DNA results, I checked our data with CODIS. Found out the report I'd given you had been altered. I knew it had to be Ortego."

De'andray's story was virtually the same as the one Pappajohn had heard on the drive to Newport. Except in this version, the dirty cop was Ortego, not De'andray.

"It was rough after his wife left with the kids. She wanted a one-woman man, Ortego always liked sampling the buffet. Seemed almost manic about it the last couple of months. He just wasn't the same guy I used to know." De'andray puffed out his cheeks and let out a long, slow breath as if to expel his disappointment.

"Anyway, lucky for us, he was using a take-home car yesterday instead of his Mustang. All the new police cars are outfitted with GPS," De'andray explained. "I was able to pinpoint your exact location on our computers."

Pappajohn shook his head. "Technology. Would have been great if we'd had those gadgets when I was with Boston PD."

Sammy looked at De'andray with concern. "You must be exhausted."

"No rest til Y2K," he said. "Fortunately, the Newport crime lab is officially handling the case. But I plan to stay in the loop."

"Any leads on the Miller character Ortego and uh—" Pappajohn glanced over at Jeffrey before lowering his voice, "the madam mentioned? Seems they were both working for the guy. If he's behind Sylvie's murder, he could still be after Ana."

"So far nothing. Ortego never mentioned him to me. But the chief's pulling Ortego's phone records. See if we come up with anything that fits. I've asked Newport PD not to release names of survivors of the blast for a few days. No point in alerting whoever's behind this. In the meantime, keep Ana close."

"She's staying here tonight with Teddy," Sammy said.

"Then she'll be fine. Hospital's one of the safest places in town. Always quiet on the holidays. Plenty of people around to watch over her." De'andray shook Pappajohn's hand before walking over to Jeffrey. "Sorry about your wife, sir."

"Yeah, thanks," Jeffrey responded and looked away.

"DA wants to talk to you, but I told him to wait another couple of days. Get that shoulder better and your head clear, okay?"

Jeffrey nodded and managed a weak smile.

De'andray patted Jeffrey's uninjured arm, then waved at Sammy and Pappajohn as he headed for the door. "Gotta get home and get a little shut-eye before my shift tonight. See the family. Wife's already pissed that I'm working New Year's Eve. Again."

"I've been there, partner." Pappajohn said with a sad laugh as De'andray left the room.

"That look again, Gus," Sammy declared an hour later. She'd been sitting by her father's bed while he dozed, watching Pappajohn's facial contortions. He seemed to be struggling with a thought. "What's on your mind?"

"That text message Sylvie sent to Ana the night she died. The one Ana e-mailed me. We know that's what Kaye and Ortego were after. What's in it that's worth killing for?"

"Ortego said something about military secrets getting out."

"I need to look at it again. Do you have your copy?"

"Sure," she said, pulling her notebook from her purse and flipping through until she found it. She tore out the sheet and handed it to Pappajohn. "It's these numbers. 34.058710–118.442183."

He stared at them for a long time. "Damn!"

"What?"

"Should've thought of this before. De'andray mentioned Ortego had a GPS in his car."

"What?" Sammy asked.

"Global Positioning System. Pueblo Software had a subsidiary that worked satellite communications. Keith once told me about it. It's a navigational setup that can track your exact location, like where Ortego was driving the police car. If my memory serves, it involves satellites and computers that determine latitude and longitude of a receiver on Earth."

"Beam me up, Scotty."

Sammy saluted Reed now standing in the doorway. "Hey, captain, ER still busy?"

"Finally quieted down, so I thought I'd come by to have another look at you, Gus," he said, entering the room. "Dr. Bishop should be here soon. If he agrees, we'll discharge you first thing in the morning."

"Can't be too soon for me."

"What's all this about satellites and computers?" Reed asked, taking out his stethoscope.

"We're trying to solve a puzzle." Pappajohn showed him the text message after Sammy explained its source, pointing to the line: 34.058710–118.442183. "I'm thinking these numbers are GPS coordinates, latitude and longitude," he said. "I'll have to give my IT buddy, Keith, a call. Have him check it out."

Reed didn't seem to be listening. He was staring at the paper, his forehead creased with confusion.

"*Oy gevalt.* Now it's you with the faces," Sammy said. "What's bothering you?"

"Op Y2K. Do you know what that means?"

"We figure it stands for Operation Y2K. Sounds military," Pappajohn said. "Why?"

Reed scratched his head. "Around four a.m. a few nights ago, I was about to go into Prescott's room to check vitals when I heard someone in there with him. Couldn't see who because the man was in shadow and when he walked out, he had his back to me.

"The conversation was muffled, but heated. That's why I stayed outside. But I'm absolutely sure they mentioned Operation Y2K."

Sammy nearly jumped out of her chair. "Prescott's involved in this? Why am I not surprised? We've got to talk to that *haleria* right away! Is he still in the CCU?"

Reed shook his head. "Dr. Bishop discharged him last night."

Just then, Bishop stepped into the room. "I did no such thing."

The mechanical room for the core's elevators as well as several other hospital operating systems extended from B2 to B3 with entry access only from B2 down a steep staircase. The older morgue attendant was reminded of the engine and boiler rooms of the merchant ship he'd served on years before. Its unwieldy layout had made the whole process of moving the bomb much harder than expected. For the better part of an hour, he and his younger colleague had maneuvered the steel gurney up and over and around a maze of machinery to reach its target at the base of the shafts. At a few minutes past nine p.m., the older man, bathed in sweat and exhausted from the strain, texted al-Salid that the job was finally done.

Reed quickly filled Bishop in on his discovery of Prescott's absence and the conversation he'd overheard outside the congressman's room. With a brusque thank you, Bishop ordered him back to the ER and strode out of the room, heading for the doctor's charting office. Closing the door, he sat down at the telephone and dialed a number he'd memorized, but never used.

The familiar voice sounded almost lethargic.

"Julia, where's Neil?" Bishop asked, his tone impatient.

"Frank? Hold on a sec. I was dozing."

Bishop waited while Julia set the receiver down, then a few minutes later, picked it up again, her voice now more alert. "Okay, what's wrong?"

"Neil's gone."

"He's not at the hospital?"

"Someone claiming to be me called in transfer orders last night."

"Transfer? Where?"

"You really don't know?"

"Of course not. Last time I spoke with Neil was just before I left the hospital last night around eight. He said he was doing fine, that I should skip visiting today and go to the Greenes' New Year's Eve party in Newport instead. But to tell you the truth, I'm wiped out and with these fires, I think I should stay close to home." Her tone took on an anxious quality. "Is Neil in trouble?"

"I don't know," Bishop said, feeling the start of a headache. "But there's trouble brewing, and I have a feeling Neil may be involved."

With the last of the programming completed, al-Salid checked the insertion and function of the worms that would alter the systems' access codes, making it impossible for ICCC staff to sign on or take control of the hospital's computers. Now, only al-Salid, Miller, and that weapon device of his would be able to enter and manage the antiseismic software's administrative levels.

Slipping the lanyard with his fake ID from around his neck, al-Salid held it up to the Omni lock and heard the click that opened the exit door from the control center. As he hurried down the hall and up the stairs to B2, he pulled out his cell phone and dialed Fahim.

"On my way," Fahim answered in lieu of hello.

"Good," al-Salid responded in Arabic. "The worm phase is done. I'll meet you at the target." He clicked off and headed toward the elevator maintenance room to join his comrades in implementing phase three.

Reed flew down the stairs two at a time and raced to the ER. Pushing open both double doors, he was stunned by the chaotic scene. Every available space in the treatment area was crowded with makeshift exam tables for those patients needing immediate care. Gurneys lining the hallways like planes on a runway held the less acute—headaches, fevers, broken bones, smoke inhalation, and minor burns. The staff appeared totally overwhelmed.

"Place was empty an hour ago. What happened?" Reed asked.

"Radio said to stay indoors tonight. Apparently they all decided this is the indoors to be," Lou answered as he handed Reed several patient charts. "Crushing chest pain, exam room three, pulmonary edema with cyanosis in five, and the 'impending apocalypse' in one. Take your pick. The interns and residents are bombed tonight." He gestured at the doors leading to the waiting area. "We're even calling in derm."

Reed peeked through the glass windows, aghast. Every seat in the waiting room was taken. The overflow sat on the floor or lined up against the walls.

An agonized scream erupted from exam room one, followed by a high-pitched shout, "The end is nigh, the reckoning has begun. It is the end of the world. Tonight everything changes."

Reed raised an eyebrow. "Y2K?"

Lou rolled his eyes. "Our seventh tonight. This is worse than the fires. Plus we have all the transfers from Orange County coming through."

Reed quickly eyeballed the woman who hurled a few predictions of doom his way, scribbled a note onto her chart and tossed it at Lou. "Call Psychiatry STAT and tell them to bring Haldol. Get room five started on IV Lasix and O_2 mask. Titrate to pulse ox at least ninety-two percent," he told one of the nurses, "I'll be in room three." Reed set off double-time toward the patient with a likely heart attack.

Twenty minutes later, Bishop was back on the phone with Julia. This time she'd called him. Her voice was decidedly agitated.

"You were right. The tower collapse was no accident."

As if he were reliving an old nightmare, Bishop felt his neck muscles tighten and his head begin to ache. "How do you know?"

"When you told me Neil was missing, I tried his cell. He took the call, probably because he saw it was me on his caller ID. Said he thought I was going out for New Year's so he hadn't wanted to bother me, but that you'd just discharged him to some private rehab facility miles away from the fires. Told me he was shutting off his phone to get some rest, and he'd call in the morning. He hung up before I could get a word in edgewise."

Her shrill laugh was full of resentment. "Over the years, I've been fed so many of Neil's cock-and-bull stories that I guess he just figured I'd swallow this one too. You know, I've always respected his privacy, but I thought about our conversation last night, Frank, and I couldn't let it go this time. So I walked into Neil's office and broke into his desk."

For an instant, Julia paused to take a breath and Bishop thought he sensed relief in her silence, as though she'd needed to complete her confession before she changed her mind. Then she plunged on. "I actually picked the lock on the file drawer with a hairpin. Like in a spy novel," she laughed again. "Routine paperwork mostly, but, at the back, I did find a report to his Armed Services Committee labeled WEAPONS SYSTEMS, EXPERIMENTAL, DESERT STORM."

Now it was Bishop who held his breath.

"A few pages describe a new weapon being tested that could bring down buildings. I don't understand all the technical jargon, but it seems as if the weapon makes structures shake until they collapse. Apparently, there've been a couple of trials in Basra, Iraq in the spring of ninety-one."

"Did this weapon have a name?" Bishop asked, afraid to hear the words he already knew.

"Yes," Julia said. "Frequency Resonance Enhancement Device. They called it a resonator, according to the signer of the report— let's see, an Albert Miller of the DOD, Department of Defense."

Miller. Bishop's head throbbed with the memory of the man who'd always been close by when desert winds blew down buildings and innocents died in Kuwait and Iraq seven years ago. The same man who'd lurked in the shadows, pulling strings when Bishop's career began its spiral toward collapse. Especially after Bishop had tried to decipher one young soldier's whispered warning: *resonator . . . murder.*

Was Miller the man Reed had heard outside Prescott's room that night, talking about an Operation Y2K? Was that why Prescott seemed so anxious to leave the hospital? Worried he'd be at risk if he'd stayed? Bishop felt a shiver down his spine.

"Frank? Are you there?"

"I'm still here," he said. "Listen, Julia, if Neil calls, promise you won't let him know we've talked. Certainly not about this."

"I'm not about to let him know, Frank." She lowered her voice. "What do you think could be going on?"

Bishop saw no point in alarming her further. "Nothing, I hope. But just in case, there's a fire shelter in Seal Beach. With Newport in flames, you might be safer spending the night there. And keep your cell phone. I'll call you if I have any news. Happy New Year."

No point in telling her that if Miller *was* planning something for Y2K, no one was safe.

You're kidding!" Pappajohn sat up in his hospital bed, nearly pulling the corded hospital phone off the end table and waking Jeffrey. "I owe you big time."

"What? Sammy asked when he'd hung up.

"Keith was kicking himself for not thinking of it first," Pappajohn began, "but when I mentioned GPS, he did some DARPA sniffing."

"DARPA?"

"Defense Advanced Research Projects Agency. Its mission is to protect national security and maintain our military's technical superiority."

"Did Keith get answers?"

"Those numbers," Pappajohn pointed to the text message, "are GPS coordinates."

"So you were right."

"That's the good news, Sammy." A troubled look settled on Pappajohn's face.

"Should I ask for the bad news?"

"The numbers are longitude and latitude coordinates for the Schwarzenegger Hospital. Whatever Operation Y2K is, it's apparently going down right here."

Sammy's eyes widened. "January first? That's tomorrow."

"Y2K could mean tomorrow, or even tonight."

"Can I see that message again?" Jeffrey asked.

"I thought you were sleeping," Sammy said.

"I was thinking with my eyes closed. Let me see those last numbers."

Sammy handed her father the paper.

"31, 12, 99, 23, 59."

"We thought it might be a telephone number or a safe combination," Sammy told him.

"No, it's a date. It's the way they do it in Europe. Trina always used that system."

Pappajohn put a hand to his head. "Of course! It's the same in Greece." He frowned. "If that's a date, then the last two numbers: twenty-three and fifty-nine could represent military time." He looked at Jeffrey and Sammy with alarm. "Something called Operation Y2K is going to take place here tonight at one minute to midnight."

"How about a little early celebrating?" Ana asked, walking into the hospital room holding up a bottle of sparkling cider. "I didn't think the doctors would allow champagne, but—" Looking from Sammy to Jeffrey to her father, she stopped mid-sentence. "What's wrong?"

Before Pappajohn could respond, the floor nurse marched in with a frown and a fax. "Tell your friend—" she checked the cover sheet, "Keith McKay, that with Y2K just a few hours away, we can't be jamming up the hospital phone lines sending pictures." She handed it to Pappajohn, disappearing out the door before he could thank her.

Sammy and Ana both moved to stand over Pappajohn's shoulder while he read Keith's scribbled note on the front sheet out loud. "Call when you receive. Fahim al-Harbi on government watch list. Alleged arms dealer. Entered U.S. on international flight from Dubai to D.C. December twenty first. Now under the radar. Could be in L.A." Pappajohn pulled out the second sheet to reveal a hazy black-

and-white scanned image of a middle-aged Middle Eastern-looking man.

"That's him!" Ana cried, grabbing the picture with shaking hands. "Sylvie's john. At the party. The night she died!"

"Midnight, tonight," Pappajohn warned Bishop, after the cardiologist returned to the hospital room. "Whatever Operation Y2K is, it happens right here in less than three hours. That's why I paged you. Figured you'd be the one to connect us with the hospital security team. I've just talked with my friend Keith McKay in Boston who alerted the feds." Pappajohn held up Fahim's picture, "Name's Fahim al-Harbi. He's a known arms dealer and he's on their watch list. And he may be in L.A."

"You don't think he'd come after me and Teddy, do you, *Baba?*" Ana asked, her voice trembling.

"Unlikely," Pappajohn said, offering his daughter a reassuring glance, "but we need to prepare for the worst-case scenario. Al-Harbi may be involved somehow in this Operation Y2K." He exhaled a deep breath. "Especially with Prescott so desperate to get out of here before tonight."

Bishop pulled out his cell phone. "I'll call in Security Chief Eccles. Your worst case?"

Pappajohn shrugged. "Arms dealers have open access to weapons—guns, explosives. It's possible al-Harbi or one of his buyers might set up an active shooter scenario, and invade the hospital. Or plant some type of incendiary device."

"You mean a bomb?" Ana's eyes widened with fear. "Could that bring down this whole building?"

"Of course not." Sammy shook her head. "Reed told me Schwarzenegger's built like a fortress, right?"

She'd directed her question to Bishop, whose neutral expression had slowly morphed into a mask of horror. "God damn. Miller. This is his doing."

Pappajohn arched an eyebrow. "You know who Miller is?"

"Albert Miller," Bishop said. "Met him in Kuwait during Desert

Storm. He was developing and testing a new weapon for the U.S. Army. I thought the project had been abandoned after—" He bit his cheek and winced as if self-induced pain would somehow overcome the pain of this revelation, "after the early trials resulted in terrible accidents."

Sammy verbalized the "But?"

"But now I have a bad feeling that he's continued the trials and," Bishop cleared his throat, "and maybe already tested this weapon right here in L.A."

"*Ghamo to*," Pappajohn muttered. "What kind of weapon?"

Bishop speed-dialed the security chief's number before responding, "One that brings down buildings. A resonator. Makes them shake and sway until they collapse."

This time they used the speakerphone on Sammy's cell to conference Keith. Though his questions were matter-of-fact and analytic, Keith's growing concern was clear from the tightness in his voice. "So based on what you've told me, Dr. Bishop, the Canyon City tower collapse may have been a trial run of this resonator?"

"Yes, but I honestly have no idea how it works and I doubt it could bring down our hospital. This facility was built with every modern specification and then some—hermetically sealed, bioterror-resistant fire doors, lead shielding, steel foundation, core struts. They even took steps to ensure it'd be able to withstand a nine Richter scale earthquake—a force a thousand times more intense than the ninety-four Northridge quake."

"Base isolation system? Active seismic control?" Jeffrey interruped.

"Of course," Bishop said. "They put in a base isolation system above the foundation, right below the ICCC in the basement. *And* a seismic-control system on the hospital's top floor. Why do you ask?"

"Because I think I know how that resonator weapon might work."

Sammy turned to her father. "You said you had nothing to do with the tower collapse."

"I didn't. But after you made your accusations, I had my engineers do an architectural autopsy, to see if we could determine exactly what happened. Unfortunately, most of the computer records of the seismic-control system sensors were destroyed when the Canyon City tower came down. They don't have absolute proof, but they suspect that somehow the seismic-control system was disabled or reprogrammed. Instead of the base keeping the building from shaking in those heavy winds by dampening the sway forces, the control system actually seemed to intensify them."

He appealed to Sammy. "I'm not proud of the fact that I never questioned my good luck when the hotel in Newport came down. Prescott reassured me it was just an accident—especially after the DA's investigation was dropped. But the tower collapse made me sit up and take notice. Along with a little nudging from you."

Keith's voice over the speaker interrupted. "Theoretically, with the right instructions a control system could amplify ground forces from a sizeable earthquake or really heavy winds. Making them strong enough to collapse a building. Your engineers are right, though. You'd have to either program the system to do that or plant some kind of worm in its software."

"We've still got that devil wind tonight," Pappajohn said, "but nothing like the day of the tower collapse. Suppose this guy al-Harbi planted some kind of—" again he looked to Ana who seemed frozen with fear, "device like a bomb. Could that be strong enough to produce the forces you're talking about? "

"Yes, I think so."

Pappajohn jumped out of bed and headed for the closet where his clothes were hung. "You better call in the FBI."

"Where are you going?" Sammy asked.

"To the ICCC with Dr. Bishop." Pappajohn put up a hand to stop any protest from Bishop. "Until the feds arrive, Keith and I can give your security team a technical hand." Pappajohn grabbed the phone. "Keith, can you stand by? I may need you to walk me through some details."

"It's past midnight here and so far our own Y2K preps have worked well. It's pretty quiet. I'll keep my phone line open."

Pappajohn turned to Sammy. "Call De'andray and have him put out an APB on Prescott. Find the congressman and we might be able to nail this Miller. Tell Dee to get an LAPD team over here as soon as he can, bomb squad, too, but not to send out a general radio alert. If potential terrorists are monitoring the police bands, we don't want them speeding up their schedule or doing anything rash."

He gave his daughter a quick hug, encouraging her in Greek to be brave, then put his arm over Sammy's shoulders and whispered, "Please go with Ana. Make sure she and Teddy are okay. Be ready to move out right away on my signal."

As Sammy nodded, Pappajohn looked at Bishop. "If there hasn't been an intrusion in the computer system, I'll be the first to pull back and let the FBI or the LAPD take over. If there has, you'll need to raise the alarm and start evacuating this hospital now."

Miller turned the L.A. Edison van onto Westwood Boulevard just as Fahim phoned to tell him the computer worms were in place. Operation Y2K was right on schedule. "Good work. The rest of your money will be in Dubai in the morning," he said, adding, "Happy New Year."

Entering the LAU Medical campus, he drove to the Peter Falk Eye Institute, a quarter mile upstream from the hospital tower. At ten p.m. the specialty facility was closed, its lot deserted, with no attendant sitting sentry at the entrance. He backed into a space that provided a clear line of sight to the hospital, turned off the engine, and hopped out.

Dressed in the utility company's uniform, Miller ambled over to the side of the van, admiring the professional lettering job his ops men had done to alter the exterior. A week ago the same vehicle had posed as a Canyon City PD van, parked next to city hall. Curious passersby tonight would assume this was an L.A. Edison repair truck on the scene in the midst of a power failure. His radiation-safe hazmat suit was well hidden inside.

Cracking the rear door to enter the cargo bay, he climbed up, bolted the door shut, and took his place at the central console. With a few flicked switches, Miller started the cascade of boot-ups of the van's computer systems. The resonator was the last to come on line. Nestled in the front of the cargo bay, the equipment relayed its first *ready* signal to Miller's monitor, cueing him to approve the wireless transmission of the Trojan horse. Inside the virus, masquerading as a "friendly visitor," were the kernels of the resonator's program. Once released from the Trojan horse software, these kernels would move in and take over the operations and functions of the hospital's active seismic-control system, allowing Miller to run the computers remotely from his van.

Miller held his breath, nervously typing a sequence of instructions on the resonator's input keyboard and entering the Trojan horse launch code into the hospital's control system's computer. Operation Y2K was a "go." Success tonight could promote the election of a new—and better—administration. And, with Prescott's support, God bless him, a new—and infinitely better—CIA Director.

In minutes, the monitor returned the *contact achieved* notification, followed by the *control established* report. Miller breathed a sigh of relief. The resonator's software had climbed out of its Trojan horse casing and invaded the hospital's seismic-control system. It was now ready to align the counterweight function with the building in a way that would magnify any shaking created by the dirty bomb's explosion. And just like the walls of Jericho, the hospital's walls would come a-tumblin' down.

Bishop motioned for Pappajohn to wait while he flashed his ID at the sensor and punched in the Omni lock code to enter the ICCC on Level B3. Hearing the latch click open, he pushed the door forward to allow them both access into the large suite.

Expecting to see the overnight technicians at their stations, Bishop was surprised to find the room totally deserted, save for an agitated and glassy-eyed Eccles. The only sounds were the bells and whistles of computer equipment whirring and buzzing on autopilot from one end to the other.

"Ventilation, oxygen, electricity, natural gas, monitors, elevators, Internet," Eccles listed. "All systems are operational." The LCD monitors along the control counter displaying shots from the multiple security cameras all showed scenes typical for the university hospital in the evening hours. "But my night shift staff is MIA."

"Where's the seismic-control system hookup?" Pappajohn scanned the millions of dollars worth of equipment that represented the heart and brain of the Schwarzenegger Hospital.

"I've got it." Eccles rolled his chair over to one control panel and began typing on the system's keyboard. His expression of intense concentration became a worried frown. "Or maybe I don't. I can't seem to access certain levels of the program."

Eccles moved to an adjacent keyboard, typed a few entries, then slammed the counter in frustration. "We're locked out."

Pappajohn put Sammy's phone next to Bishop. "Keith?"

"Yeah, I heard. If a worm's taken over access and security, you'll be blocked from entry."

"Impossible," Bishop said. "You have a firewall and screen for malware. How could a virus get in?"

"That might keep out your average hacker, but, if it's someone in the government, it's as good as a paper lock. All you need is a Trojan horse and your computer practically opens the door and invites the worm in itself. Then closes the barn door and leaves you in the cold."

"So what can we do now?"

"Frankly, your best bet is to try to shut the whole system down," Keith advised.

Pappajohn's eyes had drifted to the security monitors displaying rotating videos of the entire hospital. For a split second, he thought he recognized a man entering the hospital lobby, but the face turned from the camera before Pappajohn could be sure. Still, he'd spent too many years as a Boston street cop not to want a second look. Just in case.

"Any way to rewind this security tape?" he asked. "I want to check a face."

Eccles nodded. "One minute. Nope, can't shut it down either. I'm blocked on all fronts." He turned to Pappajohn. "What'd you see?"

"I'm not sure, but one of the visitors walking into the lobby might be al-Harbi."

Before Eccles could respond, the room was plunged into total darkness. A moment later, the transfer switch to the ICCC's generator kicked on, providing dim runner lights and ongoing power to the computers.

"Dammit! Central power's not coming back online." Eccles moved to another computer and queried system status. "Local generators are feeding critical units, but noncritical areas of the hospital are without power or light," he reported with a hint of panic.

Pappajohn noticed the security systems monitors had gone black as well.

"Elevators just went out." Red lights dotting Eccles's screen indicated cars halted throughout the hospital. "Can't get generator power to any of the lift systems."

Keith's voice came over the speaker. "Gus, it's time to get everybody out of there and bring in the bomb squad. I'll alert the feds about a possible sighting of al-Harbi. Keep your phone with you, so I can stay in touch. What about the seismic-control area?"

"Generator's still running up there." Eccles's voice rose another register as he barked, "I'm calling a level one red alert."

"Evacuation." Bishop directed as he walked Pappajohn to the exit door. "Runner lights and reflectors should guide you up to the ER on the main floor. Tell Dr. Wyndham—Reed—to implement disaster response protocol STAT, but no Klaxon. We need to get folks out as quickly and quietly as possible. We don't want to start a panic."

Pappajohn agreed. "If the attackers know we're on to them, they might move up their plans sooner than midnight." He looked over at Eccles still seated at the control counter. "Aren't you coming?"

"We'll join you in a few minutes. There's something down here Dr. Bishop and I have to do first."

Teddy had just fallen asleep. Ana and Sammy were talking quietly when the lights in his seventh-floor hospital room flickered, then died. From where she sat, Sammy could see through the open door into the hallway. The corridor too had just gone dark, except for a row of runner lights leading to the exit.

"What happened?" Ana whispered.

Sammy leaned over and picked up the bedside land line. No dial tone. "Power's out. Phone, too."

"You don't think it's the Y2K Operation?" Ana asked, her voice trembling.

"It's only ten thirty," Sammy tried to reassure her. "My guess, it's the winds again. Give it a few minutes. Hospitals have back-up generators. We don't want to wake Teddy with a false alarm."

Sammy crossed her fingers in the dark, hoping it was just that.

By the time Pappajohn had hiked up three floors to the main level and was hurrying down the darkened hallway to the ER, his wheezing had grown louder. On the way, he'd dialed Teddy's room, but surmised the power to that floor was out when no one answered. Despite his ragged breathing, he urged himself forward, until he pushed through the glass doors and nearly collided with Reed.

"Gus, what's going on? We just heard the power's out in most of the hospital. Luckily, our generator's working."

Pappajohn realized that while the ER's generators were functioning now, there was no way of knowing if a capricious computer worm might suddenly switch them off. "Dr. Bishop's still down with security in the ICCC trying to get the system up again, but he wants you all to implement the disaster response protocol right away."

"You mean evacuate the whole hospital? For real?" Reed's jaw dropped.

"Afraid so. And he wants it done quietly, so no one panics."

From the other side of the ER, Pappajohn saw De'andray wave his badge at the triage nurse, then march past her toward them. "Dee! Am I glad to see you." With Reed listening, he quickly apprised them both of the situation. "Looks like this may turn out to be a lot worse than just a power outage."

De'andray nodded, looking unruffled despite the crisis. "I could only pull a half dozen men with all the Y2K action around town. I'll send two down to the B levels to meet Eccles, get a couple searching the floors, and one's already doing recon on the perimeter. Bomb squad's on the way and the FBI's sending a field operations team." He shook his head. "They'd already been alerted by your Boston friend."

"Good." Pappajohn pulled out the picture of Fahim he'd put into his pocket. "This man's on the terror watch list. I'm not sure, but I thought I saw him enter the hospital about fifteen minutes ago on one of the security videos." He checked his watch: 10:45 p.m. "We've got less than seventy-five minutes."

Miller studied the feed from his rooftop camera into the cargo bay of the L.A. Edison van. The display had been fuzzier than he'd expected, blurred by the smoke and haze from the winds and the fires. Fortunately, right on schedule, at exactly 10:30 p.m. Pacific standard time, the worm had extinguished the lights, swallowing the Schwarzenegger hospital in instant darkness. Perfect. The elevators and dumbwaiters would be next to malfunction, and then, in a few minutes, at eleven, the oxygen supplies would be cut off.

All of these steps had the goal of both slowing down evacuations and amplifying the terror of the impending attack. A few staff and patients might make their way out, but without elevators, casualties in the adult and children's ICUs were a sure bet.

If al-Salid and his men had followed the plans, the dirty bomb should have been planted in the central core elevator shaft. In half an hour, Fahim would enter its activation code to begin the sequence toward detonation.

•   •   •

As Bishop was guiding Pappajohn out of the ICCC, Eccles remained hunched over one of the still functioning computer consoles. Luckily, his password worked on this system, allowing him access to administrator's privileges. With a heavy heart, he typed instructions for a last resort program few on the ICCC team knew about and one he had hoped he'd never need—activation of the hospital base firewalls. In case of bioterrorism, these physical firewalls would keep gases like sarin or other bioterror agents quarantined in enclosed sections until the hazmat teams could clear out the hospital.

If the attackers had a bomb, conventional or even a small nuke, the lead shielded partitions should limit the damage to a localized area, and allow the building to remain standing and stable long enough for evacuation. On the critical B-level floors, partitions had been built to slide in behind the standard fire doors, like a second set of portals, only permitting evacuees out before closing and latching again. On upstairs wards, shield doors would slide in just outside the building core, isolating the central core and elevators, but facilitating patient transport by allowing both exit and egress. If the worst-case scenario did come to pass, Eccles prayed these untested safety systems would buy the hospital and its staff and patients valuable time and save lives.

The loud banging startled Miller who'd been focused on the monitors.

"LAPD, open up."

Gritting his teeth, Miller pushed back from the console and checked the time: 11:10 p.m. This was cutting it close. Anticipating that once the lights went out, someone might approach the utility van and ask for assistance, he'd held off donning his hazmat suit and made sure the rear of the truck had been packed with equipment supporting his cover as repairman. He hadn't figured that LAPD would stumble on his truck and waste his time.

Now he stood, dimmed the interior lights, and like an actor about to enter the stage, walked to the back and cracked the door just wide enough to see and be seen. The young cop standing before him in the dark, windy night had to be a rookie, Miller guessed. No more than twenty-five. "Can I help you?" His smile was feigned innocence.

The officer flashed his badge. "Mind stepping out of the vehicle, John?" he asked, reading the name stitched over the pocket of Miller's L.A. Edison uniform.

Miller hopped out of the truck with a dramatic sigh of impatience. "Look, officer, we're busting ass trying to get power back up to the hospital. What's the problem?"

"No problem. Just a routine security check. Let me take a quick look inside, and you can get back to work."

Miller shrugged and opened the rear door so the officer could scan the bay. "We're in the middle of analyzing their transformer connections right now," he said, adding a few more lines of technobabble as distraction. "Guess you guys are up to your own you-know-what's with the fires and this millennium business."

The young officer nodded. "Third double shift in two weeks. Man, I'll be glad when midnight strikes and all the Y2K nonsense is over." He waved his flashlight haphazardly around the fake utility equipment while Miller held his breath. "You wouldn't believe the stuff people predicted would happen."

"Don't I know," Miller laughed, moving to block the view deep inside the van.

A moment later, the policeman had completed his cursory survey. "Thanks for your cooperation," he said, pocketing his flashlight, "Gotta finish my rounds."

Miller waved him off and was about to reenter the van when he heard his alias. "John?"

"Yes?" His heartbeat quickened as he slowly turned to face the policeman.

"Good luck tonight."

This time Miller's smile was genuine. "Yeah, thanks."

•   •   •

Within a few minutes, Reed had activated the medical disaster response protocol and was coordinating assignments from the nurses' station in the ER. With Pappajohn and De'andray listening, he'd explained that the computer systems were all acting up and that the hospital administration felt an immediate evacuation to be the safest approach. While some of the team appeared skeptical, most accepted the situation—perhaps because the expectations of Y2K computer failures causing trouble were so high already.

"We've halted all nonemergent medical services and started evacuating patients to the holding area in the open parking lot beyond the building." Reed shouted over the blaring intercom announcement, "Dr. Firestone, Dr. Firestone, code red in the ER."

"How many patients still in house tonight?" the on-duty nursing supervisor asked.

Reed looked to Lou, whose tracking of the daily census was legendary. It was how the clerk managed to jockey patients from the ER to hospital beds so efficiently. "Lucky for us we had lots of pre-New Year's discharges, but we're still pretty full," Lou responded. "As of ten p.m., there were three hundred twenty-two patients on eight floors. And that's not counting friends and family since we extended holiday visiting hours."

"It'll take hours to get them all out if the elevators are down," the derm resident said.

Reed forced himself to appear calm, aware they might not have hours. "We'll have to do the best we can. I need *everybody* to help the response team if we're going to have a chance to make it. House-staff," he ordered, nodding at the scrub-clad interns and residents, "you're assigned to back up the evac team for ICU and CCU."

"Just finished the last surgery an hour ago," a surgical nurse told Reed. "We can shut down all the surgi-suites."

"What about Peds?" interrupted a charge nurse. "We'll need help moving babies from NICU and children from the floors."

Pappajohn stepped forward. "I'll lead that group," he said through a loud wheeze.

"No," Reed said. "You can't climb seven flights of stairs. You'll go into full-blown respiratory failure."

De'andray volunteered. "I'll go get your daughter and grandson, Gus. You stay here and help my sergeants direct patients outside."

Pappajohn reluctantly agreed.

"Thanks, officer. I'll prepare the acute ER patients for transfer," Reed continued to the group. "The rest of you divide into teams of two, each taking a floor. Grab a flashlight before you leave. Start spreading the word to evacuate. But please, try to stay calm. We want to avoid a panic."

Lou muttered, hugging away his own shiver. "Especially among ourselves."

When the hospital lights went out, Fahim, al-Salid and his two men were already sequestered in the elevator maintenance room on level B2 in the midst of their evening prayers. For Fahim, it had become a ritual he did by rote because of peer pressure, not with the kind of dutiful allegiance to their faith these three shared.

Touching his brow to the prayer rug, his thoughts wandered far from the whispered words of the Qur'an. How had he had let himself be suckered into getting his hands dirty like these men? He was a dealer, delegating to the soldiers at the front lines. He wasn't one of them. Killing the whore had been a momentary indiscretion, an accident really, but had given Miller a murder he could use to pull his puppet's strings.

Well, Fahim had had enough. Once this operation was over, he resolved to cut those strings, even if it meant forgoing Vegas and the United States for the tamer confines of a four-star hotel in the Principality of Monaco. Exile wouldn't be fatal—Monte Carlo was filled with beautiful blondes.

Adrenaline pumping, Bishop dashed into the ER and snaked his way past harried staff escorting patients and visitors from the hospital. To his surprise, most seemed to take the evacuation in stride, a few even making a joke of it. If the building started shaking, though, he wondered how long it would be before pandemonium erupted. At 11:10, he knew they didn't have much time to find out.

Bishop searched the crowd until he spotted Pappajohn standing by the triage nurse. "Come with me." He led the way into the doctors' lounge before Pappajohn could object. "You still got your friend on the line?" he asked when they were alone.

Nodding, Pappajohn punched the speaker button.

"Keith, I'm back. I'll put you on with Dr. Bishop."

"Any luck with the system?"

"No." Bishop hurriedly explained that nothing they'd tried could override the Trojan horse and its invasive program. Left with no other choice, Eccles had finally decided to execute the untested firewall implementation built into the hospital. "It's supposed to partition and quarantine areas in case of bioterrorism or nuclear attack."

"Smart thinking," Keith said. "If there's an explosion with a radiologic dispersal device in one area, it should minimize radiation exposure to other parts of the hospital."

"*If* it works." The weariness in Bishop's voice matched his mood. "It's a new system, new construction. Frankly, thinking back to Desert Storm and the resonator trials Miller did there, all the apartment towers attacked were new construction. And they all collapsed."

"That's an earthquake zone just like California," Keith said. "Maybe they all had new seismic-control systems. Ripe for this 'resonator' to take over."

"I think so, but I still don't get how Miller could have activated the device when I know he never left the base either of those days."

"Obviously, he had a partner," Pappajohn interjected.

"Or wireless transmission," Keith added. "It could have been done remotely. How far away was the base?"

"A quarter mile, more or less. Think that's possible?"

"Not only possible," Keith said, "but if your friend Miller wanted to keep his nose clean, very likely."

The LAPD officer covering the B2 level shone the flashlight's beam up and down one corridor, while her partner did the same in the other.

"Nothing," her partner said, meeting her near the stairwell. "You see anything?"

"Nada. Only the dead down here." She pointed back toward the morgue with her light.

At the end of a corridor just beyond the elevators they stopped in front of a pair of fire doors and tried turning the handle. "Locked." The female officer peeked in through the split. "Just a black wall. Doesn't look like it goes anywhere."

"Okay, then, let's make our way upstairs to the evac zone and help Dee."

As the two climbed the stairs, neither realized they'd missed the elevator maintenance room, whose nondescript entrance was hidden in the shadows behind the locked fire door and the quarantine shield.

The black Tahoe quietly backed up to the entrance of the Schwarzenegger Hospital, and discharged the four-man FBI field team. They'd arrived in civilian clothes without their trademark company jackets, just in case the perpetrators were tracking their movements. Their supervisor, sporting the same Marine-style buzz cut as his men, waved the white unmarked van following the Tahoe toward a secluded parking spot near the ER entrance next door, and instructed, "Secure the building."

"Detective!" Ana cried, recognizing De'andray silhouetted against the doorway of Teddy's hospital room, flashlight in hand. Her voice carried a mix of wariness and relief.

Sammy jumped up from her chair. "What's happening?"

"Hospital's lost all power. We've started evacuations," De'andray said. "Just a precaution, but we need to get everyone out as quickly as possible."

Ana froze, her expression pure terror.

"We have to get moving." De'andray came over to Teddy's bed and leaned in to scoop him up.

"I can walk."

"Elevators are out, son. That's seven floors."

"I can do it!" Teddy was already sitting up and reaching for his crutches.

"Okay, but—" De'andray's walkie-talkie buzzed. He pulled it off his belt to answer. "Yes?"

"Bomb squad's here. They're working from the lobby down. We've just searched every area on B3 and B2 we could access. No sign of your suspect. Fire doors are locked beyond the elevators and the morgue. We can't get in. But neither can anyone else. We're moving to B1 and lobby. Over."

Clicking off, De'andray turned back to Teddy. "I'll finish putting the word out and meet you all on the way down." He shined the light so the three could see their way into the hall where the generator-powered runner lights provided enough illumination to guide them to the stairwell.

"We've just lost oxygen," the ER nurse told Reed as he rushed back into the treatment area. She gestured at the wall unit whose monitor now indicated a zero liters flow.

"Portable unit, STAT," ordered Reed, helping two orderlies transfer a heart attack victim to a rolling gurney. "Bring the defibrillator," he added, hoping they wouldn't need it. As he followed the last of the ER staff and patients to the parking lot outside, he glanced at his Casio digital blinking 11:10.

With three of the five stairwells dedicated to stretcher cases and Evacuchairs for those needing wheelchairs, more than two hundred ambulatory patients and visitors were channeled to the remaining two, making progress down to the lobby slower than expected. Stopping to let the more able-bodied pass, Teddy, leaning on his mother's arm, had only arrived at the fifth floor by the time De'andray reached them.

"Sammy's not helping you?" De'andray asked.

"She's gone to get her father," Ana explained, checking her watch. Eleven fifteen. "You said midnight, right?" Hesitating, she added, "We're doing good. You need to help the children who can't walk at all. We'll be down in five minutes and meet my dad outside."

De'andray patted her on the shoulder as he hurried down the stairs. "I'll be back."

Whipping winds made it hard for Bishop to maneuver the LAU Med golf cart as he rounded the perimeter of the hospital for the second time. Through the hazy darkness, he strained for signs of Miller, so far with no success. After his conversation with Keith, Bishop was convinced the resonator had to be activated remotely. That meant the bastard must be somewhere close by. Despite LAPD's all-clear report. Even if Miller wasn't running the show this time, he'd never be far from the stage during a performance.

This was one performance Bishop had to shut down. He glanced over at his Army-issue Beretta M9 pistol laying on the seat beside him. Since he'd received the strange warning call the other night, he'd taken the gun from his closet and locked it in the trunk of his car. A premonition that he'd need to use it soon? Perhaps. All he knew was that Miller had to be stopped. Should have been years ago.

When Bishop had volunteered as an MASH unit commander for the U.S. mission in Kuwait, he'd sworn an oath to protect his country. Then he'd met Miller and seen that patriotic mission perverted. This resonator Miller had helped develop was not a weapon that would protect innocents at home and abroad. The device that took civilian lives was instead a way to create fear, making foreign and domestic control and conquest easier. Bishop understood that now. Men like Miller were traitors, not patriots.

How many innocent lives might have been saved if Bishop had continued to pursue the doubts inflamed when the dying young soldier whispered *resonator, murder*? Instead, he'd climbed inside a bottle. He brushed his hand over the pistol as he accelerated the golf cart. This time, he wouldn't give up his pursuit. At eleven twenty-three, he had less than thirty minutes to stop Miller.

By eleven twenty-eight, Sammy and Jeffrey finally caught up with Ana and Teddy shuffling onto the second-floor stairwell. Groggy from his pain medication, Jeffrey was leaning heavily on Sammy, slowing her down. "Keep going," she told Ana as they stopped to rest. "Your father will be getting worried."

"No, you saved our lives." Seeing that Teddy was taking the steps one by one on his own, Ana moved to Jeffrey's injured side and gently put an arm around his waist to help hoist him up. "We're not leaving you now."

De'andray found the FBI team supervisor outside near the holding area and shared the status of the evacuations and the bomb squad's searches.

An FBI technician stuck his head out of the back of the parked white van, signaling for attention.

"What's up?" The supervisor hurried over with De'andray at his heels. Inside the open door, they saw the tech staring intently at a series of monitors hooked up to several computerlike machines.

"Sir, scan shows a hot footprint on Level B3." He indicated a large patch of bright red at the base of an overlaid map of the hospital. "Better call back your search teams."

De'andray asked for clarification.

"Nuclear radiation leakage," the supervisor said. "Seems we're dealing with a dirty bomb." He surveyed the clusters of patients, staff, and family crowding the holding area, watching the police activity. "Better start moving everybody back. *Way* back."

Reed was busy rolling a stretcher across the parking lot when he saw Pappajohn hurrying toward him, waving his arms and shouting. It was impossible to hear above the blustering winds and the din of the crowd outside.

Reed handed off the patient to a nurse and ran over to meet Pappajohn halfway.

"Have you seen Ana and Teddy and Sammy?" Pappajohn gasped and coughed.

Reed propelled Pappajohn over to a nearby bench. "Slow down or we'll lose you too."

"I've been all over the triage area, the lobby, the ER," Pappajohn wheezed. "I can't find them anywhere. Didn't they get out yet?"

"If Sammy's with them, I'm sure they're fine." Reed pointed to the hordes of people being herded to a more distant parking lot. "They're probably there, looking for you. Sit and catch your breath. I'll see if I can get away or send someone to find them."

At precisely eleven thirty p.m., Fahim picked up his PDA and began typing in the code Miller had given him, setting the bomb's timer controlling countdown to detonation. In less than thirty minutes, as Y2K crept over the horizon, the bomb, packed with nuclear residue, would explode, taking out much of the hospital's central core along with every escape route for hundreds of patients and staff remaining in the floors above. Those who did avoid injury in the initial blast would later wish they'd perished instantly. The radiation released in the explosion would blanket at least an entire city block, poisoning thousands more in the next few weeks and months, and changing the landscape of the American empire.

A shame so many people would die, but not my problem. This was the doing of men like Miller and al-Salid. By midnight he'd be in the Bentley, hightailing it away from the disaster, toward San Diego and, if needed, the Mexico border. After a short snooze at that Oceanside motel, he would catch the seven a.m. flight to Montreal for his connection to Paris and points south.

Entering the last number, Fahim nodded to al-Salid who walked over and gave him warm goodbye kisses on both cheeks.

"*Ma' Alsalam.*"

"And to you, my brother," al-Salid said. "A safe journey."

Turning to leave, Fahim wondered where the terrorist leader's next assignment would be. Asia perhaps? No matter, al-Salid knew how to reach him whenever he needed his next buy. Fahim didn't really care to know this much about what his customers planned to do with their weapons ever again. In fact—

The flash lasted only a microsecond, searing over Fahim with the pain of a thousand knives. A millisecond later, all that was left to identify Fahim, al-Salid, and al-Salid's cell were fragments of tissue and DNA. And several intentionally hardy counterfeit ID cards.

The resonator's seismograph recorded the explosion at exactly 11:40 p.m. Miller swore that the ground waves even jostled his truck some distance from ground zero. Al-Salid, his men, and especially that fool Fahim, would not have known what hit them. Fahim was a vicious bastard, not worth one shed tear, and al-Salid had become a man who knew too much. Both men had outlived their usefulness. Safely dressed in his hazmat suit, Miller smiled at the thought that the last of his "loose ends" were out of the way.

He typed in the codes that would activate the resonator's wave amplification, launching the program within seconds. Instead of dampening the quake-like vibrations caused by the bomb blast, the resonator's wireless remote control of the top floor sensor and counterweights would enhance them. Minute by minute, the shaking and swaying of the building would grow stronger and stronger, and the ride would begin.

De'andray watched the FBI team supervisor don his hazmat suit.

"Radiation's localized to the B3 level," the technician said, studying his monitors. "There's shielding that's partitioned off the blast area."

"Good," his supervisor responded, "not everybody's out of the building yet."

The LAPD rookie ran over to De'andray. "We moved the triage area back three hundred yards," he reported, peeking in the open door of the FBI van. "Great setup. Looks just like the L.A. Edison van I saw a couple of hours ago. Wish we could afford equipment like that."

De'andray frowned. "When did you see an electric company van?"

The rookie scratched his chin. "Around ten, I think. In the parking lot south of the Falk Building. Repairman was trying to fix the power."

De'andray looked at his FBI colleagues. "Any of you ever seen L.A. Edison get to a site within minutes of a power failure?" He didn't wait for their answer.

The explosion extinguished even the dim lights and dissolved all sense of calm among the dozens of evacuees still struggling down the stairwell. Pandemonium. Cries of pain and terror filled the air. People tumbled over one another, first from the sudden violent shake, and then as they pushed and shoved to escape from the building.

Sammy, Teddy, Jeffrey, and Ana had just reached the mezzanine and now lay next to each other in a crumpled pile on the landing. Jeffrey writhed in pain after jamming his injured arm against the cement where he fell.

"Teddy!" Ana screamed, reaching out blindly for her son.

"I'm okay," came a whimper from the darkness. "But I lost my crutches."

"Earthquake!" someone yelled as bits of plaster from the ceiling above began raining down.

Sammy hadn't experienced an L.A. quake yet, but somehow she doubted this was one.

"It's not a bomb is it?" Teddy whispered.

"No, no," Sammy said gently. The luminescent dial on her Timex read 11:45 as she felt the building shake again, more violently than before. Wasn't it early for the worst-case scenario Pappajohn and Bishop had discussed—the resonator that would make buildings sway and collapse like the Canyon City tower? The groaning sound of joints between the stairs twisting and the walls cracking made her wonder if this hospital would become their tomb.

Her face slick with sweat, Sammy inhaled a deep breath, forcing herself not to panic. Still one floor to go if they were to make it out to safety. "Get up," she ordered the others. "We've got to keep moving. Dad, come on. Ana, let's each take an arm with Teddy and help carry him down. Time's running out."

Miller observed his camera feed, knowing that in minutes the glass-and-steel hospital tower would reach its breaking point and crumble to the ground like unstable Pick-Up Sticks. His plan was unfolding before his eyes like the well-orchestrated drama he'd envisioned. So far everyone had played their part. Fahim, al-Salid, and his men. Now it was time for the rest of the cast.

He typed in the keyboard commands to ramp up the resonation and pressed *Enter*. At this highest level, the resonator would make the weights amplify the vibrations and sway of the building, causing its steel beams to snap at their joints. All the signals were go. The monitors scanning from his truck showed the resonator operating flawlessly. As soon as the hospital itself collapsed in a ball of steel, concrete, and dust, the Santa Ana winds jostling his van would spread the radiation from the dirty bomb over the entire West side.

Panicked residents would be calling for drastic security measures to protect the health and safety of the country. Plans already drafted and ready to be implemented by his party as a new administration dawned. Happy New Year, Los Angeles! Happy New Century, America!

In the dark, Ana tripped and tumbled down to the next landing, grabbing the railing to avoid banging her head. Her sharp cry of pain and a new limp made Sammy fear she'd twisted her ankle. Teddy clung to Sammy as hard as he could. The shaking and swaying of the building made every step treacherous—even for the able-bodied.

"Can you walk?" Sammy shouted.

Several people dashed past them, unwilling to stop and lend a hand.

"It hurts, but I have to." Ana's voice became higher pitched as the swaying threw her against the stairwell wall. "We're not going to make it!"

"We'll make it," Sammy said. "Dad, can you keep going on your own?"

Jeffrey's reply was weak, but audible. "Yeah. I'll go down and bring help."

Sammy waved him on and turned to Teddy. "Okay, hang on to me." One more set of stairs. They were so close.

The building pitched to the other side and Teddy's inertia pulled Sammy off balance. Stumbling over a step, they were both flying. She threw out an arm to catch Teddy and braced for a hard landing.

After circling the perimeter a third time, Bishop realized that the L.A. Edison van he'd seen parked near the Eye Institute hadn't moved, despite the fact that the hospital had been dark for more than an hour. Driving closer, he noticed the small dome on its rooftop—a camera *and* an antenna. Damn, how had he missed it? If Keith was right and the resonator was being operated remotely, this would be the perfect location.

Hopping out of the golf cart, Bishop grabbed his gun and raced over to the back of the van. He tried the door handle, but it was locked. "Open up, Miller, I know you're in there," he shouted, banging on the door.

No response. Angry, Bishop fired his Beretta into the lock, blasting it open. He stuck his fingers in the joint, pulled the door wide, and climbed into the back of the truck with his gun ready.

Seated at his console dressed in his hazmat suit, Miller didn't turn his helmeted head to acknowledge Bishop. "Thought I might never see you again, Frank," he said with icy calm.

"So this is it." Bishop waved his gun at the large box at the end of the cargo bay that resembled a mainframe computer. "Your resonator."

"Took a long time to get it right, but we finally did it," Miller acknowledged, eyes focused on his keyboard "Tonight is the gala performance."

"Shut that thing off now!" Bishop ordered.

"Or?" Now Miller turned his head and nodded dismissively at the gun in Bishop's hand. "You'll shoot me? Really, Frank, you don't have the guts. Besides, you're too late. The die's been cast. There's nothing I can do to stop it."

"You always were a liar. Telling me what I'd heard from that soldier in Desert Storm was all in my head." Bishop released the safety on his pistol. "Not this time. I won't let you do to my hospital what you did to me and my army career."

Miller looked as though he might laugh. "Don't be pathetic," he said, turning back to his monitors. "You did it all to yourself."

Bishop aimed the gun at Miller. "I'm serious, shut it off. Now!"

Ignoring the warning, Miller typed in a few more instructions.

Bishop pulled the trigger, at the last second redirecting the gun barrel from Miller and emptying the magazine into the resonator instead. All nine bullets struck the equipment, setting off a cascade of electrical shorts that sparked and flamed like fireworks on the Fourth of July.

"You shouldn't have done that, Frank," Miller's voice was low, but full of rage.

Bishop glanced from the resonator to see that Miller had pulled out his own gun, now aimed squarely at Bishop's heart.

The sound of the shot resonated throughout the Eye Institute's parking lot.

Sammy and Teddy rolled as they hit the concrete. The ten-year-old was almost her size, so she'd been unable to carry him alone, but leaning on each other, they'd made it to the ground-floor landing. Fortunately, this time they'd only fallen a few steps, and somehow managed to escape serious injury.

Ana, at Sammy's instruction, had already hopped to the bottom of the stairwell and shouted up anxiously, "Are you okay?"

"We're good." Sammy replied, wondering if it was her imagination or had the violent shaking begun to slow. She looked over at Teddy who was starting to slide down the last part of the stairs on his rear.

"Follow me," he said as if it were a game.

Sammy nodded and bump by bump, they slid to the lobby level into Pappajohn's waiting arms.

The bullet had found its mark. Miller fell back against his chair, blood spurting like a rose-colored fountain from the middle of the pierced hazmat suit.

De'andray stood in the doorway of the L.A. Edison van, his .38 aimed at Miller, ready for a second shot. The FBI agent who appeared right behind him also had his gun raised.

Gasping, Miller tried to speak.

Bishop laid down his weapon and, ever the doctor, rushed to examine the dying man. De'andray's bullet had been a clean hit. Miller would be gone in seconds. Bishop pulled off the helmet and leaned in close to Miller's lips, straining to hear his last whispered words, "It's not over—"

Standing tall, Bishop gazed at the destroyed resonator, then back at the now-lifeless body slumped in the chair, and shook his head. His voice was firm, but with a weary edge. "This time," he said, "it's over."

Despite his wheezing, Pappajohn refused to rest. By sheer force of will, he'd managed to carry his grandson most of the way from the lobby to the parking lot in his arms. Sammy followed close behind, with Jeffrey leaning on one side and Ana hobbling on the other to avoid putting full weight on her twisted ankle. Only when he'd reached the triage area did Pappajohn step out of his policeman's role. Overcome with emotion, he encircled Teddy and Ana in an embrace, whispering hoarsely, "Dear God, I thought I'd lost you again."

"We're okay, now, *Baba*," Ana sniffled.

Teddy pulled himself up to his full four-and-a-half-foot height, balancing on his braces. "See, *Pappou*, I don't even need my crutches."

Taking a seat on an empty stretcher, Pappajohn drew them both to his side. His breathing easier, he glanced over at Sammy and Jeffrey as they approached. "*Efharisto*, Sammy."

Wincing in obvious pain from his reinjured shoulder, Jeffrey nodded. "If that means thank you, ditto."

Reed rolled up with a wheelchair for Jeffrey, then swept Sammy in his arms, holding her close. "I almost thought I lost you too," he whispered.

"That'll never happen again. Don't you know?" she whispered back. "You and me? It's *beshert*." She tightened her embrace. "Our destiny."

The sounds of a synthesizer version of Kenny G's "Miracles" floated around them before Sammy realized it was her phone.

Pappajohn reached into his pocket for the cell and flipped it open. "Keith? Yes, it stopped. We're all safe." He hit the speaker button just as Sammy added, "Thanks, friend. We couldn't have made it without you."

"I guess I can officially wish you all a Happy New Year."

Sammy looked at her watch. Keith was right. It was exactly twelve a.m.

By one a.m., Bishop along with Reed and the disaster response team had evacuated the last acute patient to Cedars-Sinai hospital in Beverly Hills. Dick Eccles, manning the ICCC, had suffered multiple fractures in the close-by bomb blast, but his prognosis was hopeful. The massive firewalls had done their job and contained the radiation from the dirty bomb within the core—and away from the rest of the hospital and the ICCC.

The less seriously ill had been triaged to a number of smaller, local community hospitals. And, to the eventual delight of their families and their health insurers, at least a hundred more were given an early discharge home.

The building insurers would be less sanguine. Though the hospital hadn't collapsed, there had been significant damage to its lower levels. Reconstruction would likely take millions of dollars and many months—and that was only if the dirty bomb's radiation now trapped on level B3 could be reduced to adequate safety levels or permanently sealed. Most likely, the old standby, the trusty fifty-year-old hospital up the street, would have to abandon its new mission as an alcohol treatment center to resume its former role as the main hospital building for the LAU Medical Center.

The first of the media vans had arrived a few minutes after twelve, while De'andray and the FBI were still debriefing Bishop. Alerted by hysterical patients and sightseers with cell phones, reporters had heard the night's disaster attributed to everything from a meteor shower to a major earthquake to an atomic bomb. Bishop joined the hospital's spokeswoman in front of the microphones at two a.m. to address the news crews.

"Exaggerated rumors," he said calmly in response to the more alarming scenarios suggested. "A natural gas explosion in the basement caused some structural damage. Probably a pipe damaged during the building's construction. Certainly not a Y2K terrorist attack. This was nothing more than an unfortunate accident."

"How many killed and injured?" one reporter shouted over the din. The coroner's van could clearly be seen parked outside the ER in front of the hospital entrance.

"We've had a few injured, but all our patients made it out or to other hospitals safely. No patients or visitors were killed. Sadly, we do believe a couple of maintenance men working in the machinery room died in the explosion. We're working with the LAPD and the FBI to identify them and notify their families."

Bishop gazed at the sea of reporters and closed the impromptu press conference with an air of cool confidence. "It's time to move along, there's nothing to see or report. We'll know more next week. Y2K is over and we wish you all a Happy New Year." He nodded at the spokeswoman, turned on his heels, and walked slowly toward the ER, closing its doors on the trail of reporters.

Two hours after the stroke of midnight, the Gulfstream waited at the edge of the John Wayne Airport runway for the green light to begin its takeoff run. The flight plan had been filed to include a stopover in Mexico City. From there, the plane's final destination would either be Washington, DC or Buenos Aires.

The call with the all-clear signal hadn't come through as expected. After monitoring TV news and Internet reports, the congressman seemed unusually anxious to get the bird in flight.

The pilot watched the twinkling lights of the Airbus 340 approach the airport from a distance of several miles. Runway A3 12 L was the only landing strip lit. They would have to wait until Lufthansa Heavy had touched down before they could launch their own trip. He could see the drawn faces and strained expressions of the politician and his brother-in-law as they sat nursing martinis and staring at the cabin's TV.

The Lufthansa jet rumbling overhead floated out of the sky onto the ground a half mile downstream and, engines thundering, braked to a smooth stop. Good. As soon as the bulky elephant moved off their strip, they could depart.

The pilot eased the Gulfstream onto the runway and turned to face the mile-long track. A few final instrument checks and they were ready to go. Hand on the throttle, he listened for the air traffic controller's signal to roll.

It never came. Instead, a horde of red-and-blue-lit police cars, black SUVs, and other vehicles labeled LAPD, Orange County Sheriff's Airport Police, and FBI appeared like fireflies out of the murky darkness beyond the runway lights, buzzing into the plane's path and blocking its way. A tall African-American LAPD officer and a husky buzz-cut Fed in an FBI jacket emerged from one of the vans and approached the plane together as the air traffic controller instructed the pilot to shut down the engines and allow law enforcement access.

For just a moment, the pilot wondered if he had enough runway to reach T1 and clear ground before hitting the vehicles. He glanced back at his passengers and decided it wasn't worth the chance. Shutting off the Gulfstream's engines, he radioed the tower, "We're letting them in."

CHAPTER EIGHTEEN

Emerging from the Byzantine Greek Orthodox Cathedral into the bright sunlight, Sammy impatiently brushed a wisp of hair from her brow. The winds were already gentler this afternoon, the air less smoky and almost breathable. The last of the fires that had plagued Southern California were expected to die out by the end of the day.

Dressed in her green sheath and high heels, Sammy walked carefully behind Pappajohn and Teddy, down the steep church steps to the patio outside. Sylvie's memorial had been lovely, she thought, marveling at how Pappajohn had convinced the old priest to perform the service. It wasn't Sylvie's profession that had been the conservative clergyman's initial objection. Nor the fact that Dr. Gharani had illegally cremated her remains. "I need proof that she was baptized, that she was a Christian."

"She was my daughter's friend and she has no other family. That trumps bureaucratic stonewalling in my book," Pappajohn had argued, refusing to back down.

In the end, the priest had given in, and, Sammy had to admit, had memorialized Sylvie's too-short life with sensitivity and respect. Sammy supposed it hadn't hurt that Pappajohn had contributed a thousand dollars to the church's building fund from the Y2K salary he'd earned working in Boston for Keith McKay. Or that her own father had added another ten thousand to the pot. She watched

Jeffrey standing in the far corner of the patio talking with Reed. There was much they had yet to discuss and learn about each other.

Sammy followed Pappajohn and Teddy over to the other side of the courtyard where several of Kaye's "girls" surrounded Ana like a surrogate family, raptly listening to her plans to become a nurse in Boston. She was urging her former colleagues to consider leaving the "profession" too, now that their madam was gone. These young women clearly envied Ana, but judging by their expensive-looking attire, Sammy sensed they weren't ready to call it quits for a nine-to-five minimum-wage gig. Hopefully, they wouldn't end up like Sylvie before discovering the allure of glamour and money was just a façade to which they'd become addicted.

"Have a minute?"

Sammy barely recognized the conservatively dressed young woman who stepped away from the group. Out of jail one day and Courtney had already trimmed her dark hair into a neat bob and toned down her makeup. From her clear eyes and sure steps, she also seemed untypically sober. "I hear you're back on the air Monday," she said just as Jim came over.

Jim nodded at Jeffrey. "Sammy's father made some calls to America First Communications this morning to "trump" his late wife's orders, so to speak. "You're NOT fired!" he joked, affecting a poor "The Donald" imitation.

"Think I could talk my way onto your show as a guest? I'm putting together a charity concert with my old band and some industry friends. We'd like to help out the homeless in Southern California, especially those displaced by the Canyon City disaster. Kind of want to drum up some business and donations."

"Absolutely." Sammy caught the reflected enthusiasm in Jim's eyes. "That's really a nice thing you're doing."

"There's a lot of people out there who need nice," Courtney said. "And, it's about time I gave something back." She pursed her lips. "You get pretty sheltered in the business, but in a way, it's just another kind of prison. I'm going to work on trying to stay 'free.'" She mimicked a drinking gesture. "Of any prisons."

"Natural high," echoed Jim. "I'm all for that."

"See you Monday night then." Sammy grabbed Jim by the hand and led him over to Reed and her father. Jeffrey slung his good arm around her shoulder and gave her a half hug.

"You're pretty chipper, all things considered," Sammy said. "Did you meet with your lawyer this morning?"

"Yup, Neil Prescott's being arraigned this afternoon on multiple counts of bribery, corruption, conspiracy, you name it. They're talking immunity for me if I turn State's witness." Jeffrey sighed. "I can see the old boys' club doors slamming in my face, but frankly, I didn't know the half of what Neil and Trina were doing, and I'd like to think I wouldn't have gone along if I had." He smiled. "Guess I'm going to have to start all over and do it Susan's way—one reasonable investment at a time." He locked eyes with Sammy, as if trying to gauge her reaction. "Come to think of it, that's not a bad way to re-build a relationship with my daughter either."

Sammy's cautious smile let him know she was willing to give it a try. "My door's open. Anytime." Easing out of his hug, she turned to Reed. "Thanks for taking the Pappajohn crew to see the Dardens this morning."

"Good people," Pappajohn said, joining them. "Teddy really wanted to say goodbye before we head back East. And we all needed to say thank you. We stopped off at the West L.A. precinct to see De'andray as well."

"Any news?" Sammy asked.

"Classified ongoing investigation, you know, but Dee did say Prescott's definitely looking at hard time and the loss of his con-gressional seat. With the new Orange County DA talking about re-opening the investigation of the Palacio Real prosecutor's fatal car accident, he could even be facing an accessory to murder charge down the road."

"That's got to be hard on his family."

"It was Prescott's wife who notified the feds that her husband was about to fly the coop last night," Reed said. "We were rounding on our cardiac transfers at Cedars-Sinai this morning when she showed up to talk to Bishop. One of the nurses overheard him offer to drive her to some big-shot law firm later. The way they were looking at each other, I wouldn't be surprised if those two have a past."

"And maybe a future," Sammy suggested to Reed, who raised a surprised eyebrow.

"Dee did say they'd be taking a closer look at Madam Kaye's client list over the next few weeks," Pappajohn added. "Ana's willing to serve as a witness. Plenty of heavy hitters in this town on the hot seat."

"Did De'andray give you any buzz on Miller?" Sammy wondered.

"Just what's on the record," Pappajohn said. "According to the FBI, he was ex-CIA, kicked out of the agency after Iran-Contra in the eighties. But reading between the lines, I'll lay a bet he was still with the Company as black-ops."

"What's black-ops?" Jeffrey asked.

"James Bond meets *Mission Impossible*. Plausible deniability." Jim had walked into the conversation. "On the payroll, yet off the books. They do the dirty jobs, the false flags, the banana republic coups, Oklahoma C—"

Laughing, Sammy interrupted. "Thanks, for that *Conspiracy Corner* minute. Whether Miller was a rogue agent, or a loose cannon, I'm just glad his plan failed and his resonator was destroyed."

"Or was it?" Jim wondered aloud in his most dramatic voice.

Like a mother with an errant child, Sammy shook her head. The idea that someone else would build such a weapon to bring down buildings was too horrible to contemplate. Scaring people to boost ratings—that might be for the Fred Ferals and Rush Limbaughs of the world, but it wasn't *Sammy Greene on the L.A. Scene's* style. She had just one word for such crazy conjecture: "Meshuga."

"Hey, Y2K is over," Reed said, wrapping his arm around Sammy's waist. "We're safe, and together."

Sammy noticed his eyes glistening and whispered, "Michelle?"

He'd just learned about her fatal car accident in the early morning hours as he was working on the disaster response team cleanup. It was still so hard to believe.

Reed nodded. "Called my father this morning. He's agreed to help her family fund a scholarship for medical students in her name. She loved being a doctor."

Sammy held Reed tightly for a few moments of silence. When he finally looked down at her, she saw a deep abiding tenderness in his lavender eyes and felt her own unexpected tears. "We won't forget," she said softly. "It's a new year, and time for new beginnings,"

He cupped her pixie face in his hand. "I can't wait, Sammy."

"You won't have to," Sammy said as she looked up and their lips touched.

Epilogue

The fires in the hills of Los Angeles burned low as the sun set on the first day of the second millennium.

Ten days after the initial ember blew onto the chaparral, the flames had destroyed nearly twelve thousand acres and hundreds of homes, killed twelve people, and caused total losses estimated at more than five hundred million dollars.

Nevertheless, by tomorrow, for the survivors of Tinseltown, the disaster would be a mere memory—nipped and tucked away like the pain of a plastic surgeon's knife. Earthquakes, floods, even riots were the price they willingly paid for the pleasure of living in paradise.

Eventually, the scattered drops of winter rain would rinse the denuded hills with cleansing flash floods and the mesquite and chaparral would grow back on the hillsides, brittle and dry, to await the next spark, the next flame.

In a few months, the humidity would fall again. And then, down over the hills, would sweep the parching devil wind.